THE VATRA WITCH

BOOK ONE: THE LOST SOULS OF ERAPHON SERIES

G.V. HEXT

POPPY AND JUNE PRESS LLC

Book Cover by Alex McLaughlin at Nox Studios

Editing by Elyse Lyon

First edition 2026

CONTENT WARNING

Please visit GVHext.com for a complete list of content warnings.

THE CONTINENT
HUMAN KING
OKATERTH
VALBURN
CROWPASS
EGERTON
CITADEL

CEASEFALL
IRONOAK
THE
MANOR
PORT SIDNAH
EMERALD
GLADE
DEADLANDS

DEDICATION

This book is dedicated to my husband, and to those who never thought
they were good enough.
I promise you are.

CHAPTER ONE

SERAPHINA

All she saw were their small bodies burning.

Children, their faces dirty, their screams joyfully shrill under the hot sun, were burning one moment, and normal the next. Ablaze in black flame while kicking up dust in plumes. Then laughing while they dueled each other with stalks of straw for the honorary rank of Mesar.

It wanted them to burn.

Seraphina Wildrick leaned against the corner of the weathered notice board in the middle of Jedan Quarter. The graying wood groaned beside her as she pressed her thumbnail so hard into the center of her palm that she shook.

The elixirs were barely working anymore.

Now the only thing to suppress the abomination within her was pressure points or pain. And Sera would rather let Jedan Quarter burn—with its dilapidated buildings and less-than-level roofs—than look like an idiot with her thumb pressed between her eyes in front of a mass of children on their way to Darine Hall.

So pain it was, and she sank her nail deeper.

"Excuse me, Keeper Wildrick?" A young witch tugged on her cloak. "Mama told me to give you this."

The girl held up a white rose.

Sera turned to face her. "I don't know who your mother is." The girl's warm brown skin was washed in freckles, not so unlike her own when she was a witchling.

"She said you might say that. Anyway, she told me to give you this and to say thank you."

A flash, and the girl was alight. Her mouth open in a scream, her hair curling in flame.

Sera blinked away the image.

"Your mother has nothing to thank me for." Sera lowered herself to her haunches and broke off the thorns and half the stem. She pushed the rose behind the young witch's ear. "You keep it. Go on, you'll be late."

The witchling beamed at her and hurried to catch up to her classmates. Such a young little thing. Her whole world was in front of her, if she was lucky enough.

Sera stood and observed the new bartering posters crowding the notice board. So many. There were so many who were in need, and what did the Council do?

Nothing.

Darkness surged under her palms, begging her to devour the poorly constructed buildings. The papery silber bark they used in the slums would all go up in a matter of seconds. A voice deep in Sera's mind asked her, *Why not let them burn?*

The upper classes avoided this part of the white city as if it were a disease. Jedan class wasn't afflicted. They were born with shallow wells.

Sera ripped one of the pleas from the board, folded it, and shoved it deep into the pocket of her navy cloak. Later this evening, she'd supply this family with whatever they needed.

It'd be her penance for envisioning their children burning.

"Hello, beautiful," Dominick called out, jogging toward her. His floor-length gray oracle robes fluttered behind him. The reddened bags under his eyes against pale skin made them twice as blue, and his light blond hair was tousled in a way only rolling in a bed could achieve.

"I hope your tryst was fun. Galene's going to shrink me and lock me in one of her glass cabinets if I'm late again." Sera charged toward the center of the Citadel.

Dominick smiled, quickening his gait to match hers. "And you'll look so adorable as a figurine."

"Easy for you to say." She sank into the weight of his arm around her shoulders, grateful that the rattling inside her was finally beginning to calm.

"Moons, you've been so cranky lately. When was the last time you got laid?" he asked, shaking the Jedan dust from his hem. "Not counting that magical appendage you keep under your mattress, that is."

She smirked. "That's none of your business."

"I'm wounded. It's absolutely my business. Otherwise, what's the point of being best friends? Didn't you go on a date two nights ago?"

"I canceled it."

They crossed the quarter line and stepped from dirt onto the cobblestones of Dobro Quarter. The buildings went from shacks to stone constructions with perlin beams and thatched roofs, and the sweet aroma of cinnamon and sugar from the bakeries and shops at the ground level perfumed the air. Sera's stomach growled. She'd forgotten to eat... again.

"Why?" Dominick asked.

Slipping out from under his arm, she rubbed the damp from her brow and picked up the pace toward Darine Hall. "Because after the tenth time he brought up his mother on the last date, I decided it was never going to work."

Dominick opened his mouth, then closed it again and shrugged. "Can't really fight with that logic."

She raised her dark brow at him in surprise. She'd expected he would shove another one of his friends in her path. Someone broody, maybe, or like the last few—pretty to look at, but dumber than the gulls. Regardless, Dominick wasn't the kind to give up.

"Oh"—he chuckled—"I have to tell you about Sam last night..."

They turned toward Citadel proper, and Sera stopped short.

A *Congratulations, novices* banner, painted in perfect looping script, swayed lazily in the breeze above them. Decorative bows and ribbons correlating to the colors of the robes the different occupations wore bedecked each of the posts and balconies toward Darine Hall. Joyous coven members kissed their lead novices goodbye and wished them luck on their trial day.

She ignored Dominick's prattling about his rambunctious evening, which involved positions she hadn't even considered, and stared up at the banners.

The day had finally come, and as much as she wanted to be happy for her baby sister, Sera had been dreading it.

"Are you listening to me? I said that he screeched like a gull."

"Sorry, Dom."

Dominick followed her gaze and huffed. "It's been almost four years. You're still not over it?"

"No."

Each banner they passed under squeezed a little more life from her lungs. Every jovial remark and colorful bow or wreath made her sweat. It didn't help that she and Dominick had discussed this dozens of times.

"You made Dobro, what does it matter now?"

"It matters," she said, pulling her cloak tight around her shoulders like a shield, and followed the crowd of coven members toward Darine Hall. All while Dominick shuffled behind.

If it were any other day, she'd longingly admire the stunning white buildings with stone arches at every entrance. She'd appreciate the massive domes with their golden-dipped spires piercing the sky.

She'd think to herself about the time she told her little sister Nora that the reason they needed the spikes was that without them, monstrous birds would claim the tops of their buildings and rain shit around them.

But this was not the day.

Sera crossed the white marble entrance of Darine Hall and stepped into the vast courtyard. The blue wisteria, heavy with blooms, wove its vines around the third-level balcony spindles. The florals draped the walls, showering the lead novices congregating in the gardens below with stray petals, making the air sickeningly sweet.

So many white robes.

The look of them all sent a chill up her spine. Sera ran her fingernails back and forth across her palm and surveilled the clusters of novices, seeking her sister, when Dominick finally caught up. "Do you see Nora?"

He extended to the tips of his toes. "I don't think she's here yet."

Sera frowned. Her sister should have already arrived. It was unlike her to be late to anything. "I'll try and catch her before they line up. Meet me in the Menage later?"

"Wouldn't miss it," Dominick said, then waved to a handsome warlock across the courtyard—his latest obsession. Sera didn't anticipate it lasting long.

They never did.

Soon, most likely in the next week or two, Dominick would make the excuse that he was bored. She knew, deep down, that anytime someone got a little too close, a little too comfortable, Dominick would run in the other direction.

She shook her head.

Moons, she *was* miserable. Not that Sera would ever admit it, but maybe he was right. Maybe she did need to get laid. Shadow knew she needed a good distraction—a good distraction and a decent night's sleep.

Her legs burned with each step up to the designated Dobro floor. The middle level of Darine Hall wasn't as opulent as the Daedeth floor above it, but it was still lovely. Every day, she followed the same path, passing the gold letters stamped into crisp white stone: *Keepers of the Artifacts.*

The clacking of fellow keepers' boots faded away as she beheld her name painted on the wooden door.

Sera loved her placement. Each new artifact satiated her curious mind. The texts were like windows into lives so unlike her own. They held knowledge about the rise and fall of empires that had collapsed long before her.

The texts proved that the demon race had ruled over witches and warlocks since the dawn of time until the rebellion.

And yet every morning as she walked through the door in front of her—with her name emblazoned in gold under her position of junior keeper—a bittersweet stone settled in her chest. An unpleasant reminder of how her mother had petitioned the Council to move her from the position of a Glom witch in Jedan to that of a keeper in Dobro.

How, after her first solo assignment, she'd needed her mother to cover up her disaster.

If she had been left to rot in Jedan, then none of it would have happened.

Blazing flame warmed the cage she kept around that dangerous well of magic. It writhed and pressed against the walls she'd built. Sera leaned her head against the door, trying to blink away the spots racing across her vision.

The abomination surged in defiant answer. As if it were screaming at her: *How dare you keep me caged.*

Her lungs burned against the bubbling well of unchecked magic. A second well. One she was never supposed to have.

Sera pressed hard into the pressure points on her wrists. The one between her eyebrows, then below her ears, and the rattling subsided a bit. Though she was grateful to the healer who had taught her this move, Sera still felt guilty about the lie she had told to learn it.

It wasn't anxiety that rolled through her.

It was death.

CHAPTER TWO

SERAPHINA

Sera was late, and this time she couldn't blame it on Dominick. With Nora's trial looming over her and the constant rattling in her chest, Sera sighed. *Just don't burn the stacks down.* The door handle was cool in her scorching hand. She envisioned herself locking the chains, hiding that well of death once again. One more deep breath.

Sera pushed open the door to her workspace.

The signature fragrance of time and dust helped calm her a little, but knowing she was in a room with ancient relics and tomes had her biting her cheek to keep her magic in check.

Surrounding the worktables, stone walls held shelving, and upon it ancient masks, globes, and broken bottles. Mage lights danced across the ceiling. Half were back in the stacks, most likely following her mentor, but the remaining ones perched above the wooden tables reflected their light in the golden-framed mirror at the front of the room.

"Seraphina?"

"It's me," she yelled back, noticing the ledgers from the previous day were still stacked at her workstation. Sera sighed. Apparently, for Galene to have miraculously changed her assignment during the night was too much to ask. The ledgers often held endless counts of livestock and crop yields: hardly exciting.

"Come back here, please." Galene's voice was strained. Sera swung her cloak from her shoulders, hung it on the back of the door, and went to find her mentor.

Her fingertips snagged on the rough bindings and spines as she walked back into the stacks. The distinct scent of vanillin permeated the pages of ancient tomes and ledgers, settling the last bit of her magic back inside its cage. And finally, Sera let her shoulders drop.

Tomes and more tomes. It'd been tomes forever. As a witchling, huddled in the library, looking at the monstrous beast forms of demons. Reading about the ancient sacrificial rituals of witches and warlocks. The wars, the mythical beasts that dwelled deep in Eraphon's oceans.

But the one she'd wanted to get her hands on since the moment she set foot within these stacks was protected behind glass. Weathered and moth eaten, its delicate leather cover depicted the world giving birth to a god. Sera had begged Galene to read it countless times, but the answer was always a firm no.

"Seraphina, stop feeling the books and come help me," Galene crowed at her. "Grab the stool and bring it here. The Vase of Ornelle is waiting."

"Considering that it's over two thousand years old, I don't think another few minutes are going to hurt it." Sera grabbed the stool and faced her mentor.

Galene's short stature, beady eyes, and white hair that never seemed to stay in place made her look gnomelike. She retrieved the artifact and delicately placed it onto a secured transport cart.

"You"—her mentor glared at her—"are the safest solution for retrieving items on the higher shelves, due to your height." Galene waved her hands, whispering a spell, and further secured the vase with magic. "It is why I have let you stay so long."

Sera snorted. "You're not sprite-sized."

"I still believe you taller witches have access to better air quality than I do. I should petition the Council about that."

"I think you're just afraid of heights." Sera laughed, pushing her heavy black curls off her shoulder and returning to her workstation.

"That comment doesn't warrant a response," Galene said.

Sera readied her notebook and opened the top ledger.

Crudely drawn creatures coated the pages—on one, depictions of woodland goblins with their giant eyes and even bigger ears. On another, the mighty elken with their massive antlers. A pleasant surprise considering she was expecting tallies of crop yields and livestock.

"I heard a few Daedeth-class members whispering that the ceasefire will end. That maybe the war would end." Sera kept her eyes down, made an attempt to make herself look studious in her meticulous note-taking for the archives but really, she was avoiding Galene's glower.

The witch hated to talk about the war. Honestly, her mentor hated to talk about anything other than the pieces surrounding them. But Sera had worn her down after three years.

"And?" Galene asked.

"Do you think the demons have finally given up?" Sera shifted in her seat.

Since the coven founders had defected from the underworld, Gehenna, they'd been at war. The fact that they hadn't been retaken was claimed a miracle. Some said it was proof that witches and warlocks were meant to break free of the demons' oppressive reign. Sera had a suspicion there was more to it than that. Though in the three years she'd been preserving pieces of the past, she hadn't found her proof yet.

"The start of the truce was not long enough ago to reconcile with Gehenna. Twenty years is a drop in time to demons."

Sera flipped the page, revealing three separate pictures of the same bird in different phases of flight, all drawn in incredible detail. She had to admit that whoever this artist was, they were talented. "How old were you when the war started?" She bit her cheek to keep from smiling.

"Witchling." The scowl that formed on her mentor's face rivaled those of the ancient statues of demonic deities. "You know I am not two thousand years old. Do not insult me, for if you continue, I will send you to another office." Galene huffed so hard dust motes floated through the room.

"I'm not a witchling anymore. I'm about to be twenty-four," she said and turned another page in the ledger. A wolf with terrifying eyes stared back at her. Dark shading came off the beast like a shadow. She shivered for a moment, then looked at the name printed beside it: *Vuk*. Well, that was a creature she'd never seen before.

"Four years out of your schooling? You're still a witchling."

Careful not to damage the page, Sera used both hands to turn the thin paper. As she did, another image was revealed. She gasped.

"What is it?" Galene asked.

A being with giant feathered wings protruding from his back took up both pages. An aliato, light-bringer, a being of sun and sky. They were the soldiers of the human god, myths among her people, despite the evidence provided by the old tomes. No one had ever seen one in person, but here the warrior was depicted along with a sword and shield.

"Nothing... nothing."

Galene pursed her lips.

"Will you attend Honora's trial?" Galene asked. Sera turned another page, grateful it was empty.

"As if my mother would let me miss it." Sera sighed. "Nora's creating a portal. Our uncle will be on the other side."

"Artemis? Is he not deployed?"

"He is up in Valburn, but you know how my mother can be. Her goal is to get Nora into Daedeth."

Galene's eyes widened. "Impressive distance for a portal, let alone for a novice. Lavinia must be proud."

"Well, Nora is impressive." The words tasted sour in her mouth. Her mother had always been proud of Nora. One of her daughters had to be powerful, and it certainly wasn't Sera. At least not in the way that was acceptable.

And when Lavinia Wildrick had watched Sera present what little magic she had to the Council... it had been just the tip of her mother's disappointment. Sera had stood in the middle of the Menage as three Council members and a quarter of the coven watched. She'd thought she was used to the scowls Lavinia gave her, but when the coven and Council had realized just how little magic she held...

A surge of scalding heat ripped through her.

Sera bit her cheek hard to keep from yelping out. As if her very thoughts had insulted that *other* magic. She closed her eyes.

"Are you all right?" Galene asked.

When she opened her eyes, instead of her mentor standing before her, it was a Legion soldier. Sera trembled as she watched the soldier's body snap tight, his muscles and tendons constricting from the dark blaze that engulfed him. His eyes were milky rivers, running down his cheeks into his silent screaming mouth.

She was going to be sick.

The abomination roiled in her gut.

"Seraphina?" Galene's voice barely made it through the rushing of blood in her ears.

It wanted out. Those black and terrible flames scorched every one of her arteries in defiance. She couldn't let it happen. The quill.

Sera grabbed her quill and pressed the sharp point into her thumb. There was pain... always pain... but with it, a bit of release. Pushing a great breath out through her nose, she said, "I'm all right. Just had a headache come out of nowhere."

"Do you need to visit the healers? I will walk you, my dear."

She wiped the drops of blood on her uniform, right on the underside of her bicep. "I'm fine... better now."

If they found out, if anyone knew, she'd be done for.

That's when the chimes rang through the Citadel.

Chapter Three

Seraphina

Sera stood and followed Galene toward the golden-framed mirror hanging on the front wall. Council Chair Renata appeared in the glass, sitting regal in her golden throne. "Attention, coven members. Trials will be canceled this evening and resume tomorrow. Lead novices, please report to your professors for your new time."

As quickly as the Council elder's face had appeared, it disintegrated.

A second later, Sera's glowing blue sign appeared.

"It's not for personal use," Galene huffed toward the incessant pulse of magic on the mirror.

"Well, Galene, not to pull rank or anything, but if it's my mother on the other side, it's going to be bad for both of us."

She hated to do that, but it was true. Her mother was the master mastria; no one denied Lavinia.

Galene grunted. "Make it quick."

Sera swiped the mirror, and her sister's face appeared. "Sera?"

"Nora?" she said in a tone a tad more sarcastic than she'd intended.

Nora had twisted her hair into tight shoulder-length curls. Her brown skin radiated in golden undertones that made her glow. Her cheeks, chin, and lips were rounded and soft, contrasting with the sharp tilt of her amber eyes.

Nora was the sunshine to Sera's darkness. This, of course, was according to their mother. Nora excelled at everything.

"Would you mind getting a hold of Mama and finding out what is going on?" Slews of novices with their white robes rushed back and forth behind her in a panic.

A shameful part of Sera wanted her little sister to fail during her trial today. That same part hoped Nora would be assigned to Jedan, like she had been, if only to see the look on their mother's face. To mar her sister's golden image, just once.

"What was the point in contacting me when you could have gone straight to her?"

"It's chaos down here. Everyone is trying to find out the reason for the delay. We got one connection, and I knew you'd answer. Please?" Nora asked.

Sera sighed. "Fine. Meet me at Mystic's with Dom, later." She knew the conversation with her mother wouldn't go well. They never did.

Once her sister's face had disappeared, she traced her mother's symbol on the glass and waited, staring at herself in the empty mirror.

Dark bags had lived under Sera's eyes for three months now. Her brown skin was dull, and she patted down the frizz from her curls. Only her irises were vibrant, almost full of a life she didn't remember anymore. They'd always been her favorite feature. Swirls of emerald and sage stared back at her, bright and astute against her pallor.

As she admired them, they turned to amber. Sera's long, curling hair morphed into braids wrapped high in a blue scarf. Her ashen skin transformed into a glowing, rich shade of ebony.

"Seraphina." Her mother raised one pointed eyebrow at her. Even through the mirror, she could feel her mother's claws bite into her mind.

"Mother, do you know what's going on?"

"With Honora's trial? It's been postponed. I figured that was obvious. Why? Did the news cause your flickers?"

"No, nothing happened. I haven't felt a flicker in weeks." As she whispered the lie, Sera ensured the walls in her mind were solid. Her mother didn't need to know that a few moments ago, she'd experienced what she referred to as "flickers"—isolated moments when her magic flooded her body.

"Artemis is fine with the delay." Lavinia waved off her concern like it was a gnat. Her black robe's sleeve stirred in the air, revealing her favorite golden cuff. "He reached out this morning and will still be available for Honora. He understands the urgency and importance of her trial and will ensure she is placed in Daedeth class."

Of course she had already known about the change in trial date, and it was typical that she had chosen not to share it with her daughters.

Satisfied that she'd done enough to appease her sister, Sera didn't prolong the conversation. "Thank you for responding. I have to go."

"Seraphina," her mother's voice rang out, but Sera wiped the symbol from the glass, and Lavinia's face disintegrated.

Galene muttered to herself for the rest of the day, setting Sera even more on edge. As soon as she'd completed her assignment to log the sketches of forest creatures, she wished her mentor goodnight and hurried to meet Nora.

Mystic Mond was her favorite tavern, tucked away on the border between Jedan and Dobro Quarters. The brew was strong, the entertainment lively, though often off key. The best part was that no one from Daedeth would be caught there, except Dominick.

Sera smiled at the barkeep and headed to her table, Nora in tow.

Ithar nodded, prepared two glasses, and carried them toward the pair. He'd insisted this was Sera's table—the one in the far back, hiding in the shadows, a thank-you for the good she did in Jedan. She had stopped fighting the warlock after a while and accepted his charity, despite the fact that she could more than afford to pay for a reserved table.

Ithar had promised her this seat for as long as he had the ability to do so.

"Dom should be here any minute," Sera said to her sister. On the walk over, she'd shared the minuscule amount of information she'd gathered from their mother, and, no surprise, Nora had huffed and said she should have just had the conversation herself.

Sera took a seat on her stool and thanked Ithar as he set down the two glasses of purple brew and winked at her. The tavern was quiet tonight, most likely because of the rain, but Seraphina still enjoyed the soft melody of a single lute playing in the corner.

Dominick appeared through Mystic's swinging door. His eyes were red rimmed and strained, and the drizzle outside had darkened his light blond hair.

"You look like shit." Sera moved to the next stool over, giving Dominick the outside seat.

"The master had us staring into the pools all day. And if I had to guess, I'll be staring at colorful water every day until the end of my sorry life."

"That is your duty." Sera smirked and sipped her brew. The purple liquid was pleasantly sweet on her palate. Hints of peach and orange blossom coated her tongue. The bit of magic it was laced with, along with the warmth of the alcohol, was making her insides hum.

"Did you see anything? Any reason for the delay?" Nora asked.

"Other than the weather and some hideously decorated festival the humans intend to throw, no. I didn't see anything." He rubbed the back of his neck and palmed his eyes.

Dominick had explained the mirroring pools to her a few times. An oracle searched for strands of the future in the water. When they found one, the oracle would pull it forward, revealing images of what had happened or what was to come. No matter how often Dom described it, Sera never quite grasped the mechanics of it all, nor why only certain witches and warlocks could pull the strands.

"Blackwell probably had the case of the runs," she said, hoping to break a bit of the tension.

Nora scoffed. "The Council is up to something. There has never been a trial delay before. I looked it up myself. Never."

"I agree with you, Nor," Dominick responded. "I heard today that the Mistresses of Arcane spoke with senior oracles about a witch, shunned sixty years ago, who was the best strand reader in a generation. She had never misinterpreted a reading, not even once."

"Then why was she shunned?" Nora asked.

"I have no idea. This one wasn't a public shunning either. It was kept quiet. She left in the night. I also heard that the Council has been searching for her since the master oracle has been... inconsistent." Dominick took another large gulp.

Why would a shunned oracle be the cause of a delay in the trial? The Council shunned witches and warlocks frequently. Usually, the reasons were serious offenses. Thievery, insubordination, and causing harm to another coven member. What was so special about this one?

"Interesting..." Sera muttered. The sky was growing dark on the other side of the rain-pelted glass. "You need to go, Nora. Mother is going to be pissed if you're home much past sundown with your trial tomorrow."

Nora gave them a perfect pout. "Is this another leave-so-we-can-talk-without-Nora situation?"

Sera glared at her sister. "No, this is a situation where I don't want to be blamed for your lack of proper rest."

"Hmm..." Nora squinted at the pair. "Fine," she said and stood. "The last thing I need is a verbal lashing from her before the most important test of my life."

Sera did love winning against her sister. The few times circumstance allowed it, of course. "You still want to show a portal?"

"Why do you keep asking? I've practiced nonstop. Even if Uncle Artemis isn't on the other side, it'll be clear that I've pinpointed his office. He has a life-size portrait of himself hanging above his desk," Nora huffed.

Of course he does. "Relax, I just want you to be sure. I have complete faith in your abilities. And... it is possible that Dom entered me into a bet with a few Daedeth members that you'd make arcana."

Nora rolled her eyes as she pulled her robe tight around her dress. "Really, Dominick, getting her into gambling?"

"Your sister is a grown witch and makes her own decisions. I just presented an opportunity," Dominick said.

"Mother will ban you from the house for a month," Nora said.

"And wouldn't that be a treat?" Sera hid her smile by taking a sip of her brew.

"Whatever. I'll see you two tomorrow." Nora shook her head the entire way out of the tavern.

"You should tell her what you're using the coin for. I'd like not to be seen as an asshole our whole lives." Dominick pushed his glass back and forth across the wooden table.

"Never." The pitter-pattering of rain turned into a drumming as the sky opened up on the stone tile roof. A cold chill sank over the tavern, and Sera downed the rest of her drink, hoping for a bit more warmth.

"Come on, Sera. She'd understand. Shadow, I understand, and I'm an idiot." He twirled his glass, flicking condensation across the top of the table.

It would be considered a shunned offense if the Council found out that Sera was actively helping those below her in the hierarchy. "Nora has never been around Jedan members, not really, and she never will be. The only reason I told you was because I threatened a nasty and terrible death if you let it slip, Dom. My sister *would* find it commendable, and with it, she'd have loose lips praising me as some savior of the lessers."

Dominick rolled his eyes, his fingers finding the spot below his ear—the place he rubbed every time he was upset.

"Something else is wrong," she said. "What is it?"

He glared at her for a moment. "I'm worried about Colton. They've moved his battalion's position. Why?"

"You think it has anything to do with the rumors of the ceasefire ending? Or maybe something to do with the oracle?"

"I don't know, I'm still waiting for his response."

Dominick didn't typically concern himself with woes such as military movements. He was laughter and fun, the brightest spot in her heart.

The last time he had looked this concerned was a few years ago. He'd approached her with shaking hands and sweat pouring down his temples, explaining how he wasn't attracted to witches—a fact she'd already known.

A dark flicker twirled inside her.

Guilt coated in a layer of shame and swirling darkness rose up her throat. She'd kept secrets from him. Would he be as forgiving if the time came to tell him?

"I'll make an offering to Shadow for Colton. You have my word."

"Thanks." He rolled his shoulders, closed his eyes, and took a deep breath.

She wanted him to find someone to love. Really love, not fuck and throw away. But she was one of the only people with whom he truly let his guard down. So many warlocks came and went without knowing the true Dom. He had so much to give. But not only that, Dominick deserved it. He deserved everything.

"I've got to get home." She wrapped her navy cloak around her shoulders and pulled out the paper she'd ripped from the notice board that morning, giving it a quick read.

"What do they need?"

"Unfortunately, something from the healers. I'll have to get it in the morning." Dominick nodded, following her out of the tavern and into the rain. With a wave of his hand, a green covering materialized above her head, protecting her from the downpour.

"Be careful getting home, okay?"

"Thanks for this." Sera pointed up. But Dom hesitated, assessing her. "I'm okay, I promise." She hoped he didn't push; she didn't have the energy for it, and they'd already been in a heated argument two weeks prior. Another one wouldn't make things better. Right now, the last thing she wanted to do was fight with him.

Dom nodded, created a matching covering above himself, and jogged toward Daedeth Quarter. "I'll see you tomorrow in the Menage," he yelled back before turning out of sight.

CHAPTER FOUR

DOMINICK

He needed a drink. Stronger than the brew at Mystic's, something that would burn, make his mind pleasantly numb, and put him into all sorts of trouble. Dominick needed it because Sera was lying.

Rain pelted the green covering that surrounded him. His and the one he kept in place above Sera. He could sense where she was, turning onto her street now, all the way in dirty Jedan. Dominick understood why she chose to reside there and commended the help she was giving. But when would she start living for herself?

A strain on his magic had his skin heating, and Dom let the covering above his head fall away, focusing squarely on hers, making sure it stayed put until she reached her door. That single room with a tiny fireplace and bed, the bathing chamber shared with the rest of the tenants, in one of the only boardinghouses in the quarter. Shadow, she could be living so much better.

Fat droplets of water ran down his cheeks. He didn't mind the rain, not today at least. The news he'd received from his brother had been concerning, and this incessant drizzle matched his mindset. Add in the fact that it was now dark, and the clouds had fully shrouded the moons Nitheon and Nubenia in the sky... Well, at least he knew fate had a sense of humor.

The letter he had received seemed rushed, and although Colton wasn't the most elegant with his writing, his penmanship had a tilt to it. They were moving outside of Valburn, and the question was… why?

The Solarni coven had been at war with Gehenna for two thousand years, and in a ceasefire for only twenty. Dominick had been five when everything went from worried brows to genuine smiles. Colton had seen more, though. Four years older, he understood more, too, and Dom still remembered that determined look on Colton's face when he decided he'd present his magic in a way that would guarantee placement in the Legion. He and Alistair had practiced for what seemed like years. It was no surprise they both quickly moved up through the ranks.

There was nothing he could do for Colton, regardless of his opinions on the Council and how their coven was run. Dominick was an oracle. Not a general, not a Council member. His voice wasn't enough to enact any type of change. Moons, he'd been trying to get switched out of his pool for months now and still couldn't convince the master to let him.

No, there was nothing he could do for his brother; Sera, however, he could do something about. Shadow, the bags under her eyes. Her twitches. The way she'd stare off into space. Her usually vibrant brown skin would pale during those episodes. She was fucking lying about something, and he didn't know what to do about it, because the more he pressed… the more she pulled away.

They hadn't hung out nearly as much in the past three months, and that wasn't like them. He and Sera had been inseparable from the time they were young. Sitting together in their classes while they were novices, running the streets of Daedeth, constantly getting into mischief.

Dominick sighed and shook out his shoulders. He pushed his hair back in one sweep and approached the only acceptable tavern in this part of the Citadel.

Mage lights hovered below the ceiling and lined the walls, casting a warm glow throughout the space. The brew at Mystic's hadn't been nearly enough, and as he scanned the room, his eyes roaming over the iron chairs and posh tables decorated with golden candelabras, he found what he was looking for.

Or whom.

A glass full of brown liquor was already sitting on the bar beside the handsome warlock. Sam had ordered for Dom, it seemed. Impatient to get on with it, was he?

Dominick threw on his most flirtatious grin and strode forward.

"Shadow, you're soaked. What, were you hanging out with that keeper again?" Sam handed him his drink.

Dominick slammed back the whiskey and motioned for another to take its place. He supposed he could explain himself, but what would be the point? Truly, few people in the coven understood his relationship with Sera. He didn't care that she was below him in the eyes of the coven. Sera was his. Not in any physical sense, but their lonely souls had found each other, and that was enough for him.

Dom had a feeling he would be holding on to Sam for only a few more nights anyway. The warlock was getting clingy and, to be honest, too comfortable. He'd left one of his red guardian robes just lying across his bed last week. No. It wasn't going to work, but it'd be enough for tonight. Sam would help keep his worries buried.

Dom lowered his voice. "You know, the last time we were together, you used some very colorful language when I stepped out of the tub. I just figured you had a thing for me being wet." He took a large gulp of the second drink, happy for the burn all the way down to his gullet.

Sam leaned an elbow on the bar, his brown eyes heavy lidded and his smile easy. "You want to get out of here?"

"Thought you'd never ask."

CHAPTER FIVE

SERAPHINA

The two and a half cups of herbal tea should have calmed her. She'd cut it this morning with some of her sleeping elixir, but her palms still stung as she passed under the massive amphitheater's entrance.

The Menage was the most impressive structure within the Citadel walls. Five stories high, showcasing arches that mirrored the architecture throughout the fortress city.

Along the archways on the upper levels were balconies and designated boxes for the Daedeth-class families. As a witchling, Sera had marveled at the structure's acoustics and ability to seat so many. How the crowd cheered at events. And, of course, the view.

It struck her then that she would never see the Menage from that height ever again; she would be confined to the lower levels. Over the past four years, Sera had avoided coming here, no matter the event, due to the terrible memories of her failure at her own trial. Now, as she took in the earthen arena and peered up at the boxes for the Daedeth members, an overwhelming sense of sorrow came over her.

Her mother had great accommodations above, but she had agreed to sit with Sera so she could see Nora better. Sera didn't remember where her mother sat on her trial date, only that it had been surprisingly close to the arena floor. What was now entirely too vivid was the smell of the same dirt field, the constant shaking of her hands, and the memory of her sweat-soaked robes.

The crowd seemed to echo her unease. They aimed whispers and sideways glances at the novices and their family and friends who were hoping for a high placement. The anxious cloud could almost be cut, and none of it was helping her keep her abomination contained.

It had thrashed and raged inside her the past twenty-four hours. She'd barely gotten any sleep. When the healers' quarters opened, she had been relieved—not only for the family in Jedan, but also for the extra batch of elixirs she picked up.

"I'm only staying until your mother gets here." Dominick's robes billowed with dramatic flair around him as he flopped onto the bench beside her. "Then I'm joining the other oracles."

"Wish I could say the same," Sera said, rolling her shoulders and relaxing a touch.

Dominick pointed to the novices standing in a line along the arena's dirt floor. "How many do you think will place in the Legion?"

It didn't surprise her that he was concerned, considering their conversation last night. Colton's movements were bizarre, and worse, upsetting to Dominick. "I'd guess no more than any other year."

She couldn't read the expression on Dom's face as he gazed over the crowd, but she settled her head on his shoulder. Dominick always smelled like rain to her. It must have been from the water in the Ogdelo pools, but anytime there was moisture in the air, it reminded her of Dominick.

A long desk had been erected at the viewing level. Behind it were two thrones. Typically, three or four Council members assigned the novice placements. Only two was unusual.

Sera spotted Chair Blackwell conversing with some Daedeth members near a side entrance. Blackwell had been at her trial four years ago, in the same outfit—red robes that reached the ground and a black bongrace atop his balding head. What hair he had left ringed his skull from ear to ear, cut down to a stubble.

She remembered the way he'd frowned at her presentation. How Chair Briar had looked genuinely shocked, and Chair Renata had searched the crowd for her mother, looking for some sort of explanation. How could one of Lavinia Wildrick's daughters have such little power?

Sera's stomach churned, and she took a deep breath.

"He looks ridiculous, doesn't he?" Dom whispered. "That stupid hat and those robes. You'd think he's getting ready to pose for a statue to be placed in the Council chambers."

The corner of her mouth ticked upward. "Dom, you wear full-length robes every day."

"True, but at least you gave me a little smile," he said, bumping his shoulder into hers.

"I don't deserve you." She didn't, not really. Not after all her secrets, the lies, and the horrors she'd committed, whether consciously or not. Sera leaned into him while pressing her thumbnail hard into her palm, biting deep.

"I said I would stay until Lavinia arrived, but..."

Sera turned to see the same handsome warlock from yesterday waving at Dom.

"Just go. I'll see you later. Make sure you bring my winnings," she said as Dominick turned to leave.

Sera looked for her sister in a sea of white robes. Her eyes settled on Chair Thorne, speaking with a few of the younger novices.

Thorne's red hair was cropped just below her chin. A streak of white sprouted from her forehead and swept effortlessly behind her ear. Amethyst robes framed the plain floor-length black dress she wore underneath.

Sera always thought Thorne looked more pleasant than the other chairs. She smiled freely and often, revealing the apples of her cheeks. They were dashed with just the right amount of cosmetics to set her pale skin aglow beneath her freckles.

It was good that Thorne was there to view Nora's presentation. The former mistress of arcane was loyal to her old occupation, and Nora was the best this year had to offer.

"Sera," her sister called to her, bounding up the steps. "Where's Mama?" Nora had pulled her hair back into a high puff, making her eyes as sharp as glass.

"I haven't seen her come in yet. Is Artemis ready?" Sera smoothed out the creases pressed into the white satin fabric of her sister's outer robes.

"He's in his office. Mama threatened to walk through the portal herself and hunt him down if he wasn't visible for the entire Menage to see." Nora giggled.

"Well, I wouldn't put it past her." Sera couldn't remember the last time she'd giggled unironically. Even before her disastrous trial day, her mother had kept a tight rein on her. "Speaking of which, she just got here."

Lavinia Wildrick descended the stairs toward her daughters, oozing grace, stone faced and regal in her black mastria's robes. Today her mother wore her braids down instead of having tied them up like she usually did. The ends almost reached her elbows, and every few had a charm or a bead attached. There was intention in her steps toward her daughters, but when she saw Nora, her poise cracked into a radiant smile that reached her eyes.

"Darling, I am so proud of you." Lavinia reached for Nora, pulling her into a tight embrace. "And what a blessing from Shadow it is to have Chair Thorne here."

"Thank you, Mama. I couldn't have done it without you or Seraphina." Unshed tears lined Nora's eyes.

Sera's stomach hollowed out from the display of gratitude. Nora's kind heart had always tried to repair the damage between Sera and her mother. But this hurt was buried too deep. It would take more than a few tender moments to fix. Lavinia broke the moment by touching Nora's cheek.

Sera clenched her teeth and stared at the ground. Darkness snapped inside her. No matter how many times she told herself that Lavinia's approval didn't matter, the stinging viper of jealousy reared its head. The events, the time her mother and Nora had spent together training. The mother-daughter outings that Sera was never invited to. Moons, why wasn't she numb by now? This wasn't going to go away. Especially with Nora assigned to Daedeth.

Lavinia hugged Nora again. "All right, my love. Go down and take your place. Your sister and I will be right here watching."

As Nora left to take her spot in line with the others, Lavinia's face morphed back to stone.

"Your memories, Seraphina. I was able to slip in much too easily."

Shit.

"Yes, Mother." Sera reinforced the barrier in her mind as Chair Blackwell walked to the podium.

"Witches and warlocks gathered here today"—Blackwell's voice was amplified to every corner of the arena—"we view and celebrate the annual novice trials." The crowd cheered. Sera kept the wall around her mind reinforced and clapped her hands. "Every trial date, I am reminded of the responsibility of practicing magic and what a gift the coven founders gave us when they rebelled against the demon king so long ago. How our life above ground is the way the Solarni coven was meant to live.

"You have honed your skills and developed your magic through your studies, and soon, you will emerge as a valuable member of the coven."

Valuable. The word made Sera shift in her seat. What was the value of a witch or warlock to its coven? Every member of the Jedan class would be forced into a life of servitude, their occupations nothing more than cleaning and cooking for the upper classes. Dobro held the healers and, like her, the keepers—the holders of history. The Daedeth class, with their four occupations—mastrias, guardians, arcana, and oracles—played with magic, pushing it to its limits. Then there was the Legion, who followed its own brutal hierarchy.

"But let us not forget," Blackwell continued, "magic is a responsibility. As you enter the coven as adults, you must wield your abilities with wisdom, compassion, and integrity. May your incantations be true, and may Shadow watch over your souls." Blackwell held his palm to the sky and sent a kernel of magic to the goddess.

The trials began with a young warlock, short and riddled with acne, initiating what Sera thought was supposed to be an illusion. Blue light snapped tight between his hands. The warlock struggled, twisting his wrists and reciting his incantation over and over. With a burst that looked like a lightning strike, the energy was gone.

"Legion," Blackwell yelled.

The warlock's shoulders sank low, his head hung. Sera's chest grew tighter.

Her mother crossed her legs beside her, and Sera could feel her trying to claw into her mind. She ignored the rattling in her chest and worked to reinforce that wall. This was a test, and she wouldn't fail this time.

A tall witch with rosy cheeks and strawberry gold hair walked forward and took her place before the Council members. An almost perfect replica of the witch stood beside her, showcasing an ideal example of echo projection. Impressive, truly. Even her mother clapped at that.

"Daedeth, arcana," Chair Thorne proclaimed.

Anyone would be lucky to go into arcana. It was the most versatile occupation. Studying the way of magic, teaching novices, and creating new spells. They even oversaw the healers and practiced alchemy. Nora belonged there.

Another warlock, red haired and pale skinned, with an outrageous number of freckles across his attractive nose and cheeks, approached the center of the Menage. His shoulders were hunched, and his hands hung limp at his sides.

An ache formed in Sera's throat. She knew with every fiber of her being what it felt like to be out there, with the scrutiny of your classes, loved ones, and the Council bearing down on you, knowing that no matter what form you displayed, you'd never make it out of Jedan.

Sera had wanted to be placed in the mastria occupation since she was a witchling. She had prayed to Shadow and dressed in only black for years. As if that alone would have guaranteed her place.

Her cheeks burned with embarrassment at her idiocy. Her mother had known it would never happen. Still, Sera had wished that it could have been the bridge between them.

The novice looked like she felt. Defeated.

He took a broad stance, his hands reaching forward with palms facing the ground. The novice closed his eyes, whispered his spell, and shot green bolts into the dirt. Several large pine trees erupted from the ground, climbing rapidly skyward. The rich pine scent wove its way through the crowd, and Sera inhaled, reveling in the smell of the winter solstice.

Esoti in Jedan. That's where he'd be placed. Anyone with the power to grow plants landed there.

"Legion," Blackwell yelled.

A hush fell over the crowd.

"What do you mean?" The novice asked, taking a step toward Blackwell. "A Legion warrior? I should be in esoti." His hands were clenched, and clumps of grass sprouted from under his feet, crawling along the Menage's dirt floor.

Sera bounced her knee and rubbed her palms together. Every beat of her heart echoed in her ears, and the cage rattled hard against her ribs.

"Warlock Stoll, you will not question our decision. You will still be with the rest of the esoti, but you are needed with the Legion." Blackwell motioned to the exit. "Now, please step aside for the next novice."

Stoll didn't move. The green sod grew wider. If he stood there much longer, the entire arena floor would be a meadow.

"Novice Stoll"—Thorne's voice was soft—"your magic is needed to help feed our warriors. Your power is imperative to the war effort and the livelihood of our kind. It is a great honor to care for those who protect us. Do you agree?"

The grass at Stoll's feet retreated. He nodded and then knelt before the Council members. "Yes, Chairs, please forgive me for my outburst."

The next novice was placed in Dobro, but the following two went to Legion. Sera whispered to her mother, "More novices are being ordered to the Legion this year than I expected. Are our ranks so depleted that we need so many? We aren't even in conflict."

"Who cares about the appearance of the Citadel grounds if our world is extinct?" Her mother's amber eyes bore into her. "Survival is imperative."

Sera tightened the barrier around her mind and sat straighter as Nora took her place in the center of the arena. She looked like one of the statues of the founding witches: standing tall, shoulders back. She bowed to the chairs.

Her sister would do well, but still, there was a nagging ache in Sera's gut. A burning heat. A rattling lock. Sera clasped her hands together to stop the shaking while Nora prepared her portal.

Nora had practiced for months, and Sera knew firsthand the amount of power she held. She still had the scar from when they were children. Sera had given her sister a little zap in jest, nothing more than a harmless spark. Nora, unfortunately, didn't have control yet and left a raised burn on Sera's thumb. The healers had offered to remove the scar for her, but Sera decided to keep it.

Despite her heart pounding in her ears, Sera smirked. No, Nora wasn't going to fail, and Sera was going to clear that notice board tomorrow. Fill every order for the Jedan members in need. It'd be like winter solstice in spring.

A circle of blue light flickered in the middle of the arena and expanded evenly in all directions. The light bent and shifted with perfect control.

Oohs and aahs swept through the crowd, and Lavinia smiled. Nora's portal warped and ceased its horizontal movement, then raised itself to create a perfectly arched doorframe.

Even the frame Nora had created around the portal was stunning. It looked to have roses and birds carved from magic. That alone would have gotten her into Daedeth.

Sera swallowed.

As each figure formed around the portal's frame, Sera's core grew hot. She tore at her wrist to make it stop. Her darkness thrashed and beat against her skin, over and over. Sera closed her eyes and swallowed the nausea. If she lost control now, it would be the worst possible moment. So many spectators, and two chairs to witness her abominable secret.

She took a deep breath through her nose and out through her mouth. When her mother wrapped her hand around Sera's limp palm, cracking her knuckles from the pressure, Sera's eyes snapped open. A cold terror lined every one of Lavinia's features.

Sera glanced down and swallowed her gasp. A thick, bubbling fog, black as night, circled around their hands. It moved and thrashed. A steady stream trickled down the stone stairs, slithering toward the Menage center. Toward Nora.

No. No. NO.

The magic seeped from the cage she'd built around that never-ending well. Sera watched frozen as her darkness slunk to the Menage floor. Something was calling to it, pulling like a magnetic force straight for her sister's portal. She tried to pull it back, gritting her teeth, and yanked with all her might. Held on to that burning through her skin so she could lock the door and throw away the key. Closing her eyes, Sera tried to focus, but her mother let out a cry.

"Mama, let go."

Lavinia shook her head. Sera watched in horror as her darkness stripped the ebony of her mother's skin. The tops of Lavinia's long, elegant fingers were now blistered white, and the darkness, her darkness, was ripping away the pigment.

Sera shoved against the foreign well of magic. "Please," she whispered, "Shadow, make it stop."

Screams broke out through the crowd. She was done for. They'd lock her in the tower, or worse, kill her.

When Sera glanced up, she expected to see Chair Blackwell before her, ready with a set of manacles or a sword pointed at her throat. Instead, every witch and warlock in the crowd was staring at Nora and the portal beside her.

Sera's dark magic had curled its way around the frame, morphing the roses and beautiful birds, which had seemed carved of light, into monstrous creatures. Skulls, beasts with horns and sharpened fangs. The blue of Nora's archway was now wholly black.

There was no office.

No Uncle Artemis, no study with a life-size portrait.

A tall figure materialized and sauntered onto the arena floor.

Shadow. It was so much worse.

Chapter Six

Seraphina

"Hello, little witch." A deep, unnerving voice grated her ears, sending shivers from her neck all the way down to the backs of her thighs.

Sera had never seen a demon draped in flesh. Massive horned beasts covered in talons and wings... yes. Some of them with skin the color of blood. Others had thorned and plated armor. All of them were terrifying.

But this demon's outer form wasn't what scared her.

His salt-and-pepper hair was cut short, and a shadow of a beard covered his face. The cut of his jacket was sharp, resembling finely tailored formal wear dipped in a dye so black that looking at it felt like being sucked into a void. Power radiated off him in waves. Sera could almost taste it, like a faint tendril of smoke lying heavy across her tongue. Like *ash*.

"Demon! You do not belong here!" Blackwell bellowed and threw a solid wall of magic toward the enemy, barely missing Nora. Witches and warlocks in the stand screamed.

Sera homed in on her sister, and that raging heat she'd felt before was nothing compared to what the abomination was doing now.

I see you. I feel you.

Her mother slammed her palm on Sera's forehead and whispered, "Out of the darkness and into the light." A rush of frostbitten air went through her. Tears pricked her eyes with the ease of breathing, and she knew she needed to thank her mother, but when she turned, Lavinia was throwing out spells across the Menage.

"Go back to your realm and meet us on the battlefield if you wish a fair fight." Blackwell was standing now, circling the table, and threw a beam of magic toward the demon.

Sera didn't know what she was expecting. An explosion? For him to disintegrate? Instead, the intruder walked right through it. Untouched.

Coven members tripped on their robes as they rushed up the steps to escape.

"Come on," she gritted and dove deep into herself. She hovered over that well of dark power: "Come back to me." There was no spell for her to complete. No way for her to pull this... thing... back inside her.

The demon's power thrummed over the amphitheater. The ring on his finger, a silver skull with sapphires for eyes... She'd seen that ring before, and others like it. Always a skull, just different metals and stones sketched beside the forms of the horned beasts. Her breath caught in her throat.

This was a lord of Gehenna.

"Blackwell, you should know better than to use your magic on me. Try it again, and I'll kill this little witch here." He pointed to Nora.

No.

Sera took a step toward her sister, toward the danger in the center of the arena floor. Somehow, Nora kept the portal open, even with the darkness feeding on it. Sweat dripped down her sister's temples. The demon stroked her face with two fingers.

Fury prickled through Sera like needles. The chains she had wound tight were barely holding on. Soon, they would be a cage of twisted metal lying between her ribs, and everyone in this arena would be dead.

"Seraphina, do something!" Her mother pointed and cast, pointed and cast.

More of the abomination seeped from its cage and darted through her veins.

Pain. If she wanted to control it, she needed pain.

Sera clawed at her fingers and demanded that the magic return. She put her tongue between her teeth and bit down until her mouth filled with the taste of iron.

"Ahh, yes," the demon said. "I know all your little magic tricks." He looked at Blackwell and then Thorne. "You've been up here too long. You forgot *who made you*."

"Demon, return hence to where you came." Blackwell's voice cracked.

Sera spat blood on the floor between the benches, and slowly, her magic obeyed. Where were the other Council members? The Mesar? Where was the fucking Legion? Her mother let out a shuddering breath, silent tears tracking down her cheeks. Lavinia grabbed her arm, keeping her there.

"You can do it, Nora. Keep it open." Sera willed her sister to hear her words. She was twisting her magic around her wrists, pulling as one would a rope, and as her darkness receded, the top of Nora's portal returned to blue.

"Demon," Chair Thorne said. "This is a novice witch. You're committing a war crime against our coven."

"And who said I was going to kill her?" the demon said. "After all, a witch wouldn't be able to call to me unless she had magic that sang to Gehenna."

In a heartbeat, he grabbed Nora, and her sister screamed.

No. No. NO! Sera sprinted around her mother's barrier toward her sister, her black magic bending to her will.

Her sister clawed, struck, and screamed.

"Let her go!" Sera shouted. Her legs burned as she tried not to trip down the steps leading to the dirt arena. He couldn't have her. She wouldn't let him.

The demon pulled Nora flush to him and dragged her back into the black abyss.

"Mama!" Nora screamed.

He was pulling her through the beautiful blue frame. The black center reached around the demon, thousands of hands pulling him back to the depths from which he came.

Sera's heartbeat thundered in her ears. Hard stone turned to soft dirt of the Menage floor. The air around her pulsated with static.

Dominick's voice rang out. "Sera, behind you!"

She jumped, her arms outstretched, extending, reaching for her sister. A purple projectile singed the ends of her hair, heading straight for the portal.

The last image Sera saw as she hit the dirt was Nora's face frozen in a silent scream. Then there was nothing but an explosion of magic.

He had taken her. A demon, the mortal enemy of her coven, had taken her sister.

The cage rattled. It rattled and cracked within her chest. Her arms shook with the tension of holding it closed. They burned with it. She gripped the dirt in her hands and cried out.

"Sera!" Dominick's face was taut, his mouth moving too slowly for her to comprehend. A roaring of flame turned into booming in her mind.

I see you. I see you.

Chimes. "Attention—initiating lockdown—remain indoors—trust the Council."

"We need to run, Sera." Dominick held out his hand, and she took it. "Come on, before we're locked out!"

Her head spun. Sera spat out a mouthful of blood and rose to her knees, but that black vortex within her raged.

Nora gone. Nora gone. It seemed to chant within her, and she couldn't bring herself to move. It wasn't until there were hands under her and a sharp shoulder in her middle that she realized Dominick had her.

She built her usual mental brick wall around that well of darkness. It wasn't working. The void absorbed each layer.

Dominick put her down for a moment and pushed open a door leading to a quiet hallway. Books and quills lined the floor, waiting for their students to come back to them.

Sera sank to her knees in the hall and trembled. It was agony. How was she ever going to control this? Her face burned as the flames of her darkness pressed against the inside of her skin.

The vision of her mother's hand stripped of its color, blistered and scorched, flashed through her mind, and behind it, like a bloody chorus, was the sound of screaming humans from Feybury.

"It's my fault," she heaved. "They took her. She's gone."

"It's going to be all right," Dominick rubbed her back.

Sera pushed him away and crumpled further into herself. Her body seized. Just like that Legion officer, just like those people. The roiling inferno roared again. The smell of smoke lingered in the air. Her breath burned.

"Breathe." Dominick pushed out a wave of magic. She knew he meant to soothe her, but as the humming green light touched her skin, she cracked.

"Shit," he hissed. "Sera, what's happening?"

Nothing mattered. Nora was gone. Dominick saw what she truly was: a monster. She couldn't stop the sobs that racked her body. The flood of shame in her heart.

"Wait, you need to stop. *Stop, Sera!*" The panic in his voice was enough for her to look up. A solid pillar of mist encircled her from floor to ceiling. Twirling around it were achromatic flames, a blaze of black, gray, and white.

It flared wider. Sera lunged for a quill atop a pile of books. Pushed the sleeve of her keeper uniform to the elbow, gripped the quill, and stabbed.

Sera yelped and pulled the metal tip, letting it rip her flesh and, with that, calming the raging magic around her. She called to her magic, and finally, the mist and flame listened. Sera consumed the defiant abomination, sucking it in like a desperate breath of air.

Dominick's face was white. The books around her had been reduced to ash.

Sera pulled down her uniform sleeve and pressed on her fresh wound. Down, down, down her well of power went. It was so much worse than she thought. Sera closed her eyes and wrapped her arms tight around her knees, welcoming the sting.

Dominick slid closer. "Sera," he whispered. "What happened?" He was still pale.

"Do you hate me?"

"Hate you? I don't even know what you are."

All she could do was nod. He was right. She had kept this from him after everything they'd been through. "I deserve that." She wiped tears from her face. "I don't know what I am either."

"When did you know you possessed foreign magic?"

"Galene sent me on my first artifact retrieval trip three months ago. I was supposed to recover documents and ledgers from a small human village near the borders. The officer indicated an artifact was sticking out of the ground in a field."

Sera scooted herself until her back hit the wall across from Dominick. "I went to see what was there and dug." She ran her trembling hands through her hair.

How would she explain this? What she did to those people? That Legion member? It was unspeakable.

"When I started digging, I found something hard in the dirt. I did my best to follow protocol and retrieve it. I started using my tools, but I got impatient. I used my finger to brush away a clump of dirt, and when I did..."

"What happened?" His gaze was glued to the ground.

It was tempting to lie, to tell him something else had happened, anything but the truth. Sera bit her cheek and lowered her head, hoping some fabrication would come to mind to get her through this. She clenched her fists at her sides. No, it didn't matter now.

"When I touched whatever that piece was," she continued, "it was like the world ended. A black mist covered the entire town like a death fog, and then flames engulfed every structure. I had no control, no idea what was happening, only the feeling of being burned alive. Like every inch of my body was aflame. I... I passed out." She refused to look at him, not wanting to see his reaction to what came next. "The entire town was on fire, Dominick. So many humans died, and the Legion guard..." Her nose burned from holding back tears. "My mother, she heard me somehow. I can't describe it, but she knew. She threw me through a portal, and that was the end of it. I don't know what she did, I don't know whose minds she melted to erase the memories of that day, but she did enough so the Council didn't catch wind of it."

Dominick was still. "So you don't know what it is? The magic, I mean?"

She shook her head, the movement swirling her insides. They were both silent. She pictured the flames snaking down her arms and incinerating the guard, how the fire melted his skin in a matter of seconds. She thought of the woman who called her a creature, but wasn't that precisely what she was?

A monster?

For three months, she had searched any records she could, within the archives and without, for knowledge of witches or warlocks who could wield flame black as night. After weeks of searching, she'd found nothing, not even in the ancient demon tomes, at least the parts she could decipher.

She'd tried talking with her mother about it, but Lavinia kept telling her to bury it. Any conversation about the abomination was evidence of guilt.

Dominick cleared his throat. "Why didn't you tell me?" She heard how hurt he was by the tone of his voice, and her heart cracked a little more.

"I don't know. I was so ashamed. I had killed so many people. It changed me. What it did, what *I* did."

Dominick's mouth was set in a grim line. "I could have helped you cope, shared this burden with you. Sera, you've been a fucking shell lately. You don't sleep, you barely eat... I could have done something."

"I didn't want you to," she whispered. "I didn't want you to know what I did. I'm a monster, Dom. I've researched the traits of each race and found no information on this power. I can't find anything about mist or black flame. Beings like me don't exist, and the scariest part is that I think this was in me all along."

"I see," he said.

"That's it?" That couldn't be it. She was unnatural. A defective magic wielder. A liability.

"What are we going to do about Nora?"

"I don't know. I imagine my mother has already forced her way before the Council and demanded a rescue squad."

"Okay," he said and stood.

"Dom? Do you hate me?"

He huffed a laugh and looked at her. "Of course not." He ripped a long strip off his robe and motioned for her to come closer.

Sera stared at his outstretched hand.

"You going to let me wrap that or not?"

"I don't want to hurt you." All she could think of was the warrior she had incinerated. The one who'd grown up in Jedan. The one for whom missing posters were pasted throughout her quarter—the sole reason she had started helping the lessers to begin with.

"If you do, I wouldn't even be mad. Just make sure to spell out *Fuck You* with my dust on the Ogdelo floor, yeah?" Sera extended her arm, and Dominick got to work. "You're going straight to the healer."

"I can't." Dominick raised his blond brows at her. "What if one of my mother's memory spells missed? What if they are already reporting me to the Council?"

"You and I both know she didn't miss a single coven member. Me included. The first time I saw anything weird was in this hallway." He stood, extended his hand, and Sera took it.

She shook on wobbly legs. "Thank you," she whispered.

"Did you hate me when I told you my secret?" he asked.

"Of course not. Who you love doesn't matter to me."

"Then why would I turn away from you and yours? You're still my Sera. You're still my best friend, and I will always love and be here for you."

She hugged him hard. "Are you sure you don't like witches?" Dominick wrapped his arms around her. "Because I could kiss you right now for that."

"If I did, Seraphina Wildrick, I would have wrecked you for anyone else years ago."

CHAPTER SEVEN

SERAPHINA

As much as she hated it, she was grateful that Dominick had insisted she see a healer. Her reasoning for the cut on her forearm wasn't the best, but they didn't dare raise their brows in front of a member of Daedeth. Dominick was above them, and who were they to question a warlock on a higher level?

Such a dangerous policy.

When Sera got to her mother's street, it was eerily serene compared to the rest of the Citadel. She stood at the base of the stone steps leading to her mother's row house. It was made from the same white stone as the buildings in Citadel proper—all the homes in Daedeth Quarter were.

Fifteen years ago, Nora had picked out the color of the door. Red, for their father's placement, and their mother had kept it that color ever since.

Sera couldn't help that it reminded her of blood. Suddenly, every bad thing she ever heard or read about Gehenna wasn't happening to a stranger. They were happening to Nora.

Was her body being ripped apart and fed to lesser demons? Burned alive? Mutilated and tortured? What foul experiments could a lord of Gehenna conduct on a witch? A sob left Sera's throat. She gripped the stone post, steadying herself, choking down fear and bile.

Nora would be all right. She had to be. One sorry step at a time, Sera climbed the steps to her mother's door. When she beheld the purple rose petals, meant to signify Nora's decision to go into arcane, the tears she'd worked so hard to keep back fell like anvils from the Citadel's walls.

She turned the knob to her mother's row house and stepped inside.

Her sister's robes and cloaks hung on the hooks neatly, below them a few pairs of shoes and beaded slippers in a row on the floor. She almost lost herself again when her mother rounded the corner.

"*Teesina*," her mother said, casting a barrier to muffle the sound. "What have you done, Seraphina!"

Sera's breath shuddered. This exchange was so familiar to her that it was almost comforting.

"We both know I didn't do anything on purpose." Sera kept her voice even, despite the urge to scream. The well of darkness inside her was noticeably quiet despite her rising anger, a slight relief.

"Your abomination! You manipulated that portal. There is no other answer for it. Your utter lack of self-control has endangered more than you or me this time."

Her mother's words left their mark right where intended.

It was true. Her strange magic had wrapped itself around Nora's portal, turning it from blue to black, cursing it with darkness.

"You think I wanted this?" Sera clenched her jaw. "Why would you think I'd ever do anything to hurt Nora? Why would I want a demon to steal my sister? I can't control this."

"It doesn't matter now." Her mother's voice was like a stone under-water—deep and unmoving. "You'll get her back." There was something more fathomless than rage in her mother's amber eyes. A storm of anger and panic just below the surface.

"I'll do anything. Just tell me what to do." She opened her palms and let her arms drop to her sides.

"I don't think you understand, Seraphina Wildrick. You will go to Gehenna and bring her back where she belongs. I do not care if you die doing so, but you will get her, and you will bring her back to me."

Her words felt like a slap, the verbal handprint purpling across Sera's mouth. "Mama," she whispered. "How do you expect me—"

"Spineless," Lavinia spat. That storm in her eyes hadn't wavered, even though Sera had let down the walls in her mind, revealing every tortured thought and emotion. But that didn't matter. Lavinia didn't soften for her. At least she hadn't in a very, very long time. "That's all you've ever been. Sniveling and deficient. You've been a burden since you came into my life. I don't care." Lavinia threw her hands up. "We meet in front of the Council in an hour. You will volunteer and get your sister back."

"This is suicide! The Council would never let a Dobro-level witch enter the underworld. If that's even where Nora is!"

Her mother paced in the small sitting room. The cream-colored walls pulsed inward with every step she made on the sage carpet—closer, closer—until the breath in Sera's lungs stalled. How would she get to Gehenna? And once she made it, what was she to do?

"Did you think I just stood and watched that monster take my daughter?"

"Of course not. The crowd you—"

"Not just the crowd, Seraphina." Lavinia threw her hands out. Her black robes swished around her with each step. "I ripped into that demon lord's mind. If I had moved to save your sister, he would have snapped her neck."

Sera knew her mother was powerful, but to dive into a demon lord's mind without cognizance was a skill unmatched by any other mastria. Surely, if that lord had known what her mother was doing to him, he would have ripped them all to shreds. A shiver of fear snaked around the column of her spine.

"I've done so much more than that to protect you. You think the Council missed your defect? You think they didn't notice the dark magic seeping out of you?" Her mother crossed the room and opened the front door wide. More purple petals tumbled across the steps and into the entryway.

"I will not keep them waiting." The golden glass beads in Lavinia's braided hair clinked as she descended the steps. She was right. Nora needed to be rescued as soon as possible.

A chilling breeze whipped down the street, and Sera looked out onto the quiet Daedeth corner.

For so long, she hadn't wanted to believe it. Had told herself that somehow, someday she'd figure out a way to master this darkness within her. Every single day had been a fight.

The elixirs didn't work.

The pain didn't work.

And now she'd harmed her mother. Sera's utter lack of control had gotten her sister taken to the underworld. And Nora... Sweet and young Nora didn't deserve this.

Only with magic who sang to Gehenna. That voice... What was it?

"Let's go," Sera said and followed her mother toward the Council chambers.

She had walked these halls more than most coven members. The first time was when her mother had been appointed master mastria ten years ago. Then on her trial day, when her mother had demanded Sera's placement be in Dobro and not Jedan. Now they walked the halls again, hoping to save her sister.

Sera's gaze was fixed on the grand wooden doors.

The chambers hadn't changed. Exotic greenery draped tall columns of white marble. Lush leaves, roaming flowers, and ivy that didn't grow anywhere else in the Citadel flourished here. It was a disservice that most of the coven members didn't get to witness the beauty of it, to breathe in the soft scent of the blooms.

Between the displays of plant life were the faces of the first rebellion leaders, woven into the weft threads of tapestries lining the walls, celebrating the freedom they'd gained two thousand years ago.

It was all beautiful, but Sera couldn't look away from the mess she had made of her mother's hand. On the walk over, her mother's fingers had swelled to twice their size. Blisters had erupted, along with angry pink patches of missing pigment.

She had done that. Guilt choked her, but she forced herself to not look away from the damage.

Sera had harmed her mother in such a way that the beautiful pigment of her skin had been stripped. She was a monster. A fucking abomination that deserved to be locked away.

Sweat rolled down the length of her back, inch by inch, with every step she took toward the carved arched doors.

If her mother had missed even one person in that crowd, if they had seen what Sera was and reported her, this would be the last time she would see the light of day. Too many times, Sera had heard of witches and warlocks being tortured for not adhering to the coven's requirements, seen them dragged from their homes. What would be the punishment for her? She could imagine that if they ever found out she had burned an entire human village to the ground, the first place they'd throw her would be the tower.

Lavinia and Sera reached the doors, which opened wide of their own accord. Then closed shut behind them.

The deliberation room was circular, its vaulted ceiling ribbed in crisscrossing marble. The farthest portion of the curved wall was made entirely of floor-to-ceiling windows.

Sera wished she could admire the view. Take in the vastness of the ocean beyond. This was the only room that she knew of in the entire Citadel that allowed for a break in the walls to view the sea. But blocking that view were five Council members sitting in their golden thrones.

"Solarni Council." Sera bowed deeply, sinking to one knee. Her heart pounded as she kept her eyes on the floor. She was centered in the blazing mosaic sun.

"Rise." Chair Briar's voice was like tumbling gravel. Her dark jowly cheeks drooped to her neck.

Sera stood and acknowledged each Council member. Blackwell and Thorne were pale. They looked as rattled as she felt. She wasn't surprised, since they were the only Council members who had actually seen the demon. Chair Renata sat in the center, poised as ever, while Chair Corbin had his usual scowl. Off to the side, in the only shadow the windows allowed, stood a figure. A guard.

"Council." Sera kept her hands clasped in front of her. "It is my greatest wish to be granted permission to leave the coven and rescue my sister."

She'd do anything. Take Nora's place, be knocked down to Jedan, anything. But she wasn't leaving this chamber unless they approved her to go, or locked her in the tower.

Silence blanketed the room. Swallowing its thickness, she waited. Chair Blackwell's red robes rustled as he changed position. "Witch, do you think yourself capable of this task?"

"Yes, sir, I believe I am—"

"From what I remember of your trial date, you were placed in Dobro only after your mother petitioned us. Is that correct?" Sera snapped her attention to Chair Thorne, who was giving her a quiet smile.

"That's correct, ma'am."

"What skills do you have now as a Dobro witch such that you believe slipping into the underworld and rescuing your sister will end successfully?" Chair Corbin's gaze cut her to the bone as surely as one of Sera's keeper's trowels would.

"Sir, I am knowledgeable about artifacts, magical objects, ruins, and demon history. I also have barrier magic and am resourceful." Her darkness began to heat in her gut.

So little faith. Sera winced at the phantom voice. What was it? And how?

"The witchling is barely four years out of her trial," Chair Thorne added, pointing to Sera.

Corbin adjusted his grip on the arms of his throne. "Renata, do you think losing another witch is a good idea?" He leaned over, giving the lead chair a pointed look.

Renata barely moved. She tilted her head, her long blond hair falling from her shoulders.

That heat from her magic snapped through Sera's veins. She took a deep breath.

"The power Honora carries is not something we can ignore. We do not know what the demon lord will do with her. They could use her against us." Briar's shaky voice sounded more frail than minutes before.

"A novice with portal magic already so advanced," Thorne said, more to herself than the room.

Sera could feel the annoyance radiating off her mother. Lavinia whispered something behind her, but she couldn't make out what it was. The figure hiding in the shadows seemed to stiffen, but the chairs carried on with their conversation as if Sera weren't even there.

Sera clenched her fists until her knuckles screamed.

"That is doubtful, Briar," Chair Blackwell said. "Honora Wildrick has no formal training other than basic schooling. Regardless of her skills, she never received a placement."

"Blackwell has a point," Chair Briar said. "The demons have not had consistent access to witches' or warlocks' power in two thousand years."

Sera followed the conversation until Renata's piercing blue gaze beamed into her. A condescending smile coated her lips. Sera couldn't look away fast enough.

"Out of everyone, I didn't expect you to be so naive, Briar." Chair Corbin curled his lip. "There are those who do not claim the Solarni coven as their home."

Lavinia stepped to Sera's side, and the chair holders stopped arguing. The figure in the shadows straightened and moved into the light. Sera couldn't make out who it was, only that they were outfitted in a Legion uniform.

"Council members, I also wish that my eldest daughter retrieve my youngest. Honora is too talented to be in the enemy's hands. Seraphina may not be the strongest, but her mind and her bond with her sister make her the most motivated."

Lavinia sank to her knees, placed her forehead on the mosaic floor, and spread her hands before the Council members in complete submission. Shock washed through Sera. Her mother never submitted, never backed down from anything. She was poised and powerful. Many had fallen under her scrutiny, Sera included, and here she was with her face on the floor.

Then she heard it. Her whispers.

"Master Mastria Lavinia Wildrick." Chair Renata's voice cut through the air. "We thank you for your input and cannot imagine the devastation you must be feeling, but surely you have thought this through and know you may lose both of your daughters in this task?"

Sera realized this was the first time Renata had spoken.

Her mother stood to answer Renata's question. "I would ask to go in her stead, but as we agreed earlier, I am unable to leave my post due to the current political climate."

Of course her mother had already approached them to retrieve Nora. But why hadn't she shared this information earlier?

"You are more than just a Dobro keeper, aren't you?" Renata's gaze pierced Sera. "You know prewar demon customs, do you not?"

"I—I know many, yes."

"And tell me, are you familiar with the old maps?"

Sera was hesitant to answer. Yes, she had researched and looked at the ancient scrolls containing maps of the continent, the ones that originated from the demon realm. Renata's question had to be a trap, for junior keepers weren't supposed to access those texts. Not even Galene had access. Sera had used her mother's influence to read them, along with anything else that might explain this dark magic she held.

"Go on," Renata said. She pushed her blond hair off her shoulders and readjusted her gray robes.

"Yes, I am familiar with the scrolls you are talking about."

"Wonderful. Captain Alcott, please bring the scroll."

Sera froze. Alistair Alcott marched forward with the scroll clenched in one hand, but he didn't turn his gaze to her. He was bigger now, so much bigger than she remembered. She hadn't seen him since he and Colton left for the Legion. But she'd remember that dark hair and smug look anywhere.

She'd kill him for the way he was handling the artifact. It might have been protected by a preservation spell, but it was still ancient. At least he was wearing gloves.

Renata commanded the scroll to unroll, and Sera saw a crudely outlined drawing of the continent. North of the Lanac mountain range lay the human territories, sectioned off into their respective kingdoms. Dense forests had taken over the eastern side of the continent, though there were more now than there must have been when this map was made. And along the eastern coast were the Deadlands.

"Can you point to me where the Citadel is?"

On a peninsula spearing the ocean on the southwest shore was their fortress. As Sera moved forward to indicate it, her arm brushed against Alistair's. A fluttering went through her as he worked the muscle in his jaw.

Sera raised her shaking hand and pointed to the Citadel.

"What other landmarks are you aware of?" Renata continued. Some of the other chairs murmured and grumbled.

"Here"—she pointed—"is the Emerald Glade. Here is the Lanac mountain range. Then over here are the Deadlands." The map clearly depicted the barren scorched earth. Gehenna was entrenched deep below the surface, making the land above uninhabitable.

"Renata, why are we playing this game? Can we continue with our deliberation? I have more important things to worry about."

"I am trying to make a point, Blackwell. Do not rush the witch." Renata didn't even look at Blackwell—no, she kept her gaze glued on Sera. "What cities do you know of that are occupied by demon rulers?"

Sera swallowed. Her darkness swirled inside her. "Ceasefall is located here." She pointed to a spot directly in the center of the Deadlands. "Then here is Port Sidnah."

Her mother let out a sigh of relief.

"I propose we allow Seraphina Wildrick to assist the captain with retrieving our oracle. If she is as resilient and knowledgeable as Lavinia claims, she could also help find the doorways into Gehenna." Sera shivered under Renata's piercing blue gaze. The scroll rolled itself up, and the Council elder handed it back to Alistair. "If you complete this task, we will provide you with a team of elite Legion warriors to accompany you to extract Honora Wildrick."

None of this was making sense. Find doorways? For what? Sera needed to get to Nora. She could be hurt. Demons could be torturing her sister right now. "But, Chair, no one has ever—"

"She will do it," Lavinia said from behind her.

Renata's smile was triumphant.

"Captain Alcott, would you be able to bring Witch Wildrick with you and still succeed in your mission?"

"If that is what the Council wishes, then it will be so," he said matter-of-factly. The baritone in his voice gave her an involuntary shiver. His blue Legion uniform accentuated his biceps and tapered waist. Standing at ease with his feet shoulder-width apart, he was almost a full head taller than her. Heat rose from her neck to her cheeks.

"Then I call for a vote," Chair Renata said. "All in favor of allowing Seraphina Wildrick to accompany Captain Alcott on his quest to find the oracle, say aye."

She held her breath. Three months ago, she'd thought the destruction of Feybury would be the event that got her killed. She'd been expecting Legion soldiers at her door, but that never came. But now, as the chairs were about to seal her fate, she couldn't help but think she'd never see the Citadel again. She'd never see Dom or Nora or her mother ever again.

"Aye." Blackwell.

"Nay." Corbin.

"Nay." Thorne.

"Aye." Briar.

"With my vote of aye, the motion is approved. Seraphina Wildrick, you will report directly to the barracks within twenty-four hours to Captain Alcott. Please ensure your affairs are in order. Your occupational mentor will be alerted," Chair Renata announced.

That was it.

"Meeting adjourned." Chair Blackwell stood from his throne.

Her mother turned on her heel and exited the chamber, not sparing Sera a second glance. She'd gotten what she wanted.

"Thank you for allowing me to save my sister," Sera said, and bowed to the chairs. She glanced at Alistair. He kept his face forward, his chin high, not even a hint of acknowledgment.

Seraphina bowed once more and left.

CHAPTER EIGHT

SERAPHINA

Dark clouds hung over the stalls and tents of the open market in the middle of Citadel proper. Petrichor hung heavy in the air, and if Sera was to guess, the sea on the other side of the Citadel walls was probably raging.

Dominick was uncharacteristically quiet. She'd told him about the meeting with her mother and the Council the day before. About her new assignment and the bickering between the chairs. The only part she'd left out was who was taking her. It was not going to make him feel any better about Colton.

"What about a scarf?" Dominick asked.

"During summer?" She had no idea what she needed or what would be provided to her. All she knew was that she was grateful Dom had agreed to tag along, even if that meant a mark against him.

"Good point." Dominick shrugged and wrapped the hideous blue lace scarf around the front of his head, tucking it behind his ears. He loved reenacting that old joke from when they were children—his poor substitute for long hair.

"Put that back," she hissed, hoping the vendor didn't see him. Dominick smirked, folded the scarf haphazardly, and placed it back on the table.

The market was set up along a side street. Fluttering flags danced in the sea breeze. The Jedan workers displayed the Council's goods on racks with signs that seemed to change color with every passing moment.

Sera greeted the Jedan member manning a tent with leather goods.

"Is there anything I can help you with, Keeper?" The warlock kept his eyes averted, but she knew who he was. How he'd been sleeping in the Jedan streets beside the buckets of ash and waste.

"Just these," she said and pointed to a pair of black gloves.

"What in the world do you need gloves for?" Dominick asked and rolled his eyes.

Needing them wasn't the point. It was the fact that *this* warlock had now brought in a sale. And though profits were meant for the city, not a Jedan member's pocket, he'd be incentivized with better lodgings if he sold enough. "You never know," she said to Dom and winked at the warlock, who handed her the gloves as if they were precious.

Sera slipped a few extra coins into the warlock's empty tin cup and followed Dominick down the row, passing a booth selling pocket mirrors. "How am I going to talk to you?" she asked. "I don't think these can be used over long distances."

"Maybe you can sweet-talk your captain into using whatever he communicates with." Dominick winked at her.

"About that..." Colton and Alistair had been inseparable most of their lives. Out on the streets, causing chaos among the quarters, bloody from fights, and then accepting their punishments. The two had entered the Legion together. Sera assumed that they'd been placed in the same battalion. Apparently this wasn't the case, or at least not anymore.

But that wasn't why she hadn't told Dominick. She worried that after the conversation they'd had at Mystic's, he'd be upset, or worse, worried. "The captain is Alistair."

Dominick stopped walking. "Alistair is taking you on this adventure to find the doorways? He shouldn't be out of the Legion ranks. He's supposed to be with Colton."

"I'm aware." She chewed on the inside of her cheek while her friend fretted and scratched that spot under his ear.

"I'm going to send another message to Colton tonight. Wait—didn't you?"

"Please don't say it." As if the curdling embarrassment churning in her gut wasn't enough. It had to be *Alistair*.

"Oh, is Shadow punishing you, Seraphina?"

"Seems like it." She groaned.

"For what it's worth, I'm glad he's the one protecting you. At least I can threaten him to keep his hands to himself, or… you know… if you want, I could—"

"Don't you dare!"

Despite Dom's jokes, Sera didn't feel any less guilty, like she was responsible for separating Colton from Al. Every move she made lately was leaving a permanent scar on the people she loved. Nora taken, her mother harmed, Dominick worried: When would it end?

They continued through the market, while worry furrowed Dom's brow. "How did he look? I'm sure he's hot now. He never stopped by during their leave."

Sera cursed under her breath. "I only saw him for a moment," she said, passing a vendor who sold candied nuts. The mouthwatering scent of spices and sugar had her wishing she could bring some with her.

"Oh, I bet there was something to see." Dom kept a steady pace, his hands in the pockets of his gray oracle robes. Whether it was meant to get rid of his anxiety or hers, she wasn't sure, but this string of teasing wasn't going to end until they reached the barracks. "See, I know how the Legion likes to bulk them up. It's always better to have a sword for backup if you're close to burnout. Colton came back looking like he had been lifting boulders all summer, eating eight meals a day."

"Your brother was always exceptionally tall for a warlock, so it doesn't surprise me that he bulked out." The cobblestone changed to smooth white pavers as they crossed the threshold into Daedeth Quarter.

"I'll be sure to tell him just how bulky you think he is next time he's home."

Sera smacked his arm with the back of her hand as they continued down the street. "I need to stop at my mother's to say goodbye. You wouldn't be willing to come with me, would you?"

"I'll meet you at the corner when you're done and walk you to the barracks. There's something I forgot at the market." Dominick wiggled his eyebrows and turned down a side street.

Before Sera could knock on the door to her mother's row house, it swung open.

"You've finished packing," Lavinia said with her typical cold tone. Her dark skin still had a contrasting white patch covering the back of her hand. But the blisters and swelling had disappeared. It seemed even the most skilled healers couldn't return the color Sera's abomination had leeched from her skin. The sight of it caused a thickness in the back of her throat. "How about you worry less about what my hand looks like and focus on saving your sister?"

Sera huffed. "I wish you wouldn't do that."

"I wish you would learn to keep your walls up," Lavinia snapped, pressing a finger to her own temple. Then she turned and left her daughter in the entryway.

Sera rebuilt that wall around her memories and held it there. It was so similar to the cage she kept around her darkness. With such a small well of magic, maintaining both the wall and the cage drained her more than usual. She had tried do something with the abomination, utilize it in a way that might be useful. She'd tried building stronger defenses around her memories with the sometimes inky, sometimes flaming darkness. It didn't work—every time, her mother powered straight through it.

The pressure in her chest increased with each step her mother took toward her. Lavinia's arm extended with something dangling between her fingers.

A stone raven hanging from a cord.

"Your father wished me to give this to you one day. I suppose today is as good a day as any," she said with a grimace. Sera could have sworn her mother shuddered, but that wasn't possible. Lavinia Wildrick wasn't afraid of anything.

"Father left this for me?" Sera asked and held out her hand. Her mother dropped it, then snatched her arm back to her side. Sera rolled the small bird in her palm. It was cool and lighter than she'd expect a solid stone pendant to be.

Her father had died when Nora was still in their mother's belly. Sera had been only three. Her mother explained years later that he had died in the last skirmish before the ceasefire. Sera barely remembered him. Sometimes, she saw flashes of his kind brown eyes in her dreams. She remembered how he would spin her around in circles, sending her into a fit of giggles. He was safety and love, and when he was gone, their home froze over.

Sera tied the cord around her neck.

"Get her back, Seraphina. Bring her home." Lavinia put her whitened hand atop Sera's head and whispered her departing words. "Out of the darkness and into the light." Her mantra she'd repeated for her daughters since they were witchlings. All the times Sera had left the house, her mother stopping her with that phrase—a kiss on the cheek before leaving for studies. Even now, as an adult, Lavinia would place a palm over Sera's head in goodbye after their monthly dinners.

Lavinia's lower lip quivered, her amber eyes cased in glass. If only those tears were for Sera. For just one moment, she wished she could read her mother's mind. See the terrible things that she'd witnessed in that demon's memories.

"I'll do whatever I can," she said. "Even if it's barely anything at all."

She left and slammed the door behind her.

A roaring crashed in her ears, wave after wave of fury, whipping her abomination into a frenzy. She was surprised the lock on the well held tight.

Dominick was waiting for her at the intersection with his head tilted, squinting as if he could see her inner conflict brewing. He started to speak, but she held her hand up to stop him.

Years and years of insufferable comments and shame poured onto her day after day from her mother. Always, Sera had held her tongue. Did she owe her mother everything? Yes. Was she sick of being treated as a failure? Also yes. But that nagging sensation in the base of her skull, telling her that she still needed Lavinia's protection, was boiling over. Sera was sick of needing anyone. She wanted to be self-reliant and strong. She wanted to be... like her mother.

"Give me a minute," she said to Dom and turned toward the barracks. For once, Dominick listened.

When had her relationship with her mother changed? When had the attention she so craved as a child led to dismissal? Sera didn't remember exactly, but nighttime tales as she was tucked into bed had turned into slammed doors and a dark room. Since then, she'd been chasing her mother's approval.

All Nora had to do was breathe, and she was blanketed with praise—the best of everything. The newest dresses, the prettier dolls; meanwhile, Sera got what she got. She'd been agreeable, even grateful, but that had turned to resentment as she grew older. And now that little voice in her head screamed and raged for the witchling she had been.

As they rounded the corner, the barracks came into view. Half the massive building held the living quarters for the soldiers stationed in the Citadel. The other half was littered with training grounds and offices. Travertine pillars supported the domed roof, and one set of marble stairs ran the length of the building.

She'd never been inside. And although she had always been curious to see the layout and the training grounds, Sera wished that she were witnessing it under different circumstances.

"All right," Sera said.

Dominick exhaled like he'd been holding his breath for days.

"You're very dramatic, you know that, right?"

"So you tell me all the time. Spill it."

"Just my mother. Nothing out of the ordinary." Lavinia hadn't even offered her a hug. It stung. Her mother knew she'd be leaving the Citadel walls. Still, she'd denied Sera affection. Or deemed her unworthy of it, and Sera wasn't sure which was worse.

"You need to stand up to her," Dominick said sharply.

"Why? So she can tell the Council I'm an abomination? No, I'd rather take her verbal lashings and get on with my life. Maybe one day, I won't need her in it." Sera cleared her throat and stopped before the steps leading to the barracks. "Plus, she gave me this necklace."

He winced. "It's... nice?"

"Apparently my father wanted me to have it. Honestly, I think it was too ugly for Nora to wear." Sera said this but thought of her mother's outstretched, trembling hand, the way she'd stepped back quickly as if the pendant would harm her.

"If anyone else told me their mother treated them this way, I'd never believe them." He reached out and lifted the raven tied around her neck. "Interesting..."

"What?"

"I don't know," he said, rubbing the pendant between his thumb and forefinger. "There are strings—threads like I see in the pools. I can't manipulate them, but they connect the bird with your heart."

"Maybe it's enchanted?"

"Speaking of enchanted." He grinned and pulled something out of his robe. "I got you something. Well, I got us something." Dominick handed her a leather-bound journal. "I had them enchanted, so when I write something in mine, it will show up in yours, and vice versa. That way, I can always be in contact with you."

Sera flipped through the blank pages, then cradled the notebook to her chest. "Thank you." The corners of her eyes stung, and she knuckled away her tears. Dominick hugged her close and kissed her cheek. She was going to miss him. Writing wouldn't be enough; she needed him. Dom was her home, and for the first time in sixteen years, they'd be apart.

"I can't wait to tell you how hard I railed Sam tomorrow," he whispered in her ear before letting her go.

Sera laughed, wiped her nose, and tapped him with the journal before placing it in her bag. Moons, he was impossible.

"I need you to do something for me."

Dom stood there rocking on his heels, his hands deep in his robes, waiting for her request.

"Under my mattress is some money. I need you to get it to Ithar. Tell him it's from me, and he'll know what to do with it."

"Give it to him when you come back."

"Dom..."

"Fine! I'll keep your little crusade of feeding the poor going while you're gone, but I'm not doing anything past that."

She couldn't help but smile at him. "Thank you."

"Shh, shh, here he comes," Dominick said with a smirk.

She quickly smoothed out her frizz before turning toward the captain. She had grown. They were no longer children. She could be mature about this.

"My, my, he does look delicious in that uniform."

Sera sighed, mostly because Dom was impossible, but also because he was right.

"I would climb him like a tree and ask him to carry me home after. Seraphina, you, my friend, are in deep trouble." Dom straightened his robes. She couldn't help but roll her eyes at him. "Alistair! Wonderful to see you. I thought you would still be in placement with Colton?"

"Dom, been a while." Alistair pulled Dominick in with a big slap on the back that left Dom coughing, then stepped back and pointed his chin toward Sera. "You were due at the barracks thirty minutes ago, and now we're behind schedule." Alistair crossed his arms, his body rigid, displaying his heavily muscled biceps. Some sort of intimidation tactic, or did he want her to notice them?

Sera's cheeks heated. Long gone was the scrawny, lanky warlock of their youth.

"Oh, come now, Al. We're all old friends here," Dominick said.

"I'm just saying my goodbyes. Mind giving me a little bit of privacy?" Sera had laced her question with more venom than she intended. Al shook his head before taking a few steps back.

Dominick gave her a wily grin.

"Don't say it."

Dominick tilted his head. "Don't say what, Seraphina Wildrick?"

She ran a hand through her hair again. "This is going to be a nightmare."

"Listen to me," Dominick said, hugging her again. "I love you. You will do this stupid quest, and then we will get Nora back. I'll even petition to go with you next time." It was easy for him to say: Dominick had access to a deep well of power. She had a little barrier magic and an abomination that needed to be suppressed. "I will write to you every day. I promise to pass along anything I find that may be helpful. Just do me a favor?"

"What?" she asked.

"Try not to catch feelings when he fucks you into oblivion."

By the time the words registered, Dominick was running toward Citadel proper, and she prayed to whatever deity might be listening that Alistair hadn't heard him.

She turned slowly to meet Alistair's gaze, and the smirk he had plastered on his face told her he absolutely had.

CHAPTER NINE

DOMINICK

He snickered all the way past Darine Hall. Sera was going to kill him, or maybe kiss him, depending on how her journey with Al went. Regardless, Dominick couldn't help planting the seed, or whatever they said.

The streets were empty in front of the Ogdelo. A few coven members hurried from one building to the next, creating a well-worn path from the grand Council chambers to the massive barracks. It wasn't until a flash of red barreled toward him that he took any real notice of the people around him.

"Dominick," Sam yelled.

He winced. Moons, he should have ended it last night. He almost had. Then, well, Sam had done that thing with his tongue that Dominick so loved, and Dominick was a weak warlock.

"Samuel, what are you doing out of your perch? Don't you have a ward or something to reinforce?" Dom turned away from Citadel proper toward Jedan Quarter. He wanted to get his task completed before he had time to reconsider. The last thing he needed was to get caught helping Jedan members. Even though he was high on the chopping block, the Council wouldn't hesitate to throw him in the tower.

"We were called for a meeting at the barracks. You want to get dinner after?" Sam reached out and squeezed his bicep, and Dom swallowed his disgust. One thing he hated was public affection among lovers.

"Oh, Sam. Listen." Dom leaned in a little closer. He'd learned that if he lowered his voice, they usually didn't cause a scene. He lowered his head and took in that hopeful look in Sam's eyes. "I think this has run its course."

And as if the dark clouds had opened above them, shock rained over the warlock. Sam's eyes widened for a second, his mouth open, but then, there... Anger. "You fucking prick."

Dominick tried not to smile and backed away slowly. "It's been fun, truly."

"I hope you turn to dust, you asshole," Sam called out, louder than Dom would have preferred. But he wasn't following him, and Dom was grateful for that. Too many messy situationships ending in the middle of the street and he'd have an even worse reputation. He didn't mind, not really. Let them think what they wanted. It still didn't stop him from attracting admirers, at least not yet.

"I'd rather turn to dust than be burned," he said under his breath and continued toward Jedan.

***

"Where the fuck is it..." The doorframe was in rough shape, and he had already gotten one sliver feeling for that blasted hole she'd shown him. She didn't have enough magic to hide a key away, nor had she given him a spare for whatever reason, but Sera had mentioned on more than one occasion that there was a slit between the wall and the frame, and she'd stuck the spare inside.

He had to get her out of this place. When she got back, he'd put his foot down and get her into a nice place in Dobro. The hallway, despite looking clean, smelled musty. He'd refused to use the single bathroom, opting to piss outside if he ever had to. The last time he'd been here was half a year ago. Sera'd had to carry him out of Mystic's, and they'd slept side by side all night, cramped and hot.

There.

He wedged his finger into the space and pulled on the metal. Fitting the key into the lock, he pushed.

"Shadow…" He didn't know where to look first. This wasn't Sera. He checked the symbol on the door and confirmed he was in the right room.

Empty elixir bottles were littered everywhere. Her bed was unmade, clothes strewed about. He had known she was hiding something, and it had broken his heart when she finally told him what it was. But this—Sera's darkness was destroying her.

Dominick grabbed a cloth bag Sera used to carry her books in and placed all the empty bottles inside. Then he wiped the dust from the mantle and swept the ashes from the small fireplace. How had he been so blind? She was practically begging for help—screaming, if her room was any indication. Sera had destroyed an entire human village: no small feat. But this felt like staring into her soul. One that was suffering, disheveled, and lost.

When the room was at least maneuverable, he approached the bed. The sheet bunched under his hand as Dom heaved the mattress up.

"You have got to be kidding me, Seraphina," he whispered to himself, although if she were there, he'd scream it.

Cut into the bottom of the frame was a hole, and in it a large wooden box, filled to the brim with coins. The mattress pressed into his shoulder as he lifted the box, trying his best not to drop any of its contents.

The coins clinked, and a few rolled under the bed when he set it on the floor. She must have been saving for years. There was more than enough here to live comfortably in Dobro.

This was all too much. Sera was unwell. Did Lavinia know this?

He needed to calm himself before making a mistake and cornering the witch. Master mastria or not, one day, he was going to finally give Lavinia Wildrick a piece of his mind.

Dominick reached under the bed, swiping out the few coins that had rolled under it, but instead of his fingers brushing gold, he grabbed a notebook. Opening the first page, he read:

Family Klein... a dozen swaddling wraps for newborn
Family Meulen... fresh produce, asked for a crate, gave them three

He flipped through pages and pages of the palm-size book, the words blurring from the tears collecting in his eyes. She was making a real difference, and every line he read indicated she wasn't paying for frivolous things. She was gifting food, building supplies, and essentials that should be provided to them freely by the Council.

"Shadow bless you, Sera," he said, and sent a kernel of his power to the goddess.

CHAPTER TEN

SERAPHINA

Despite having wanted, in the past, to tour the barracks, Sera was missing a lot of the scenery. It was hard for her to admire the statues and ancient weapons while Alistair Alcott walked in front of her. He collected parts of a coven uniform from one of the many rooms they journeyed through, draping the pants and shirts over his forearm. He nodded to every Legion member who passed, showcasing the line of his overly chiseled jaw.

She needed to get herself together. It'd been years since she'd thought of him, but now, in his presence, she was every bit as awkward as she'd been when they were young.

He turned. His eyes swept her up and down, and damn if she didn't want him to smile at what he saw.

Instead, his face stayed impassive.

Well then. Guess even now, she wasn't his cup of tea.

He continued into a room with stacks of shelves that reached the ceiling. Not unlike her workstation in the keeper wing, but instead of priceless artifacts, the shelves held brown leather boots.

"You won't need anything you packed," he said over his shoulder and led her to an empty table.

"And how do you know what I need?"

"Oh, Minnow," he sighed. Sera wished she would turn to dust right there on the spot. "This isn't my first assignment. And based on how full your pack is"—he held up a gloved finger—"the length of time we are going to be traveling"—he held up another—"not to mention the fact that I'm holding your uniform, I can almost guarantee you won't need anything you packed."

Minnow. It had been years since she'd heard her old nickname. She wished it had been an endearment—that he had given her the name as a sign of playful flirting. Alas, she'd been awarded it because she'd fallen into one of the garden pools, and being compared to a tiny bait fish wasn't particularly sexy.

"You will need armor," he said.

"Armor? I'm not appointed to the Legion. Isn't that what you're for?"

He regarded her again, then chuckled, raspy and deep. "I'm here for a lot of things," he said, and handed her the uniform and a pair of boots. "Go in there and change, quickly. We have a meeting with Chair Renata to review our assignment. If you delay me further, I will leave without you."

"How do you know these will fit?" she huffed, entering a changing area. She closed the curtain behind her and peeled off her shirt.

"I've got a good eye." There was a smile in his answer, and she ignored her fluttering insides.

And of course, they fit.

The brown pants were made of thicker material than her usual keeper uniform and slipped easily over her hips, tying comfortably under her belly button. Her new tunic was long-sleeved but breathable, falling to mid-thigh and dyed coven blue, with the Solarni sun embroidered on the chest.

"The other Council members won't be there?" she asked.

"This is Renata's mission."

Sera pushed back the curtain and emerged. Alistair was leaning casually against the wall, arms crossed, scanning her from head to toe. His nostrils flared for a moment, his full lips pulled to a straight line. Without a second look, he crossed the room toward the table where he'd placed her things.

"Let's see what's in your bag." Alistair gave her a conspiratorial grin and set a Legion rucksack on the table.

"What? Why?" Sera gripped the strap tightly. He didn't need to know what she'd brought. He just needed to get her there.

"Because, as I said, you're most likely carrying nonsense, and it's my job to ensure you can walk long distances."

"I'll be fine. We can go."

He held out his hand. "Give it, Seraphina."

She shivered at each syllable of her name exiting those full lips and handed over her pack. He rifled through her things. Sera all but bit her tongue off as she watched him throw her journal, leather gloves, and comb on an empty table. He'd pulled out the few pairs of pants when she stopped him.

"I'm bringing those."

"These are not thick enough. They're going." He ripped them out of her hand, and three glass bottles of elixirs pinged across the table. Sera caught two of them, and Alistair grabbed the other. He lowered his voice. "Sera, what are these?"

She snatched it from his gloved hand and swallowed hard. "They're for sleep," she whispered.

"Are they contraband?"

She shook her head. "I got them from the healers." She turned one over so he could see the underside where the healer's mark was scratched into the glass. He glanced at the bottle, then right at her. His crystal-blue gaze pierced right through her.

There was pity in that stare, and it was piquing her darkness. He didn't know her anymore. He had no right to judge what she was going through. No one else had to deal with this power, this destruction running through their body every second of every day.

Sera threw the elixirs into the bottom of the rucksack and turned away. He kept glancing at her while he folded an extra pair of brown pants, another Legion-issued tunic, and two pairs of socks. He left the table, giving her a moment to breathe. How was she going to explain this? How could she hold herself together for weeks? Especially under his scrutiny... his pity.

Alistair returned with a brown cloak. He folded it with more care than she'd expected and placed it inside.

"The rest will be returned to you when we get back."

"I need this." She reached for the notebook Dominick had given her. Alistair grabbed her forearm. The abomination snapped inside her, wriggling under the surface where his hand bunched the fabric of her tunic.

"I am a captain in the Solarni Legion, and as of twenty minutes ago, you report to me. I had hoped you had matured more than the last time we interacted, but don't make me pull rank. Minnow." The side of his mouth tilted upward with each stroke of his thumb against her uniform. Her darkness thrashed. "You will follow orders."

Every fiber in her body vibrated with rage as she ripped her arm from his grip. The darkness rolled in her stomach, and she clenched her hands so hard that her knuckles cracked.

Alistair continued rubbing his fingers together, inspecting his hand, then looked back at her. His face puckered as if he'd eaten something sour.

Sera lowered her voice. "Keep your hands off me."

She grabbed the journal Dominick had gifted her and threw it on top of her cloak, making quick work to close her new Legion rucksack around it.

Alistair's face was stone while he continued to rub his fingers together. She'd seen how he'd done that in the throne room the day before. Some weird tic he must have picked up from the Legion. No wonder they had kicked him out of Colton's battalion.

Sera crossed her arms and raised a brow, waiting for him to snap out of whatever trance he was in. He straightened, puffed out his annoyingly broad chest, and walked past her. With no choice but to follow, Sera walked into the hall.

The Council chambers were less intimidating without the other four chairs present. Empty and echoing, no crinkle of robes or murmurs. But the sea beyond the glass was raging. The gray peaks were white with foam, so angry she wondered if the mer were having a hard time with the currents.

Chair Renata sat sharp in her throne, waiting. Her blond hair was slicked back in a bun. Sera noticed two golden wings were clipped behind her ears. An odd hair ornament for a witch, let alone a Council member.

Sera followed Alistair's lead and bowed, keeping her eyes on the floor.

"Captain Alcott, you've outfitted your recruit in our uniform. Wonderful." Renata clapped her hands together and stood.

Sera's chest tightened at the casual use of the word *recruit*. Surely Renata couldn't mean Sera would be commissioned to the Legion even after completing her quest? She had nothing to offer.

"Yes, Chair, I have." He stood up straight and held his hands behind his back.

"I'm sure you are curious about the details of your mission."

"I am," Alistair said. What a diligent soldier he was. Only spoke when spoken to. Standing at ease.

"This is what I have for you. The oracle's name is Ophelia Fray. She was last seen in Ironoak, a human settlement on the southeast side of the Lanac mountain range. She is presumed close to the area, but this information is a few weeks old." Chair Renata picked at her long nails, looking utterly bored. "She has been moving from settlement to settlement every few years. It would be wise to use caution when approaching her. I can't imagine she wants to be caught."

"How did you find this information?" Sera asked. She bit her tongue as soon as the words were out.

Chair Renata squinted at her. "And why do you think it is your place to know? Do you think you should have the privilege, Seraphina Wildrick?"

Sera bowed her head. She knew better, but once again, her curious nature had taken over. It was fascinating to her how the Legion collected information. She couldn't help but think that in two hundred years' time, the next group of keepers would be digging up the lost transcriptions in her same office.

"No, Chair, I do not. Please forgive my outburst."

Renata pursed her lips. "You will report to Captain Alcott and follow his every command. It is imperative that the oracle is secured and brought back to the Citadel. The future of this coven depends on her knowledge and the doorways."

Sera took a deep bow, resisting the urge to look up as she responded. "Yes, Chair."

"Now, as far as the doorways to Gehenna are concerned, once you find them, you will need to mark their locations accurately on a map that Alistair will make available to you."

"But how will I know what the doorways look like?"

Renata turned her back on Sera and glided to her throne. "That is not my job, Witch Wildrick. Surely you must have some idea of what they would look like?"

Very few texts mentioned the doorways. The ones that did were often in the old language, and although Sera was more proficient in it than most, there were still gaps in her comprehension. Still, she knew they were direct lines under Eraphon's surface. Ones that would bring you to the halls of Gehenna.

"I will do my duty, ma'am."

"Good. Now that that is taken care of, Captain Alcott, please pack enough provisions for however long you deem necessary. Everything will be at your disposal."

Sera recognized the smile plastered on Chair Renata's face—one an owner would give a pet.

"You are dismissed," Renata said. Alistair gave her a curt nod and turned to leave the chamber. "Oh, and Seraphina," Renata called out. "If you hope to use the coven's resources to rescue your sister, you'd best ensure you don't hinder this mission."

Sera's mouth went dry. She nodded, then turned on her heel and followed Alistair out of the Council chambers.

CHAPTER ELEVEN

SERAPHINA

Their footsteps echoed through the halls, an unnerving sound amid the silence of the officers' wing. This section of the barracks seemed to have been constructed similarly to the rest of the city. White marble tiles on the walls, and skylights above let rectangles of sun shine on every coven emblem stamped into the floor. It was understated compared to the chambers they had just left, but still beautiful.

Alistair opened his office door, and Sera stepped inside.

"Take a seat," he said as he sat behind a desk that occupied most of the room. There was nothing around the office that indicated it was his. No trinkets or souvenirs, nothing. His father had died serving the Legion, that much she remembered. She had attended the lighting ceremony with Dominick and Colton. She still remembered the hollowed look on Alistair's face when he lit his father's pyre; he couldn't have been more than sixteen.

She sat across from him, wondering how this was going to go.

"You seem nervous," he said.

"Why would I be nervous?" she squeaked, then quickly cleared her throat. He smiled at her then, a real smile revealing a single dimple on his cheek. Heat rose up her neck. As if the warlock wasn't handsome enough, he had that fucking dimple.

"Hmm." He smirked.

"Dominick seems to think you should be placed with Colton. Why are you in the Citadel?"

Alistair leaned back in his seat, entwining his fingers behind his head, lounging. Oh, he knew what he was doing all right, showcasing the lines of his muscled body, tilting his head so the light would bounce off his sky blue eyes. But as he considered her question, his smile dimmed a bit. "I was placed here." He shrugged. "You wanna talk about it?"

"About what?"

He gave her a pointed look, and if she could have melted into the floor, she would have. "Sera." He leaned forward over the desk, as if he were about to reveal her deepest, darkest secret. "I know you had a crush on me when you were younger. Is that going to be a problem?"

She scoffed. "I'm not a witchling anymore, Al."

"The blush across your cheeks might say otherwise."

She rolled her eyes. "It's a little awkward, okay. There, does that make you happy?"

"A little." He shrugged, and that dimple lit up again.

"You're a real ass, you know that?" She pushed her hair back off her shoulders. Sure, she'd had a crush on him when she was younger. Most of the witches did, and he looked half as good then as he did now. He probably had women lined up for him every night. "I was a witchling, and you broke my naive little heart when you turned me down for the solstice ball. Woe is me. Give me a break, Al."

"Oh, come on, Minnow." His jesting smile faded.

"No." She pointed at him. "Don't Minnow me."

"Okay. Serious business only." He held up his hands in surrender. She shifted in her seat and crossed her arms. "Now that we've got that out of the way, what is your magic again?"

She gritted her teeth, and as if the darkness had heard him, it awoke. She clenched her stomach to try and calm it.

"*Barijara*," she said, and pulled her barrier forward. Her skin turned from brown to a shimmering blue light.

His face was blank. "You got to Dobro level with that?"

Sera launched from her seat and turned for the door.

What an entitled prick. He'd teased her relentlessly as a child, but she was done with this.

She'd almost made it to the door when Alistair hissed behind her, shaking his hand as if she had burned him. She hadn't even felt his touch, but her magic must have done its job.

"All right," he said, "I'm sorry. I guess it's kind of useful. Would you please sit back down so we can finish the brief?"

She didn't enjoy hurting people, especially after the incident in Feybury, but she couldn't help but feel a slight sense of pride that washed over her. And how the smugness had been wiped clean from his face.

"I'd never thought I'd hear you apologize," she said and returned to the plush chair, waiting for him to be seated again.

"One of my magical abilities is travel," he said. "I've never been to Ironoak, so we'll arrive near Crowpass tomorrow."

"You're a traveler?" Travelers were exceedingly rare. They could move at great distances within the blink of an eye. But she didn't remember hearing that Alistair was one of them.

"From there," he continued, "we will go to Ironoak on foot, or horseback if we are lucky. Once we find the oracle, I will bring her back to the Citadel."

"Okay, sounds like a plan."

"And your plan is?"

She scrunched her brows together.

"The doorways, Seraphina. Moons."

"If I had been awarded a little more time, I would have done extensive research." Sera crossed her arms. They had to be in the Deadlands or near it. That was where Gehenna's underground kingdom was. The heat from below warmed the land above it, making it barely habitable. At least that's what the texts she had accessed said. "Do you have the map Chair Renata mentioned?"

Al nodded and opened a drawer on the desk. He unrolled the map, using magic to keep it in place as she reviewed it. This was a more up-to-date map than the one Renata had quizzed her on. The locations of the cities she had pointed out had been labeled, as had the human kingdoms. Sera placed her palms on the map and traced the border lines, searching for inconsistencies. She didn't know why, but even now, this felt like a test.

"What do you see, little fishy?"

Sera peered at him through her hair. He was staring at the Deadlands. "I see a map, you troll."

He lifted a brow at her. "Troll?"

Seraphina smiled to herself and pointed at the area in the center of the Deadlands. "Ceasefall was the largest aboveground fortress the demons held in the first six centuries of the war. There had to have been a way into the fortress without moving their army across the land."

Alistair sighed. "That's deep into the Deadlands."

It was. Deeper than she'd ever dreamed of going, but if Nora was being held there or below it, she had to try. There were more ruins besides Ceasefall. "Does the Legion know for certain that Ceasefall is abandoned?" Sera asked.

"No."

She traced her nail down the line where the supposed forest met barren wasteland. "There are outlying ruins, yes?"

"There are a few, but I can get information on others."

Sera nodded. "Then that is where we will start." She'd never thought she'd be headed that far east. Digging up artifacts was a dream, yes, but in the ruins skirting demon territory? It took effort to pull in a lungful of air around the weight that seemed to be sitting on her chest.

"The oracle first, then your doorways."

"Nora is down there. Don't you get that?" He wasn't smiling now. "I need to get this map back to the Council as soon as possible if I have any chance of getting her back here alive."

"This mission, first and foremost, is to find Ophelia Fray and bring her back here. The doorways are a side mission, and frankly, not my responsibility."

Fire burned through her. How could he not care? He knew Nora. Sure, she had been much younger than him, but he'd seen her play and tag along with Sera and Dominick for most of their youth. She was real, not just another casualty. "How dare you—"

"We leave at dawn. You're dismissed." Alistair's face was a cool mask, one that said his word was final. It was written in the hard line of his jaw.

She wouldn't fight him, not now. Not while she needed to calm down before she burned the prick alive. Exiting his office, she searched for a sign indicating the location of the sleeping quarters. Her skin was boiling. She needed to distance herself from him. His face, his smart mouth.

"It's left," he said. Sera couldn't help the scowl as she stomped down the left hall.

CHAPTER TWELVE

SERAPHINA

He was late. Mister High-and-Mighty Captain was late.

Alistair had said dawn, and the sun was about to rise, so where was he? She dressed in her new uniform and leaned on the doorframe of the witches' sleeping barracks, waiting.

Sera ran her fingers through her curls, doing her best to separate the knots from them without creating too much frizz. The thought had crossed her mind more than once that Alistair was doing this on purpose just to fuck with her, all while his comment from yesterday grated in her ears.

I know you had a crush on me when you were younger. Is that going to be a problem?

How conceited could he be? She hadn't seen him in years, and the first thing he did was tease her when Nora was in danger? Then his comment about how the oracle came first? Even now, it made her blood curdle.

She thought storming out of his office yesterday had been an act of defiance. Unfortunately, she'd gotten lost almost immediately and wandered around corridors for an hour or more. A witch had seen her staring down the fourth set of hallways she'd come across and took pity on her. She led Sera to the sleeping quarters and pointed out an empty bunk.

The moment Sera had lain down, she'd wished she'd just gone home and risked being late. At this point, it wouldn't have mattered, since she was waiting for *him*.

Sera's stomach grumbled.

A group of three Legion members passed her in the hall, looking regal in their uniforms. She was dressed the same, but they looked better, stronger. Not even in matching clothes could she fit in. Sera stepped out behind them, hoisted her pack, and hoped they'd lead her to the dining hall. The soldiers were whispering to one another about their orders and exchanging gossip. Nothing too scandalizing: something about a warlock getting demoted, another about a witch being ordered to the demilitarized zone.

While she followed the group, she passed more drawings of the Mesar, displayed at random throughout the halls. Last night, she'd even seen one stuck to a mirror in the witches' washroom. Red-lipped kisses marked the paper, as well as hearts and inventive phrases full of innuendo. It seemed the Legion worshipped the famed demon hunter.

She guessed she would have had more appreciation for the Mesar if she'd been placed in the Legion. He was a sign of strength against their enemy. Only one person at a time was selected for the role. When the Mesar died, another was promoted—but there was no glory in it, since the Council kept the Mesar's identity secret. No ceremonies or medals, just killing. Why anyone would want the position was beyond Sera.

When they were children, Colton and Alistair used to take turns pretending to be the famed slayer. Sera and Dom were *always* low-life demons responsible for dying dramatic deaths.

As she rounded the corner, the scents of breakfast wrapped around her, and her mouth watered. The sounds of cheerful conversation between soldiers filled a large room of tables, some occupied and some not. Along the front wall, an array of food was stacked high. Any breakfast dish you could imagine.

Sera grabbed a tray and piled cinnamon buns, a cup of tea, a taste of oatmeal, and her favorite—a chocolate tart. She found an empty table in the corner of the dining hall and sat, savoring the bliss of the cinnamon bun's sweet frosting. As it hit her taste buds, she closed her eyes and gave a little moan.

"You need meat."

Her eyes flew open to Alistair sitting across from her, straddling the chair backward, his dark hair freshly cropped, his blue eyes striking under his brown brows. Frosting stuck to her cheeks and chin when she pulled the bun away. Frantically wiping her face, she said, "You're late."

Alistair gaped at the pile of baked-together dough and sugar in a heap before her.

"I've been here an hour already, Minnow. I got sick of waiting for you to wake up."

She'd told herself not to let him bait her, not to react, so she focused on other things. His uniform was different. The sun emblem was missing; a basic straight-collared navy shirt with rolled sleeves showcased his tanned forearms. His boots and pants were the same brown as hers. She glanced at the sun on her shirt and then back at him. "Why do you get a plain shirt?"

"Because I've been here longer."

She scoffed and sipped her tea.

"Really, though, you should eat something with more substance. In a few hours, you'll wish you listened to me." He rose from his seat and stopped at several tables to converse with other soldiers. All of them greeted him with a smile or a laugh. Shadow help her; she couldn't keep her eyes off him, the way he moved, commanding the entire room.

Instead of sly jabs, he patted his comrades on the back, gave them sincere congratulations. He allowed his colleagues to tease him. When she was fifteen, she would have sold her soul to get that kind of attention.

A moment later, he smiled at her from across the room and tilted his head to the door.

And now he's caught you staring, Sera. Great job.

Sera wrapped the chocolate tart in a cloth napkin and placed it in her pack. Clearing off the rest of her lonely table, she followed Alistair Alcott outside.

The walls around the Citadel fortress were as white and pristine as the buildings themselves. When they were little, Dominick and Nora would join her in sneaking up the ramparts to glimpse the sea. The walls blocked most of the cool ocean breeze, knitted with brine and mist, from reaching the city streets. Dominick always tried to spit on the sentries below, no matter how often his father punished him when he succeeded.

Sera adored the time she spent watching the waves and would stay as long as she could before Nora made an unconvincing birdcall to warn them of guards.

Nora. Was she eating? Was she hurt? Sera's chest ached with the thought of her baby sister afraid and alone. The sooner she found this oracle and the doorways to Gehenna, the better.

Alistair led her through a steel-gated archway set into the northern wall and waved at the guard to let them through. The screeching of iron chains rang out as the gate lifted just high enough for her and Al to duck under.

"Why aren't we traveling from inside the walls?" she asked. The area surrounding the Citadel was desolate swampland. The briny water that flooded the ground during storms killed the trees' roots, leaving skeletons of twisting branches bleached corpse gray.

"Most coven members don't know I'm a traveler, and I plan to keep it that way," he said while mud sucked at the bottoms of their boots. The sun had started to rise over their part of the world, its pink and orange hues glossing over the pale blue of the morning light. She rarely watched a sunrise. She'd forgotten how beautiful they were.

"I'd think being a traveler would give you all kinds of special privileges."

"My position requires... subtlety."

Of course he would squander his power's privilege. Sera grunted against the mud gripping her boot and pulled her foot free seconds before she stumbled.

"Are you ready, Wildrick?" Alistair held out his hand. She hesitated, lifting a brow at him. "Coven founders, Sera. I have to be touching you to travel."

The darkness in her gut began to twirl. She swallowed and glanced from his hand to his face. This was it. She was leaving her home.

Alistair stood there, assessing her.

Sera beheld the golden spires glinting in the sunlight. She took in the white domes peeking above the tall walls that protected her coven from the outside world, and breathed in one more deep breath of the ocean wind.

Her sister needed her. It didn't matter that she was terrified or that everything was about to change.

"Okay," she said, but instead of putting her palm in his, she looped her arm through his elbow and waited. She could almost feel his eyes roll.

"Don't puke," Alistair said.

"Wha—"

Chapter Thirteen

Seraphina

Traveling felt like standing up too fast. Her heart slowed as the blood rushed to reach her brain. She breathed in through her nose and out her mouth to keep from expelling the dough and sugar she had inhaled earlier. Meat wouldn't have stayed down any better than cinnamon rolls, though, and despite the churning in her stomach, she didn't regret her decision.

Somewhere in the pocket of the universe, she went from having her arm looped through Alistair's to hugging him tight around the middle, keeping herself upright. Her nose was buried in his tunic, enveloped in his scent of sage and sea salt.

Of course he smells good.

"Are you all right?" Alistair asked.

She opened her eyes and looked into his. The light blue outer ring held a golden center that burst from the pupil, lined by dark lashes. She wished she could swim in them. "I think so," she whispered.

"Can you let go of me then?" His arms splayed wide.

She stepped backward and dusted off her uniform, desperate to look anywhere but at him, and hid her burning cheeks. So incredibly stupid. They had been out of the Citadel all of ten seconds, and she was already embarrassing herself.

"Which way do we go?" she asked.

The forest's canopy reached to caress the clouds. Some of the trees successfully dipped their leaves in the cerulean sky. Their bark was thick and rough, with protruding knots from the damage of fallen branches. She'd never seen a tree trunk that thick before. The trees near the Citadel were skinny and easy to chop down, with papery bark that peeled with a gentle breeze. These looked like they would take forever to fell.

Even the air smelled divine here. The forest's essence was ancient and organic, leather and loam. Sera basked in the mossy tang, all while a cool breeze caressed her cheeks and rustled the greenery around her.

"That way." Alistair pointed forward and hoisted his pack higher on his shoulder.

"Why didn't we just land inside the town? Wouldn't that have been easier?"

"I always arrive a few miles outside a location. It allows me to assess," he said.

"You mean make an appearance, in your case." She gave a little snort at her joke.

He didn't seem amused. "Right."

The walk to Crowpass was quiet and slow. Each step became more painful as her new boots rubbed her in all the wrong places, but she still delighted in the gentle hum of the trees. The leaves entranced her. The way they rustled as they walked through the underbrush and over dead logs, the vivid greens and browns—it was unlike anything she'd seen before. The Citadel was almost sterile compared to the calm beauty of these woods. She couldn't help but stare at the high branches.

"There are bigger trees in Ironoak, I've been told," Alistair said, interrupting her admiration of the forest around her.

"I can't imagine it," she said.

"Well, we'll see for ourselves soon enough. The eastern companies often tell me it's the hardest wood on the continent."

"What came first? The name of the trees or the town?"

Alistair peeked over his shoulder at her, revealing a small flash of a smile and that damn dimple. "I think it was the trees."

Sera couldn't stop the fluttering in her chest. When he was young, he'd been so skinny that the natural soft hollow hadn't fully formed when he smiled or smirked, not as much as it did now, with his jaw so well developed.

"Do you meet with other companies? Travel to other bases?" she asked, ducking under a low branch.

"Sometimes," he said. "Lately, I've been running confidential missions for the Council. They typically don't require me to have a team. Or a tagalong."

"Sorry to ruin all your fun." She took a step and hissed. Alistair glanced at her again. "I'm fine," she said, biting her cheek. It would be ugly when she removed her boots, but she wouldn't give him the satisfaction of asking to stop, blisters or not.

Alistair grunted and continued walking.

A road of reddened clay, heavily worn by wagon tracks, cut its way through the trees. Alistair threw out his arm and stopped her right before they crossed.

"Do you know how to glamour?"

"You mean to make myself look dull, tired, and ugly, like we were taught in year ten?"

"That's a yes, then?"

"No."

"Shadow help me. All right, stay here." He threw his pack down on the ground. "I'm going into Crowpass and will try to find transport to Ironoak."

Sera slipped off her pack and sat beside their supplies, happy to finally rest her aching feet and calves. "I've got this," she said, motioning to their rucksacks.

He stared at her, suspicion painting his features. In an instant, his dark brown hair was dulled and lined with silvers, his skin marred with spots and deep wrinkles, and his uniform drab and full of patches. He even put on beat-up work gloves to round out the ensemble. But his glamour did nothing to shrink his size. The humans she'd encountered in the past didn't have his physique. She hadn't remembered any of the ones she'd met being quite so large.

He lumbered off, and with Alistair finally out of sight, she slipped off her boot with another hiss. The skin was raw and ripped at the back of her heel. A bloody mess already, and who knew how much farther they had to go.

Not even high sun, and she was a disaster. At this rate, she'd be finished by sundown.

This wouldn't have happened had she been allowed to wear her keeper boots. Leave it to Alistair to make sure they matched.

She sighed. No, the reason for all this was her. Her defect, curse, whatever it was.

Fluttering darkness beat against her rib cage. The walking and pain must have helped keep it calm.

Her mother had corresponded with some tutors, casually mentioning traits of Sera's power to Lavinia's peers in Daedeth class. Every one of them told her to report someone with magic like that to the Council. There was a time Sera had been grateful her mother never followed their recommendations, but maybe Lavinia should have. Then Nora wouldn't be gone.

A chattering yip and the scraping of tiny claws across the hard bark drew her attention as two rats scurried up and down a tree trunk. Instead of having naked pink tails, theirs were plumes of fur and curled as they moved. Unlike the rats that lurked in the alley outside the boardinghouse, these were cute.

All kinds of birds began to appear. Some with red feathered heads slammed their beaks into the thick trunks. Blackbirds with fire-red shoulders pecked at the ground not far from her aching feet.

Thump.

The darkness vibrated within her, straining against its cage.

Thump.

A slow drumbeat pulsed through her veins.

Thump.

Sera placed one hand on her chest, the other on her stomach, and pulled in deep breaths. With every exhale, the forest grew quieter. Birds ceased their singing, and Sera couldn't shake the sensation of eyes on her.

She flinched when one of the rats bolted up the tree. Though Seraphina was not in tune with the ways of the wilderness, she could sense there was a predator in these woods. And she was alone and unarmed.

The abomination snapped and twirled. Each hair on the back of her neck stood, one by one.

Sera rose to her bloodied and swollen feet.

"Barijara," she said and snapped her barrier into place, turning the woods a shade of blue. Her heart pounded in her ears. She should run straight to Crowpass and find Al.

One step, then two. She paused when the sound of hooves against clay thudded toward her.

It was—*he* was— Sera's hands shook so hard her barrier trembled around her.

There was no making out his eyes within the void of his hood. Just the tip of his nose down to a smooth half smile. Beneath the elegant drape of his black cloak was a silver chest plate. Arm guards led to silver gauntlets, their knuckles tipped like spears, holding the reins of the biggest horse she'd ever seen.

The greaves on his shins were polished to a brilliance that reflected the blue of the sky and the green of the leaves. He wasn't human, couldn't be. The pure power in his form that leached into the air around her screamed of something magical.

Sera knew what he was by the color of his cloak. By the rushing wave of magic that flowed over her, through her—the taste of it… Ash. Fear, as suffocating as the heat from the hottest death pyres, ripped the air from her lungs.

"Are you lost?" His voice wrapped her like velvet. If she could lean into it, she would, and the abomination spun circles begging her to do just that.

Let me out. Let me out.

She willed it to listen. *Stay.*

"I'm fine."

"Do you need a ride to Crowpass? Maybe Ironoak?" He tilted his head, and she could feel his eyes trail her from her hair down to her bloody feet.

"No." Sera clenched her fists, desperate to keep her magic at bay, to keep her barrier in place. There was no helping her now. If he wanted to take her, kill her, he could. She'd never get away quickly enough.

Burn them.

Moons, why on sweet Eraphon was her magic whispering to her? It swirled and moved as if being coaxed out to play. She was tempted to let it, but the images of smoky black plumes over Feybury flashed in her mind. There'd be nothing left of this forest. Nothing but ashes.

"Please, move along. I'm fine." She swallowed and raised her chin to the man in front of her.

A flash of glowing red eyes peered at her from beneath his hood. Terror stitched her mouth closed, but the burning red orbs kept her stationary.

He chuckled at her, and for a split second, there was relief. The cloaked stranger gripped his reins tightly, shifting his weight on the noble beast.

In the months Sera had dealt with this cursed magic, she'd experienced pain. Burning, scorching pain. But when Sera looked into this stranger's glowing eyes, agony tore through her.

"Fuck!" she screamed and sank to her knees, clutching at her chest. It was ripping—her heart was tearing itself apart. This wasn't the same sensation her magics gave her, either of them; this was rupturing flesh and muscle and blistering torture.

"Sera!" Alistair was running full speed toward her.

"You?" the stranger asked. His eyes glowed a shade brighter, and he held out his gloved hand toward her. "Come with me."

The darkness thrashed. Her palms were on fire, and although she tried to stop it, tried to ignore that pulling sensation, Sera extended her hand.

Closer, the thing within her chanted.

No!

Alistair materialized between them, sword in one hand, shield in the other. He was no longer glamoured, instead in full coven armor.

"*Na prelaz blizt, demon*." Alistair snarled.

"Are the syllables of my own language supposed to scare me?"

Sera shivered at his smoky utterance, and that ripping in her chest stitched back together—all but one thread, open and raw.

Al threw an iridescent ball of power at the demon, followed by a charge of swinging steel. The stranger ducked the flaming projectile.

"You are making a grave mistake," the demon snarled, his horse prancing and snorting.

"I think not."

Sera's hands were deeply rooted in the clay; she was still and gasping for breath. Between the pain in her chest and the fight before her, she was boiling. She should run as fast as she could away from there. Alistair could travel. He'd find her. She needed to run.

With grace, Alistair charged, the sword an extension of himself. But he was met with a blade of gleaming black stone. Alistair grunted, and the demon laughed as the pinging of steel on stone echoed through the wood.

Sera stumbled to her feet. Her blue barrier winked out.

For a moment, the demon's head turned toward her, his red eyes blazing, his mouth in a snarl. Her flesh crawled under his gaze.

Alistair locked eyes with her and took advantage of the distraction to swing his sword for the horse's throat. Before the blade met flesh, a force unlike she'd ever seen sent him flying backward.

"Al!" Sera froze.

A sickening crunch sounded as Alistair hit the tree, then fell limp to the forest floor.

"*Te sie moj, Subdina.*" The demon's eyes blazed red, and he aimed his horse toward Al. "He will die..."

Show him. That voice, her magic, it was right there. Boiling heat seared through her arteries straight to her palms. "Don't!" she cried.

A whip of dark mist materialized, and in one snap of her arm, she struck. Her magic sang through the air in the form of a whip, and the tip of that conjured scourge sliced into the demon's hood.

A screaming whinny pierced her ears when the demon raised his gauntlet and touched his cheek. The silver steel came away coated with fresh black blood.

"*Neve,* Ponic," the demon hissed, and the horse galloped toward Crow-pass.

"Fucking moons." Sera ran to Alistair, the scourge disintegrating into mist.

She collapsed beside him.

Al's eyes were closed, his neck bent back, revealing the bob of his throat before he let out a groan. Her hands hovered over the Solarni sun embroidered across his broad chest, unsure of what to even do. "Alistair, can you hear me? Are you all right?"

A grimace, then a deep breath, had him squinting his eyes at her. "Did he say anything to you?" Alistair's voice was grating compared to the lure of the demon's, but she'd never been so damn happy to hear it. "Sera?"

"You're worried about what he said to me? You're fucking bleeding, Al!"

Al rolled on his side and raised a hand to his head, and a shining light raced over him. He let out a sigh of relief. "I need to know what he said so I know if he enthralled you."

One, two, three beats of her heart, and she glanced toward Crowpass. Sera rubbed at her chest. The demon's outstretched hand... his blazing red eyes. It was entirely possible. And enthralling—the blood drained from her face—meant to be forced into obedience, to be watched and instructed to tell every secret she ever held. Had he enthralled her? Would she even know if he did?

"He—he asked if I needed a ride into town and if I was lost," she said.

Al rose to his feet. "Look at me."

His gloved hands were warm on her cheeks, keeping her head still. Her only view was the blue outline and yellow center of his eyes, his brow damp with sweat. A few strands of dark hair clung to his temples. Shadow, he was handsome. Sera's heart pounded in her chest, and she was pretty sure he could feel her pulse through her cheeks. His hold grew softer, and his gaze dipped to her nose, then her lips.

"You're fine," he said and let go. "But Sera, you need to tell me... What made him run?"

His question was a punch to the gut. There was no time to process the fact that not only had Sera been able to conjure her darkness without burning down the forest around them... she had conjured a weapon from the abomination. A whip that had drawn the black blood of a demon lord.

Fear slithered up the column of her spine.

Never in her life had Sera been able to do more than create a barrier around her until this well opened. Then there had only been destruction. But if she *could* manipulate it... it would change everything.

Only... Alistair couldn't know.

He was a captain in the Legion who reported directly to the highest chair on the Council, and despite their history, this wasn't something she would be willing to share as a test of loyalty. "I don't know... You hit the tree, and he just took off."

Al was quiet, his face a cool stone. "Let's get going."

"And what if he follows us?"

"Then he follows us, Minnow." He sighed and pushed his hair back. "I'll figure that out when it happens."

"I think we should have a plan—"

"My plans don't normally involve looking after a witchling, but here we are." Al picked up his sword and shield and sent them into some pocket in the universe he had access to.

Silence. It was all she could give him because now she knew what her presence meant to him. A fucking burden.

Sera collected her boots and bloodied socks. The leaves crunched under her as she sat to put them on. Stubborn. Such a stubborn warlock. She hadn't wanted to go on this mission, to find doorways and an oracle. All she wanted to do was save her sister.

"Here." Alistair knelt beside her.

"I'm fine," she said.

"Give me your foot, Minnow. I'll heal them for you."

If she were a stronger witch, a more spiteful one, maybe she'd refuse just to piss him off further. But the truth was, her feet were killing her, and the longer they sat on the side of the road, the greater the chance the demon would be back.

Sera lifted her leg, and Alistair tenderly held her heel in his gloved hand. A burst of white magic coated her sole and oozing skin. Cooling and calm, his magic was like dipping her scorching toes into an ice-cold stream. Sera bit her lip to keep from groaning as the layers of her skin knit back together. His jaw ticked, and he grabbed the other foot.

So much magic. Such a wide variety of uses as well. Most coven members had occupations and worked within their designated roles. Mastrias focused on developing their mind reading abilities; healers concentrated on healing. But Alistair... he could travel. He could heal, glamour, and summon objects. She'd never met anyone this diverse.

When her foot no longer burned, he dropped it into the clay dust. "Put on two pairs of socks. It prevents blisters," he said, and grabbed his pack. "There's a transport to Ironoak, but it doesn't leave for two weeks. We're walking."

"Wonderful," she said and hoisted her pack onto her shoulder.

As Sera crossed the road, she couldn't help but glance toward Crowpass. She could have sworn she saw the demon astride his horse, watching her. But she blinked, and the vision was gone.

Chapter Fourteen

Seraphina

Dusk settled over the forest. Crickets chirped, and glow bugs pulsed with illumination between the low branches. Her calves throbbed, and although she was happy—the pain from her feet had been lessened, thanks to Alistair—she couldn't help but focus on a new ache that pushed forward. One new, one old. Demon. Her magic.

Nora had been taken by one of them. He'd slammed Al into a tree like a leaf in the breeze. What chance did she have?

Sera refused to cry. Crying didn't help. So she bottled it up just as she had her darkness, as she had her hopes and dreams of becoming something more.

Alistair found them a place to camp between a set of ancient oaks. He was methodical. Cleared the ground, gathered the wood, and set a fire. He must have done this a hundred times before.

Was this what life on the road was like? The Solarni coven of the Citadel wasn't the only band of witches and warlocks on the continent, only the largest. She'd heard about the Suma coven, which dwelled in the forest. It was one of the traveling covens, which would stop at various places to sell goods and wares. Their evenings must have looked similar to this one—a troupe gathering around a fire, settling to the sounds of the woods.

Alistair had a stick in his hand. He mumbled his spell and drew a circle about eight feet from the center of the fire. A thin barrier surrounded them. It was clear, unlike her blue, but Alistair's almost glittered in the light of the flames. She could make out the prism of colors only from the corners of her eyes; when she stared directly at it, they disappeared.

"This will keep us safe through the night," Al said. Thunder crackled in the distance, and faint blasts of light lit up the sky between the gaps in the leaves.

Rain sprinkled on the dome around them before beading and rolling off the side.

"You've got a deep well, don't you?"

Al grunted. He'd been quiet and moody ever since they left Crowpass. Thankfully, there had been no sign of the demon or any other danger.

Sera shook out her bedroll, claiming a spot on the opposite side of the fire from Al, and leaned against a fallen log. She grabbed her notebook and opened it to see Dominick's spidery scrawl.

1. We are having a conversation about the state of your room as soon as you're home.

2. Ithar hugged me when I handed him your box of treasure, which wasn't as skin-crawling as I imagined.

3. Please tell me you fucked Al... and don't spare details!

She hadn't wanted to ask him to help with Ithar, but she'd run out of time. She supposed she did deserve a hard conversation about the fact that she'd let herself go, let her lodgings go. There were so many other important things to worry about. Most of all, Nora.

Things have been dreadful without you here, and it's only been a day. I have no one to gossip with or ogle warlocks with, and my life is utterly dull without you. So, for selfish reasons, I request that you find that oracle quickly so you can return home to me.

P.S. I broke up with Sam... he didn't take it the best

Sera slid her pen from its holder and wrote her response:

Thank you for taking care of Ithar for me. As far as my boarding room goes... you try dealing with this magic in your veins on a daily basis.

I miss you, and no, I haven't fucked Al, and don't plan to. Also, for him being as close as a brother to you, you seem to have a weird fascination for details.

We made it to Crowpass. Al went into the town, but when I was waiting for him, another demon lord appeared. I swear it had me enthralled. I couldn't move, and if Al hadn't come running, I'd be gone. The forest is beautiful, but there feels like a lingering darkness. It could be my imagination or the demon, but I'm terrified.

If you hear anything about Nora, please let me know. I'm relying on you, so please don't get yourself shunned or do something stupid.

—Sera

She closed the journal, then reopened it. The pages had cleared her words.

"Here," Alistair said right before a ball of fabric smacked her in the face. "Since you can't glamour, you need a disguise."

The lavender garment was made of coarse material, with uneven and lopsided stitches around the hem. But she noticed the small smirk on Al's lips. She wanted to be happy for this break in gloom, but his mood had been a boulder in her gut. One that seemed to stay put.

"Is this the best they had?" she asked. The dress was hideous—about three sizes too wide, and it would hang at an awkward length below her knees.

"You don't like my taste in dresses?"

"This isn't a dress, it's a tent."

"Are you worried I won't find you pretty enough to ask you to the solstice ball?" He winked.

Sera couldn't help her scowl. Maybe he was over the events of the afternoon, but she remembered what he had said, what he had implied. "Now you have a sense of humor? Over our little incident with the demon?"

That struck a nerve. His blue eyes pinned her where she sat, his mouth set in a grim line. "Do you have any idea of what could have happened? What could he have done to you?"

"Believe it or not, I am very aware of the different varieties of demonic torture." Sera threw her notebook into her rucksack and pulled out her Legion cloak, rolling it into a ball to be used as a pillow for later.

"So glad you're well read." Al stretched his arms above his head. She didn't want to watch him; she hated how her eyes lingered on the lines of him, envisioning what all that muscle looked like under his clothes.

Sera restrained herself from going further down that thought line and stood. This wasn't some opportunity to reconnect with an old crush, and how dare she lose focus on the real reason she was here?

"This is not a game to me! Nora is gone. They have her. How would you feel if they had Colton?"

His lip curled. "I know more than most what it would be like to have someone you love ripped apart by demons."

Sera swallowed hard. His father. Of course. How could she have forgotten? "Then you know exactly how I feel right now. The only difference is that I don't know if she's dead or not." Sera slapped her hand over her mouth. "Al, I'm sorry—"

"At least you have a fucking chance." The dead leaves on the ground crunched under each step he took toward her. "At least there is some hope that Nora is alive down there. Maybe beaten, maybe bloody, but *alive*."

Her heart sank. She recognized the pain in him now. The anger, yes, but also the helplessness.

She could barely hear what he said over the thunderclaps around them. "Never assume what I may feel about a situation. I promise you'll always end up wrong."

The back of Sera's knees hit the log behind her. Scrambling for a moment, she landed atop the log with Alistair hovering over her. Still, Sera held her chin high. "Fine," she gritted out.

"Fine," Al repeated back to her and strode back to his bedroll on the other side of the fire. He lay down, keeping his back to her.

Downing her sleeping elixir, Sera let her silent tears fall.

CHAPTER FIFTEEN

DOMINICK

The Ogdelo—or pool house, as most oracles called it—had once seemed to Dominick a wonder to behold. The building was one of the reasons he had wanted to be an oracle. The murals painted on the ceiling in the great hall depicted the sky—the sun, moons, stars—in such detail that he thought he would be able to caress the fabric of the universe if he could only reach the paint.

A shallow viewing pool greeted each oracle as they entered, with fountains of colorful threads spilling over each other in a synchronized dance. Beyond it, rows of exquisitely carved pillars, each marble column emulating the same starry theme from the ceiling, led to the grand pool, where dozens of platforms abutted the water.

It was beautiful. But the longer Dominick worked there, the easier it was to see the cracks.

He marched through the corridors of the Ogdelo, pushing past some oracles lingering outside the main chamber, and headed toward the grand pool.

Helping Sera was his top priority, and right now, she needed to know if Nora was alive. Dominick wasn't advanced enough to read lifelines himself. No, he was currently stuck reading upcoming crop yields and weather. Basically useless. So to help his best friend, he'd have to do what he did best.

Flirt.

There had to be someone he could convince or manipulate. It didn't matter which, as long as he got what he needed, and he needed information. Sera had to know. Shadow, he had to know if Nora was all right, and knocking on Lavinia Wildrick's door was a worst-case-scenario situation.

"Dominick?"

A face he recognized. One that he saw lingering around his usual haunts. Tanned skin, icy sea green eyes, and light blond hair. "Theo! It's so funny seeing you here. I was waiting for one of my friends. I didn't know you were promoted to lifelines. Congratulations."

Theo's tanned nose pinkened. "It was just a few weeks ago," he said, his smile stretching wider.

"We must grab drinks tonight. You have to tell me how you excelled so quickly." Dominick placed his most charming smile on his face and dropped his eyes to Theo's lips. A strawberry hue climbed Theo's throat.

Perfect.

"Okay," Theo said, almost too eagerly.

This was going to be far easier than he'd planned.

"Perfect. I'll meet you at Radost at seven. Promise not to leave me hanging?"

"I promise," Theodore said.

Dominick winked at him and strolled to his pool chamber to learn whether the brown beans would be bountiful this year.

The brick wall in the alleyway behind Radost was wet. Moisture seeped into his palms, which he'd placed on either side of Theodore's head. Dom kissed him, deep and full of tongue.

Theo wasn't bad looking. Quiet—timid, even—but not ugly. Timidity usually turned Dom off, but Theo wasn't a half-bad kisser.

The conversation over dinner had been dull. Dominick made sure to look interested and hung on to each of Theo's words between the clinks of crystal goblets and scrape of silverware on delicate dishes. It was an exhausting task in light of the situation, but he'd accomplished what he needed to and had Theo in his trap.

Dominick wrapped his hand around the back of Theo's neck, pulling him closer, and pushed his body into the front of Theo's robes. He didn't doubt the warlock would be putty in his hands. Shadow, he might even enjoy it if Theo fucked as well as he kissed.

But that wasn't the primary mission. He wouldn't let it get that far tonight. "I'm sorry," he said, pulling away. "I can't do this right now."

"What do you mean?" Theo tugged him back toward his lips.

"I have a lot going on. It's not fair to you."

"Last time I checked, I was consenting." Theo's hand squeezed Dom's hip, and heat washed through him.

Dominick raised a brow at the warlock, taking note of the heavy lids over his sea-colored irises. His ruffled blond hair made an attractive contrast to the tan of his skin, and now Theodore was showing some spunk.

"I've just…" Dominick looked down the alleyway to the street. "I've lost a lot of people recently, and I'm scared." He hadn't meant for his tears to blur everything. He hadn't meant to open that part of him up. He cleared his throat, trying his best to keep the emotion from bubbling to the surface.

Everything was happening so fast. Nora gone, Sera gone. Colton, who knew what… Dom hadn't received a message back from his brother in days. And he was alone. Despite the trysts and late-night drinks with acquaintances, this was the first time in years he'd felt truly alone.

"What happened?" Theo asked.

"You remember my best friend, Seraphina? Her sister was the one taken by that demon last week. Sera and I are worried sick, and we can't get the Council or her mother to tell us if she's even alive." His airway constricted slightly. Saying it out loud sparked more of a reaction than he'd expected. "I should go. I'm sorry I started this." Dominick palmed Theo's cheek. "It was nice to catch up."

He turned to enter the side door of Radost.

"Wait."

Dominick smiled to himself before turning to face the lifeline oracle.

"I can search for her," Theo offered.

"I couldn't ask you to do that."

"I'm offering, you're not asking," Theo answered.

"It's against protocol. I don't want you to get in trouble." Dominick took a step toward him. He didn't really care if the warlock got caught, though future pulls, if needed, would be easier if he wasn't.

"I won't get caught. I'll look for her tomorrow."

"Shadow, you're amazing," he muttered as he took Theo's chin, pushed him back up against the wall, and devoured him once again.

Chapter Sixteen

Seraphina

The wind whipped her heavy curls. The ground trembled. A chasm opened, extending as far as the eye could see, wide and deep. The ravine went down to the core of Eraphon, and Nora dangled high above it, wrapped in shadow and black flame, shrieking in silence. One second, she was there; the next, she was swallowed whole.

Down, down, down she went.

"Seraphina."

Her name carried on the wind. The demon, in all black with glowing red eyes, appeared and called to her by name.

"Sera, wake up."

Her eyes snapped open. A thud was followed by pain. Sera grabbed the side of her head, cursing the warlock. Alistair held his cheek and sat in the dirt, staring at her, dumbfounded.

"Moons, you have a hard head," he said as the white healing of his magic zapped into his skin, leaving behind a raised red welt.

Sera stood, frantic, searching for her sister and the chasm. But there was nothing. No Nora, no demon, just Al. It had all been so real. Such terror etched into the lines of her little sister's face. She supposed that was the consequence of taking a smaller dose of her sleeping elixir, but she only had three, and who knew how long this mission would last?

"Morning to you too." She pressed her fingers into the side of her head and winced. As if she wouldn't have woken with a headache after their argument last night, she had to awaken to being smashed on the skull. The spot was already tender and would bruise before long.

"Come here," Alistair said. He held out his large gloved hand. She grabbed it and yanked to get his hulking frame to his feet. "That's not what I meant, but thank you."

Sera focused on him, confused and disoriented from waking in pain. Before she could object, Alistair reached for her and settled his gloved palm on the side of her head. His lips were straight, eyes focused on her. Her skull throbbed for a second longer, until a cool rush overtook the warmth of blood that had traveled to her scalp.

She held on to him and leaned into his palm, much like a cat begging for attention. It felt amazing. "That healing power is pretty useful," she said, gazing up at him. Her insides melted. Alistair had a flush across his cheeks, his eyebrows raised high, those full lips parted. A second later, he dropped his hand and cleared his throat.

"It—uh, it's useful when you're on the road."

Sera couldn't stop herself from smiling as she turned away to rummage through her pack. Somehow, throughout their journey, her chocolate tart had remained relatively intact. She unwrapped the cloth napkin and slid the confection into her hand just as Al offered her a piece of jerky.

"You brought a pastry?"

She took the jerky from him and placed it in the napkin to save for later.

"I'm not sharing," she said before taking a giant bite, and followed Alistair into the forest.

Sera didn't quite know how to move on from their argument the night before. Tensions from the demon, worries over her sister, and heartbreak for Al: It was all a convoluted mess. She supposed she should apologize, but Alistair had said things that burrowed under her skin. Call her stubborn, fine, but her sister had been captured, and what sliver of hope she had was fading rapidly day by day.

Nausea surged, but Sera forced down another bite of chocolate pastry. She needed this mission to be over as soon as possible. She needed to save Nora.

"The ruins that line the Deadlands—do you know how many there are?" she asked.

"Do you always talk with your mouth full?"

Sera took care to step over a fallen log and followed Alistair on a deer path through the forest. "An answer would work just fine, thank you."

He turned, giving her a look of pure annoyance. Sera shoved the rest of her breakfast into her mouth to keep from smiling. She rather liked irritating the warlock.

"I requested some additional information. There are at least twenty, probably more. I'm waiting on correspondence to come back on names and locations."

Twenty? Moons, each outpost could be equivalent to a small village. "You think there are more?"

"Bound to be. That's your theory, then? Doorways and ruins coincide?" Al lifted a branch above his head and motioned for her to go under it. Sera brushed past him. The contact of her shoulder against his chest sent a jolt through her, one she didn't mind one bit.

"I think the doorways must have been created to get a large number of troops in and out of Gehenna." Sera gasped when a cold shower of lingering raindrops from the trees above hit her. She glared at Al but was met with a sly smirk. "Anyway," she said, wiping the water from her forehead. "Gehenna is entirely underground except for its outposts, Ceasefall, and Port Sidnah. They must have tunnels leading to the surface near each area to keep them manned during wartime."

"Let me go first," Alistair said, stepping around her. She couldn't help but notice he was careful not to make any physical contact with her this time.

A whirring sound emanated from deep in the forest.

"Al, what's that—"

Before she could finish, Al's hand shot in front of her face. The tip of a dagger punctured brown leather, slicing through Al's flesh.

"*Stit*," Alistair gritted, and an iridescent shield was up before them. The thunking of a dozen knives as they broke against his shield almost overpowered his cursing. Al winced as he yanked the blade from his hand.

Sera stood frozen, the blood drained from her cheeks, her darkness pulsing like a drumbeat through her veins while Alistair healed himself. The world spun, black dots peppered her vision, and in that downward spiral of dangerous power, darkness seethed.

How dare they... her power said.

Sera shook away the voice. Trying to rid herself of the burning and rage building under her skin, she sank her nails deep into her palm. It wasn't going to be enough this time, even if she drew blood... it wouldn't be enough, and if it seeped out... if her mist caught an ember of her flame...

Alistair's eyes were dripping down his chin... the ground, the trees, her... everything was black flames roaring, destroying, killing... Sera bit down on her cheek to keep the images from flashing.

Her magic laughed.

"Crag!" Alistair screamed. The only answer was a hoot of laughter. That was when Sera caught movement between the shadows of the trees. She counted twelve Legion members in total, each one covered in dirt and splatter, but something about the stench made her pause.

That wasn't mud.

The burning had almost reached her palm then, and when Alistair released his shield, she did the only thing she could think of to make her abomination stop.

Sera picked up one of the daggers by the blade and squeezed. Sweet pain lanced through her palm up her forearm, and the burning rage lingering beneath the surface paused.

"Shit," she whispered.

"How'd you know it was me?" A warlock trudged into a gap in the trees where sunlight broke through. His overgrown stubble could nearly be called a beard. The rest of his head was bald, and like his fellow squad members, his attire was browned and stained, except for the arrangement of daggers strapped across his chest. Those shone with brilliance.

"You're the only one I know who'd pull that shit," Alistair seethed.

Hot blood dripped from the cut on Sera's palm, but finally she was able to breathe, and her abomination slowed its swirling. Was it so much to ask for a little control? And when would hurting herself be too much to bear? Dominick had already noticed what she was doing to herself, and Sera would prefer no one else found out.

There is no control, only acceptance.

"Shut up," Sera hissed to herself.

"Your recruit should have known better," Crag said, picking up his dagger from where Alistair had thrown it. "Looks like she can't even pick up a dagger from the right end."

Sera huffed, and Alistair whipped around toward her. He cursed while wading through the dense bushes to her side and lowered his voice. "You all right?"

"I'm fine."

"Let me see." Sera gave up her palm to him, and he pressed his gloved fingers to the wound. His touch was like a gentle breeze on a sweltering day, and she'd be lying if she didn't think about what that would feel like everywhere. Brushing across her navel, those hands sliding up her thighs.

Alistair's eyes widened for a second, and Sera couldn't help but wonder if he had mastria abilities too. She shook the idea away. He surely would have said something by now. Still, she glanced around at the other witches and warlocks in the squad and built that wall around her mind brick by brick.

"She's not a recruit," Alistair yelled back at Crag. He searched her face again, his expression questioning if she was all right. Sera could only nod. "She's not even in the Legion, Crag."

Alistair charged straight for the squad leader, gripping the warlock by the collar.

One by one, the other members picked up their daggers. A few apologized.

"I didn't know," Crag rasped out. "Captain, let me go."

Al let him fall to the ground.

"You know them?" Finally, her words came forward.

"Unfortunately," Al said. "Meet the Kader Squad." He pointed at the witches and warlocks surrounding them.

She felt something scrape against the wall of her mind and directed what magic she had on the barrier around her memories. She scanned the witches and warlocks that surrounded them, trying to figure out which one it was. None of them looked directly at her, though.

"Don't worry, we won't bite," their leader said.

Despite the attempt at reassurance, Sera wasn't convinced. The Legion members' movements were too jerky. The hollowness of being on the road for too long had set into each line of their faces, and the ones who did smile had a wide-eyed look about them.

"The name is Crag." The leader reached around Al, offering a soiled hand.

"Eager, are we?" Al mumbled.

"Not every day you see a beautiful witch on the road."

"Where are you coming from?" she asked.

Al raised a brow at her.

"East."

The shink of daggers being sheathed surrounded her. The squad members shifted side to side, seemingly ready to move on.

"Near the Deadlands?" she asked. "Have you heard of any movement beyond?"

Crag furrowed his brows at her. His curious look told her she'd maybe said too much, but Sera didn't care. She needed information, and if the squad had been near the Deadlands, near anything that might resemble a doorway, she needed to mark it on her map and find more of them.

"We have." Crag turned from her and looked at Al.

"You may speak freely. We're on a mission for the Council."

The stained fabric of Crag's coat crunched when he crossed his arms. "There is talk that Ceasefall has been reoccupied. Rumbles of marching hordes have reportedly been felt below the surface. Something is brewing."

So she was right. The demons did move their armies through tunnels underground. It had only made the most sense. She'd read texts discussing the first battles; though speculation was minimal, they'd hinted at it. Most of the relevant pages were missing, as if the authors of those diaries didn't want the information leaked.

"Thank you, that's useful. Can you tell us exactly where you felt the rumbling?" she asked the squad leader. He sucked on his teeth before answering.

"South of Ironoak. Can't quite say how far south—maybe a day or two's travel?"

"Thank you, that's helpful," Alistair said, crossing his arms. Clearly, he was ready for this conversation to be over.

"We'll be off, then." Crag saluted Al.

The troop walked past them, and Sera released a breath when the clawing around her memories ceased.

"Crag," Al called out to the squad leader. "Be mindful. A demon lord is hanging around Crowpass."

"Aye, Captain. We'll journey south, then."

The two soldiers nodded to each other in farewell.

"He's below you in rank, then?" Sera asked Al, who'd already started eastward.

"I'm the youngest captain in the Legion," Alistair said so matter-of-factly that she would have thought the rank didn't mean anything to him. But she noticed a tightness to his shoulders, a more stilted way of walking.

"He's so much older than you. How do they determine rank?"

Alistair glanced at her over his shoulder, and his jaw flexed. Then he said, "By the depth of your well... and the number of demons you kill."

At mid-sun, they'd taken a break. Alistair was hunting for their evening meal somewhere deep in the forest. Sera settled at the trunk of a tree, the damp from decayed leaves seeping into her trousers. She leaned against the bark and took a moment to open her journal, enjoying the tweets and chirps of faraway birds.

I have successfully seduced a lifeline reader to spy for me. You're welcome. Also, let's keep away from the demon lords for now? I really can't handle losing a second Wildrick. Actually, that's not true. Your mother could turn to dust for all I care.

Sera responded.

And here I thought you'd go through a dry spell without me to wing-woman for you. Funny how you don't share your details.

She could almost picture Dom's indignation through the page. And oh, how she wished she could see it.

A crashing of branches, breaking sticks, and whipping leaves had her snapping her barrier into place.

Alistair emerged from a thicket holding a screeching green creature high above his head, then dropped the thing at her feet.

The creature curled into a tight ball, its ears enormous compared to its tiny head. Large brown eyes almost bulged from their sockets, above a button nose and wide mouth.

"I found it sniffing around." Al crossed his arms, disgust on his face.

A sickly-sweet smell of fear rolled off the creature.

"A goblin?" Sera kept her voice low so as not to startle him.

"You know what he is?"

"I'm a keeper, remember?" The goblin held itself tighter and shivered. His brown eyes barely peeked over his protruding kneecaps. "It's okay," she said, softening her features. "Come here." She extended her hand, holding out the piece of jerky Al had given her that morning. The goblin straightened his neck, and Sera dared to move closer. "It's all right, little one, I won't hurt you."

The goblin eyed the dried meat in her hand, then swiped it.

"He must have been following us for a while," Alistair offered. "I've been sensing demon magic for miles."

"I don't know what's more concerning, the fact that you can now smell demons or that you haven't told me you're sensing them." She lifted her brow at him, and he glared at the ground.

"Don't feed it," Alistair said.

"He's half starved." Sera reached into her pack, looking for more food. "What's your name?" she asked the little creature.

"I doubt it speaks. They aren't known for being the most intelligent beasts." Alistair picked up his pack and swung it onto his shoulder. The wind swayed the crowns of the trees along the skyline.

The goblin looked at Alistair and hissed.

"I think he's smart enough." Sera giggled and patted his head. "Do you have a name?"

"Sssssnnnnnnkkkkk," the goblin sounded.

"Ssnnkk?" Sera tried to repeat.

"Sssnnniikkkk."

"Snik?" Sera asked. The goblin smiled. The corners of his mouth almost reached the base of his ears in an expression she assumed was supposed to be endearing.

"All right, Snik. I can't give you any more. We have to leave now." Hoisting her pack onto her shoulder, she followed Alistair into the forest.

Snik followed them for hours, prompting Alistair to comment multiple times on how terrible an idea it was to have him around. Whenever they heard a rustle, Sera would turn back and wink at the green beastie.

"Stop encouraging him."

"Stop saying that," Sera responded, her voice echoing through the dense forest as they continued on a deer path.

"We don't have time or resources to keep a pet," Alistair countered while lifting a tree branch above his head and holding it for Sera to pass under. "Plus, he is considered a demon."

"He's a creature in need. Not a pet. A being of Shadow." If she had to insist on it, she would. She glanced back at the goblin, and he mimicked her wink from earlier and closed the distance between them.

Snik seemed determined to accompany them along their path, and she wouldn't turn him away.

CHAPTER SEVENTEEN

DOMINICK

It was far too early. The sun had barely risen, coloring the clouds a violet gray. The angle of the sun, the hue of the clouds: It was unnatural, all of it. But here he was, witnessing the Citadel waking, when he should be fast asleep. The things he did for his friends.

Dominick propped himself up against one of the pillars outside the grand pool to wait for Theo.

Last night, after their date at Radost, he'd been enlightened, to say the least. It turned out that Theodore Sano wasn't as shy as he'd made himself out to be, and even though they hadn't made it all the way, they'd both finished the evening satisfied.

He'd tried being his smooth self but couldn't help the grin that crept across his face. Not only on the walk over, but also now. A job well done, if he dared say so.

Theo had been in the pool, pulling, for half an hour, according to the sundial perched in front of the Ogdelo. It was a fickle business. Dominick had watched countless oracles complete the ritual during his three years here. Not every pull was successful, especially if the oracle had no ties to the person they were pulling. It took decades of practice. As far as he knew, Theo didn't know Nora from any other witch in the coven.

Yet a creeping thought kept slithering into his mind, saying that maybe Theo was avoiding him. Maybe it was because Nora couldn't be found. Dom jerked his shoulders, shaking the thought away.

Instead, he wondered what kind of kiss-ass oracles even came in this early. No one loved their occupation this much.

Dominick lifted the back of his hand to hide his yawn, wondering if he could make it to a bakery before he was due back to check on the future squash harvest. He'd never been so grateful to stop staring at beans.

The sound of quick steps on marble had him turning. Theo's brows were creased. He was frowning and walking too quickly, as if he were...

No.

This couldn't be happening. She couldn't be dead. How was he going to tell Sera? Did Lavinia know? If Lavinia knew, he was pretty sure she would have found a way to burn down the Council chambers with the chairs inside. Poor Nora. Moons, Sera was going to kill him.

Theo finally met his eyes. "No, no, it's all right. She's all right."

"Oh, thank Shadow." Dominick breathed and curled forward, but there was still a frown on Theo's face.

"Her threads are strong, which means she's not even badly injured. I almost can't believe it."

Neither could Dom. Who knew that Nora could survive being captured? "You're the fucking best." Finally, he could relax, or at the very least be relieved that he didn't have to break the news to Sera that something terrible had happened to her sister. He'd thank Shadow for that later.

Theo rubbed his eyes, still frowning.

"What else is wrong?" Dominick asked.

"Nothing. Lifeline business." Theo glanced back at the pool.

"All right, spill it."

Theodore sighed, his gray robes rustling in the breeze as he turned toward the entrance. Dominick followed him, assessing his tight shoulders and brisk pace, wondering what could be so troublesome that they needed to leave the building. When they rounded the corner and were hidden in the shadow of the Ogdelo, Theo finally stopped.

"Is there a reason we need to be sharing secrets in the shadows?" Dominick asked.

"You know when you're pulling what you have in your mind's eye?"

Dominick nodded. An oracle envisioned what they wanted to come forward. For him, working in weather and crops, he just had to think of the day. A thread would shoot out of the water, and he'd pull it and view what he needed. He assumed the same system worked for lifelines. You envisioned the name or the person, and they just popped forward.

"I searched for Nora for a while. She was hazy at first. Then I started to search through those who encountered demons recently, and there were many."

Dom's heart dropped. "Do I want to know what they were wearing?"

Theo bit the pad of his thumb. "If you thought a Legion uniform, you'd be right."

Shit. He still hadn't heard back from Colton, and if there had been a skirmish... Dominick itched below his ear. "Any fatalities?"

"That wasn't what I was searching for, but I assume so. I'm only telling you this to warn your friend."

Sera had already mentioned a demon lord. It was possible that a squad had gotten into a skirmish with him. It was on the tip of Dominick's tongue to ask, but he paused. Was this even something he wanted to know?

Determined to push that feeling down, Dominick did a quick scan of the area before grabbing the front of Theo's robes and kissing him. The warlock's sea-green eyes lit up for a second before closing. Dom didn't typically participate in public displays of affection; honestly, the thought of being caught made his skin crawl. But he'd been thinking of the way Theo tasted on his lips ever since they left his apartment that morning.

Dominick broke their kiss and observed the oracle before him. All oracles had light hair and eyes. They were linked to the recessive trait needed to view the threads in the water—at least that's what the Council said. Having them almost guaranteed your placement as long as you had the power within you to manipulate the threads. But Theo's tanned skin, sun-kissed against the blond of his hair, made him look otherworldly.

"I've got to tell Sera. Meet me for dinner? I want to know what you find out."

Theo smiled. "Wouldn't miss it."

Chapter Eighteen

Seraphina

She's alive.

Those words, those beautiful words, lived on a single page in Sera's journal. Dominick hadn't elaborated further than that. He didn't have to. Her baby sister was alive. Sera let out a trembling breath. She wanted to know everything Dom had uncovered, but it seemed like she'd have to wait for more information. It was going to be torture.

Damp from dew, Sera shook off her sleep. Alistair was noticeably absent across the fires' smoldering embers. And her new green friend, who had curled behind her knees and kept her warm all night, also seemed to be missing.

Al's pack and bedroll were still laid out, so he couldn't have gotten far. Sera took a moment to relieve herself in peace. As she meandered between ferns beaded with large droplets of dew, dampening her boots, Sera was happy for a moment alone. To take in the wind and the swaying branches of the canopy above. To appreciate the way the sunlight danced through the trees. Normally, Sera would have wished for her cloak in the chill of the shadows, but her sister was alive, and the brisk air filled her with a new purpose.

She had time, or at least she hadn't failed Nora yet. And even though she knew she shouldn't, Sera let herself release a little bit of that guilt.

The air had a sweet scent. She'd bottle it up and send it to Dominick if she could as a thank-you for this gift.

The ferns in their feathered greenery swayed around her with every step she took toward a trickling stream. She stripped off her tunic and proceeded to wash, scrubbing at the grime embedded in her knuckles.

The doorways. They needed to be her priority. This evening, she'd get the map from Al and review it. See where the trio were in relation to the Deadlands and where the ruins might be. If demons were beginning to reoccupy Ceasefall, then things couldn't be getting better between the coven and Gehenna. She needed to hurry.

Sera barely caught herself before she face-planted into the stream. A buzzing sensation was pulsing right from the center of her chest, and it... pulled.

"I swear..." she said as her dark magic rolled forward, almost asking for permission to exit. Strange. That had never happened before. The abomination swirling under her skin almost seemed polite. Releasing it slowly hadn't ever been an option, only keeping it in, buried deep down. But what if she let it out? A quick glance around confirmed she was still alone.

"Just a little," she whispered to her darkness.

A steady stream of black mist flowed from her fingertips into the wood. It slithered in an almost sentient manner, curling around the trunks of trees and weaving through the woody flora. Magnetic, just like it had been in the Menage...

Branches snapped. Snik ran for her on all fours, yipping excitedly at her magic. She pulled at the mist, and for once it obeyed, disappearing into her skin.

If only it were this easy every time.

"Our little secret," she said to Snik. The goblin nodded and pulled at her with his mud-covered claws.

Hello... her magic said.

Sera peered through the thicket. "Come on, Snik. Let's go find Al."

Trudging through the forest was getting exhausting. Her feet were sore, which was to be expected, considering her boots still hadn't broken in, regardless of the miles they'd covered. Her hips ached, her knees throbbed, and even her sides felt bruised.

The enticing wonder the trees initially brought her had faded with the monotonous trek through crunching leaves, as she scraped her forearms on thorns and low-hanging branches. Sera was even getting sick of her fuzzy rat friends.

Alistair, though, didn't seem to mind in the slightest. Not the walking, nor the bugs. It was like he actually enjoyed it. He snuck a glance at her from over his shoulder as they walked. "You've never learned how to use a weapon, correct?"

"We aren't exactly allowed to use the weapons we find in the keepers' wing." Sera swatted at a fly as Snik handed her another token from the forest. Raven feathers, shiny pebbles, a rodent skull: all little offerings she assumed were thanks for the meals and warm bedroll she shared with him. Sera kept every one.

Alistair sighed. "You should learn to wield one. Burnout is real, and having a backup—or, in your case, any form of protection—is crucial in a fight." He picked up a stick and cracked it over his knee, then threw the stubs to join the other decaying foliage.

Sera rolled her eyes. "Next town we get to, I'll be sure to hire a trainer."

Al stopped short, giving her a forced smile. "I will teach you the basics if you're inclined to actually listen to me."

"You'd teach me?"

He cocked a brow at her, and the first time in a few days, that dimple made its appearance. "If you don't want to learn, I won't waste my energy on you. But if you do, yes, I'll teach you. Unless you still have a reason to hate me."

Why did this feel like a trap? She wasn't completely helpless. Sera had been the one to save *him* when the demon lord attacked. It had been her abomination that frightened the demon off. And as troubling as those thoughts were, that *she* could be intimidating enough to scare away a demon lord...

Still, knowing her way around a simple blade couldn't hurt, could it?

"All right," she said.

"Good. We'll start tonight. I suspect we'll reach Ironoak in a few days."

Al had a menacing look of determination on his face. He circled her, his large hands clasped behind his back, and scanned her as if she were prey. "You're small, weak, and to put it plainly, out of shape."

Sera crossed her arms. "You're a shit teacher, you know that?"

He grinned. "Maybe, but it's the truth." He stopped before her. "Your greatest strength as a woman is that others will underestimate you." He stepped closer. "You'll have to evade, be quicker"—another step—"and learn how to fight at close quarters."

She didn't have a moment to breathe before he was on her. She was wrapped in his arms, the fabric of his uniform bunched between her throat and his bicep.

"What the fuck, Al!"

"Fight, Minnow."

She ripped at his arm, but it was like trying to grip a single brick in a wall. Alistair squeezed tighter. Unease slowly grew into terror.

Thump. Thump. Thump.

"Come on, Minnow, do something," he whispered in her ear, which made her shiver for a completely different reason.

Sera tried to elbow him in the stomach, which was just as firm as the bicep curled around her throat. But there was something lower that was quite soft. Sera picked up her leg and aimed straight for his balls.

"Motherfucker..." Alistair let her go and cupped himself before hitting the ground.

Sera heaved in big breaths and sank her nails into her palms to stop the swirling. "That's what you get!"

Alistair groaned. "Okay," he said, sitting up. Leaves tangled in his hair as he attempted to right himself. "That was a low blow."

"You said fight." Sera crossed her arms and eyed him.

Al brushed off the dirt and got to his feet. Sera couldn't help but smirk as he limped over to her. "Make a fist."

He grabbed her wrist and rearranged her thumb so it lay below the second knuckles of her first two fingers. She wondered how often he had to adjust the grip of his soldiers and if they also experienced the fluttering in their stomachs when his hand enveloped theirs.

Was she ever going to get over this crush and act like an adult? Sera bit back her sigh. Every skip of her heart brought her back to the slight glance he'd given her when she was fifteen. The time he'd been close enough to kiss before he'd pulled her hair and run away.

"I'm going to try to hit you. I want you to move your forearm to the side of your face to block me like this." He made the motion. "Ready?" He swung his arm, aiming for her left cheek.

Sera blocked.

"Again."

He swung. She blocked. They did this repeatedly, switching sides while he corrected her form.

"Okay, now I want you to hit me." He pointed to the center of his chest.

"You want me to punch you?"

Alistair smiled, showcasing his perfectly straight teeth in a look that could almost be called flirtatious. "I want you to feel what it's like to make contact with your fist." Sera glanced below the belt. "Do not even think about it, Minnow."

She snorted. "What if I hurt you again?"

He laughed. Moons, he was gorgeous. Sera couldn't look away from his corded neck, the way his throat bobbed with every chuckle, then that chiseled jaw. "I'll be all right. I've sparred with bigger warlocks than you."

"If you say so." He came straight for her, and she punched him as hard as she could. It was like hitting a brick wall—a very handsome brick wall, a brick wall that smelled like her favorite parts of the Citadel.

"Oh, you've got some power in you, Wildrick." Al rubbed his chest. The look he gave her made her stomach flip.

A mistake.

A movement in the corner of her eye had her lurching backward. "What the fuck!" she screamed at him, her back end now firmly planted in the dirt.

"Don't let your guard down."

Sera swatted his gloved hand away as he tried to help her up. She slapped the dirt from her pants and set back up to continue the lesson. He threw punches, and she blocked until she was slick with sweat and her chest was heaving.

"Starting tomorrow, we're running part of the day." He wasn't even winded.

"Excuse me?"

"You're huffing and puffing from a few sparring exercises. I haven't even given you a weapon to hold yet."

"Sorry I'm not made of muscle like you."

"Oh, Minnow, are you saying you noticed my muscles?" The bastard flexed, and she swore. Of course she'd noticed them. How could she not? The damn moons probably noticed them.

"You know, Alistair, I never knew you to go fishing for compliments. Has your well of eligible witches so dried up you need to pull tributes out of me?" She smirked, thinking she'd won.

She didn't expect his eyes to grow darker and his smile more wicked. "My well is never dry." He winked at her. Her core temperature rose a few degrees.

"Such a shameless flirt," she said and flopped onto her bedroll.

Alistair shrugged, worked that powerful jaw on a piece of jerky, and tended to the fire. Settled, she reached into her pack, looking for her journal.

Dominick's words fluttered to the page.

Sorry for the short message, but I wanted to let you know as soon as I heard. Thank Shadow, she is still alive. I'll have Theo check every day if I can. There are some other weird happenings going on in the lifeline pool. Theo and I are working on figuring out what exactly it is. Right now, all I can tell you is that there seems to be an uptick in demon-coven interaction.

Also, in response to your comment concerning potential sexy time with Al, it's semantics. Alistair is like *a brother, but he* isn't *my brother, so in this case, I am demanding details even if you refuse to share them.*

Your mother has kept her head down in the mastrias' wing. I've no doubt that she knows more than she would ever tell me, even if I could get her to give me the time of day. But I'll keep trying to spy. Hugs and kisses.

That didn't sound good. Increased interactions with demonkind? She needed to find those doorways, at least one, before Al brought the oracle back to the Citadel.

You have no idea what relief I felt when I read your words this morning. I owe you your weight in brew at Mystic's, but something tells me I'll ask for a few more favors before I return.

I hope you didn't break the poor lock's heart. Please thank him for me.

Have you heard from Colton?

Sera closed her journal and sent the goddess a kernel of her power. The blue spark floated in the air for a moment, then fizzled out, accepted by Shadow herself, as the saying went. An offering. A prayer.

"Who are you praying for?" Alistair asked over the crackle of the fire he was feeding.

"Colton."

Alistair was silent. He didn't offer any words of assurance when she met his gaze. Out of anyone, he must know what it felt like, not knowing if your friends would return alive. A piece of her heart cracked at that, and a little more as she watched him rub his chin before pulling a kernel of power and releasing it into the night.

"For Colton," Alistair whispered.

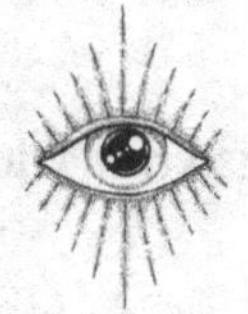

CHAPTER NINETEEN

DOMINICK

"We're going to Jedan?" Theo asked him as they crossed over the threshold into the slum quarter.

Dominick tried not to bristle at the question and increased his pace toward Sera's boardinghouse. "Have a problem with Jedan members?" The words came out accusatory. Sera wasn't even a Jedan member, but she lived here, she cared for these people, and by default, that meant he did too.

Dom turned down her street, passing a group of novices huddled together, throwing dice at the end of an alley. Quietly, the two warlocks snuck into the house.

"I don't have an issue with them," Theo said. "I expected you would, though."

Dominick couldn't help but raise a brow at Theodore. This was a pleasant surprise. Who knew there was at least one more Daedeth-class member who didn't hate the lower class?

He pulled Sera's key from its place and thanked the moons that he didn't get another sliver. He'd felt like a fool for going to the healers last time. "You said you wanted a place to talk where no one could hear," Dom said, pushing open the door. "Ask and you shall receive."

Theo rolled his eyes and stepped inside. Dom shut the door behind him and crossed the room. With a sweep of his hands, he made sure the space was soundproof. Sure, he could have done this in his own apartment, but in this quarter, the presence of a Daedeth member who was stronger than him… was highly unlikely.

"It's cute," Theo said. "This is your friend's house? I didn't realize she was in Jedan."

"She's not." Dom flopped onto Sera's bed. "She's a keeper, but it's a long story as to why she's staying here. Anyway, what did you find out?"

Theo let out a breath and pulled a small notebook from the pocket of his robes. "Today alone, there were twenty fatalities." Dominick straightened. A sour taste coated his tongue. "All Legion. Looks like there have been pocket skirmishes."

"Do you know where? Who?" Dom was going to be sick. Shadow save him if his brother was harmed. He was still waiting for a reply to his letter. He shouldn't panic; it could take weeks for the post to reach Colton's new base, and the battalion was moving, the last he heard.

Theo shook his head. "It would have taken too long. There are specific readers appointed for the Legion. I shouldn't have even been looking, but they aren't reporting it to the coven. Have you heard of families receiving death notices?"

"No." Dom raked his hand through his hair as he stared at Theo, who was obviously as troubled as he felt, judging by the way he was pacing back and forth. Dominick couldn't blame him. This was news dangerous enough to get you executed, let alone shunned. Dominick shivered. "You said Nora's thread was still strong, though?"

"It is."

"Okay. Well, we keep notes. We work on our mind barriers or whatever, and we keep it secret and see what the Council does." Dominick shrugged. What else could they do? Dominick and Theo had no power, no way to hold the Council responsible for the discrepancy. There had to be a reason.

"You've got any place I can keep this safe?" Theo asked, tapping his notebook on Sera's counter.

Dominick got up from the bed and lifted the mattress. "I know just the place."

CHAPTER TWENTY

SERAPHINA

It had been three days of burning shins and bleeding toes, and the bastard was laughing at her. Sera realized Al was downright elated now that running had been added to their daily itinerary. Between running every morning and spending her nights examining the map while marking potential ruins and doorways, she was going to hurl.

Bent over, forearms on knees, she was desperate to catch her breath. Snik stood beside her, whining at her discomfort, but Sera was too busy sucking down precious air to soothe him.

"You know if we were being chased, you would've died hours ago." A light sheen on Alistair's forehead had dampened his hair just enough that it stayed in a perfect dark wave when he pushed the strands back. Those blue eyes were startling in the sunlight.

"I'm fine," she said between heaving breaths.

He smirked at her, that dimple mocking beneath the shadow of stubble. Apparently he could grow a full beard now, too, unlike the scraggly mustache he'd had in their youth. "You don't look fine."

"Has anyone ever told you it's rude to comment on a witch's looks?" Sera plopped on the ground and held her stomach. The dark well inside her was restless, despite the running, despite her exhaustion. The abomination swirled, making her chest tight. Sera couldn't help but wonder if it was a bad omen. Was something coming? If so, she didn't know how to prepare. What she wouldn't give to feel a semblance of control.

She'd had control when she created that scourge and whipped that demon lord. It had been as natural as breathing. "Maybe it was the jerky we had for breakfast," she offered as an excuse. Snik whined.

"Tasted fine to me."

"Well, maybe I'm a little more sensitive than you." Sera unwrapped her curls from a high bun, rubbing hard at her scalp.

"You're most definitely more sensitive than me." He held out his gloved hand. "Come on, we're on the outskirts of Ironoak."

It was odd how he kept his hands covered. She could understand it when they sparred, but while running? Shadow, every inch of her was sweating. She couldn't imagine wearing gloves.

"Does that mean I get to sleep in a bed?"

"You'll be sleeping in a bed tonight, Minnow. You'll also need to wear that dress I bought you."

"Never mind, I'll sleep on the ground."

"Oh, come on. It's purple. I like purple."

At least he was trying. It had been days since they'd had even a tiny spat. If anything, she had started to think he enjoyed her company.

"It's lavender, and if you like it so much, you wear it. Purple isn't my color." Truth be told, the only color she liked wearing was black.

"Give me the dress," he said.

"Can you glamour it? Make it look halfway decent?" Sera reached into her pack and threw it at him.

"Something like that." Al threw the lavender monstrosity to his feet and stomped it into the dirt. She'd catch flies with how far her jaw dropped. Once the tread from his boots was visible, he picked it up and handed it to her. "There. Now it's purple and brown, and since you can't glamour, we'll have to get creative."

Alistair bent down, dragged his gloved hand through the soil of the forest floor, and approached her.

"No." She backed away. "No, Al, *don't*."

He was snickering. Outright snickering, and if her palms didn't already itch with the abomination begging to be released, she would have pummeled him.

You can't burn him alive. He's your only way to save Nora. She repeated her new mantra while they trudged into the outskirts of Ironoak. Alistair had glamoured himself well enough. There was a dullness to his skin and reddened marks on his cheeks and under his eyes. His beard was much longer, but he still couldn't hide all that muscle.

"Did you really have to wipe dirt over my entire face?" Sera asked. She was sure a grain of dirt had burrowed its way into her tear duct, and rubbing was only making it worse. Also, this dress's blind seamstress had made the sleeve so uneven that the arm kept twisting with every movement she made.

"Humans don't have flawless skin," he said, keeping his gaze on the city before them. She supposed she should take that as a compliment. "Try not to gag when we get to the tavern."

Sera was already missing Snik. She hoped he was out having fun, gallivanting with the furry tree rats... or eating them. He did like to eat them. The little goblin had seemed so sad when she'd told him to go.

Sera was pulling at the twisted fabric between her armpit and her pack's shoulder strap when her toe hit a rock. Before she could hit the ground, Alistair was there, gripping her around the waist.

"Coven founders, Minnow. Watch where you're stepping, won't you?"

She couldn't breathe with his hands on her like that, with the low baritone of his voice in her ear. She gripped Al's hand as they turned onto the main road.

Ironoak wasn't as grand as the Citadel, but it was more impressive than Feybury. Sera tried to swallow the lump forming in her throat. There were so many more people here. Which meant more casualties if she had an incident.

Just don't lose control. The magic laughed at her, and she shook her head.

Alistair's grip on her hand tightened. The streets were a combination of smoothed rock and packed dirt. Jedan Quarter didn't even have the privilege of stone mixed with the dirt of their roads. Would that help keep the street from becoming a muddy mess in the rain? Her irritation flared as she realized that humans had better materials than the lowest magic-born.

"Wait, why would I gag?" she asked, trying to divert her attention from the hypocrisy of her own coven.

"Humans are dirty and smell."

"I've been in a human settlement before. They didn't seem that bad."

As Sera and Al moved through the city, dense with tightly clustered houses, children ran after each other, hopping over fences, and dogs happily chased them.

With each person they passed, Sera felt her airway grow tight. She hadn't anticipated the physical reaction to being in a settlement again. Everyone she passed—the children, the old women gathered around a washbasin, the men guiding their carts to market—she imagined melting before her and crying out in pain.

"Have you been to a human city?" Al asked.

"Well, no. It was a small farming village. That's usually where artifacts are found, buried in large fields." The leather of Al's glove was absorbing her hand's sweat, but she didn't let go as a group of men stumbled around the corner.

"Oye," one of them called out to her. "Handsome pair." He collided with two of his friends, who struggled to stay upright themselves. Al moved his grip to her elbow, using his body to shield her. He was all but snarling at them as his heavy palm rested on the small of her back. The slight touch sent a wave of warmth through her.

It was so much easier to hate him when he was being an ass. Not this new, protective, rugged version of him.

Sera tried to focus on Ironoak's charm. Wooden posts with metal candle holders lined the streets in front of timber-framed cottages with brick chimneys. Al led her toward a quaint-looking two-story building, which was washed yellow—or, she supposed, it could have once been white, but the surface was now imbued with dirt and sand. Green shutters framed a few windows. Its peaked roof was shingled with slate, and a wooden sign above the door bore a carved barrel design.

Alistair entered the doorway, passing into the darkness beyond.

Sera followed and immediately gagged.

A briny odor of rotting onions and something almost living, like a fungus, invaded her nostrils. Her eyes watered, and she coughed, refusing to leave the doorway.

An *I told you so* grin was plastered on Alistair's face as he approached the barkeep.

Sera squeezed her nose shut, pulling desperate breaths through her mouth. This was more than smelly—it was damned putrid. How on Eraphon did they not smell themselves?

Alistair had that twinkle in his eye every time he glanced at her, the side of his mouth inching upward. She supposed it was her discomfort that brought it out in him, but she couldn't deny she was drawn to it. His confident movements. The way he commanded a room. Sera sighed.

"Give me your pack," he said after talking to the barkeep. She swung it onto his waiting arm, happy to relieve her shoulders. "What do you have in here? Rocks?"

"Guilty," she said in her nasal tone, refusing to release her nose until they were at least a floor above the vileness of the tavern. "Can we stay somewhere else?"

"No. We've got the last room in all of Ironoak, apparently," he replied and nodded toward the stairs. Once they'd mounted them, Alistair led them to the end room of the upstairs hall.

The air didn't smell as foul here, considering the filth on the bottom level of the establishment. And there was a desk. "Al, give me the map."

He sighed and pulled it out of his pack. Sera unrolled it and traced her finger south. "According to this, if we walk maybe twenty more miles south, we'll run into this section here. There's a clearing in the trees, you see?"

The colors of the parchment indicated elevation, forests, and beaches, but right under her finger was a section that seemed bare. If she had to guess, it was possibly a ruin, and with it, a door. Alistair leaned over her. The heat of him was nearly driving her insane when she realized that their sparse room held only one bed.

Sera snapped upright and hissed at the sharp pain at the back of her head when she hit Alistair's chin.

"Shadow almighty, Minnow. Will you stop with that?" A light flashed behind her, but her mind was already running through every uncomfortable yet delicious scenario where she was lying in a bed beside him.

"Where's the other bed?"

"There isn't one."

"I'm not sleeping next to you," she said, moving around the desk. There needed to be something between them. For some reason, sleeping next to him under the stars didn't quite feel so intimate. Sera backed away until she was stopped by the mattress in question. An expression was all over his face, and she didn't quite know if it was annoyance, but it looked like it was. Something sharp poked into the back of her leg. "This is straw."

"Did you expect clouds?" Al gritted, still rubbing his jaw.

"I don't know what I expected. I've only ever stayed in an enchanted tent on assignment."

Al rolled his eyes, crossed the room, and opened the door. "It should feel better than sleeping on the hard ground. Come on, let's get something to eat."

There was no need to be nervous. She was grown, mature, completely capable of not making this something that it wasn't. Right? They were on a mission, and she'd have to suck it up.

Heat climbed her neck and across her cheeks as she followed Al downstairs.

CHAPTER TWENTY-ONE

SERAPHINA

A hundred years of grime stained the table in front of her. Sera did her best to breathe out of her mouth as Alistair placed two mugs full of amber-colored liquid down. Amber. The color of Nora's eyes.

Her stomach sank. At this rate, she'd never get to her sister in time. Every day, Dominick assured her that Nora's thread was strong. He also mentioned "strange happenings" but kept quiet about them for now, promising he'd fill her in more later.

"Drink," Alistair said. "It makes it a little more manageable."

She raised her brows at him, impressed by his intuition until she realized he was referring to the humans. In the corner of the room, a musician tuned his lute. The sound was a melodic counterpoint to the belching and grumblings of the patrons. Sera would be relieved once it started to drown out a bit of the other noise.

She'd never been this close to this many humans before. They had scraggly hair and threadbare clothes, many were missing teeth, and some were barefoot—a disgusting observation, considering how her boots peeled away from the floor. Already she was getting used to the ripeness of the place. Now, that was a fact that needed to be washed down.

The ale was cool on her tongue and had a full tang that stuck to the back of her throat. It was so different from the brew she enjoyed at Mystic's. She preferred something sweeter, but this wasn't bad.

She leaned over the table, doing her best not to touch it. "Al?" she asked. "What's a wank?"

Alistair choked on his ale, drawing attention from the entire room. "What?"

"A wank. When we walked into the city, I heard one of the men say that he'd give me a pretty coin to wank on my toes."

His eyes were wide, and the pink in his cheeks turned crimson. "Umm..."

She raised a brow at him. Never in all the years she'd known him had he ever looked this flustered. Al leaned closer and whispered, "Someone pleasuring themselves."

"Oh, for fucking Shadow's sake."

"Watch the Shadow talk," he said through his teeth. "We're becoming more friendly with humans, but that doesn't mean they won't throw us out. And I really don't feel like threatening anyone this evening."

"What do you mean, we're becoming more friendly with humans?"

She'd heard no rumors or whisperings about this in the usual circles. It seemed like information about friendlier relations with the human kingdoms would have spread through the Citadel like wildfire. At the very least, she expected her mother would have complained at one of their monthly dinners. Lavinia hated the race and wasn't afraid to share her opinion.

Al kept his voice low. "The Council has made strides to communicate more with human leaders. I've been on more diplomatic babysitting assignments lately than anything else."

Now, that was interesting.

"Are you sharing super-secret coven information with me, Al?" A slight twitch of panic lined his face before he turned stony. She bit her lip and delightedly noticed that the motion drew his eyes. "I'm not going to tell anyone, don't worry."

The slight quiver in his sigh made her smile harder as two wooden slop bowls landed on the table. He pushed one to her.

Ugh, the texture. Fat, gravy, and hunks of something unrecognizable swirled under her spoon.

"It's not that bad," Alistair said.

The room hushed as the musician strummed a pleasant tune. Sera took a bite of her stew. Al was right. It wasn't awful, and with the amount of dried jerky she'd eaten on their journey here, well, turns out she didn't mind the grease and root vegetables as much as she'd thought she would.

"So tomorrow, you think we could work toward the ruins? Maybe find out if there's a doorway there?" Sera decided she needed to find at least two of these mythical doorways. That's what Renata had said: "doorways to Gehenna." On her morning runs with Al, she'd think about the texts she'd read about Gehenna. The gates would be shrouded, maybe by a cloaking spell, or possibly covered with rock or otherwise disguised. Regardless, she should be able to feel the magic, taste it, sense it... Something.

Alistair shook his head. "We gather information here." He kept his voice low. "This was where the oracle was last seen, so we stay until we know where she went."

"I could go alone, you know." Sera scooped up another bite of her stew.

"Oh really, Minnow? You think you've trained enough to go alone, in the woods near the Deadlands, to a ruin that may or may not have demonic spells covering it?"

She hated that he was right. Thankfully, the next song picked up in tempo, and she didn't have to voice that fact. The crowd was whooping and clapping to the beat. Robust, strong-armed women slammed mugs of ale, five in each hand, down on wooden tables already slick with foam. Boisterous and loud, the crowd stomped and cheered as the musician played.

They seemed so alive.

"Why so much ale?" Sera yelled over the noise.

"We needed information, didn't we?" He smiled and finished one mug while grabbing another.

"You did this? The whole tavern?"

"People are much looser with their lips when they're slick with drink, wouldn't you say?" Al's smile crinkled his eyes. "Drink up, Wildrick."

He seemed to be enjoying this. The laughter, the smells. Alistair, captain in the Solarni Legion, enjoyed spending time in a hovel like this. This was worse than some of the lowliest establishments in Jedan Quarter. And Al was a traveler. He should have been awarded a stately house close to the Council chambers.

"You don't like the music?" he asked.

Sera scanned the crowd. Liking the music wasn't the issue. It was lively—infectious, even. The beat was fast, and merriment twirled through the space just as the women's skirts did with each spin. Their faces were smiling, and she took in their laughter, but somewhere deep down in her cold, lonely heart, she thought of Nora. Of the terrible things Sera had done.

Guilt dropped like a stone in her gut as she pictured the portal Nora had created and Sera's black magic turning it ugly. Char marks still stained the walls of her mind as she thought of Feybury. Of the apparently permanent loss of pigment on her mother's hand. Of lying to Dominick for so long. The weight was so incredibly heavy.

This type of happiness wasn't meant for someone like her.

"It's nice," she said and sipped on her ale.

"Oh, come on. You're not too good for this, are you?"

Sera scoffed. "It's just different."

If only he knew how defective she was. What she had done to save him from that demon. She could feel his gaze upon her, but she refused to meet it. He wouldn't understand.

"Lighten up, Wildrick."

A sharp twang from a very different instrument cut through the room. Al must have seen the shock across her face, for he said, "It's a fiddle," and finished his second mug of ale.

The instrument created vibrating waves of music, which were followed shortly by the sound of a drum. Men and women left their seats, their meals untouched, and small, grimy children ran in, taking random bites from abandoned bowls. Couples swung in sweeping circles in a dance so dizzying that Sera wasn't sure how they were still upright.

"Duty calls," Al said and rose from their table, crossing the room. After slapping a patron hard on the back, he let out a loud whistle.

Sera knew that if his beard were its regular length, both dimples would be fully displayed. He raised his hands and clapped in time with the beat, and every few moments, his gaze met hers across the crowded room.

Moons, she was done for. Why fate had decided that *he* should come back into her life, she would never know. But damn it, did she enjoy looking at him, even with his glamour.

No one bothered her. Not that she was upset about it. She was pretty sure the reason was that Alistair shot death glares at anyone who walked close. He'd made his way around the room while Sera enjoyed a second mug of ale.

Her cheeks were hot, and she knew she had an idiotic smile plastered on her face as Alistair began twirling a little girl in a circle. Al, almost a full head taller than anyone else, was hunched over and smiling as the child laughed. Her blond curls wrapped her as the music drummed on.

It wasn't hard to notice how every woman's eyes were on him. Many approached, asking for a dance, something Sera wasn't too happy about, but he politely declined them all. The child's request must have been innocent enough.

Sera tracked his every move. She was a fool.

Al stalked toward her, his shoulders relaxed, and for once, he seemed to feel like the world could wait. She knew it was for show, that he had been gathering intelligence all night, but right now, as he flopped back in his seat before her and swigged down another mug in what seemed like one gulp, he seemed unburdened.

"You seem to be having fun," Sera said.

"Ah, you're not jealous of little Dahlia there, are you?" As if on cue, Dahlia waved, and Al waved back.

"Not in the slightest, Alistair Alcott," she said.

"Dance with me."

The corner of her mouth twitched.

"Come on, Minnow…"

"I don't know these dances." She crossed her arms but couldn't stop her smirk.

Alistair's face cracked into a rakish grin. "It doesn't matter." He held out his gloved hand.

Sera stared at it, half expecting to be struck down if she took it.

She wanted to take it, to feel a bit of joy. Her heart ached for it. For so long, she'd felt alone while navigating her power, her family, even when she helped the Jedan members in the middle of the night. Always alone, completing those small acts to help fill the aching space.

But now, here, in this rotten tavern, reeking of filth, Al stood with his hand extended. That smile, those brilliant blue eyes staring back at her with a single question. A dare, even.

His voice was so low she almost missed it over the merriment of the crowd. "Seraphina, will you dance with me?"

Her breath hitched as she stared at him. And there, between the glamoured crow's-feet framing those beautiful eyes, was his unguarded truth.

That if she said no, he might feel it, and as much as she loved the thought of having that power over him…

She caved.

Sera stood, finished the rest of her ale, and slammed the mug down before taking Alistair's hand.

He about ripped her arm out of her socket as he dragged her to the middle of the dance floor and started her in a series of spins under his arm. Her hideous lavender dress flared among the sweaty bodies. She wasn't immune to the death stares from the other women waiting for their turn with him around the room.

Sera relished it.

"Does this make up for the solstice ball?"

Sera smacked his arm, and he laughed. After a few songs, her cheeks were tight, a pleasant warmth spread through her, and not even a flicker of her abomination stirred in her gut. When was the last time she had felt this free?

Alistair stilled with her in his arms. That twinkle was back in his eye, and as he held her, she could smell the sea and spices of the Citadel on him.

His fingers brushed her temple, pushing a few heavy curls behind her ear.

"What?" She was breathless and hot, her mind fuzzy from the extra sips of ale she had taken. She didn't know how many songs they had danced, only that sweat slicked Al's hairline, and she didn't want this to stop.

"If I'd known you danced like this, I might have said yes to you."

"Oh, shut up." She pushed him before grabbing his hand and twirling herself under his arm once again.

❧

Sera didn't know how much ale she'd drunk. Her head swam in a pleasant warmth of hazy edges and giggles. As she attempted to climb the stairs, Alistair, not much steadier beside her, held her under one shoulder and outright snorted when she almost fell for the third time.

"You're a menace," he said before sweeping his arm under her knees and carrying her the rest of the way up.

"Do not drop me," she said, resting her cheek on his chest. Shadow, his arms were so firm, so solid. She could fall asleep just like this.

A few steps into the room, the comfort of his warmth was suddenly gone.

Sera screeched and tried clawing at something to catch herself before she landed on the straw mattress. Alistair's baritone laugh was infectious as she stretched out like an overgrown cat.

Al removed her boots, then her socks, and swore.

"Why didn't you tell me?" His gloved hand healed her new blisters in a flash of white light. A tingling went from her feet to her calves and higher and higher. She moaned at the sensation. "Careful, princess." The crowd below was still going strong, but she didn't miss the way his voice lowered, the breathy undertone. His gaze explored her, warming each place his eyes landed like the sun's rays. Her face, her chest, the curve of her hip beneath lavender fabric.

"I'm grown. You should call me a queen." Tingling pleasure rolled through her, and suddenly she wasn't so concerned about the one bed.

"Whatever you say, Seraphina." He shook his head, then hovered over her, and those sky-blue eyes settled on her lips. She arched toward him, just enough...

Al reached behind her head, stole a pillow, and settled at the foot of the door.

Sera sighed in her drunken bliss, turning onto her side. Alistair was staring at the ceiling, lost in thought.

"Why do you wear gloves all the time? I don't remember you doing that when we were younger."

He rolled on his side to face her.

"I'm sensitive." He furrowed his brow. "My magic developed, and certain things can irritate my skin."

"Like what?"

"Demons," he said with a shrug. "It's been pretty fucking itchy with Snik around."

"He can hurt you?" The straw mattress crunched under her elbow.

"All demons can hurt us. I'm fine as long as I don't touch him with my bare hand. Really, anything demonic, hence the gloves." He wiggled his fingers at her.

What a strange reaction.

Sera flopped onto her back. "Do you ever wish you were different?" She sighed. "I wish I was better. Not so afraid to be happy."

Sleep pulled at her.

"Why are you afraid to be happy?"

"I don't think I deserve it," she whispered.

"You deserve it, Seraphina. You deserve to feel every ounce of joy."

"Maybe I'll try harder," she said, closing her eyes. "You're pretty easy to be happy around." The rolling darkness was quiet as she drifted. She almost missed his reply.

"You are too."

CHAPTER TWENTY-TWO

DOMINICK

The days were getting longer, the air warmer, the breezes carrying sticky salt across the Citadel. Dominick took in the setting sun as he sat on the pool house steps and waited for Theo. The air, the humidity, all of it reminded Dom that summer was coming.

He was looking forward to the solstice festivals and the after-parties. The late-night dancing, with early-morning trysts. He and Sera stumbling around the streets of Dobro singing too loudly, too drunk, but together and whole.

Yes, summer was coming, and things would be better.

Dominick nodded to a few of the departing oracles as the pools began to empty for the night. Just as the clouds above turned a molten orange, he smiled to himself. He had been looking forward to taking Theo to dinner all day. While thinking of the warlock, he'd caught himself smiling more times than he'd ever admit to anyone, even though their findings were becoming more and more troubling. It was annoying—in the best sort of way, he supposed.

Normally, using Theo to pull threads wouldn't bother him. Maybe that's why he dove headfirst into this mission of finding discrepancies between the lives that perished versus those being reported. It relieved some of the guilt he was feeling. But no matter how many times he asked Theo to pull Nora's thread, Theo never seemed to mind, and as long as Theo kept going along with it, Dominick thought it might be good to have a little fun too.

Dominick stood, brushed off his robes, and peered between a group of oracles scraping their feet against the beige stone as they exited. Beyond them was the warlock he was looking for.

"Fancy meeting you here," Dominick said, taking in Theo's slightly crooked smile and strong chin. The oracle's eyes were red rimmed and glassy; he'd done too much today.

"Hey." Theo approached him and kissed Dom on the cheek.

Dom reared back. Heat climbed his neck to his cheeks as he looked around to see if anyone had seen, before clearing his throat.

Theo turned rigid. "I thought after this week..."

"I just wasn't expecting it, is all." He could feel the embarrassment creeping from his cheeks to his ears. He must look like an utter fool. Dom couldn't help but itch the spot below his ear in the nervous tic that Sera constantly made fun of him for.

Public affection was never his thing. His reputation was built on the cool mask he kept in place, which—at least he thought—made him seem mysterious and appealing. Cheek kissing didn't really fall into that category.

"Point taken." Theo's voice was stone. His bloodshot eyes furrowed before he rubbed them.

Great.

Dominick grabbed Theo's wrist and pulled him away from the flow of foot traffic. This was not how he wanted the day to end. He couldn't fuck this up, and the last thing he needed was for Theodore to tell the other lifeline readers that Dom was desperate for someone to pull the lives of his friends.

Plus, besides the time they spent on their little mission, Dominick was actually starting to like the warlock. That in itself should have been a red flag, but alas, here he was, dragging a warlock through the streets, trying to figure out how in Eraphon he was going to fix this.

"Dominick, let me go. I'm tired."

Dom pulled Theo into the gardens between the Ogdelo and Council chambers. Safe behind a cluster of trees, he finally let Theo go.

"You're upset." Dom brushed his hair back and stood with his hands on his hips. Shadow help him.

"What do you need, Dominick?"

"I don't *need* anything. I *wanted* to know how your day went and if you still wanted to grab dinner. Based on how bloodshot your eyeballs are right now, it doesn't seem like it went well." Why was he so bad at this today? Usually, he just fucked them and moved on. But keeping someone interested in him until Sera got back was going to take work. Work he wasn't exactly qualified for.

Theo crossed his arms. His gray robes whipped around him, and the way the sunlight moved over the planes of his face...

"I guess I see clearly now what you really want... for me to pull threads for Nora, and a good lay after? Excuse me for thinking this was a little bit more than that."

Coven founders...

"Just... stop, okay. Stop. It is. I do." Dominick groaned in frustration, wiping his hand down his face. He lowered his voice. "Theo, I do like you. I've been looking forward to taking you out all day. I was just surprised, is all..." Dom ran his hand through his hair again. "I'm not good at this shit, okay?"

Theo raised a brow at him, and Shadow help him, he'd beg Theo if he had to. For Sera, for Nora... for him.

Dom's groveling was interrupted by the sound of boots on stone.

Chair Renata passed the gardens, leading four human men. Their pock-marked and wrinkled skin, along with their strange clothing, gave them away—tights with heeled shoes, thick velveteen jackets, and fluffy collars tight around the neck. Only one wore white robes, and he carried a tome.

Dominick gasped at what was behind them.

Massive winged beings, men bigger than any Legion warriors he'd seen, with white wings edged with gold held high above their shoulders. The gilded tips, like their armor, glinted in the sunlight. Their wings were large enough for flight, which must be a feat, since the bodies attached were thickly wrapped in muscle.

Giant swords fastened to the warriors' hips, some down the center of their backs, didn't look light either. The weapons shimmered with magic—wisps of white and iridescence escaped the scabbards and sheaths. A dozen of the winged warriors followed the humans and Chair Renata while every coven member in the vicinity gawked.

Not even the birds dared to chirp in the presence of their harsh faces.

Chair Renata led the parade to the front steps of the Council chambers, and after a few moments, they all disappeared inside.

"What are they?" Theo whispered.

"I have no idea."

CHAPTER TWENTY-THREE

SERAPHINA

There was movement in their room above the tavern. Alistair was up and about, but Sera wondered whether if she kept her eyes closed and lay still enough, he'd leave her alone.

Her head was pounding. A piece of straw jammed into her cheek through the flimsy fabric that was... wet? Drool, not piss, thank Shadow.

"Wake up, *Queen Minnow*."

Sera wiped her face. With a groan, she rolled over. "No, thank you," she said, pulling the itchy quilt over her face. Why did her head hurt so much?

"We're wasting daylight because you can't hold your ale."

Ale.

That's what that drink was called. She wished it had been laced with magic like the coven breweries' was. That's what must prevent this incessant throbbing.

Al ripped away the quilt, and the sun shining through the filthy window was brighter than she'd thought. "Just go without me. We both know you could finish this mission faster if I didn't get in the way. So let me not get in the way."

Alistair's eyebrows were almost at his hairline when she peeked through one eye. He was smiling and clean shaven. Those fucking dimples would be the death of her one day.

"Don't be too surprised, but I actually need your help today." He crossed the room and rested his forearm on the doorjamb. "There's bread on the table. Eat it. Then meet me downstairs. Soon. Don't make me come get you." And Alistair Alcott, captain in the Solarni Legion, gave her a look that immediately made her thighs clench. Then he shut the door.

A few minutes later, she descended the stairs in her stained lavender dress, bread in hand, slowly working the hard crust between her teeth. She sat opposite Al, and he handed her a bowl of last night's reheated stew.

"Eat," he said.

"I don't think my stomach will like it."

"You've lost weight." There was a hint of concern in his tone.

"Didn't we talk about commenting on appearances?" She held her head in her hands.

"Your uniform was getting loose before we got here. And when I carried you up the stairs last night, I could feel your ribs."

Sera didn't know what to do with that statement. Didn't know if she should throttle him for even mentioning her body, or if she should be impressed that he paid close enough attention and realized she was suffering. And she was suffering. The guilt was beginning to eat her alive. Nora, Feybury... all of it.

"In case you haven't noticed, I'm dealing with a lot right now."

"I know, but you're no good to anyone if you're dead from starvation," Al said.

She glared at him, but he continued to watch her. She tried to eat a spoonful of stew, and just as she suspected, her stomach protested. Though its flipping could have been from the shame of being sloppy enough that he had to carry her. She hadn't realized she'd been that far gone.

But from what she remembered, he'd stumbled a bit too.

"You were quite lively," Alistair said. Her cheeks burned as she shoveled another spoonful into her mouth to try to hide her embarrassment. "You looked happy. Well, the happiest I've seen you."

She sneered. "Glad I could entertain you on this dull adventure." She choked down another spoonful of slop. "From what I remember, you were quite chummy with the locals."

Alistair leaned forward. "You really are jealous of little Dahlia, aren't you?"

Sera rolled her eyes. "You're impossible, you know that?"

"Maybe that's why your eyes are that lovely shade of green... You're just full of envy." He winked.

She knew she was blushing, and there was no way to stop it, but instead of ducking her head to avoid his gaze, Sera rested her chin in her hand and admired him. The lines of muscle beneath his shirt, the way his forearms were so well defined, all the way down to his leather gloves. Then she lifted her gaze right back to his, and his cocky smile widened, deepening those perfect dimples.

Al lowered his voice and leaned closer. "I don't know if you'll win this game, Minnow."

Sera shrugged her shoulders. "We'll see," she said and took another bite of her stew.

"There's a market a few streets away. I want to try and get some information from the traveling covens."

Now *that* was something she was interested in. The Solarni coven liked to think they were the only coven on the continent, but she remembered how the traveling covens used to venture to the Citadel when she was younger. Their magic wasn't so different, but it was more organic. They chanted under the full moons. Used poultices and brewed potions naturally, with foliage directly from the ground. They were more in tune with Eraphon.

"The Suma or Staraji?"

Alistair tilted his head. "You know, every time I think you can't possibly be more adorable, you spit out a fact. Makes my heart race a little, Minnow." Sera choked. "I don't know which coven. Assuming Suma, since they are within a human city, but I guess we will see."

She needed to get out of that room, away from him and that lingering gaze that was doing far more than making her heart race.

"If I were a snarkier witch, I would tell you that I'm surprised you'd be interested in someone with a brain. But because I'm not, how can I help you get information from the traveling covens, Alistair?" she asked.

"I'm going to ask a few leading questions. I don't expect them to share anything with me—I scream Legion—but once I leave, they may whisper information we could use. That's where you come in."

"You want me to spy?"

"You get it. Good job!"

It was way too early for this...

Wagons, humans, and dust congregated around the market. The tents were a splash of color against the dulled landscape. Everything had a thick coat of dirt here. Even Sera's skin was gritty.

It was easy to distinguish Alistair from the humans. Was he unable to shrink his size? Or did he just like being the tallest man in the room? He lumbered from stall to stall, catching everyone's attention as he went.

Al had been right; it was the Suma coven. She could tell just by the color of the tents. Greens and browns similar to the forest she had trekked through for days. Not to mention their wares were a bit outdated. They wore talismans and carried around animal feet for protection. Their way of life fascinated her.

There was danger on the road, sure, but it couldn't feel much different from the constant fear she'd been in since before she left the Citadel. At least they saw the continent. Sera shielded her eyes and watched Alistair enter a tent. Once he'd left, she entered.

Rows of animal feet on rickety shelves stared back at her.

"The rabbit is for luck." A hunched witch pointed her twisted finger at the display. She was weathered, deep grooves cemented between her brows and around her mouth. The witch sucked in a bit of drool that had escaped her lips and limped to a stool behind a table. "Mole is for a toothache, and badger will give you fierceness."

"Thank you. I was just looking."

"You are seeking something? Something I do not have?" The old witch sniffed the air. "See, I know. I know what you need," she said, sucking her spittle. "A bone. You need a bone."

Sera backed away slowly. "No, I'm fine."

"But you must, I insist. I can taste it on you. Ash."

Sera froze. She'd tasted ash in the air only a handful of times. Once before Feybury, and the other in the Menage when Nora was taken. One time involved a demon relic, the other a demon lord.

The old witch was muttering, reaching for something behind the flap of the tent, when a tingling hum of power raked over Sera. The vibrations shifted with an unnerving familiarity.

You run and run, her magic whispered in her mind.

"Stop it," she said back. She had to get out of there. Sera exited the tent and hit a wall.

No, not a wall.

She sucked in a breath. There before her, inches away, was *him.* Beneath a dark hood, a pair of red eyes gazed from below dark brows. A barely healed pink scar slashed across his right cheek. This close, she could make out the sharp lines of his face and the sensuous curve of his lips. He had a violent kind of beauty, one that promised pain wrapped in pleasure.

"Hello again." His voice, a deep rumble, skittered through her. She stared at him, unable to move or unwilling. Mesmerized by how his irises changed from bloodred to steely gray. "Do you always walk around with dirt on your cheeks, Subdina?"

Speak, the voice in her head said. She was too stunned to say anything. Too terrified to move away from the obvious danger in front of her. The demon tilted his head as he examined her. Her body, now trembling, held her waiting magic within her. Waiting and watching.

The only thought that crossed her mind was that she wanted him to speak again. His voice was a ballad, brushing her raw nerve endings in a caress. She'd read about a demon's ability to enthrall a victim, but to feel it? This felt like a homecoming, something she had been missing her entire life.

When his gaze left her, she could finally breathe. The top of her head reached just below his chin, so dangerously close she was, and the power that came off him washed over her in waves. Ash, but something deeper, earthen, woody.

The demon gave her a half smile. "Your bodyguard is on his way." He lifted her hand to his lips and said, "Until we meet again."

Then he was... gone.

"What are you doing?" Alistair called to her, his hands on his hips.

"You didn't see him?" Sera could still feel him, the vibrations of his magic. She reached out a hand to see if this was all some insane illusion, half expecting to touch his cloak. But there was... nothing.

"See who?"

Sandalwood and ash enveloped her. He had to be there, somewhere. "I just— Never mind."

"The sun must have gotten to you." Al linked his arm through hers.

"We still need to get information." She pulled her heavy curls over her shoulder, desperately wishing for a gust of air to cool her.

"I've already got something. Demons were seen searching for something south of the forest," he whispered to her.

Searching for something, or coming from? South of Ironoak was that empty space on the map. There had to be a ruin there, and with it a possible doorway.

Sera wasn't sure if it was Al's whisper in her ear, the hallucination, or the thought of being close to a doorway that led to the underworld; whatever it was, she shivered under the beating sun.

CHAPTER TWENTY-FOUR

SERAPHINA

Alistair had let her nap. She was grateful for it. All day, ever since she'd apparently hallucinated, she'd felt off. Too hot, then shivering. Hungry, but when food touched her lips, she wanted to vomit. Sinking further into the pillows, Sera opened her journal in her lap, still captivated by how Dominick's script appeared on the page.

Something strange is going on.

Chair Renata led a group of winged beings. Fucking white-and-gold feathered wings. The Citadel is in chaos, but I'll let you know what's going on as soon as we know more.

I miss you, and Theo is a hell of a kisser. I think I'll keep him around.

So mythical beings had come to the Citadel. Sera had read about them—an old foe from before the rebellion. The archives contained limited entries about their species, so most assumed they didn't exist. But here they were, in the flesh, in the Citadel.

As she mused on the news, unsettled, voices cheered in the tavern below. She sank further into the straw mattress. Another rowdy night of bard entertainment. As much as she longed to escape her mind and the constant smell of ash, Sera didn't want to drink the ale again. This afternoon's hallucination had already embarrassed her, and she didn't need to push that further by falling up the stairs.

But was it really a hallucination? She could have sworn it was real. *He* was real.

Alistair was partaking in the activities. He'd said it was to get additional information, but she was skeptical. Regardless, it gave her a much-needed moment alone. A luxury she hadn't been able to indulge in lately.

Sera picked up her pen and wrote:

They're called the aliato. Soldiers of the human Creator, widely thought to be myth.

Why they are in the Citadel is a little concerning.

Speak with Galene if you need more information. She'll have access to older texts than you'd be able to find in the library.

I'm glad you found someone who doesn't bore you to tears. You deserve it. He's lucky to have you.

Her script disappeared from the page.

Galene would have the answers. Sera had once brought up the aliato to her mentor, who'd looked petrified and intrigued at the same time. After working with the witch for years, Sera had learned that was the face she used when Sera brought up a subject that Galene had no intention of discussing.

But buried in the archives were depictions of the winged soldiers, and if anyone knew their way around a library... it was Galene.

Heavy footsteps sounded outside the door.

Shadow help her. If Alistair had locked himself out, she'd never let him live it down. Sera slid off the bed and fluffed her hair for a moment before approaching the door.

"Al, you can come in," she said. She was turning the knob when the door slammed against the wall.

Sera stumbled backward.

The man's beard dripped with ale. He had a pungent stench about him and wild, bloodshot eyes. "Ah, there ya be, lass. Was lookin' for ya to be alone since last night."

She sprinted around the bed, grabbing one of Al's hunting knives from atop the map on the desk. She couldn't let him near her. He'd overpower her in a second. No training was going to help her here, not with her heart beating frantically like this and her veins burning.

The man's lips were stretched so tight over his teeth that they seemed to disappear. "Don'tcha do that now. I just came to give ya a little kiss." He licked his lips. Sera noticed a bulge in his pants and swallowed the hard lump in her throat.

The music picked up again. Sera could hear stomping and whooping below. Even if she screamed, they'd never hear her. Al wouldn't hear her.

"Get the fuck out," she spat at him, gripping the knife with both hands. She couldn't stop the steel from shaking. He inched closer.

You are more than steel. Her magic whispered and surged. Moons, she was burning. Raging and burning and ripping. Sera tried reaching for her barrier magic, but the abomination snapped inside her like an asp in a mighty flood of heat.

The corners of her vision began to fade as the man came closer. The swing of her arms was met with his maw of a hand over hers.

Before she could scream, before she could even register what was happening, the intruder was on the ground—with a feral Alistair above him.

"She said, *Get the fuck out.*" Al had the man gripped by the throat. He clawed at Alistair's forearm for release.

"You can't keep her for yourself. The whores are passed round 'ere."

Alistair snarled, and then they were gone.

The knife clanged to the floor as every cell in her body vibrated.

No.

Shouts of terror rose from the tavern below. Black mist poured from her, pooling around her ankles, leaking between the floorboards.

A single gray drop of flame fell from Sera's palm, and they were burning.

Smoke curled up the stairway and into the room. It was unnatural how fast it worked. Sera squeezed her eyes shut. With its lid removed, that well of darkness went down, down, down. So deep, she'd never imagined someone could hold that much power within the confines of their body. The screaming—Shadow, the screaming.

Stay. Feel them.

She shook. That burning scorched her veins. Sera cried out, pulling and pulling it back, down, to lock it away. But what if... what if this time she stopped? Stopped running, stop trying.

Her pulse raced. Her lungs choked on the black smoke with each inhale. She could almost sense the way her flames licked up their bodies, consuming them, the walls, the tubs of ale.

Another town destroyed. Sera couldn't bring herself to move. Mist and flame engulfed the room around her. She could sense the walls cracking and burning, people's flesh melting.

Someone shook her. When she opened her eyes, they met his blue. Alistair's arm circled her waist. His hand on the back of her head pushed her face into his strong shoulder.

Sea salt and sage.

Not ash.

As she flipped through time and space, her stomach lurched. No longer in a room aflame, but in a small clearing in the forest. Al sank to his knees and set her down gently on the ground.

"Breathe, Sera."

She was trying. Trying to tell him, but Al disappeared. Her lungs burned. It was fucking excruciating how her own magic could harm her in this way. Dead leaves crunched between her fingers as she tried to hold on to something. She couldn't get enough air. Shadow, she was going to die here.

As she lifted her head, panic seized her, shortening her already shallow breaths. "Al... Snik..." she wheezed.

Heavy tears rolled down her soot-caked cheeks. In the dusk light, across the clearing, was the man who'd attacked her.

His mouth hung open, his neck bent at an unnatural angle. The forest scavengers were already circling high above.

Sera heaved up the contents of her stomach. The pressure in her head was excruciating, and every second, she worked to slow the flow of magic through her body. She was dying.

"You're all right. It's all right." Alistair had his hands on her shoulders, was pulling her hair away from her face.

She gasped and clung to him.

"Shit," he said and lifted her to a seated position. He knelt in front of her. "I'm going to try to heal your lungs."

Sera gave him a shallow nod. It was like her body had forgotten what it was like to draw in air.

Ripping off his gloves, he settled his thumbs on her breastbone, his palms and fingers spread along her ribs as white light seeped from his fingers.

His eyes were closed in concentration.

Sera tried to memorize the planes of his face. High cheekbones, strong brow, and the way his lips quivered in concentration.

"Breathe, damn it!"

Cool air flooded her chest, and on her exhale, she sobbed.

"Well, your lips aren't blue anymore," he said after a few moments and let her go. She instantly missed the warmth of his hands around her.

Before she could thank him, Sera puked again.

"Fuck," Al said. "Can I carry you?" he asked, barely a whisper.

She nodded and reached for him. He scooped her into his arms, grabbed both packs, and threw them over one shoulder.

"We'll make camp a little further south," he murmured into her ear.

Sera stared over his shoulder at the man who'd started this. Crows had landed around him, and she didn't look away when they plucked out one of his eyes.

CHAPTER TWENTY-FIVE

SERAPHINA

It wasn't the prodding that made her panic. It was the pops and crackles from the fire that caused Sera to wake up screaming. Snik slithered his way into her arms. His whines reverberated against her chest like a soothing purr.

"Snik? You're safe," she croaked. Her throat was raw from either the vomiting or the smoke she'd inhaled.

He's safe. Yes. The people? She'd done it again, and every pop of a stick against flame made her twitch.

"Are you all right?" Alistair asked from across the fire.

Sera ran a shaky hand through her hair. She didn't remember being set down on her bedroll, nor Al making camp. The last thing she remembered seeing was the empty eye sockets of the man who was going to rape her.

Sera nodded.

"I moved us south. You won't have to see him again," he said, breaking off a piece of a stick and tossing it into the flames. He must have been doing that for a while. A pile of burning stubs lay near his side.

"Thank you." Snik was warm in her arms, a blessing, since she wanted to be as far away from that fire as possible. Flame and death, that's what she was. Destruction... an end.

Al wouldn't meet her eyes. "I shouldn't have let him approach the stairs."

"It's not your fault. How would you have known he was coming to our door?" *Our door*, like this was something permanent, like they could go back and spend their whole lives drinking ale and dancing the night away. As if the entire world wasn't crumbling around them and she wasn't burning and killing and ruining everything she touched.

"I'm supposed to protect you."

She froze at that word. *Always needing to be protected. Defective, spineless, incapable.* Her mother's words churned through her head, causing her darkness to rouse. Sera quickly bound what magic she had, envisioning the cage and locking it away. "You're supposed to find the oracle. If I survive, great, but your mission isn't to protect me."

Too much talking. Her lungs protested despite Al's healing. They were bruised, the muscles around her rib cage sore.

"You think I'd let harm come to you, Sera?"

She didn't have an answer for that.

"Why didn't you run?"

Sera stared into the fire. The movement of the flames matched what had licked up the tavern walls. Instead of the reds, oranges, and blues, all she could see were black, gray, and white—mist, fog, and burning.

"Sera, when I traveled back, you were just standing there. Why didn't you try to get out?"

Her palms itched as she willed the darkness to stay in the cage within her. She'd never wanted this. Of all the times she had, as a witchling, prayed to Shadow for more power, this had never been what she wanted. "I thought maybe I deserved it. That I should die there."

"How could you think that?"

"Who would care if I went up in flames?" She swirled her fingers in the soil.

"Are you insane?" Al wiped a hand over his mouth.

Her mind jumped from one thing to the next. A useless waste of space. Too tiny a well. She didn't even know why the Council wanted her to try to find the doorways to Gehenna, and she'd been too cowardly to ask. A barb of hot anger ripped through her. She set Snik on her bedroll.

"Wouldn't it have been easier?" Her throat protested. "Or were you too worried about leaving a recruit behind? That if I died, you wouldn't get a promotion?"

"How fucking dare you," he growled at her. "How fucking dare you think all I care about is a promotion, Sera. What the fuck even is this?"

She wanted a fight. To rip him limb from limb, to feel something other than the constant pressure of limiting herself. To stop struggling.

"Like you know me so well?" she huffed, slamming her hand on her bedroll. Snik winced as she stood and began to pace. She was overheating, and it was fueling her anger.

"We may not have been friends the last seven years, but I know you matter." He stood before her. His gaze was intense, sweeping over her face and mouth. "Not just to me, but to Dominick, Honora, and your mother."

"My mother doesn't care about me," she hissed. "All she cares about is the seat on the Council that she's been working toward half her life, and Nora. Her instructions were to give myself up to save my sister. A bargaining chip, a trade, and a fucking poor one."

Alistair grabbed her wrists and pulled her forearms to his chest. She could feel his heartbeat galloping at the same speed as hers.

Alistair leaned down, his breath scorching her skin just below her ear. Sera shuddered at the sensation. "Get over yourself. You're not the only one who had a hard life."

He let her go. And there, in the middle of each palm, was a burn. Al wiped his hands on his pants and swore, leaving her beside the fire.

She rifled through both packs, hoping her journal had been tucked between pants and tunics, or somewhere else where she couldn't see it. She needed Dom: a balance, her anchor, someone to keep her from spinning out of control.

The longer she rummaged, the more panic set in.

Alistair walked into the camp, shirtless and wet.

Very wet.

Water dripped from his hair down his corded neck, shoulders, and chest.

He was made for battle. Every inch of him was hard muscle. His defined abs had a trail of hair down the center, leading below the waistband of his pants.

His hands... The injuries were so similar to what she had done to her mother's. Not as severe, but moons, they had to be painful.

"What are you doing now?" he asked.

"Looking for my journal," she said. "Have you seen it?"

Alistair shook his head and threw his shirt down amid the other clothing and trinkets. "I'm going to assume by this"—he motioned with his damaged hands to the mess strewn around her—"that it wasn't in your pack?" He reached for a roll of bandages and slowly wrapped each palm.

"I was writing in it before... Did you grab it, by chance?"

"The room was in flames. I barely got your map in time."

"Fuck," she whispered. "Fuck!"

"I'll buy you a new journal," he said, tenderly putting his gloves on over his bandaged palms.

"It was enchanted." This couldn't be happening. That was the only way to communicate with Dom and get information about Nora.

No control. She had no control and no way to figure out how to fix that. Ironoak was probably soot now.

She wiped the tears from her cheeks.

Failure. Disappointment. Spineless.

"Have you cried since Nora was taken?" he asked softly.

"I feel like I haven't stopped."

An air of melancholy surrounded him, and he traced the palm of his glove, clenching his jaw, his dark wet hair flopping across his brow. Shadow, what was wrong with her? She was bitching about her journal, and he was in pain.

"How are your hands?"

He flexed his fingers in his gloves. "This isn't anything to worry about."

"Why did they do that when you grabbed me?" She was terrified to hear the answer.

"Could have been anything. That magic was… unnatural, and you were surrounded by it; you inhaled it. I've never seen a demon use that kind of power before, but that doesn't mean they aren't evolving. It also doesn't help that you're constantly cuddled up with that beast over there."

Snik responded with a snore. The goblin lay curled in her bedroll like a sleeping cat; he hadn't even moved when she'd tossed the clothes on top of him.

Alistair thought it was demon magic. Sera held her head in her hands. She felt like she was being pulled from the inside out, raw and frayed. She pulled Snik closer, curling around the goblin. She wanted to waste away, to be free from carrying these burdens. The killing of innocent humans. The harm done to Nora, Dom, and now Alistair was all because of her. She was alone in this.

She reached for her pack and downed one of her elixirs, praying for a soundless sleep.

Above the chirping of crickets and the crackling of the fire, she heard Al moving something around. Then he lay beside her.

"What are you doing?" she whispered.

"If you think I'm going to let you sleep unguarded, you're out of your mind."

If she took a deep enough breath, the planes of her back would brush against his. She didn't want to admit that the thought soothed her. No matter how many times she'd wanted to refuse his help, anyone's help, she knew now she couldn't. She needed Alistair Alcott in more ways than one.

That fact clawed at the back of her mind like a rat trying to escape flames. And there was nothing she could do about it.

Safely tucked between Al and Snik, she wondered what it would feel like to fall asleep in his arms, to feel truly safe, to let herself be taken care of.

But a desperate witch was never safe.

The calm rise and fall of Al's breathing could have lulled her back to sleep. Snik had rustled her awake before venturing out into the woods for his morning hunt, leaving her to stretch, turn, and tap Al on the shoulder.

He startled and threw his arm in the air. Suddenly a domed white barrier surrounded them.

"How many powers do you possess?"

"Shadow, Sera, stop touching Snik, then me. I thought I was stabbed." He dropped the shield and rubbed sleep from his eyes. He was still shirtless from last night, and goose bumps now rippled over him.

Where her fingertips had touched him were raised purple welts.

"Sorry," she said. Al covered her delicious view of his far-too-chiseled chest with his shirt. "And thank you," she added.

"For?"

"For sleeping next to me." She got quiet. "For saving me."

"Always," he said, holding out his gloved hand to help her up. "You're going to need more training, though."

"I do." She sighed.

"We'll work on that," he said, looking at their clasped hands with a furrowed brow. The muscle in his jaw twitched as he turned her hand in his, inspecting the grooves of her palm. Sera ripped it away from him. "For now, let's eat... and I mean eat. There will be no more sharing with Snik. He's proved he can hunt for his own meals. I'll cook them if he wants, but you're wasting away."

"Again with the commenting on a witch's figure," she said, rolling up her makeshift bed. He handed her a piece of bread, and she took it and began to chew. "Butter would make this edible."

"I'll get some butter for you in the next town, *Queenie.*" Alistair glanced at her sidelong, and she bit back a smirk. "We're headed to Port Sidnah. I overheard talk last night about an oracle holing up there."

"We need to stop at the ruins first. Port Sidnah is almost to the sea."

Al nodded in agreement. "Well, it was the lead we needed. I just wish we'd learned a little more before... well, before the night went to shit."

She forced down the dry crusty bread. Her appetite had evaporated at the mention of the tavern.

"Don't do that," Alistair said.

"Do what?"

"Get quiet like you did something wrong. That wasn't your fault."

In another life, she'd be relieved he hadn't figured it out. In this moment, all she wanted was to be seen.

He'd saved her twice now.

He offered protection and power, but she lied to him. Hid this abomination that ran rampant through her veins.

Dominick had been forgiving, but a captain in the Solarni Legion?

Taking in his gaze, the concern on his face, the way the side of his mouth crept upward with every passing second, she stared at him. She wondered what his expression would be when he realized she shouldn't be permitted to live.

She thought of how his features would change—a scowl, then tight manacles around her wrists. Sera had no doubt he'd report her. He had a duty, and that duty wasn't to her.

No matter how much she wanted it to be.

CHAPTER TWENTY-SIX

DOMINICK

The dawn light streamed through his curtains, bathing sleeping Theo in golden sunlight.

Dominick had begged for forgiveness last night, something he'd never done before. And it'd been worth it. After those winged soldiers, and then dinner, it seemed important they stick together and figure out why the Council was lying to them.

And why were so many Legion soldiers dying? Dominick hoped that the swords on the winged soldiers' backs were to help coven members, but... he couldn't help but wonder if something far more sinister was afoot.

He settled further into his pillows, trying very carefully not to disturb Theo, and opened his journal to read Sera's entry.

Aliato.

Of course Sera would know what they were. There was no one better to find out the origin of a species than Seraphina Wildrick. When they were young, she'd always had her head in some crusty book.

The aliato had spooked the entire coven. Not that they hadn't been uneasy already. He'd checked in with his mother a few times already this week. She'd been worried, and if he thought she had the ability, he was sure she'd be pulling strings herself to check on his brother. No word. There had been no word for weeks, and Dom couldn't stop a pit forming in his stomach.

A blanket of paranoia and rumor had descended on the Citadel, affecting everyone but the Council of Elders, it seemed. The entire situation was fucked.

Theo's hair was strands of yellow silk across his pillow. He stirred as Dom brushed his fingers along Theo's brow. A feeling somewhere between fear and longing tumbled through him every time he looked at the warlock, and this moment was no exception. It was unnerving.

Theo inched closer and wrapped an arm around Dom's bare waist. Dominick smiled before sliding from under the duvet to get dressed.

"What are you doing?" Theo's groggy voice called to him.

"I've got to talk to Lavinia today."

"We're off today. Go tomorrow... Come back to bed."

"I'm going to try and meet her at her house rather than the office. Maybe the element of surprise will get her to tell me something."

Theo sat up. "Do you want me to go with you?"

"No. Get some more sleep. I'll be back soon." Dom kissed Theo's forehead and left his flat.

He had trouble stopping a smile from creeping across his cheeks as he walked to the Wildrick residence. It was unnatural the way Sera's mom could be so calm in a scenario where demons had kidnapped one daughter and the other was outside the fortress walls.

The entire situation was fucked. One day, Shadow help him, he would tell Lavinia exactly what he thought. That no mother had the right to treat her daughter that way. It didn't matter that Seraphina wasn't as powerful as the rest of them. She was still part of their family. She was *his* family.

Dom did his best to build a barrier around his mind, walked up the stone steps, and rang the bell.

Lavinia opened the door. Her usual braids were wrapped in a black head scarf, making her look even more regal and somehow more menacing at the same time. Her upturned eyes assessed him.

"Come in," she said, standing aside.

He hated that she already knew why he was there. He hated that he couldn't hide his thoughts from her. Sera had taught him once how to put walls in his mind, but he'd never practiced. Until now, he'd had nothing to hide.

Lavinia gave him a disapproving stare. "I see you have been in communication with Seraphina. You know that my daughter is still alive, so what you can tell Sera is this: I am working with the Council to arrange an elite squad to save Honora. I also communicate daily with the master oracle regarding Honora's lifeline and daily activities as best as the pools will show. She has not been gravely injured and is still being held captive."

Dominick shivered and worked to keep his mind blank. "Thank you. I've been very worried."

"You should be. The destruction these beasts have unleashed on the world is catastrophic."

Movement over Lavinia's shoulder caught Dominick's gaze. One of the warriors. His wings were tucked in tight as he moved at a slight angle down the hallway, careful not to knock into anything. He was massive.

"Everything all right, ma'am?" the aliato asked.

"Everything is fine," she called back to him. "Oracle Benero was just leaving."

Dominick nodded and headed to the door.

"They're called aliato, Dominick. Light-bringers. Be sure to remember that." Then she closed the door behind him.

This wasn't working.

Galene.

Sera had instructed him to seek Galene for information on these beings. Instead of going home, he turned toward Darine Hall.

Jedan members were using their magic to clean the bleached white pavers. He did his best to stick to the sides of the street, keeping out of their way as he marched toward the Citadel proper.

After providing Ithar with the initial chest of coin, he'd checked on him once more. The barkeeper almost kissed him when he'd entered Mystic's and had assured Dominick that what he'd done was enough. It didn't seem enough. Ever since he'd helped Sera, he couldn't ignore the conditions in Jedan or the divide between the coven's classes.

Three chimes rang, and Chair Renata's voice greeted the Citadel fortress.

"Coven members, it is with heavy hearts that we announce the end of the ceasefire. Hostilities with the demon realm have resumed. As of this moment, our coven is back at war. We urge all coven members to remain vigilant and, above all else, trust the Council. There will be further information shared soon in a gathering in the Menage."

"Fuck."

The Jedan members around him froze. He could smell the fear coming off them. They knew the rules. Jedan was the first class to be conscripted, the first to die. Then Dobro. Daedeth was the last defense against a siege. They stayed within the walls to protect the Council and the coven's very way of life.

The most powerful hide behind tall walls.

Dominick rubbed his face. Colton was already at the front. That's why the Council had moved the Legion.

"They knew," he whispered. They'd been fucking preparing.

He ran back to his flat in a blur. Sprinted up the stairs and flew through the door.

Theo ran into his arms. Dom pulled him tight to his chest, breathing him in. They were both oracles, protected by their class. But Colton? Nora? Sera?

"This changes everything," Theo whispered.

"I know, I know," Dom said. "I've got to tell Sera." He crossed the room, picked up his journal, and scribbled:

WE ARE AT WAR.

Chapter Twenty-Seven

Seraphina

Sera and Alistair walked south. The air was warmer, and the breeze carried a hint of brine, reminding her of home.

But was it home if Honora wasn't there? Her sweet sister. She hoped Dominick would have gotten her more information, anything to help this overwhelming pit of shame from swallowing her. Any hope left had been burned with her journal a few nights ago.

Alistair was wrong. She wasn't losing weight thanks to sharing her food. She was losing weight thanks to the images of Nora being tortured over and over again in her dreams. The fear of finding her sister dead. The guilt that Dominick was waiting for a reply that would never come. She hoped that those humans were right, that the oracle was near Port Sidnah and she and Al could go home.

Sera had insisted they stop at the spot on the map she swore was the ruins. They were close now; she could feel it. Chair Renata had said *doorways*, plural, but she'd decided the night she burned the tavern in Ironoak that she'd provide the Council with one. That would have to be good enough.

Snik galloped between the trees and underbrush, squealing and carrying on, driving Alistair mad. Earlier, the goblin had given her a rabbit, and ever since, he had been yipping cheerfully with the birds.

Sera was pretty sure she'd heard Al smite Snik when he tied the rabbit carcass to his pack. She never understood men's egos. So sensitive. And the one in front of her... she didn't know what to make of him.

Her eyes betrayed her by continually seeking him out, taking in those strong shoulders, his manly beauty. Al carried his pack on one shoulder. He'd stripped off his tunic early in the day, leaving him in only a sweat-slicked undershirt. His back muscles moved with as much grace as a mountain cat's, fluid and powerful. And Shadow, his ass...

Sera wiped at her brow as they trudged through the woods. The summer solstice was drawing near, and the days were getting longer. She wrapped her hair in a high bun, pushing the loose curls behind her ears.

"Let's take a break," Alistair said. "I want to try something." He ripped off his undershirt and rummaged in his pack, then stood with something in his hand.

Her breath caught in her throat. The sun actually glistened on his chest. He didn't even smell, if that was possible. She was pretty sure she did, after the way they'd been walking and the few streams they'd passed.

"Eyes up here, Minnow." He smirked at her and held out a leather cuff with a stone in the center. Hanging off the cuff were two chains with metal rings fastened to the end. She'd heard of enhancers before; each one was a little different, tailored to the witch or warlock meant to wield it.

"These"—he held up the enhancer—"are for recruits. Give me your right hand."

She laid her hand on his gloved palm. "How did you know I'm right handed?"

"I pay attention," he said, much too smoothly. His eyes smoldered, turning her core molten as he slid the two rings down her middle and ring fingers. Once he'd attached the cuff around the width of her hand, the purple amethyst was centered and strapped to her palm.

"The chains give you freedom of movement, while the magic concentrates here." He tapped the amethyst. "Put your arm up, palm facing out." He stepped behind her.

"Now what?"

"Where does your magic come from?"

She peered over her shoulder at him. "Me? Where else would it come from?"

"Coven founders save me," he muttered. "Where do you feel it in your body?"

"My chest."

"Put your left hand on your chest and keep your right extended. Take a deep breath. Instead of creating a barrier around your body, try to push the power out of the enhancer. Ready?"

This wasn't a good idea. The darkness within her was quiet now, but would it stay that way?

Barijara. She whispered the spell in her mind. Inhaling, she pulled at her blue barrier magic, imagining it wrapping her arm and emerging from the stone in her palm.

"That's good," Alistair said behind her. "Keep going."

She clenched her teeth, picturing her blue barrier as a beam of light instead of a second skin. The magic barely expanded past her hand. Her arm shook, and her body temperature rose as black flame churned behind its cage.

Alistair stepped closer. "You can do this," he whispered, reaching around to support her extended elbow. She pushed her magic, refusing to let him distract her. Then his gloved hand was on hers, planted right above her heart. "Come on, Sera."

His breath on her ear made her shiver. Lost was the concentration she needed to push magic through a stone in her palm. It was taking everything she had not to lean back into him.

"Focus," he whispered again, a hint of a smile in his voice. She was about to be putty.

"You're rather distracting," she said, closing her eyes. Her darkness thrashed at his proximity. It was irritated, but Sera refused to let it escape. Not this time. She couldn't let it happen again.

Thankfully, the enhancer didn't call to her darkness, only to the small well she'd been born with. Sera locked her elbow, and her muscles screamed in protest.

"That's it," he said. "Keep going." But the well only went so deep, and she was burning. She was sure that the only reason she wasn't dust was because of her darkness. That's how coven members' magic worked... If the well ran dry, the witch or warlock ceased to exist.

Her breaths were uneven as she pushed that bit of blue barrier magic through her arm, calling up every ounce.

"Open your eyes." Al's breath tickled the skin below her ear.

A blue dome surrounded them. Sera yelped a laugh, viewing the trees, the sky, all of it through a turquoise-tinted layer. "I did it! I made something."

The dome fell, and Sera couldn't help herself; she leaped into Alistair's arms. Turning in dizzying spins around and around, she couldn't stop the bubble of laughter that broke through her. She'd done it. She wasn't defective.

"Ahh, fuck." He dropped her to her feet. "Shit, no more petting Snik."

She laughed at the two handprints that marked his shoulders. He couldn't have been too upset by it because he stepped closer and gripped her waist.

Every inch of her body went taut, his face serious as his eyes roamed hers, then dropped to her lips. Sera tilted her chin up to him, a blatant invitation that she refused to be ashamed of making. The planes of his face held a hint of suspicion, but she wanted this. She wanted to know what he tasted like and how his lips would fit on hers. Wanted him to make her forget every bad thing she'd ever done, and that the world was burning around her.

Sera could see the hesitation in his eyes before the soft leather of his glove cupped her cheek. "Sera," he whispered.

"Al."

"YEEEEEEEEEEEEEE!" Snik barreled into the clearing, screeching. The goblin stopped and snarled. Not at Alistair. Snik was growling at something deeper in the forest.

A wave of magic crackled over Sera's skin. The forest was silent, and she couldn't shake the feeling of something watching her.

"Get my dagger from my pack... slowly," Alistair said in an almost whisper.

There was nothing she could see in the underbrush, but Snik was there, snarling and spitting. She'd never seen the creature act so rabid, but he stayed with her, guarding her.

The cool metal of the dagger's grip was firm in her hand, but Al... She squinted. Somewhere in the space of a few seconds, he had changed.

Standing before her wasn't the warlock she'd spent her youth pining over, or the Legion captain who'd saved her more than once on this journey.

No. Before her, holding a sword in one hand and a white-hot ball of power in the other, dressed head to toe in black, was the warlock whose image was plastered over every wall in the Legion barracks. The same one that had been stained with red lip prints in the witches' bathing room.

"You're the fucking Mesar, Al?!"

A group of terrifying beasts emerged from the trees. The sound of their throats clicking made her shiver. Their limbs were long, the ends of them tipped with sharp black talons. Tattered cloaks covered the beasts' bodies, and beneath their hoods the dried skulls of deer and elken covered their faces. Beady red eyes peered through the empty eye sockets.

These were something other. Sera had never seen a species of demon like this.

They clicked to each other, their bodies twitching. Two reared back on their haunches and lunged.

Alistair threw out a beam of blinding light at the beasts, then swung his sword. He was a work of art. The black Mesar uniform had extra padding around his middle, shoulders, and upper arms. His hood and mask were in place. It made sense, knowing how sensitive he was.

Snik crouched before her. She had her enhancer on one hand and the blade in the other. The two beasts who weren't attacking perked their heads, and their masks' mighty antlers scraped the hanging branches of the trees. Their clicking turned to snarling.

Al blasted out another streak of power, searing the beasts, whose screeches echoed through the trees.

"RUN!" Al screamed.

Snik snarled in approval and grabbed her hand. Her heart pounded, her magic thrashed in defiance, but she focused on following Snik.

In the web of bushes and branches, her feet slipped on high piles of leaves. Snik whined. "I'm coming," she hissed as a thorny vine ripped the sleeve of her tunic. She crawled into a dense thicket and waited. Barely audible over the beating of her heart was the sound of a sword slicing through the air and howling cries. She'd known he was lethal, but Al was the Mesar. The ruthless demon butcher. She'd kill him for keeping that from her if the beasts didn't do it for her.

"Shit," she whispered. "Shit shit shit."

There were four of those things. Sera unclipped the snaps holding her enhancer to her palm and placed it on her other hand. If she was going to have any success brandishing a weapon, she needed her dominant hand free.

Al yelled, and she froze.

"He needs help."

Snik pulled at her uniform and whined.

"Stay here. I'm going to check on him."

Was she out of her mind? Quite possibly, but she'd be damned if she let him die alone. Crawling on her hands and knees, she crept out of the thicket and back toward Al. Each step had her heart pounding, her magic rising to meet her palms through her veins, but Sera poked the tip of the dagger just deep enough to draw blood from the pad of her thumb and sighed at the relief of her darkness retracting.

I will not be smothered forever, the magic whispered. "Oh, shut up."

On silent feet she stalked. The sound of Al's heavy breathing grew louder. Two of the beasts were dead on the ground. Al was dodging the other two as they circled him. Sera crouched behind a tree and watched.

Twist, block, slash. Over and over, he deflected their talons. Black blood circled him in great sweeping arcs across tree trunks and the forest floor. He was destruction in warlock form. Sera had never witnessed him train. She never realized how much it looked like a deadly dance.

The beasts' clicking grew louder. Alistair raised his sword, but the creature behind him swiped.

"DUCK," she screamed.

Al's eyes went wide, but he listened, saving his head from being torn from his shoulders. But there was panic there, and he missed one of the beasts' lunges. A claw ripped through the reinforced padding of his uniform, and Al swore.

Gripping the dagger, Sera snuck behind the monster he was engaging. She was going to help; he needed help. Sera jumped, flung her arm around the beast's throat, and stabbed. Over and over, into anywhere soft. The dagger shifted and slid in her hands as the beast fell to its knees. Hot black blood smeared her hands. Her face was dotted with it as she tugged the dagger out, readjusted, and sliced the beast's neck. Deep, through tendon and cartilage, then skirting bone.

Her darkness was thrashing, burning... Sera nicked herself again. Her red blood mixed on the blade with the beast's black.

Al swung his sword, alight with shimmering flame, and slammed it into the last monster's gut. Sera's whole body was shaking, her breaths coming too fast. She had killed again.

Al pinned the beast to the ground and ran to her.

"Are you hurt?" he panted, looking her over and noticing the tiny trail of blood down her arm.

"It's nothing, but you..." Blood leaked from the wound at his side. Through the reinforced stitching, a steady red stream was flowing.

Al ripped off his mask.

"I'm fine. We need to keep moving. Grab your pack. More could be out there."

She could barely grip the straps in her shaking hands.

The sound of brush moving made her snap her head to the woods, but it was only Snik racing to her side. He grabbed her thigh and cried. "Hold on, Snik." As she swung her pack onto her back, she heard a wet squishing sound behind her.

A gurgle. Then there was something that sounded like bone rubbing against bone. The dead beast on the ground twitched.

Al blasted a healing flare into his side and yelled, "Run!"

Chapter Twenty-Eight

Seraphina

Sera's heartbeat drummed in her ears as the beasts on the ground twitched.

"Sera! Run!" Al screamed again.

He raced by, his grip like steel on her arm, and she moved. They shot through the trees, Snik ahead of them on all fours, howling a battle cry.

Sera ducked under branches, everything a blur of brown and green. Her lungs burned, and she pushed her legs to move, to hurtle over logs. She barely felt the stinging on her arms, the sharp pulling in her thighs, as she moved.

"Faster," Alistair yelled.

The trees thinned with every step forward. She stopped short and looked up. A wall of solid granite blocked their path, reaching at least sixty feet into the air. A straight drop. They had to be close. The ruins could hide them.

Or kill you.

Sera followed Al. They sprinted along the bottom of the cliff. Her side cramped, and she hissed, trying to breathe through it. Something thudded behind them. Claws pounding dirt.

"Grab Snik!" Al yelled between breaths.

Snik stopped short and jumped into her arms. Before she could register what happened, they were on a deer path much farther ahead. Nausea rolled through her. Her abomination's cage rattled, and dark spots crept into her vision.

"Keep going." Al pushed her forward. "They will not stop."

"How are they alive?" she managed to ask, choking down her bile.

"They fucking regenerate," he said through gritted teeth. A bright white light blinded her as Al healed his side, then turned, whipping his arm through the air. His glorious glimmering magic whipped out like a fan behind them. The demons' flesh smoked as the beasts fell onto their backs.

He stumbled. Sera gripped his arm, but blood still streamed from his side.

"Go."

They continued around the cliff face.

Clicking all around her... above her. Sera glanced up, where a dozen of the monsters stared at them from the cliff's edge. Raising her hand above her head, she grunted, getting a barrier in place just in time to prevent boulders and rocks from crushing them.

A beam of white light sailed through the sky, knocking a few beasts down. Then, to her horror, they jumped, slamming into the canopies of the giant ironoaks. The tops of the trees swayed violently under the weight. The raven pendant tied around her neck thumped hard against her chest.

"Fuck," Alistair growled from behind. His breath was ragged.

"Why aren't you healing?" The snarls grew louder, the clicking rising to a near-deafening level. She gulped down precious mouthfuls of air. "Snik, you need to get out of here."

Snik shook his head, his oversize ears swaying with the motion. The goblin set his chin like he was ready and willing to die by her side. She didn't know why he'd given her such loyalty, but it broke her heart when she said, "It's an order! Get out of here!"

Snik whimpered, then veered off.

Sera threw down her pack, snatched Al's, and tossed them into some bushes. Maybe she and Al would come back for them if they made it through this, but right now they needed to run.

"Al, travel us."

Al nodded and grabbed her arm. She gasped, barely getting a moment to prepare for the dizzying fold through space.

Sera slammed to her knees. But when she opened her eyes, it wasn't the white Citadel walls that surrounded her. Instead, they were still deep in the forest, just a few hundred yards from where they'd been. The beasts no longer in front of them, but behind.

Alistair panted and took a perfect warrior's stance, his sword raised to the sky. With a pained grimace, he unleashed a wall of power. An instant later, at least two dozen of the creatures lay dead... for now.

Al fell to his knees.

"Holy shit," she said and stumbled to him. "That's the reason they wanted you as the Mesar." She swallowed. The carcasses smoldered, but it didn't look like they were moving. Al fell forward on his hands and knees, panting. She pulled his hood back; his hair curled with sweat.

Sera draped his arm over her shoulder and pulled him up.

He'd given them a chance, and clearly he was too hurt to travel. He looked at her then, and Sera saw how much pain he was in. His skin pale, his eyes bloodshot. He was close to burnout, had to have been, and if they didn't get out of this forest soon, they were going to die.

The ruins had to be there somewhere.

"I need you to put whatever magic you have left into healing that wound at your side."

He nodded. A white flash burst into his skin, and he winced but stood upright.

"Let's go." She pulled him.

A break in the wall of stone ahead had her rounding a corner, entering a path lined by low stone walls. This had to be the right way. The farther they ran, the tighter the sides closed in. If they could hide, even for a short time, then Alistair could regain enough of his magic to travel them out.

Sera dragged him behind her. His magic whirred, and she knew it wasn't being directed at healing his side. Glancing over her shoulder, she sucked in a breath as she beheld the horror behind her. The beasts' numbers had doubled.

Crumbled piles of rocks and wood littered the sides of the path. Sera ran ahead of Al, looking for a cave, a cove, somewhere to hide. She'd fucking climb into a doorway straight to the underworld right about now. But...

Sera sagged to a halt. There were no ruins, no doorways, just a solid rock wall that was too high to climb. They were trapped.

Her lungs spasmed as she heaved in air. When Alistair rounded the bend behind her, their eyes locked, and sorrow crossed his face. He grabbed her, pushed her back against the stone using his body like a shield.

"Throw up your barrier," he rasped.

"I don't think it will hold."

"Do it!" He pulled her to his chest, and she threaded her arms through his and pushed a blue wall out the enhancer. It was the only thing between them and the beasts. The horde of demons watched. Their jaws snapped, drool raining from beneath their skull masks.

"I'm going to travel us out of here," he said between gasps.

"You don't have enough left. You'll burn out." Her arm trembled.

"I just need another second. I'll be fine." Blood was actively flowing down his side. The bottom of his tunic and his pants were soaked with it. Al closed his eyes.

He wasn't going to make it. No matter how strong he thought he was. They might get out of the ravine, but not alive. There had to be another way.

"You can't," Sera begged.

His eyes met hers, and she watched them take in every inch of her face. Her arms strained from holding her barrier out around them. The demons snapped their jaws and growled.

"It will be fine, I promise. I'll just get us over this cliff."

"No," she said, unable to stop her tears.

"You can't hold this forever," he said and made a pained sound. "They aren't going to keep their distance much longer. It's the only way." His eyes settled on her lips.

This was it. She would be at the top of a cliff, holding on to dust. And he would be gone.

"Please," she begged.

He lifted his hand, cupped the back of her neck, and slammed his mouth into hers. Every emotion was in that kiss: Desperation. Want. Hope. Need. She opened to him, and he kissed her deeper. It wasn't soft... it was the wish to survive so that they might do this again.

She whimpered, then her barrier dropped. Sera clung to him, waiting. Waiting for the rush, for his life to drain from his body and his magic to take over.

A scrape across her back had her gasping, and instead of falling up, they fell backward.

"Oh fuck," Al groaned, barely catching himself before he crushed her. Still, in the chaos, somehow he'd cradled her head to keep it from smashing on stone.

Another scrape and the sky disappeared, leaving them in complete darkness.

"You okay?"

She didn't try to stop her voice from shaking. "Yes."

Slowly, the heat of his body left her. "I've got you." Reaching for him, she felt his hand and clung to it. Al hauled her to her feet. "I'm going to guess you can't make a mage light right now?"

"No." She shivered. The cave was cold. She couldn't see a thing, but she could hear water dripping, smell the damp musk of the earth.

"A witch and a warlock in my cave. How interesting."

CHAPTER TWENTY-NINE

SERAPHINA

Deep in the cave, a single bead of light cast a glow around a woman walking toward them. Shadows danced off the rough walls of the cavern, which glittered with damp. Sera allowed Al to guide her. She was grateful they weren't dead, but something was telling her that whatever was in this cave—*whoever* was in this cave—could be twenty times worse than the horde outside.

The feline voice that called out to them didn't sound menacing, but...

"Stay behind me," Al whispered.

She wanted to respond with snark. To say that of course she was going to stay behind him. But she held her tongue. They were a unified front; they had to be, if they were going to get out of this alive.

The woman was closer now. Sera could make out blond hair, so light it almost glowed, and she was wearing blue robes. Coven blue.

Her disembodied voice wrapped them. "You're a very long way from home."

"Who are you?" Alistair demanded, gripping Sera's hand so tight in his she was sure blood no longer flowed to her fingertips.

"I'm the one you've been looking for," the witch said, a hint of a smile in the shadows beneath her nose. The woman raised her arm above her head and clenched her fist.

Sera gasped as they descended back into darkness. The abomination rose to the surface of her skin. Al stiffened, but he didn't let go.

The witch's voice echoed around them. "You may have been looking for me. But I've been waiting for you. Come, bring your soldier, Seraphina."

Seraphina.

A clap echoed off the stone walls, and the darkness lifted as hundreds of candles lining the floor lit in a burst of flame. Sera squinted against the sudden glow and took in the cave. The cavern they stood in was humid, the air thick with the scent of groundwater seeping along stalactites, each dripping, covering the ground in artificial rainfall that made the stone slick beneath her feet.

Sera shivered, envisioning Al as a pile of dust on top of that cliff. He had been willing to die to get them out of there, get her out of danger. Another flash of light, this time coming from Al's hand into his side.

"Are you all right?" she asked.

"I'll be fine once my magic replenishes." He squeezed her hand, and she took that as a demand not to worry. But she was worried. He'd lost a lot of blood, and she'd never known a wound like that, one that didn't heal.

The oracle stepped into the great room they stood in. Delicate wrinkles framed her eyes and the corners of her mouth and spread across her forehead.

"Ophelia Fray, you are hereby summoned to the Citadel," Alistair said.

"I'm aware of what the Council wants to do with me."

"I must insist on taking you back now."

Ophelia tilted her head and observed Al. "And how do you propose to do that, warlock? You're still actively bleeding." She raised a white-blond brow at him. "You have traveled far to find me. Come, then." The witch turned and strode back down the tunnel she had come from, leaving them only one choice. Follow.

Sera was silent. But questions ran rampant through her mind. How did the witch know Sera's name? Why had she been waiting for her?

"I'm glad you both made it in one piece," the oracle said. "There were quite a few instances when I didn't think it'd be the case."

Sera straightened at that. "You've been watching us?"

Ophelia glanced over her shoulder. "So, she can speak. Come along. I'll take you to your rooms."

Deeper and deeper they walked under Ophelia's mage light, until the familiar flicker of candlelight indicated the corridor's end.

Al's hand was still tight in hers as they entered a room. The walls had been smoothed, and black candelabras as tall as Sera lined their path, which changed from stone to black carpet beneath her feet. They walked through an arched hallway into another space.

Tapestries of a type she'd never seen hung on the walls, and in the corners were carved statues like the ones Sera had seen depicted in texts from the keeper wing. Al had to pull her to keep her from inspecting them closer.

"Before I bring you to your quarters, I will take you to meet the lord of this underground manor."

Alistair went as still as a wraith in front of her. Her heart pounded in her chest. She was going to be sick, for the term *lord* was only used for one thing: a demon lord.

A rush of warm air greeted her, with it a familiar scent that seemed to follow her. Alistair flexed his jaw—in pain or irritation, she wasn't sure. Then he sent another wave of magic into his side.

Sera finally let go of his hand and wrapped her arms around herself. She'd lost her dagger while she was running, but she had her enhancer. Not that it would do anything against a demon lord.

But... deep down, her darkness bubbled and churned.

Watch now, it sang to her. She tried shaking that voice away, but it lingered in the forefront of her mind. Neither she nor Al could defend themselves, unless... unless she released her darkness. And she would. For Al, she would. Damn him if he reported her, but she wouldn't have his death on her conscience.

Al opened his palm, and in a moment, his sword was in his hand.

Ophelia pinched the bridge of her nose. "He will not harm you."

"And you expect us to just take your word? A shunned oracle who's been on the run?"

He's here, he's here. Sera peered past the oracle, and there, moving in the darkness from the tunnel beyond, was a figure. He sauntered toward them, hands in his pockets, shoulders relaxed, and stepped into the light.

He was taller than Alistair, though not by much. His hair was pure white, cropped short on the sides and longer on top, a bright contrast to his straight dark brows and the pallor of his skin. She was too far away to make out the color of his eyes, only that they were deep set, hidden in the shadow of his brow bone.

But a strong chiseled jaw led down his strong neck... and those lips. Sera knew exactly who he was.

"I'd prefer if you didn't brandish weapons in my home." His voice curled around her like smoke. Called to her like a song she'd been desperate to hear her entire life.

Alistair practically snarled. "And I'd prefer to collect the oracle and leave."

The scent of sandalwood and ash swirled around her. Her eyes fluttered closed as she breathed him in. It was no coincidence; it couldn't be.

Al pointed his sword at the lord, who just... chuckled. "First you use my language to scare me, then try to attack when you can barely stand?" The demon lord clicked his tongue and stepped beside Ophelia. There was a twinkle in his gray eyes that didn't match the vicious grin he gave Al. "Some Mesar. I could have killed you before."

"But you didn't," Al said.

The lord's gaze focused on her then, and Sera saw the silver scar on his cheek. The mark she had given him when she'd finally controlled her magic. Her heart pounded. She hoped—no, prayed—that the next words out of his mouth weren't about her or what she'd done.

The demon raised a brow and tilted his head in curiosity. "No, I didn't see the need to."

Ophelia clapped her hands together. "That's settled then. No killing. And let me formally introduce you to Lord Vasso."

Lord Vasso gave a slight bow. "Welcome. Make yourself at home within the residence. Do not hesitate to ask if you need anything." Vasso's predatory gaze was still on her. She felt bare, even with Alistair partly blocking her from view.

Alistair reached back with his free hand, and she took it. Vasso's eyes homed in on the motion, and his smile dropped.

"Ophelia, I'll leave you to show our guests to their rooms." Vasso walked past them, glaring at Alistair with so much vengefulness, she swore his eyes glowed red. And just as he passed them, Al fell to his knees.

"Fuck," he gritted.

Sera stared daggers into the demon lord's back. She'd kill him, rip him to shreds for whatever he'd just done, and all the lord did was give her a sly smile over his shoulder.

"Come on," she said and helped Al to his feet.

Ophelia led them through another set of tunnels. "Just there is my pool, should you ever need me."

Sera was still trying to figure out how in Shadow's name the oracle knew who she was. How on Eraphon had they ended up here, in this manor, with this lord?

In a hall that had been constructed out of stone blocks and lined with ornate sconces, Ophelia pointed to two doors. "These will be yours while you recover. I shall return after you bathe, and take you to dinner."

Without another word, Ophelia left them.

They were so fucked. So utterly fucked.

Al threw open the first door and pulled her in behind him.

The room was spacious. Near the entrance, a small writing desk stood against the wall. The stone floor was covered by a lush bloodred carpet.

Then there was the bed. Iron posts curled toward the ceiling, with a canopy above. And pillows, so many pillows, atop a velvet duvet the same color as the carpet.

The only thing that stopped her from jumping onto the bed was what she saw on the far wall.

Tapestries depicting ancient magic. Their style was similar to those that hung in the Council chambers. But these depictions... she'd never seen before. Threads twined together, creating images of light and magic being released from a bottomless pit of stone. She walked toward them, reached up, and touched the flames in the depiction. They were black, just like hers.

There was also violet for arcana, the green glow of plants, and blue for protection. This... this was the birth of magic. Moons, she wished she had her notebook, even if just to capture a rough outline.

Alistair cleared the room around her. Checked every corner, even under the bed. But she couldn't move, just stare, in awe, because she, Seraphina Wildrick, was somehow in the presence of the world's history.

Al's grip on her shoulder was firm but comforting as he guided her to sit on the edge of the bed. Sera lay back. As she'd imagined, it felt like a cloud. Alistair entered what she assumed was the bathing chamber. She supposed she should be more concerned about what could be lurking there, but the lord of this manor, *Vasso*, could kill them with a flick of his wrist.

He'd made that clear with whatever he'd done to Al.

The amount of power that came off him... Sera shuddered, just as she had every other time she'd encountered him. What didn't make sense was why Ophelia was here. Why would an oracle associate herself with a demon lord?

Being shunned for sixty years probably didn't give her much of a choice regarding allies. But why not kill her? To even consider Lord Vasso safe would make her a fool.

"Seems clear," Alistair said. "You hurt?"

She lifted her head off the bed. "You're the one who was about to reach burnout to save us."

He huffed a laugh. "Maybe you're right."

"That's the smartest thing you've ever said to me."

Al wiped his hand over his mouth. There were burns over his face, down his chin. That kiss, the heat between them. Sera touched her lips and pulled her hand away. Her face was covered in blackened demon blood.

"You're the fucking Mesar?"

"Yes." He was tense.

"Why didn't you tell me?"

"It's not really something I'm allowed to announce." He wiped his mouth again. The burns, the sensitivity to demons. Of course he would be the perfect fit. He could tell who his target was without question, with a brush of his hand. "Sera, I think we should leave."

"How do you suppose we'll get out of here? You're not strong enough to travel. Did you pay attention to which tunnels get us back to the main entrance?" She shook her head and grabbed his gloved hand. "Did you forget about the horde of beasts that almost ripped us apart?"

The muscles in his jaw flexed. "This place feels wrong. Don't you feel it?"

"Other than the pit of anxiety swirling in my gut, knowing we are in a demon lord's den, surrounded by things that want to kill us, and the fact that this lord probably controls them? No, I don't feel anything else." He didn't smile like she wanted him to. Sera scooched herself off the bed and stood. "Stay here, rest, and keep healing that wound on your side. I'll bathe and get this blood washed off me, and *then* we can make a plan. Together."

"You shouldn't be alone."

"Are you asking to join me?" Sera raised a brow. Al's cheeks turned bright red as he sat on the edge of the mattress, holding his side again. She held out her hands, and he took them, deep concern drawn on every inch of his face.

"I'll be a room away," she said and let him go.

"You'll knock on the wall if you need me?" he asked as she entered the bathing chamber.

"I promise." She closed the door behind her.

Safety wasn't her first thought while she was undressing. It was the fact that she was naked and Alistair Alcott was steps away.

And all she wanted was his hands on her.

She supposed she should be embarrassed, considering the immense danger they were in. But all she wanted was to escape for a short time. And being wrapped around Al sounded like a great way to do that.

Then there was the lord.

Heat burned through her as she thought of him, what he had done. The arrogance, the nerve, after saying they were welcome… to ask if they *needed anything*. Sera swore the water in the tub rose a few degrees from the amount of heat running through her. She picked up a cloth and scrubbed.

After Sera had changed the water twice, her body finally lost the sheen of grease and grime caked into the creases of her elbows, knees, and knuckles. She slipped back into her dirty pants and Legion tunic, wishing she had her pack with a less dirty uniform. She unwrapped her hair, then rubbed hard at the roots before letting her curls air-dry.

Shadow, please keep Snik safe. She sent a kernel for an offering and prayed he'd make it home.

"There's plenty of hot water. Go clean yourself up," she said, leaving the chamber and using a towel to scrunch the water from her curls.

"Do not leave this room."

Sera rolled her eyes. "I won't. Now go. You smell."

He gave her a small smile and closed the door behind him. Once Sera heard the water running, she tiptoed to the door and peeked into the hallway.

Her eyes met Ophelia's.

"Shit," she said, her heart pounding.

"My intention was not to startle you. I wanted to make sure your accommodations were acceptable."

Sera released a breath. "Yes, they're fine, thanks."

A second later, Alistair barreled out of the bathing chamber, wearing nothing but a towel around his waist. The wound on his side was still raw and angry. "I heard something."

Sera took in every inch of hard muscle and swallowed. She admired his pectorals and his abs, and her eyes stopped at the V that dropped below the white towel.

Alistair cleared his throat.

"I'm fine. Ophelia just startled me, is all." She did her best to give him a reassuring smile, trying to lessen the heat building between her legs.

He nodded and looked at Ophelia before turning back toward his bath. "I'll be another moment. Don't go anywhere without me." He closed the door behind him, leaving a puddle of bathwater and an acute awareness of desire.

"I'm assuming you're here to escort us to dinner?" Sera asked.

"I am, but you're not attending in *that*." Ophelia snapped her fingers, and a gown appeared in her outstretched hands. "Please wear this while I have your current clothing... laundered. Just leave your *uniforms* by the door. I'll make sure they're ready for your departure." The oracle looked like she had smelled something rancid.

Sera paused before taking the gown from her and placing it tenderly on the bed. Ophelia followed, laying out an outfit for Al as well.

"When you're both dressed, meet me at my pool." Ophelia gave her a look over and left.

Sera lifted the gown. It was jet black, with a square neckline and sheer black organza puff sleeves cinched at the wrists. She slipped it over her head and admired the formfitting bodice, which hugged every curve from her chest to just below her hips. From there, the skirt fell straight to the ground.

She stared at herself in the mirror, where her curls melded seamlessly with the dress, making her green eyes practically glow. She slipped on her boots, which looked wildly out of place against the elegance of the gown, and admired herself. It'd been ages since she felt pretty. Long before that abominable well of magic opened within her.

Sera cracked the door to the bathing chamber. "Ophelia left us some new clothes. I'm going to wait for you to change in the hall."

"Sera…"

"I'll be right outside. I promise."

The splash of water hitting the ground made her close the door and leave the bedroom, allowing him some privacy to change.

Sera leaned against the stone wall and waited. They'd found the oracle. Alistair's job was over. But hers? The doorways? She was no closer to finding those than she had been before.

The ruins, if you could call them that, were swarming with those *things*. And unless Al was back to his full health, she wouldn't be able to chance it. Then there was the other concern… that he'd leave her on her own.

Alistair opened the door. In contrast with the ruggedness she had been accustomed to over the past few weeks, he looked pale and uncomfortable, dressed in head to toe black.

"Black isn't really your color, is it?"

"It's not my favorite, but you look—" He paused. His eyes trailed over the gown's neckline to her waist, and then to the floor. "Beautiful. It's like it was made for you."

Despite the danger… his injury… the fact that they were in a demon lord's lair, Sera couldn't help but beam at him. "Are you feeling better?"

"A little."

"Good. Ophelia wants us to meet her near the mirroring pool," Sera said, looping her arm in his.

"So we're having dinner with a demon lord who tried to kill us?" His face was grave as he looked forward.

"We don't have a choice."
Alistair nodded, and they walked to meet the oracle.

CHAPTER THIRTY

DOMINICK

Mystic's was lively. The usual bare tavern bridging Dobro and Jedan Quarters was brimming with witches and warlocks, and their relieved chatter sounded better than any music Dom could have requested. Earlier today, they'd received word of a Legion victory with minimal casualties. It seemed every member of the coven, including Jedan, needed a brew to wash away the lingering anxiety.

When they'd arrived, Dominick had pulled Ithar aside and bought out the bar. The old warlock with his dated muttonchops and bald head had hugged him and insisted he take Sera's designated table.

Dominick settled onto the stool, reveling in how the patrons' confused looks gave way to joy as Ithar brought out more and more mugs of brew.

"You only have one sibling?" Theodore asked him.

Dominick had been surprised that Theo was willing to visit Mystic's. They needed to update the ledger they were keeping at Sera's boarding room, which detailed the discrepancies between the deaths Theo saw versus what the Council was reporting.

He was feeling nostalgic. He missed Sera, Honora, and his brother. He was also hoping that the familiarity of the tavern would give him the courage to ask another favor of Theo.

"Yep, just me and Colton," Dominick said, sipping his brew. The purple foam coated his throat, settling his nerves. Sera hadn't responded to his previous two messages. He was worried.

"Who's the favorite child, out of you two?" Theo asked.

"Well, my mother would never admit it, but it's Colton. It's no secret he's everyone's favorite. Sera had a crush on him when she was young. Then she realized he was more of an older brother to her, and her admiration turned to Alistair." Dom chuckled, remembering when she had tried to climb up onto the roof with the three of them. She'd slipped on the ladder and torn her dress all the way up her side. She was mortified. He could picture her face even now, red, with hot tears streaming down her cheeks. He'd helped her, and ever since that day they'd been inseparable.

She'd always been a little behind. Not only magically, but slow to trust herself and others. But what Sera lacked in confidence, she earned in brilliance. No one could compete with her in their classes, not even Nora. She got top marks in every course, but her lack of confidence—as he'd realized when he was older—was a result of how her mother raised her.

"Interesting," Theo said.

"Why is that interesting?"

"Have you ever..." Theo cleared his throat. "Have you and Sera, I mean..."

"Shadow, no. She knew I preferred warlocks before I did. She's gorgeous—I'm not blind. But Sera and I just clicked. We felt like two impostors taking on the world. You know?"

"I can't say I do," Theo said and looked at Dominick over the lip of his mug. "I don't have anyone that close."

"No siblings?"

"Not that I know of. Both my biological parents were killed in a skirmish before the ceasefire. Being raised under the Council's watch prevented me from growing close to anyone. We were always set against each other.

Who could be the better orphan and whatnot." Theo just shrugged at the admission and motioned to Ithar to bring over two more brews.

A life without his brother or Sera? It seemed like a life barely worth living. His fondest memories were of them all together. To be so utterly alone? Dom's heart hurt at Theo's admission. Orphans were raised in Jedan, with the same chance as any witch or warlock to change their station on their trial day. But Dominick didn't know what life was like for them. He'd been raised in a loving home.

Dominick caught his tongue before he could tell Theo that maybe... just maybe *he* could be his close someone. His old self would be making all the innuendos, but now, when he actually might want something more...

"I hate to do this..."

"I'll pull Sera's thread tomorrow," Theo said.

"I didn't want to ask... You've already done so much."

Theo gave him a half grin and leaned his elbows on the table. "Dom, I hate to break it to you, but you're not as slick as you think you are."

Dominick's brows shot to his hairline. He didn't even have a rebuttal, only a racing pulse and the need to throw this warlock against a wall and show him how slick he could be.

The crowd quieted as patrons filed out the front door. But he let none of it distract him from Theo. "Tell me about being an orphan."

"Talk about a buzzkill, Dom."

"Is it a crime that I want to get to know you more?" Dominick swirled the brew in his mug before taking a sip.

"I'm not sure. You know parts of me pretty well."

He couldn't prevent the rush of heat to his cheeks with that comment. Their time together had been more than satisfying. The smell of him, his soft skin. Theo was... addictive. "You don't have to tell me if you don't want to."

The twinkle in Theo's eyes dimmed a bit. "I don't want to talk about it right now."

Dom nodded.

"I fear... I fear there will be a lot more orphans."

It was a thought Dom didn't want. No one did. But it was inevitable. It was the coven's way of life, and even though he hadn't agreed to it, he had no power to stop it.

Ithar approached him. "Master Benero..."

Dominick put his hand up. "Ithar, I am not a master, just a humble oracle." He didn't miss the way Theo rolled his eyes.

"Yes, again, thank you... You are welcome anytime."

Dominick stood and clapped Ithar hard on the shoulder. "Then I shall take you up on it. But we will take our leave. Have a good night, Ithar."

"And you, sir... and you."

The streets were quiet. The mage lamps illuminated as the warlocks passed under them, drenching them in a hazy glow as they strolled through Daedeth Quarter.

It could have been the buzz from the brew or how Theo had looked at him all night, but either way something was shifting. He grabbed Theo's hand.

It felt... right. His hand *fit* right, and he swore there wasn't a more handsome warlock in the entirety of the coven.

"You're fine... with this?" Theo's grip tightened.

Dom lowered his voice. "I think our lives are too short now to care."

"Praise Shadow for that," Theo said.

The mirror on the far wall was glowing when they walked into Dom's flat. An unfortunate delay, as he was more than ready to get his mind off the doom and gloom of a missing Colton and Sera, and on to more enjoyable things.

Dom swiped the mirror, and his mother's round face appeared, covered in tears.

The brews he'd just enjoyed threatened to come up.

"What's wrong?" Theo asked.

"Stay here. I'll be right back." Dominick ran out the door.

He was hot, then cold, the contrast dizzying. Panic coursed through him. The sudden onslaught of shame he felt for having seen his mother's face while thinking of unsavory things was making him nauseated.

It could be anything. She could've hurt herself. Or maybe it was his father? Nothing a healer couldn't fix, he was sure. His mother had been on edge for weeks, just as he had, after not hearing back from Colton. His mother, Shadow bless her, was not the most patient woman.

Dom barged through the front door. "Ma?" he called out.

His parents were sitting at the small wooden kitchen table, murmuring to themselves. His mother, his beautiful mother, held her head in her hands, his father's arms wrapped tight around her.

"What happened?" Dominick demanded.

His father turned, and in his hand was a pink slip with a black sun letterhead—a death notice.

"No," Dominick said in a croaked whisper and pushed away from the table.

"Not him," his mother wailed. His father looked at Dom with quiet sorrow as a single heavy tear slid down his face.

"It's a mistake! It has to be!"

His father's voice, usually deliberate, strong, and steady, was raw. "It's no mistake, son."

Dom's knees weakened with every breath he took as his mother rose from her seat. Her head barely reached the middle of his chest. He held her once slender back tight to him.

"It's not him. Not Colton…" This couldn't be happening. The reports said minimal casualties. His brother was a seasoned and powerful fighter. A creeping thought poked at him. Colton hadn't responded for weeks now.

His mother's soft hands were on his cheeks.

"I'm going to fix this, you'll see. I'll prove it," Dom swore.

He ran. He ran and ran and ran until he stumbled through his front door, then tripped on his way to the bathing chamber and vomited. His hands shook harder with each heave of his stomach.

There must be a mistake. Colton couldn't be dead.

"Dominick?" Theo called for him through the door. "Can I come in?"

Dom rocked back and forth on the cool tile floor, waiting. He needed to think; he needed to make a plan.

"Dominick," Theo called again and grabbed either side of his face, forcing him to look into his sea green eyes.

This was why he didn't let anyone get too close. This was why he didn't love. What was the point when it only ended in pain? He'd learned that the first time he'd opened up to someone only to be rejected. It was why he kept everyone at arm's length. But now, the curse had gripped its claws into his family. He couldn't do this. He wanted to be alone.

"Dom, what happened? You can tell me."

The tenderness broke him. It was only then that the heavy tears began to fall.

"Shhh, come here." Theo guided him, resting Dom's head in his lap. His hands were cool against Dom's forehead, soothing him with soft strokes.

"Colton." Dom's voice hitched. He couldn't stop the despair that shook him, rousing a new set of tears. He shuddered and took a shallow breath. "They said Colton is dead." The words wove through his mind, as if saying them out loud made them true. He wouldn't believe it..

"Oh, Dom."

"I need you to look. To be sure."

"Of course, of course." Theo lifted Dom from the floor and gently laid him on the bed. Tenderly, he peeled Dom's gray oracle robes off him. And when Dominick was comfortable and under the covers, Theo wrapped around him and lay there.

A hollow numbing crept over Dom. Where was Colton? Why wasn't Sera answering?

CHAPTER THIRTY-ONE

SERAPHINA

Sera and Alistair stepped through the arched doorway leading to Ophelia's pool. The air was warm and heavy with moisture. Sera could practically feel her curls frizzing in the humidity the closer she got.

As the tunnel opened up, she gasped. It was beautiful, but *pool* wasn't the right word for it. A dull blue light glowed from the rock on the far side of the underground lake. Its rays skittered across the water's surface, lighting every part of the cavern. The stone was nowhere near bright enough to illuminate the entire room, yet everything shimmered.

She'd never been allowed to enter the Ogdelo and witness the workings of the mirroring pools, so she had nothing to compare this to. But something told her that this place, a sanctuary of sorts, was special.

Ophelia stood on the circular platform in the middle of the water. Threads of light in all colors rose and fell above the pool's surface, reaching the cavern ceiling. Ophelia sifted through the many layers of colors and the strings.

Sera would scold Dominick when she got back. The beauty of this magic had been lost in every description he'd ever given her.

When a pillar of gold formed, Ophelia let the rest sink below the surface, coloring the water with reds, pinks, greens, and blues.

"Come, witchling," Ophelia beckoned Sera forward.

Sera stepped gingerly onto the narrow stone walkway leading to the pool's center, leaving a wary Alistair behind her. The colors churned in the surrounding water like ribbons, never mixing or muddy—just infinite strings, every color she'd ever seen swirling in harmony.

Ophelia pointed to the gold pillar before her. "This is your life." An almost solid structure towered over her, made of more threads than Sera had memories. "Here is the past, present, and predicted future." Ophelia picked out a strand and coaxed it forward for Sera to inspect more closely. A black band wrapped the shimmering gold. Sera tried to swallow the lump in her throat. "I think you know what day this is?" Ophelia asked.

Sera nodded.

"And this one as well?"

Feybury. It had been the first time she summoned the darkness. Then again by accident at Ironoak. She shivered at the thought of them, remembering the feeling of her magic against the humans' skin. But before her, in the golden pillar, Sera picked out all the individual black bands, and if each one was an incident...

"As I thought," Ophelia continued. "Let us eat."

"Wait, is this..."

"I do not think it is the time to discuss. Do you?" Ophelia tilted her head toward Al, who stood at the end of the stone walkway. The oracle was strange. She had an air of confidence, but not only that, an all-knowingness about her.

"Perhaps not."

"Come then, I'm famished."

Sera followed the oracle and linked her arm back through Al's.

"What was that about?" he asked.

"I'm not entirely sure."

They followed Ophelia through the cavern halls. There was a coziness to it, between the natural geological formations that surrounded such ordinary furnishings and the drips of groundwater from above echoing off the walls in sweet melody. Somehow, by magic perhaps, there seemed to be little moisture in the air.

It was beautiful.

The three walked silently. Alistair was rigid beside her, not that she could blame him; this must have been his worst nightmare, surrounded by so many demonic things. He kept his gloves on, every part of him covered except his head and neck. She imagined that if it wouldn't have angered the lord further, he'd cover those too.

When they reached the dining chamber, shadows danced across the walls in an intricate waltz. Five black chandeliers floated across the ceiling, hanging from what looked like thunderclouds above a long iron table where crystal goblets, fine white porcelain plates, and silver cutlery lay.

Sera had never seen such opulence in one room.

"Please take your seats." Ophelia motioned to the two place settings near the head of the table and sat on the opposite side.

The doors at the other end of the room opened. The lord of the manor instantly commanded the space. He was dressed the same as he had been when they arrived, in the same dark pants and jacket with silver-embroidered lapels. His white hair slicked back, but this time on his hand was the skull marking him as a lord. It was carved from what must have been a massive red ruby.

It was the same color his eyes had been when she gave him that silver scar across his cheek.

"Excuse my delay. I seem to have found someone very attached to you." An amused smile spread across Lord Vasso's face, making him even more striking.

Sera slammed her hands over her ears as some poor creature let out a piercing howl. Then, from behind Vasso, a green goblin barreled toward her.

"Snik!" Sera ripped her arm out of Al's grip and rushed to him.

He was safe. She gripped his small body in her arms, not caring that he was soiling her gown. The goblin hugged her back and cooed.

"How did you find him?"

"He was sniffing around one of our secret passages," Vasso said, looking pleased with himself. "He probably smelled you."

"Oh, Snik." Sera squeezed him harder. The goblin hummed back, and Alistair huffed.

"He dragged some very dirty packs in. Am I to assume that they are yours and have them brought to your rooms?"

"Thank you," Sera said.

"Why don't you let *Snik* get cleaned up so we can return to dinner, shall we?" Ophelia interrupted.

Snik snorted at the oracle.

Placing her friend back on the ground, Sera asked the lord, "Could you have him brought to my room?"

"Of course." Vasso snapped his fingers, and a being half his height appeared through a hidden door. The creature was covered in silvery blue fur, with a beard that kissed the floor and elongated fingers and toes. His bright yellow eyes lit up the room seemingly on their own. The gentle creature approached Snik and took his paw, pulling him toward the doorway.

She thought she was going mad. Truthfully, she thought she'd been going mad for months now, but before her, this creature, was thought to be extinct for centuries.

"He's a domovoi," Vasso said.

"I know what he is," she replied. "I just never thought I would see one."

"You know of their kind?" Lord Vasso crossed his arms.

She could feel every place his gaze touched. Her face, her arms, her hips, like a warm static. His magic was heavy in the air, causing hers to react. It swayed in her body. "I studied them. They were thought to be extinct."

Sera had spent hours of her youth studying the different creatures of Gehenna. She remembered this one fondly. They were guardians of the home, protecting the inhabitants from harm. But many witches and warlocks grew suspicious of the gentle creatures after the rebellion and slaughtered them. Yet here in this underground manor, one lived.

"They almost are," Vasso said, the hard lines of his face softening a touch.

"Will the two of you please sit? I am famished," Ophelia said as Snik and the domovoi slipped from the room.

Alistair pulled out the chair farthest from Vasso. She let out a breath of relief that she wouldn't need to sit near him. Across the room was enough, but to be so close? Sera adjusted the cuff of her organza sleeve to a more comfortable position.

Al sat, holding his injured side. She could tell he was putting on a show, doing his best not to display any weakness in front of this threat, but his skin stayed pale.

"I understand this is unorthodox, considering the current political climate," Vasso said. "But I did mean it when I said you have full access to the manor and to please reach out to me or my staff if you need anything."

"And why are you being so hospitable?" Alistair was glaring daggers at the lord. She was sure that sitting near a demon wasn't the most comfortable position for him, what with his position as Mesar, but Shadow save her, she needed him to be diplomatic.

Dying before the first course wouldn't help her save Nora.

"Ophelia informed me of your arrival, and it is in my best interest—in the best interest of all of us—if I am hospitable instead of hostile," Vasso said. His irises flashed from gray to red as he looked at Al. "If you wish to fight, however, I'd be more than happy to oblige."

Alistair smirked. "Is that a threat... *demon*?"

Sera put her hand on Al's knee, hoping he would get the hint not to push further. He responded by making a fist. *Time to change tactics, then.*

"Ophelia, what have you seen?" Sera asked the oracle, hoping the standoff between the men in the room would end.

"I have seen much, witchling. Your births"—she looked between Sera and Alistair—"and your deaths." She looked at Vasso next. "I know what will happen to me, Eraphon, and the galaxy if we do not stay the course."

The future of the galaxy? There had never been an oracle recorded who was so powerful they could pull that far into the future. If there had been, she was sure they would have been worshipped as much as the coven founders. She would have read about them in her studies.

"I didn't know oracles were that powerful," Alistair sneered.

Sera pinched his thigh to get him shut up, but he didn't flinch.

"They usually aren't." Ophelia straightened her cutlery. "There was a reason I was sent away, warlock. It wasn't because I was unskilled."

Ophelia looked at the lord. "Vasso, please provide us with wine and the first course. I will need it to get through these idiotic questions. Also, do something about these damned chandeliers." She pointed up.

Vasso chuckled. "As you wish it."

The chandeliers stilled, lowering their flames to a glow, creating an intimacy Sera wasn't entirely comfortable with. Her darkness sat in her veins, dormant and waiting. At the sensation, she shifted in her seat.

More demons emerged from what seemed like thin air, bringing jugs of wine and the first course. A soup.

The thick cream held hints of crustacean and mollusk. She recognized it as a delicacy served in the Citadel, one she hadn't enjoyed since being assigned to Dobro. Sera tasted a spoonful and groaned, savoring the creamy, buttery flavor of the bisque.

A press of Al's elbow into her side made her stop.

"I'm sorry," she said. "I've had nothing but bread and jerky and piss-poor human stew for weeks."

"No apology needed." Vasso gave her a wink. "Ophelia insisted we have a taste of your home ready for you."

Her heart gave an involuntary flutter.

Alistair shuddered beside her. His skin had taken on a grayish tint now. A prickle of sweat dampened the hair at his temples.

"Al?" He flinched when she laid her hand on his forearm. The heat coming off his skin had her doing the same. "Excuse me, Lord, my friend here is under the weather. I think I need to bring him to his room." Sera stood, gripping Alistair's arm tight to her side.

"No reason he can't go alone," Vasso said, the corner of his mouth ticking upward as he leaned back in his chair. "You stay. Eat with us. Surely the Mesar can take care of himself."

He was enjoying this, the self-righteous bastard. If Vasso hadn't thrown whatever magic at Al in the hallway earlier, she wondered if he wouldn't be in nearly as bad a shape. "I'd prefer the company of the *Mesar* right now."

She shouldn't have provoked him, but lord or not, maybe the bastard needed to be put in his place. Still, a thought nagged at her. He could have killed them multiple times, but he hadn't. The only question was, Why?

"We'll have your dinner brought to your rooms, dear," Ophelia said as Sera dragged Alistair to the hall.

CHAPTER THIRTY-TWO

SERAPHINA

Al wasn't resisting, which meant something was terribly wrong. After ten minutes of tugging him down hallways, his crushing weight lay across her shoulders. She threw open the door to her room and dumped him atop the red velvet comforter on one side of the bed.

Snik jumped up yipping, and as delighted as Sera was to see her green friend, Al needed help.

"Do not touch him," she instructed the goblin. The last thing he needed was Snik's little demon hands all over him. "Al, why aren't you healing?"

He mumbled something she couldn't understand. Sweat soaked his shirt. Sera made quick work of the buttons down the front and did her best to peel it off him. She wasn't a healer; he needed to do that himself. But the amount of magic he'd already used that day...

Panic clawed at her chest as she slid off his boots and socks. Sera lowered herself to her knees and inspected his side. The cut was raw but seemed clean; she didn't see anything too concerning. Sera pressed lightly around it, causing Alistair to hiss. Then, right before she pressed again, something wriggled under his skin.

"What in Shadow's name..." Snik whined and poked Al with his claw. "I said, don't touch him."

There was a knock at the door.

"Where can I place this for you?"

She jumped. "Lord Vasso! I'm sorry. I thought you were a servant." Vasso cocked a brow at her and tilted his head in a predatory way, looking from a half-naked Alistair to her. She cleared her throat. "I just figured a servant would put our meals down and leave. I didn't expect it to be you."

Vasso placed the tray on the writing desk. "Seems the famed Mesar has a weakness."

Her darkness paced inside her. Vasso was utterly unbothered, hands in his pockets, the delicate cut of his jacket lying perfectly on his frame. And that tilt of a smile mocked her. "Do you have a healer?" she burst out.

Al groaned, but she ignored him.

"I know a thing or two about healing."

Sera squinted at the lord, and his smile grew. She couldn't help but feel they were sparring on another plane, as if he were daring her to slip, to show her magic in front of Al. Daring her to lash out at him, brand him with another scar. "Will you help him?"

He chuckled. "Why would I want to heal a monster who's been slaying my kind? A famed one, at that."

"You almost sound in awe of him."

He crossed his arms then and raised a brow at Al, who seemed to be drifting in and out of consciousness. Vasso's gray eyes flashed red but settled once again when his gaze moved back to hers. "You mistake my ire for awe."

"What do you want?" It was a dangerous move. She knew it, and worse, so did he.

"Who says I want anything?"

"A demon is always open for a bargain, is he not?" She stood at the foot of the bed. Snik whined and hid behind the skirt of her dress.

"I don't think you know what you're asking." Lord Vasso leaned forward, and a strand of white hair fell on his forehead. "That could put you in a very dangerous position, one I don't think Mister Mesar over there would want you to be in."

She looked at Al. His skin was a deathly hue against the red duvet. One arm hung off the bed, sweat beaded his broad chest, and his side, moons, his side...

"I'll chance it."

"Excellent." Vasso crossed the room in a few strides and approached Al. The demon knelt and poked gingerly at the swollen skin, leaving purple welts wherever his fingers touched.

"Do we shake or something?"

"We can square up after this is finished. He is close to dead already, and I'd hate to miss the opportunity to call in a favor."

Vasso prodded the swelling until the wriggling mass appeared again. Sera knelt beside him. "Please tell me that isn't a worm."

"Not so much a worm as a magic-eating parasite. They live under the claws of the agbris—a vicious beast with long talons and sharp teeth who hides itself behind an animal skull."

"That sounds like what was chasing us." Sera dared to look closer at the parasite, and Snik whined again.

"Care to remove yourself from my light?"

Sera huffed and backed away, scooping Snik into her arms. She paced. What more could she do? It was foolish—more than foolish; outright idiotic—that she'd make a bargain with him, but what other choice did she have? Letting Alistair die was not an option.

"I can help him, but it's going to hurt."

"No." Al's raw voice barely escaped his windpipe.

"Can you give us a minute?" she asked Vasso.

"Don't take too long, I may change my mind."

The demon lord took his time, his hands still in his pockets and that strand of hair drifting over his forehead. In one motion, he swept it back and then left.

"Al, you're dying. And I know you don't want him to touch you. I can see how much it hurts. But if you don't let him try, you'll die." Her voice cracked as she stared into his blue eyes, glassy with fever. "Let him help you, Al. I can't do this alone." He stared at her. And she pushed back a curl of dark brown hair. "Please…"

When he made the slightest nod of agreement, she released a breath. She wasn't lying. She couldn't do this without him. As much as that made her a coward, she didn't care.

"Lord Vasso," Sera called out. The demon lazily walked in, his hands still deep in his pockets, looking completely unbothered. She motioned to Alistair. "Go ahead." Sera stayed at Al's head, taking his gloved hand in hers.

"Say no more." He grinned and slipped out of his jacket. As he crossed the room, he rolled both sleeves up to his elbows, revealing his defined forearms. The red skull ring mocked her as Vasso held his hand above Alistair's side.

A trickle of magic leaked from his palm, dripping like ink into a glass of water as it fell from him, black and smoky. Sera's stomach dropped as she watched the magic work. The mist encircled the wound.

Alistair cried out, gripping her hand so tight she was pretty sure he'd break one of her fingers. But Sera was transfixed by the darkness that leaked from Vasso's hand.

It looked like… hers.

Hello… Her magic called to her, surging to her palms, making them itch something fierce. Sera ripped her hand from Al's and watched.

It couldn't be the same. She wouldn't believe it.

The mist formed under Vasso's instruction. Once the wound was completely encircled, Vasso hooked his finger, and a sharp talon shot out from his nail bed.

"Hold him," Vasso said to her.

Getting to her feet, Sera planted both hands on his shoulders, and Al screamed. With one quick swipe, Vasso sliced into Al's side and pulled out the wriggling thing.

Blood spilled onto the floor, and the stench... Sera choked. It smelled as if the wound had been festering for months. Sera didn't care what Vasso said. It looked like a worm; it *moved* like one.

"Let go of me," Al said through gritted teeth.

"I'm so sorry," she said and pulled away, leaving behind blistered handprints.

Vasso's lip curled with disgust as he observed the parasite hanging from his claw. Then a spark shot out of his finger, igniting the thing... in black flame.

Sera's blood hummed, the darkness just under the surface now, and she envisioned that cage wrapped tight around it. Shadow, save her... It was the same. She knew in the marrow of her bones that it was. That they somehow shared magic. That *she* embodied the same magic as a demon lord.

"You all right?" Vasso asked her. His gaze pierced her, and something pulled taut in her chest.

Sera blew out a shaky breath. "I'm fine." She hovered her hand over Al. "He's cooling already. Thank you."

The lord's face was perplexed. He stood, grabbed his jacket, and headed for the door. But before he left, he said, "When you're done here... you're to meet me to discuss terms." With that, he left.

What had she done? This... Everything. Moons, she was so fucked. Al was alive, but she and Vasso had the same magic. Her... she... Her mind swam with fragments of disbelief. She ran to the bathing chamber and splashed cool water on her face.

She had little to offer him. Her barrier magic was nonexistent. She could distort the truth, explain that she was weak and didn't carry much witch magic at all.

He can teach you. Use us. We want to be used.

Now that was a thought. *If* he could teach her how to wield, or at the very least be consistent with her magic, help her contain it...

Snik picked at the food-filled plates. The goblin looked as if he was afraid he'd be scolded, but she didn't care. She was happy he was alive, that they all were.

"Have your fill," she whispered.

"Is he eating my dinner now too?" Al's voice was weak, but she'd never been so happy to hear his sarcastic tone.

"You scared me," she said.

"I'm sorry."

"How are you feeling now?"

"Better than I was." He tried to sit up. "I thought I was going to pass out face-first in the bisque."

"You almost did." She sat on the other side of the bed.

"What price did he ask for?"

Sera stiffened. She glanced at his side, then back up to his face. "Don't worry about it."

"Minnow." Al coughed, then winced. "What did he ask of you?"

Sera pulled the blanket from under him and laid it on top.

"Tell me..." His voice was deadly quiet, and violence raged in his eyes.

"I'm going to find that out once you're feeling better."

Al shot a blast of healing magic into his side. "I'm going to kill him," he said, attempting to rise.

"Lay back down, you stubborn brute. I made the deal, not you. This is my burden to bear, and I'd do it again. I'd do it a thousand times to save you."

He grew quiet, his features softening as he lay back down. "Promise me... if it's too much, you'll let me take it."

She barked a laugh at that. "The Mesar owing a demon lord a favor? I'm pretty sure that would be a first."

"Promise me, Minnow."

Sera stared at him. His jaw clenched tight, the linens bunching in his hands. He *was* serious. He'd take it for her, and... and what was she to do with that? He was the Mesar, and if he broke the bargain, then the great demon butcher would be indebted to a demon lord.

Al shifted. She watched a wave of pain go through him as he hit his side again with another blast of healing.

"I promise."

That seemed to appease him. He lay back down, closing his eyes.

Sera watched the rise and fall of his chest slow. The tension fell from his face and shoulders as he fell into slumber.

She ached to be closer, to be held in his arms. But Vasso's magic, that darkness... Her handprints were still visible on his shoulders from where she'd held him.

It wasn't Snik.

It was her.

And although she felt safe beside him, even in enemy territory, only one question came to her mind: Was he safe with her?

Chapter Thirty-Three

Seraphina

Sera jolted awake. Sweat plastered her hair to her temples. Snik was curled in a ball against her stomach, and Al was still sleeping soundly at her back. Both the warlock and the goblin were snoring in offset intervals, like a tracheal orchestra. The three of them were piled on the bed, twisted in blankets, but neither of the others moved.

But she had slept. Without her elixir... and without nightmares.

Peeling herself from the middle, careful not to wake either, she tiptoed to the bathing chamber off the main room.

She'd certainly gotten herself into a mess.

Yes... to owe him is not good.

"Oh, shut it," she said to her magic. The water basin was cool under her grip. She needed a plan, and to find the doorways to Gehenna, and to save her sister... and, and, and. There was nothing she could give him.

There is always something.

Her stomach sank. Shadow, she hoped it wouldn't come to that, using her body as a form of currency. Sera smoothed the creases from the gown and tiptoed out of the bathing chamber. One by one, she blew out the candles in the sconces along the walls, stopping for a moment to touch the black flame in the tapestry, then headed out to meet her doom.

It must have been the early hours of the morning. The manor was quiet, but for a sloshing of water filling the halls. Sera crept down the tunnel and peered into the mirroring pool chamber. Threads lifted and sank in dizzying procession, and Ophelia, arms raised, robes whipping around her, was the conductor of it all.

"Come in, Seraphina."

Sera swallowed the lump in her throat and crossed the threshold. "Are you always looking into the pool?"

"My time here is ending, and I want to prepare as many of those who need it as I can." Ophelia waved her hands over the water, and a different set of threads burst from the surface and wound their way to the cavern ceiling, tight as bowstrings. The blue glow of the stones on the other side of the pool bathed Ophelia.

Sera approached her with caution. "Will you let us take you back to the Citadel, then?"

Ophelia's eyes rolled into the back of her head as she touched a strand, then let it go and grabbed another. "I said I would, and I keep my word. It's for the good of Eraphon." She turned toward Sera then. "But that is not your only question, is it?"

Sera wanted to ask what Lord Vasso was going to do with her, but thought better of it. "Do you know where the doorways to Gehenna are?"

"You'll have to ask Vasso that." Ophelia lowered her arms, and the threads dropped to the depths below. "He'll be here in just a moment."

"How did you—"

"I told you. I know all." Ophelia turned, leaving her platform and threads behind. "He will help you. With the doorways and your magic."

Sera's mouth grew dry. "You won't tell anyone... when you go to the Citadel?"

"Darling, that darkness will be your salvation."

If she had her mother's magic, she would have burrowed into the oracle's mind and erased every memory that had to do with her.

"Ophelia, please stop giving my guests such cryptic messages." Lord Vasso slunk from the corner of the room like a wraith emerging from shadows. He'd lost the jacket from dinner, though his sleeves were still rolled to his elbow. He was handsome, unassuming, seemingly harmless—a beautiful trap.

"I so prefer it that way," the oracle cooed.

"Well, witch." Vasso turned his gaze to her. "Shall we discuss terms?"

The darkness swirled within Sera, not in its usual irritated way but as if it was watching... anticipating.

"My lord," Ophelia interrupted. "Take her somewhere more private. I have much work to do."

The demon broke out in a wide grin. Sera swallowed her gasp; *beautiful trap* didn't do him justice. Those harsh lines evaporated with his smile, and left behind was something carved by Shadow herself.

"This way, Seraphina."

She followed him. With each step, his carved ruby ring glinted in the torchlight like a blazing beacon among the gloom of the cave.

Among Gehenna's high court, the ring wasn't just a show of wealth. It was awarded to those with immense power. Sera had studied the lords and their rings in textbooks. She'd been obsessed with any information she could gather on demons. Lavinia had banned her from researching them, but Sera had kept investigating, huddled in the darkest parts of the library, straining to see the forms on the page. Her first day as a junior keeper, she'd searched the more restricted parts of the archives just to see what she could get her hands on.

Lord Vasso motioned to a dark doorway. "Go ahead."

She hesitated.

"Don't be scared. I promise I won't bite... hard." He winked at her, and moons above did it rage through her like wildfire. As Sera entered, the only thing she could think of... was how very fucked she was.

With a snap of his fingers, the walls sconces and the candelabras on the various tables in the room burst to life. They revealed stone walls with floor-to-ceiling shelving. There were books, so many books. But also artifacts, many she'd never seen the likes of.

A small bear carved out of wood was so detailed that she couldn't imagine a regular-size knife had created it.

"The domovoi made that for me."

Sera jumped. She hadn't heard him behind her. If he hadn't been solid in front of her, she would have thought he was an actual wraith. But that smell... sandalwood. That she would forever associate with him, thanks to their meeting in Ironoak.

"Come, take a seat." He rounded the large desk in the middle of the room. She sat.

"You're being very hospitable to someone who owes you a favor, Lord Vasso," she said. The chair was plush on her back. She wished she could sink into it, but her nerves kept her upright.

"First of all, you must drop the *lord*... It's utterly exhausting to listen to day in and day out." He snapped his fingers, and two crystal glasses plinked on the desk, immediately filling with amber liquid. "A drink?"

"No, thank you. I'd rather get this over with, if you wouldn't mind."

"So touchy... but if you insist." He swirled his glass and swallowed a mouthful.

He had to be stalling, and she hated him for it. Hated that she was indebted to him at all. But Vasso had done what she'd asked. Alistair was whole and healing, and whatever the circumstance, she should be grateful for that at least. Regardless, it didn't stop her anger from curdling that darkness within her.

"I want you..." he drawled. Sera held her breath. "To show me your magic."

"That's it?"

"That's it." He smirked at her. His gray eyes twinkled behind dark lashes.

"But you've already seen it."

Vasso swiped his finger across the scar on his cheek. The one she'd given him. Her hands trembled as she waited for his response. This was some sort of sick joke. He was going to kill her for what she'd done to him.

We will not let that happen... Sera shook her head to make the voice go away zipping her raven pendant on its cord. Vasso just raised one dark brow at her.

"Well, I definitely felt it. But I wish to see it up close." He leaned back in his chair and rested his long legs on the corner of the desk as he continued to swirl his liquor.

"And that's it? You won't kill me?"

"Cross my heart and hope to die, Subdina." He downed the rest of his drink.

Subdina... her magic echoed back.

"Okay." Sera held out her hand. She'd read countless times that a bargain needed to be sealed with a handshake.

"None of that." He swatted her hand away. "Just show me."

Her magic swirled in answer, instantly heating her lungs, her skin. She could do this. Sera rose from her seat, closed her eyes, and, with a release of breath, let it go.

Her death fog fell from her palms. It bubbled and churned in a black mass over the study floor, clawing its way toward the books lining the bottom shelves.

Vasso straightened in his chair, his smoke-gray gaze darting from the mist back to her.

"There's more," she said. He worked his jaw, his brows scrunched tight. "Maybe this isn't a good idea."

"No!" Her flame thrashed under her skin. Vasso cleared his throat. "I'm sorry, I didn't mean to yell. Please... continue."

With every passing second, the crawling heat of her flames snaked through her body. Creeping... begging. "Can you control the fire?"

"The what?"

"The black flame—you can control it?"

His steel gaze bore into her, and he stood. Vasso's face was so serious it looked like a snarl. "Of course I can control it."

Sera held out her palm and summoned a flicker forward. Black flame burst from her fingertips. She breathed deep, trying to control the heat overtaking her. Perspiration dampened the nape of her neck, her chest. Moons, she was hot. This thick gown wasn't helping either.

"Bloody Shadow," Vasso whispered.

Yes...

His voice was like a switch, and her flames jumped to the floor, igniting the fog around them. "I can't control it. Put it out!"

The demon lord pointed his palm to the floor and released his magic. A dull static raced over her skin. This sensation was... strange. Although their darknesses appeared the same, there was a difference between the two. His flames danced beside hers. She dared to glance at him, not sure what to expect. But he looked curious. Not scared or disturbed, but fascinated.

Vasso gripped his fist tight, and the flames, mist, fog—all of it disappeared at once. He plopped into his chair and undid the top two buttons of his black collared shirt. "I need another drink." At once, his glass refilled, a full finger more than before.

He slid her a glass, and this time she took it. Call her a fool, but she needed one too. It had been... How would she describe it? The control he had: She wanted it. She wanted to be able to summon and extinguish like he did. To know for certain that she wouldn't harm anyone ever again. Her magic had been used by reflex, or in a rush of adrenaline or panic. Never willingly. Not since she'd harmed him.

"How long ago did you manifest?" he asked.

"A few months ago."

"What happened when you did?"

She sipped her liquor. It burned the entire way down, and she was grateful for it. Sharing this much had never been the plan, but he wasn't running or killing her. "I burned down a whole village and killed a bunch of innocent humans."

Sera choked on the lump in her throat, taking a long sip of her drink to push it down.

"Are you okay?"

Time slowed. Sera regarded the demon lord sitting before her. From his long fingers to the way his shirt stretched over his lean, muscled shoulders, to the patch of chest that showed at his collar, leading up his neck to his blade-sharp jaw. Why? Why had he chosen to ask her this, out of all the things he could have done or demanded? Why her magic? And why... why had he asked if she was okay?

No one had asked her that. Not Dominick, not Nora, especially not her mother. But here, this demon lord she had known for less than a day was asking if she was okay, and Shadow help her, she wasn't.

Her voice cracked. "No, I'm not."

"Who else knows?"

"My sister," she rasped. "My mother and my best friend."

"Not your bodyguard? The Council?"

Sera released a breath that sounded more like a strangled laugh. "He's not my bodyguard, but no. Alistair doesn't know."

"I see." Vasso swirled the last bit of his drink before swallowing it down. "I took out half the Emerald Glade when mine manifested, and I had the greatest teacher in Gehenna at my side."

"That was you?" That meant he had to be at least two hundred. Sera regarded him again. Demons aged much slower than witches and warlocks, but he didn't look much older than Al.

He chuckled and pushed back that strand of hair that seemed to always be flopping on his forehead. "You've seen what the magic does. It's not like I meant to."

He can teach you.

Sera slumped in her chair and took another swig. This was either the stupidest idea she'd ever come up with or the most brilliant.

"Will you teach me?"

Vasso barked a laugh. "That's a big fucking ask." He crossed his arms. She couldn't stop herself from admiring the curve of his cheek, the way his eyes danced in the candlelight. He had a deadly calmness to him. Even the white of his hair was a bright contrast to the dark study around him. He reminded her of a poisonous plant, made to attract... then kill.

"You're the only person I've ever seen with this power," she said. "Not just seen but even heard of. I've scoured everything I could find in the Citadel library."

"It will change you." His tone was serious, those sharp features back in place.

"My life changed the day it escaped from my body."

A muscle twitched in his cheek. "You possess witch magic as well?"

She nodded. Vasso studied her, tapping the finger with the skull ring on his bicep. Without warning, a burst of ice-cold air shot at her. Sera yelped and snapped her barrier in place. She would kill him. Rip him to shreds, slash more than just that tiny scar on his cheek.

"I'll help you," Vasso said with a smirk before she could let out a string of curse words.

"Was that supposed to be a test?"

"You can't tell your bodyguard." Vasso held out his hand.

"That's your price for helping me?" she asked.

"Afraid you'll fail?"

It seemed too simple. She was missing something. If a bargain was that simple, why would anyone not bargain with a demon? And why didn't Vasso want Alistair to know he was helping her?

Sera knew why she didn't want Alistair to know, and Vasso had already confirmed that Al didn't. There was definitely something missing.

What she didn't need was for Lord Vasso to consider a harsher price. Something that would get her into worlds of trouble, enslavement—who knew.

Sera glanced at his hand. So unassuming, a simple handshake, but this would be binding until the deal was done. Sera grasped her raven pendant, zipping it back and forth on the string.

It is the only way, her magic hummed at her. Shadow almighty, she hoped this wasn't a colossal mistake. If she broke it, if Al found out he was teaching her, she'd be bound to him.

Vasso's hand remained extended. That ruby ring stared at her, and the sly grin on his face dared her to take the deal. She'd never wanted this power, but if there was a chance she could learn to use it, keep it from harming the ones she loved over and over... she had to do it.

Sera grabbed his hand. For a moment, there was nothing. Then his eyes flashed from gray to bloodred, and a searing pain shot through her arm, down her shoulder to the bottom portion of her spine. "Moons, that hurt."

"Well, I couldn't brand your hand, now, could I? Someone might see it."

Fuck.

CHAPTER THIRTY-FOUR

DOMINICK

Dominick paced in a grief-stricken daze outside the arched doorway to the lifelines pool. He should already have reported to his post, but Theo had promised he would pull Sera's thread first thing this morning, and that he'd try to find Colton's.

He couldn't believe it, wouldn't, until either Colton's remains arrived to be burned or Theo confirmed it. He'd been up all night tossing and turning, keeping Theo up with him.

A squeeze on his shoulder had him jumping. "Shadow, you scared me. Did you find her? Colton?"

Theo rubbed his brow. "Not exactly."

"Theo, I can't do this right now. Tell me... Is she dead?" Nausea rolled up his gut.

"She's definitely alive, but... Dom, did you know she's golden?"

"Are you sure you searched for the right one?" Dominick asked. Those with golden threads could be pulled only by masters of the art. Some spell to keep others from spying on the Council members.

"Positive... I picked her out of one of yours."

Despite the relief he felt, knowing that Sera was at least alive, he couldn't help the blush that crept across his cheeks. Shadow only knew what event in Dominick's past Theo had viewed in order to find Sera. "Sera basically has zero magic. Why would she be blocked?"

Theo glanced around the main entrance of the Ogdelo. Dominick followed his gaze and noticed for the first time that morning that those winged beings, with their golden armor and giant swords, were all over the place.

"Come on." Theo grabbed his hand and all but dragged him out to the side garden. "I don't know who did it or why, but your friend has been blocked. No one can pull her strands. They're still present, so she's alive, but I can't see where she is or what she's doing. Have you ever had anyone pull her before?"

Dominick rubbed the heels of his palms against his eyes. The sky was annoyingly bright and chipper for how on edge he felt this morning. Even the birds chirping in the topiary were making him jump.

"No, she's never had to be pulled. Sera's always been here with me."

"Someone is protecting her, then, or at the very least, they don't want someone knowing whatever she may have done in her past."

"Lavinia..." Dom said. He couldn't think about this right now. His head was beginning to pound, and those damn birds wouldn't shut up. "What about Colton?"

Theo shook his head. His eyes were already bloodshot. "I... Dom, I'm sorry."

A sob broke from Dominick. He sank to the ground.

"Shh, I know." Theo sat beside him and threw an arm around his shoulders.

He was really gone. Colton. Out of the two of them, how could he be the one to go first? Colton had always followed the rules, covered his ass. He was powerful, deadly with a weapon. How could this have happened? And worse... oh, Shadow... how was Dom going to watch his brother burn?

"Dom, listen, I know this is hard, but I'm going to need you to get yourself together." The words were harsher than the sympathetic look Theo was giving him.

"How do you expect me to just pull myself together? My brother is dead, Theo... Sera hasn't responded in days... just... fuck!" Dominick's robes were rough against his cheeks and nose. Shadow, it hurt. It hurt so fucking much.

"Dom, this war is going to get a lot worse. More threads are being cut every day, and every cut we must report directly to the master. At first I thought it was because of the battle... but the threads, they're still not matching the casualty reports."

"Still more?" Dominick dared to ask.

"More. A lot more."

The skin prickled on the back of his neck and up his scalp. He tried to wrap his head around it. The aliato in Lavinia's house. Their constant presence throughout the Citadel. Sera's lack of response. More threads being cut than reported to the coven populace. Colton dead... it was too much for him to make the connections.

"We can't tell anyone," Theo continued. "Have you noticed the extra Legion members standing guard?"

Dominick shook his head. "I guess I haven't been paying attention. I'm sorry."

"It's been a lot. Don't worry about it."

"How can you be so understanding?"

Theo crouched before him and looked him in the eye. "Shouldn't a warlock be understanding of his lover?"

"I feel like I used you," Dominick answered. "I seduced you into helping me." Moons, it was good to get that off his chest. He couldn't deny that his feelings for Theo were growing stronger than with any other tryst he'd had.

Theo gave him a soft smile and wiped away a few tears. "You think I was so taken by your good looks that you conned me into helping you?"

"I don't know what I think anymore."

"You're not the first warlock to ask me for a favor."

Dominick sighed and grabbed Theo's outstretched hand. "I'm a fool," he said and kissed Theo under the sun. "Thank you," he whispered. "For everything."

"Always."

"Will you come with me... to Colton's burning?" Dominick held his breath. This would be too much. He was asking too much of Theo.

"You want me there?"

All he could do was nod.

"I would be honored."

Dominick looked at this beautiful warlock in front of him. He was unsure of how he would tell his parents about it or what his father would do, but trying to navigate the burning without Theodore would be impossible.

"We've got to get to our posts. I'll meet you at your flat after?"

Dominick nodded, and the two oracles climbed the white marble steps back into the pool house.

Chapter Thirty-Five

Seraphina

She hoped Al was still asleep. Ever so slowly, she turned the metal doorknob to their room. As soon as the latch clicked open, the door was practically ripped from the hinges.

"Where the fuck have you been?" Al growled at her, almost pulling her arm out of its socket as he jerked her inside.

"Hey!"

"I swear to every fucking god I've ever heard about, Seraphina..." He was pacing the bloodred carpet. Shirtless and pacing and angry. "Where the fuck were you? I woke up and you were gone."

"I told you I had to go see what he wanted." She folded her arms around herself, her organza puff sleeves bunching uncomfortably. She couldn't wait to get out of this gown.

Alistair stilled. "And what did this *lord* want from you?" Snik jumped up on the bed and growled at Alistair, his giant ears pinned back.

"I think you need to calm down." She backed up a step, her hip hitting the writing desk behind her. Snik snorted in agreement.

"You want me to calm down..." He placed his hands on his hips. A deadly look crossed his face. "I am surrounded by my weakness. I almost died yesterday, and when I woke up, you were gone and I was covered in these…" He turned, and Sera saw that his entire back had broken out in hives. "From your little pet over there. Sera, I thought you were dead."

Oh, she was not going to stand for it. Who did he think he was, speaking to her like that? "You leave Snik out of this." Sera rose her chin and met his gaze. "In case you don't remember, I did that to save you. And I am not dead." Her dark magic snapped to her palms. Both of them needed to calm down. He looked like he was about to burst a blood vessel. "Turn around."

"What?"

"Alistair Alcott, turn around."

His jaw fluttered in irritation, but he listened at least. Sera swiped a fork off the tray, which had been left there overnight. She felt a little bad for making him worry, but not enough for that tone to be considered appropriate.

He gave an exaggerated sigh but didn't say anything.

She inspected the nasty patches of red hives on his back. And what a beautiful back it was. Planes of thick muscle cradled his spine. His shoulders were clearly defined. No surprise there, with how tense he was. She lifted the fork and began to scratch.

Alistair groaned. Something deep and primal. She'd be lying if she said the sound of him didn't instantly make her squeeze her thighs together. "Can you be calm?" she asked, continuing to scratch.

"I'll be whatever you want me to be if you keep doing that."

"Good boy." Al shot a look over his shoulder, and she decided then and there that she would absolutely use that phrase again. "Now, if you'll stop bellyaching, I'll tell you what the demon lord wanted."

His muscles rippled under the fork she kept raking across his skin. She wished she could use her nails… her teeth. But Sera was terrified, knowing what that would do. She shared magic with a demon lord, which made being around Al infinitely more complicated.

"So, what was the price for my life?" His shoulders flexed as if he were ready to take a blow.

Sera sighed and dug the prongs into a red patch on his ribs. "All he wanted was to see my magic." Alistair spun to face her, his brows up to his hairline. "And before you ask, 'Why would he want that?' the answer is, I have no idea. He didn't share his reasoning, and I didn't ask."

"That's all? You're sure?"

She hated lying to him, but the brand on her spine burned. "That's all."

"I don't trust him. The minute I can travel, we're gone. You hear me?" He was back to pacing. Snik's head followed him back and forth, a weary look on the goblin's face.

"There's only one problem with that." She placed the fork down. "I still don't have the doorways marked."

They'd found Ophelia. His job was done... but hers? She wished the oracle had told her something more. The only thing Ophelia had told her was that Vasso would help her. It wasn't the best plan, but it *was* a plan. She could try to convince him to give her some locations.

Part of her wanted to mark the map where this manor was, just so she could say she'd found a doorway. She'd be punished for the lie, but it was entirely possible that it wouldn't be one. There could be a doorway somewhere deep in this manor.

"We can figure that out once we're not under this roof."

Sera crossed the room and sank into the mattress next to Snik. The goblin brushed his claws through her hair. "Or I was thinking maybe I could ask Lord Vasso?"

"Over my dead body you will." That rage was back in his face.

"This is my mission, Al. I should get to decide how I want to complete it. Regardless, unless I come back with at least one doorway, the Council isn't going to send a team to save Nora. You know this."

"Minnow, you don't..." He softened his voice. "You don't have any magic to protect yourself."

Her blood boiled. She should have known he'd be the same as everyone else. Would think that she was incapable of taking care of herself. That she needed help—protection. *She* had prevented Vasso from killing him in the first place. *She* had made a bargain with a demon lord to save him a second time. And here he stood, self-righteous, thinking he needed to protect her.

"This is my only chance. I won't give up saving Nora because you're uncomfortable. My sister needs to get out of the underworld, and if this is the only way for me to do it, then so be it. But you're not going to stand in my way."

He pressed his fingers into his temples. "I'm going to bathe. We'll have this conversation later."

"I mean it, Al!"

All she was met with was a slammed bathing room door.

Chapter Thirty-Six

Seraphina

Somehow—by Shadow's intervention, probably—Alistair had agreed to search the manor for a doorway. It had taken all day to convince him, but he'd finally relented last night.

She was grateful Vasso hadn't invited them to dinner; she needed a break and some rest, though she got very little of that with Alistair hovering over her like a mother hen. Any alone time she had was within the confines of the bathing room. Sera had taken a peek at the brand Vasso had given her, and although the mirror wasn't full length, she could make out its basic shape.

A dagger.

Sera had nearly fainted at the sight of it. It didn't matter that it was intricate and strangely beautiful on her skin; it was still a symbol of a bargain with a demon. One she had to keep hidden from a warlock who seemed determined to undress her, and what a fucking shame it was.

"Faster," Al demanded.

She ran back and forth across the training room they'd found while investigating the manor. Alistair had wanted her training immediately. Sera just hoped that Vasso had meant it when he said to make themselves at home.

Black candles lined the room, and more chandeliers hung from the ceiling. If thick black mats hadn't covered every inch of the floor, she would have thought this was just another opulent room. One thing she knew for certain was that Lord Vasso definitely had a thing for chandeliers.

"One more there and back," Alistair yelled out. The sprinting and stitch in her side had gotten rid of the tension between them. Al was feeling better; she measured it by the slight grab he made at her waist and the way he'd smelled her hair this morning. She wanted it, wanted him, but the realization that she had the same magic as Vasso...

Sera pushed herself, her lungs desperate for air as she crossed the mat and collapsed to the floor.

Alistair's face blocked her view of the chandelier hanging above her. "You're getting faster at least," he said and held out his gloved hand. Sera took it and let him hoist her up. He had been wearing the gloves constantly. Not that she could blame him, since they were, quite literally, within the belly of the beast.

Sera folded forward, continuing to pant, and flipped him off.

He laughed for the first time since her incident at the tavern. That smile, those dimples, a crack in his armor.

"How's your side?" she asked.

Al lifted his tunic, giving her a peek at his obliques, something she decided she'd never get sick of. But the wound at his side was still healing. This morning, they had discussed when he thought he'd be ready to bring Ophelia back to the Citadel. He didn't give Sera a direct answer, but she could tell by the slash, still scabbed over, that he was a ways off.

"Let's do some enhancer work." Al handed the cuff with two rings to her, and she strapped it to her palm.

Releasing her magic in front of Vasso had done wonders to ease some of the tension in her veins, but her darkness was itching to play again. Thankfully, the enhancer didn't call to it.

Sera lifted her hand skyward and created a barrier bubble around her. It was getting easier, and she was using less of her magic than she'd initially needed.

"Form it. Try to make it into a shield."

Visualizing the shield she remembered him holding in the woods, when he'd protected her from Vasso, she held out her hand. A shield took form, no larger than her palm, but then fizzled out.

"I'm too tired."

"You'll be tired when you're fighting, and if you stop and take a break—"

"I'll die. I got it, big guy." Sera rolled her eyes and tried again. She was pushing out that blue barrier with all her might when Alistair whispered in her ear.

"That's it."

Heat nuzzled her neck. His lips were so close.

She strained, focusing her magic through the amethyst secured to her palm, but the slightest touch of his fingertips against her side awoke a very different sensation, and the barrier fell. Her gaze crashed into his. His smile was long gone.

Sera wondered if he longed for the brush of her mouth against his. If the kiss they'd shared had only been a desperate moment of sweet euphoria before the promise of death. One they'd both been willing to lose themselves in for a few precious seconds.

He was inching closer when a clearing throat interrupted them. Vasso watched intently from the doorway, seemingly unbothered by the moment he'd just crashed.

"Lord Vasso! I'm sorry for intruding on your practice space." Sera's cheeks burned.

The demon smiled, hands in his pockets. "That's all right. I said you were free to use the manor. That included training rooms. And I thought we'd agreed on Vasso?" Vasso winked at her. Out of the corner of her eye, she saw Alistair standing so stiff he looked ready to snap. "Could I steal you for a few minutes, Seraphina?"

"Sure, I'll just be a moment." Subtlety didn't seem to be the lord's strong suit. How would she get away with training with Vasso when Al was standing right behind her, ready to pounce? Pure rage lined Al's face, and Vasso answered it with an amused smirk. The demon retreated into the hall, easing some of the vitriol in the room.

"What do you mean *you agreed on Vasso*?" Alistair fumed at her.

This was going to be far more challenging than she thought. "Relax. It was after he helped me with your wound," she huffed, then removed her enhancer and swiped her sleeve across her damp brow.

"You're not going anywhere alone with him."

"I won't know what he wants until I speak with him, will I?" She handed the cuff back to Alistair.

"I'm going with you."

"And what happens when he bursts your skull open with the snap of his finger?" she hissed, hoping Vasso wouldn't overhear. "I need you alive. Let me handle this and see if I can get some information about the doorways."

"If he touches one hair on your head..."

"You'll do what? Ruin this entire quest because a demon lord wants to talk to me? You'd prevent me from saving my sister because you're jealous?"

He reared back as if she'd slapped him. Maybe she'd gone too far, but they needed a bit of distance. She also needed to learn how to wield so she'd stop burning down entire villages.

"I'm not jealous. I'm trying to keep you safe!"

Sera sighed. "I've been with enough warlocks to see the signs." She marched out the door as Al stumbled over his words. She refused to entertain the conversation any longer. Breaking her and Vasso's bargain would make her indebted to the demon, and that was the last thing she needed.

Farther up the hall, Vasso leaned on the carved stone wall, biting his lip like he was preventing a grin. "Trouble in paradise?"

"You're not helping. You couldn't have come and gotten me when he wasn't around? It's like you want him to find out." She looked up at him. Moons, he was tall, a creature designed for pure destruction. She was used to warlocks meeting her eye; she'd always been considered tall for a witch. But between Vasso and Alistair, she felt petite.

"My apologies," he said with a sneer, turning down the dark hallway, his hands clasped behind his back. "Are you too out of breath for some real training?"

"I'm fine." She lowered her voice, making sure Al wasn't spying on them from the doorway.

"What about him?"

"He has every right to be concerned. He's been trained to fight demons his entire life, and he doesn't know *why* you're asking to speak to me."

"Honestly, I wonder if I should be..."

She grabbed his wrist. He turned and raised a brow at her. "We made a bargain." After a moment of silence, she realized her error and snatched her hand back. "Please don't maim me..."

His eyes flashed red for a second. "I won't... *this* time."

Sera followed him down the dark hallways, unsure if she should believe him or not, but at this point, she didn't have a choice. She had his brand on her back, after all.

As in the rest of the underground manor, the walls were made of stone. Sera wondered how they'd been carved and manipulated this deep underground. It must have taken centuries. The grooves of the rock skidded across her palm while she trailed her hand down the wall. This place was old. She couldn't describe it, but belowground, the rock pulsed with life.

"You're quite trusting," Vasso said.

"We made a bargain. Pretty sure the indebtedness works both ways. You can't train me if I'm dead."

Up ahead, boulders scratched, sliding against each other, and gave way to a beam of sunlight.

Vasso shrugged. "There *is* no bargain if you're dead. But still, you seem almost at ease..." His sensuous tone wrapped around her with the smell of sandalwood and ash.

She didn't know what he was implying, too tired to care; all she needed was to save Nora, and being around him got her one step closer to that. Maybe she should be more concerned. Perhaps she should have begged him to reverse their bargain. Should have figured out a way to suppress the darkness for the rest of her sorry life, tucked away in her Jedan boarding house, until it sprang free and burned the Citadel to the ground.

Her magic laughed at her then. Sera squinted against the sun beams entering the dark hall.

"Do you require that I spill all my secrets?" she asked.

"Of course not. But I do have an incredible knack for uncovering them."

"You're arrogant."

He chuckled then. "When you're as powerful as I am... you get to be."

Sera bit back a huff at the smirk in his voice.

Each step she took toward the exit, her heart ticked up a notch. Those beasts had almost torn her and Al apart the last time she'd been outside.

Vasso must have sensed her hesitancy. "I'm not letting you play with vatra magic in my home. And nothing out there is as deadly as I am, Seraphina."

The way he said her name tingled at the base of her skull, and either he was casting a spell or her subconscious idiocy was overruling her once again. Either way, she started to believe she was safe with him.

Sera shielded her eyes and blinked a few times before she stepped into a field. The tall grass was shaped into a perfect circle. Not a tree or shrub disturbed the clumps of wildflowers swaying in the slight breeze. The air was sweet. She breathed it in.

Beyond the massive ironoak trees that surrounded the training circle were the white-capped Lanac mountain peaks reaching for the sun. At this distance, they were stunning.

Vasso snapped his fingers. His tailored clothes morphed into an all-black leather ensemble that fit his frame perfectly. The tunic, tied at his throat, was reinforced at the elbows and chest and around his long torso, accentuating his tapered waist.

"No," he said. "That won't do." He snapped his fingers again, and her Legion uniform shifted to buttery-soft black leather, clinging to her like a second skin. It smelled glorious.

"How did you do that?" she asked, stroking her arms.

He gave her a deadpan stare. "Magic."

"Very funny," she bit back. Vasso's smile lit up his face. Her heart beat so hard at the sight of it, she wondered if he could hear it. "What's with the leather?"

"Harder to burn." Vasso flicked something off his finger, and an ember of black flame fizzled on her thigh.

"They're ruined now!"

"I'll make you a new pair, Subdina." He smiled again, and it felt like a lightning bolt slammed into her chest. "Stand in the center of the circle."

Sera waded through the tall grass and swore to look up what that word meant if she ever set foot in the keeper wing again. It was the fourth time he'd called her that. At this point, she wanted to know if she should be offended or not.

The blades and petals of the wildflowers tickled her palm with every step toward the center. Her hesitation lessened with each second the sun warmed her face.

"You sure like touching things."

Sera sighed. Taking a moment to engage with one of the senses, like touch, grounded her, especially if what she touched was organic. Something about the way Eraphon's life felt between her fingers... But he didn't need to know that.

"Can we get on with it?" she asked, brushing the tall grass against the hollow of her palm.

"So prickly... Burn the field."

Her mouth went dry. "I don't want to set the forest on fire."

"I didn't say the forest, I said the field. You think you can handle that?"

Sera glanced back at the tunnel they'd just come from. She hoped Alistair hadn't followed them. Moons, if he had seen *anything,* he'd flay her alive.

Vasso waved his hand, and the stone door scraped closed. "There, now go."

She took a deep breath and closed her eyes. The darkness twirled in her gut. She coaxed it to the surface, heat spreading through her veins, down her arms, and under her fingertips. She pointed her palms to the ground, let her head fall back, and released.

The tension she'd carried for months vanished from the planes of her back, released from her shoulders and hips. Even her ribs felt less restrained as she took in a deep breath.

So long she had kept this power caged.

The grass crackled, and the scent of smoke scorched her lungs. Sera winced. She was safe. There wasn't anyone there to hurt. But still, the sounds of people's screams, the feel of flesh burning... She stopped.

Peering out at the field, she yelped.

Half the field was alight with black flame, which sped rapidly toward the trees. Smoke billowed so thick she couldn't make out the entrance to the cave, and Vasso was gone. Panic clawed at her.

"Vasso!"

He stepped to her side. "I wish I could say I wasn't impressed, but..."

"Shit." She clutched her chest. "You scared me."

He kept his hands in his pockets. "How did it feel? I bet it felt good."

It did. Shadow, it did. "Are you going to put it out?" she asked.

He arched a single dark brow at her, held out his hand, and released a stream of black flame. It trickled into the darkness, ripping its way across the field.

The sensation of his magic mixing with hers vibrated deep inside her. It was strange, the flip of her stomach and the flutter in her chest. Sera glanced at Vasso to see if he felt it too. His jaw was as sharp as a knife, his eyes focused on the flames, and a soft curve pulled at his lips. He didn't seem affected at all.

The buzzing in her body intensified as he took longer to contain her mess. She crossed her arms tight on her chest as she watched Vasso work.

The reverberation drummed to her stomach, then lower. Sera clenched her thighs tight.

Vasso closed his eyes, the muscle in his jaw ticking before he made a fist and extinguished every flame. Once they were out, the vibrations stopped.

When he opened his eyes again, they were bright red. The heat of his gaze raked over every inch of her body. She couldn't contain the blush rising to her cheeks.

"Again," he growled.

Planting her feet, Sera pulled at the abomination's well. She could do this for days without burning out. It was so much easier to play with this vatra magic. This was what it was like to be powerful. To feel like you could make a difference in the world. That your life had significance, that you had the ability to stand your ground and be heard. No wonder her mother was so entitled, and Al, and Nora.

Once the other half of the field was alight, Vasso let loose his magic again. Sera bit her knuckle so hard it left marks as his magic raked over hers.

Vasso didn't take his time. Instead, they absorbed and extinguished almost immediately.

"That's enough for today," he said. Vasso ran his hand through his white hair and stalked toward the manor's secret entrance. The lord's shoulders were tense under his leather tunic.

"That's your lesson? Burn a field?"

Vasso hovered over her, his eyes flashing from gray to red again. "I said we are done." There was the promise of death in that glare. Sera shivered.

A harrowing screech came from the forest; only then did Vasso break his stare.

"What was that?" she asked.

Vasso sighed. "Looks like you just got your second lesson. Follow me."

CHAPTER THIRTY-SEVEN

SERAPHINA

Burned grass crunched under her boots as she followed the demon lord to the perimeter of Ironoak Forest. The howling was louder, and Sera couldn't help the pit opening in her stomach. All she could think of was the agbris chasing them, their snarling, the claws swiping for Alistair's middle. Whatever beast was screaming in pain, the agbris had probably gotten them too.

"Our power"—Vasso paused for a moment, cleared his throat, and began again—"is destructive. It kills, burning almost everything to ash."

"I'm fully aware of the type of destruction it can do," she said, stepping over a fallen log. "It seems like that's the only thing it's good for."

Vasso wove between the thick trunks of the ironoak trees. It was cool in the shadows of the canopy, and besides the painful shrieks of the creature they were walking toward, the forest was silent. No rustling nor chirping. Even the rays of sunlight that dared to touch the forest floor seemed to shy away from him.

"I used to think that too," he said, almost a whisper.

They approached a dense thicket full of brush and brambles, and before it lay a small fox, its leg mangled and bloody. The poor thing grew quiet as they neared.

"This magic is death. But sometimes it can be a mercy to those suffering. We dark ones wait for our souls to reach Shadow's realm. It is no different for them." He lowered onto his haunches beside the animal. Vasso petted its white-tipped ears and gray muzzle.

"You're not going to kill it, are you?" she asked.

"No," Vasso said and glanced up at her. "You are."

Sera stilled. Her darkness pulsed inside her. "I've already told you the horrors I've committed, the countless people I killed in Feybury. And now your *lesson* is to kill this poor animal?" She was going to be sick, but she worked to push down her magic, lock that cage tight around it. He'd have to pry it out of her if he wanted her to hurt this creature.

"You wished to learn how to wield? Looks like fate has granted you the chance to experience what this magic was made for." The animal sighed in relief as Vasso began petting it again. It seemed almost comforted under his touch.

"You said you had healing abilities. Why not heal it instead?"

Vasso shushed the creature, who nuzzled his head into the demon lord's hand. "This one's time is up. He wants to go home, and I can guarantee the death either you or I give him will be twice as merciful as the end he will meet out here."

"I won't." She took a step back. "I wanted to learn how to control it, not kill more."

Vasso stood. Without his comforting hand, the little fox whimpered again. "You want control?" Vasso's eyes turned bloodred; his jaw clenched tight. "This is control!"

Sera couldn't stop the tears from forming. He was cruel to make her do this. An innocent animal, and he expected her to do what? Burn it alive? No, she wouldn't. The lock rattled inside her, but she raised her chin.

Vasso took a step toward her.

"We don't get to choose our lot in life, Seraphina. Prophecies, fate—it has all been written. The only control we have is how we use it."

"Then I refuse to use it to kill another innocent thing."

Vasso's straight mouth turned into a devious smile. In an instant, he was every bit a deadly demon lord. Sera couldn't stop the trembling in her hands. Shadow, this was a mistake, all of it. Begging for his help, the bargain—all of it. She tried to get away, tripping backward when her ankle hit a downed branch. Vasso caught her before she landed on her ass, his grip punishing around both wrists. Sera's heart pounded in her ears.

"You'll do it, or consider the bargain called in," he snarled.

"You can't do that. I didn't break it!"

He smiled, and again she saw that deadly beauty. His white teeth, the flash of his red eyes below dark brows, and that single white strand of hair falling across his forehead. "You are refusing to take my instruction, and that was the deal, wasn't it? I must teach you, correct?"

He was so close they shared breath. She couldn't help but feel his gaze settle on her lips. She didn't have her books to figure out if he could do this, what the laws for bargains were. All she knew was that she couldn't chance being indebted to him. Nora needed her, Dom needed her...

Vasso ripped her forward, dragging her toward the downed fox.

"No, I don't want to." Sera tried to break free from his grip, her boots sliding in the dead leaves. The pulsing magic rang through her like a chant. It craved... it wanted. "You're a monster!"

"Oh, my dear, you have no idea."

The leaves crunched under her knees as she landed hard beside the injured animal. It was so small, no larger than her arm. She'd kill Vasso for making her do this. She'd hurt him once and could again. Her magic seemed to flare in answer.

The thorns from the bushes within the thicket tore at her arms and cheek as she scrambled to get away. Vasso's dagger brand on her spine burned in warning. It was all ruined: her time, her magic. She was tainted... wrong. Sera was halfway into the brush when...

"No, you don't," he said and yanked her by her waist.

"Let go." Sera panted, her cheek burned, but Vasso's arm was tight around her middle, holding her to him. Sera swung and scratched, did her best to try and get away.

"You'll learn your duty... just as I did... and the ones before me."

"Please, don't make me," she sobbed. He sat her in his lap right on the ground, his chest stretched around the curve of her back like a solid wall as he took her wrists in each hand. The smooth skin of his cheek brushed against hers, and his strong arms held her still. "Vasso... please."

"I think I rather like the sound of you begging," he chuckled in her ear. Sera began to thrash again. "Enough... look."

The fox raised its head, and Sera paused.

Its eyes were the color of honey. The ginger fur had long since turned white around its brows and snout. Slowly, her wrist in his bruising grip, Vasso extended one of her arms and laid her hand atop the fox.

The animal's fur was soft under her fingertips, and its wet nose tickled her palm. Moons, she couldn't pull away even if she wanted to. Vasso kept her so still.

Memories swirled in her mind. The Legion soldier burning alive. The homes engulfed in black flame and even blacker smoke, with their inhabitants watching on as their entire lives were burned to ash. Sera choked down her sickness, not caring now if her tears fell... if *he* saw them.

"Good," Vasso whispered in her ear, steadying her hand on the animal's head. "Now, *feel*."

Sera gasped at the flood of sensations that rocked through her. Pain—terrible, unrelenting anguish. She couldn't stop herself from crying out. Vasso's grip loosened a touch.

"It is suffering." His words were hot in her ear, but his tone had softened. "You can end it."

So much pain. The leg had festered. Infection had settled in, and deep in the bowels of the poor thing, maggots were already eating, destroying.

It is the way, her magic hummed to her.

"Help me," she rasped. "I don't want to do this alone."

Vasso adjusted himself behind her. He let go of her wrists, and his hand covered hers. A surge of power rolled off him, through her. That same vibration she'd experienced in the field bloomed in her chest, washing her in understanding.

"You are not evil," he whispered to her. "You are not death... you are... mercy."

Sera sucked in a shuddering breath, and the moment before she released her darkness, the fox blinked his honey eyes at her. There was no more pain running through her, only relief and thanks.

Hot black flame burst from her hands, and a second later, there was only ash, blowing away on a strong wind.

Vasso lifted her from his lap and stood. "Let's go," he said, not giving her a second glance.

How? How was this possible? Never had she done something like that, experiencing another's pain from a touch. She rose from the ground and followed the demon lord back to the field. Their magic had opened up something inside her. She couldn't place it, only knew that it felt right.

His confident stride didn't falter, nor did he slow for her to catch up. She wiped away her tears and righted herself as they entered the tunnel. Vasso flicked his wrist, and the stone door scraped closed, dropping them into darkness.

The strands around her face tickled her temple and cheeks with his breath. His body heat washed over her in waves, and the first thing she noticed as her eyes adjusted to the tunnel's darkness was the look of bewilderment across that beautiful face.

"You felt it too," she whispered. That hungering need when their magics mixed. "What does it mean?"

Conflict played across his features. He raised his hand and brushed her cheek with his thumb. "It never said—"

"Sera?!" Alistair yelled.

She peered around Vasso to a warlock barreling toward them. This was not going to be good. Vasso stiffened when her shoulder grazed his as she went to deal with the captain.

Chapter Thirty-Eight

Seraphina

The tunnels grew brisk the farther she walked from the surface back to her rooms. She marched directly past Alistair, wanting to be alone to process whatever the fuck had just happened.

The sensation when their magic touched. Relief that she didn't burn down the forest, then pain and despair for putting that poor fox out of its misery... and lastly the undeniable fact that she had a well of demon magic within her.

"Why were you outside?" Alistair demanded, keeping pace beside her.

"He asked if I could show him something." Sera forced the words out. She was terrible at lying, always had been. What good was it to lie when your mother could read your thoughts?

"And why couldn't I join you?" Agitation was evident in his tone. His hands clenched at his sides. He was definitely pissed. "What are you wearing?"

Fuck.

She hadn't thought of that. "Alistair, you don't have to follow me everywhere." She brushed off his questions and continued through the dark halls. They passed minor house demons carrying linens, each giving her a slight bow as she walked past.

"I want to protect you."

She halted and faced him. "I understand your concern. But I'd like to be alone right now." Her words were firm, maybe too firm, by the look on his face. The muscles in his jaw bulged. He'd break his molars if he didn't stop. She hated possessiveness and wondered why he assumed he could force her to do anything. Because of a kiss?

"Did he touch you?"

"No." Sera wiped a hand over her face.

Alistair summoned his sword from thin air. "I'll kill him."

"For Shadow's sake," she said. The last thing she needed was the two of them ripping each other to ribbons. "Can you please give me some space? You've been hovering over me for days," Sera huffed and walked toward her room faster.

"That's not fair." Alistair whipped her around by her arm. "You leave me to go be alone with him... show up in a completely different outfit—" He scanned her up and down, his blue eyes bright with rage. "And then tell me you want to be alone?"

Sera pulled hard out of his grasp. She was so sick of being manhandled. The dark magic—vatra magic—inside her perked, but she buried it back down. "Don't ever put your hands on me like that again."

There was a deep tug in her chest, then a wave of calm rushed over her. Like a breath of cool air on a hot summer day. Sera glanced down the dark hallway where she had just left Vasso. She swore he was there, leering at her from the shadows. There was nothing to see, but... she could sense him.

"I'm going to my room." Sera turned on her heel, and this time Al was smart enough to stay behind.

Snik's green ears perked when she walked in. Sera hardly noticed the chicken bone in his teeth as he leaped from the bed and wrapped his gangly green arms around her knees.

"It's all right," she said to him, rubbing his back.

The goblin harrumphed and went back to chewing.

Sera shed her leathers. Her arms, her legs, and everywhere else were slick with perspiration. Leather might have been the best option to protect her body from flames, but it didn't breathe. After filling the copper tub with hot water, she proceeded to rake her fingers through her curls and sank into the steam.

She hated lying to Alistair. After everything they had been through on this quest. He'd comforted her, healed her blisters and scorched lungs, danced with her... laughed. Up until the other night, she'd been safe with him. Sooner or later, though, he would realize what type of magic she possessed. If the Citadel's tower was her fate, she'd gladly go as long as Nora was out of Gehenna.

She could still hear Vasso's words. *You'll learn your duty, just as I did, and the ones before me.*

"All right." She knew she was foolish for speaking aloud, but she needed more answers. "Do you have anything to say for yourself?"

Are you talking to me? her magic whispered in answer.

"There isn't anyone else in here, is there?"

Her magic snickered at her. Darkness twirled and danced in her body. *What do you wish to know?*

Sera swallowed the lump in her throat. "Am I a demon? Is that why you came to me?"

I came for it was fated. The crossroads nears. Her magic slithered and sang. *You will know when it happens, for there is still a chance the stars do not align...*

She groaned in frustration. "Just tell me the truth. Will I hurt him?"

Yes.

The door creaked open. She could hear Snik on the other side, whining.

"You can come in," she said. The tops of his pointed ears were visible over the tub's edge. Snik reached his bony green hand toward her, and she took it and squeezed. The goblin squeezed back and curled on the bath mat, snoring not minutes later.

Heat from the water roasted her cheeks as Sera searched for an answer in the cracks of the stone ceiling.

Dom had to be furious with her. It'd been over a week since she wrote him. Moons, she hoped he was staying out of trouble. He'd been with her through every celebration, breakup, and hard decision. And even though he would be most likely amused by the predicament she was currently in, at least she knew Dominick would be understanding.

Sera held her breath and sank below the surface of the water. This magic... the control... It only seemed to listen when she was around Vasso. Then there was the tug in her chest, and that soothing calm that had washed over her when she was ready to rip Alistair apart.

Vatra. That's what Vasso called it.

Sera breached the surface and began working the soap through her curls. The release from her body. All that tension gone when the dark flames had poured from her. But it was the freedom of not hiding it, of not being afraid for once, that had been liberating.

Then there was Vasso. First, he prevented her from becoming a destroyer of the forest, but then... he was so demanding. Her breath hitched as she remembered the sensations of his magic rushing through her. Like leaves unfurling, like flowers turning toward the sun.

She sighed.

Wasn't this just a cluster of shit she'd gotten herself into? None of it was normal, and once again... she was other. Something different. Death. Or was she what Vasso had called her? Mercy?

A soft knock came on the outer bedroom door. She lifted herself from the tub, did her best to squeeze the water from her curls, and wrapped herself in a towel.

Then she gripped the raven around her neck for courage. "Go away, Alistair. I don't want to talk to you."

"It's not Alistair."

Her heart fluttered at his deep voice. She cracked open the door.

"Is this a bad time?" he asked, glancing at her towel.

"Give me a moment."

Sera ran back to the bathing chamber, padding in her bare feet across the bedroom carpet, doing her best not to wake the sleeping goblin as she slipped on her freshly laundered coven uniform. She stopped when Vasso slinked in, closing the door behind him. In his hands were the tunic and pants she'd been wearing before he'd dressed her in leathers.

"Can I help you?" she asked. Who did he think he was, sneaking into her room? Even if it was his underground manor... Shadow help her, these men wouldn't leave her alone today.

"Your bodyguard was down the hall. I figured I'd at least *try* not to get caught outside your room."

"For the tenth time, he isn't my bodyguard."

"Could have fooled me by the way he lurks around you." Vasso pushed his hair back, and a few of the white strands dropped down. He was still in his leathers from their training, which was mildly distracting, considering how dignified he looked in them.

"How is it that all of a sudden you care about what I want? You surely didn't give a shit when we were in the woods." Sera crossed her arms.

His movements were stilted. That usual grace and sway to him was gone as he stiffened. "I came to apologize for that."

She laughed. It was the first time in days, but she couldn't stop it from bubbling out of her chest. "That was the weakest excuse for an apology I've ever heard. Tell me, Vasso, what are you apologizing for?"

Vasso put his hands in his pockets, rocking back on his heels. He gave an exaggerated sigh and ran his hand through his hair again. If she didn't know better, she'd think he was nervous. But that was impossible.

"I apologize for how... *firm*... I was with you in the field, and then..."

"And then when you ripped me from the thicket? Or how about when you held me against my will... or maybe the fact that you made me kill that poor fox when I begged you not to?" Her magic flared within her. Rage roiled under the surface as she watched this *lord* attempt to say he was sorry. The echoes of that little animal's pain racked her. Up her leg, into her guts: unrelenting pain. It didn't matter that she'd helped it move on; it was that he had *made* her do it.

Vasso's jaw muscle feathered in his cheek. His eyes were a pinkish shade, somewhere between gray and red. "I didn't come here to argue with you," he said.

"Then why did you come here?" Sera approached the bed and sat upon it, pulling a pillow into her lap and twisting the tassels at its corners.

"I told you."

She huffed. "You've never said sorry for a single thing in your life, have you? Tell me, why do you care at all about my feelings?"

"My reasons are my own, Seraphina. Take the apology or don't."

He was trying. She'd give him that. And although she didn't know his true intentions, there was no denying that their magic tied them together. Could it be that he needed her cooperation? "I'll accept your apology, but I need something out of you."

He smirked. "I thought you were all done with bargains?"

"Not a bargain... more of a measure of good faith."

Vasso tilted his head. Quiet. Assessing. She could tell he was trying to find the loophole. "What is it you ask of me?"

She bit her smile back. "Tell me where a doorway to Gehenna is."

Vasso barked a laugh. "You're kidding."

"Nope," she said. She was close. She needed this, just one. Then she could mark it on the map and go home. It would take months for them to realize that the manor wasn't an actual doorway, but if she had one that *was* accurate, well then... Renata would just have to deal with that.

His face shifted, not to malice or anger but to amusement. "So you won't take my apology"—his shoulders sank back into the door, and he crossed one foot over the other—"unless I tell you how to get to the underworld?"

"I don't need to know how to get there, just an entrance."

"Interesting…"

Why did she feel like she'd just given something away? Something he could take to his commander belowground and barter with? That thread in her chest pulled tight. This wasn't her magic. It was something else entirely, like being dragged through a current, plunged like an anchor into the sea. But there at the end of it all, a steady beat of a heart…

Sera jumped at an insistent knock on the door.

"Sera, can I come in?"

"Fuck," she whispered and frantically motioned for Vasso to hide. She pushed him into the bathing chamber with Snik and closed the door.

Why did Al have to ruin everything? She was close, so damned close to getting the answer she needed. Leave it to Al to mess it all up again.

Sera cracked the door wide enough for her face to pop through. "What do you want?"

"To talk."

"We can talk right here."

"Is someone in there?" Alistair glanced over her head, scanning the room. A second later, she was staring at empty space, and he was inside, looking into every corner.

"First of all, I thought you were too sick to travel. Second, I didn't invite you in."

"I traveled four feet, hardly a strain." He was on his hands and knees looking under the bed. Sera zipped her raven back and forth on its string.

"Snik is asleep in the bathing room. That's all of who's in here. What do you want?"

Al crossed his arms. "I wanted to make sure he didn't do anything to you."

"No, he didn't do anything to me." *Liar.* He'd awoken something… given her hope.

"Sera, he could have powers that we don't know about. What if he enthralled you? You're a Jedan witch, for coven founders' sake."

Sera stared at him. "What did you just say?"

His shoulders fell. "Sera, I..."

"Get out."

He stayed put. "I didn't mean it like that."

She lowered her voice to a deadly tone. "I know exactly how you meant it. You think that because I don't have a lot of magic that I'm less than you?" Sera ripped the door wide. "Get out."

"Do I think you're less of a witch? No. But you can't deny the fact that your limited magic makes you—"

"Get the fuck out, Alistair Alcott." She gritted her teeth together so hard they squeaked.

"This discussion isn't over." He glared at her. As soon as his bootheels were on the other side of the threshold, she slammed the door.

How had he known she was originally placed in Jedan? Sera never mentioned that day, nor did she bring up the day after, when she walked onto the Dobro level of Darine Hall, evading dirty looks and whispering tongues.

A click of a door had her turning to see Vasso cradling a still snoring Snik in his arms. He set the goblin down with as much care as she would a newborn. Taking the decorative blanket from the foot of the bed, he placed it over Snik.

"Thank you," she whispered. "He gets a little heavy for me sometimes."

"He's had a rough go, this one." Vasso pointed his chin at the goblin, placing his hands in his pockets.

"What do you mean?" Snik curled in a ball, his ears relaxed as he rested his small head on his arms.

The demon lord sauntered toward the door. "Why don't you ask your captain what happened to his clan?"

With that, Vasso left.

CHAPTER THIRTY-NINE

DOMINICK

Never in his life had he seen so many pyres. Mourners gathered around the platforms arranged throughout the Menage. The wooden bases, surrounded by silber logs and hay, were ready to burn the bodies within them. Even the air seemed dry today, as if the atmosphere itself were eager for a quick burn.

The Council of Elders had declared a mass ceremony with a spare pyre for the *parts* of bodies that had come back. Dominick shivered.

Part of him had been ashamed to refuse to view his brother's body. Now the only thing he'd remember his brother by was what was in his memories, and the linen-wrapped lump among the branches.

"Shadow." Chair Briar's tumbling voice resounded throughout the arena. The Council chair, in her purple robes and jowly face, had those winged warriors on either side of her. Dominick peered around the upper levels where various coven members sat viewing the spectacle. The aliato were standing at attention every twenty feet. "We call to you on this day to ferry those we love into your realm. Watch over their souls, keep them at peace, and forever hold them in your graces."

Dom's father lowered the torch to the hay, and the flames devoured it hungrily. All around, his fellow coven members cried. Dom couldn't. Not here, not when he still couldn't understand what had happened.

A dangerous thought crept into his head, one he refused to dwell on, but still a nagging feeling that if Al had been with Colton... No. This wasn't Sera's fault. Dom swallowed hard as Colton's pyre burned brighter, his mother on one side of him and Theo on the other.

With each second, the mourning moans from mothers, wives, sisters, and daughters intensified with the thickening smoke that rose to the blazing sun.

The coven glorified death, called it turning to dust. But that wasn't truly how it worked. You only turned to dust if your magic burned you out. Roasted you from the inside, a natural sort of combustion.

But Colton hadn't burned out. His mother had prepared her son's body, and she'd said Colton had come back slashed. Death by someone else's hand left a corpse.

And Colton's had just caught flame.

A low hum left his mother. Tears streamed down her cheeks, and Dominick's heart cracked. Between her audible grief and the smell of burning hair and flesh, he was overwhelmed. He reached for Theo's hand and squeezed it tight. Theo nodded and led him away from the smoldering remains, exiting the Menage and finding some solace outside.

"How are you holding up?" Theo asked.

"As well as expected. Fucking terrible." His throat grew thick with the words, and he choked tears down again. Dominick kissed the back of Theo's hand. "Thank you." He attempted to keep his voice level. "For being with me today."

Theo's arms wrapped around him. Dominick took in the smell of his skin, burying his nose in Theo's neck. The warlock only held him tighter.

He was a mess, but he wasn't alone. The first tear slid down his cheek, then a second, and a third. Each one swung his heart in some sort of paradox pendulum. Growing and breaking sadness; then a sensation that for once in his life, he almost felt whole.

The distinct sound of his father clearing his throat prompted Dom to let Theo go.

Tristan Benero had been stern with Dom and Colton growing up. Dom supposed he had to be, with two young boys in the home who created chaos wherever they went. The day Dominick announced he wanted to try for an oracle position rather than the Legion ranks like Colton, he'd received a stern lecture about honoring their family. His father had been assigned as a guardian despite hoping for a Legion position. Tristan prided on protecting their way of life. It would be his legacy—for him, but also for his sons.

But now, his father stood, eyes bloodshot, cheeks washed with tears, reaching for him. A solid wall of chest slammed into Dom's. His father's bear-size arms wrapped around him, pulling him to his bulky frame.

Dominick didn't quite know what to do with his hands, but as his father's forehead crushed into him, as the Benero household head's shoulders quaked with silent weeping, Dom wrapped his arms around his father's broad back and held him.

"My son," his father said. "My son, my son."

Dominick glanced at his mother approaching and then at Theo. They both had grief and worry painted on their faces. And something surged within him.

Honor, maybe? Revenge? Something bubbled within. His father never wept. His mother should not have burned her favorite son. And the more he looked around at the coven members filing from the Menage in a line of misery and anguish, he couldn't help but glare at the aliato standing guard at the door. They had something to do with it. He was sure of it.

"Come home. I'll make some tea." His mother, with her puffy eyes and voice hoarse from her mourning chants, rubbed her husband's back.

"Yes, dear," his father said, wiping away his tears and with them his vulnerability.

Still, Dominick glared at the winged warriors. Not one of them acknowledged him. They looked hollow. Their wings held high, the magic seeping from their scabbards.

His mother's hand was warm and soft in his. She took Theo's in the other. "Let's go, loves."

"Yes, Mother." He let her lead him home.

Through the streets of Daedeth Quarter, Colton's face kept flashing in Dominick's mind. His tightly cropped blond hair, the slight sunburn he always seemed to have across his nose and cheeks. His laugh. Memories of his brother levitating frogs, crabs, and other critters around the house in a parade of ribbits and clicking pincers until their mother chased him with a wooden ladle.

Colton would giggle as he ran, his procession of varmints bouncing off furniture and walls behind him, while Dominick, squealing in delight, watched the madness.

At the base of the stone steps leading to the row house, his mother finally let go of his hand.

"Thank you for being here for him... for us." Fresh tears raced to Dominick's eyes as his mother kissed Theo on each cheek. She gave her son a knowing smile and climbed the steps after his father. "Theodore, you'll stay for tea at least."

"Oh, Mrs. Benero, I couldn't impose."

"Not an imposition, dear. See you inside."

"Do you want me to stay?" Theo directed the question at Dom now. This was the first time he had brought a man home to meet his family. In the light of the tragedy they had endured, his mother and father had accepted Theo with open arms.

"I'd like that." The words felt like blades against his throat. Moons, he was tired of crying, tired of being... sad. Dominick tilted Theo's chin and kissed him. His lips were soft and familiar now. They were outside, and he couldn't seem to care. What the neighbors thought, what his parents thought, any of them.

Theo broke their kiss. "I'm going inside. Take your time."

Dominick sat on the steps and listened.

To the door squeaking closed behind Theo, to the murmurs inside the house, and to the scuffing of other Daedeth members' shoes across the white stone blocks of the street.

That bit of rage sat heavy in his chest. War had been the coven's way of life since the beginning of its existence. They took the most vulnerable of their people and placed them as fodder on the front lines, claiming that it was the demons who wanted to control them.

But as Dominick looked around at the stone homes, at the iron posts holding mage lights, at the esoti warlock who trimmed the bushes across the street, still adorned with his mourning ribbons, he wondered how this war could have raged for so long. The witches and warlocks of the Solarni coven *were* powerful. But were they more powerful than a demon army?

His mother interrupted his thoughts. "Dominick, come inside, please."

He waved her off. Just a minute more.

Dominick scratched the stubble in that place below his ear, almost hearing Sera's voice: *Such a nervous lock you are.* He wondered if she was all right. If she knew—if Alistair knew about Colton. Dominick didn't think he could go through it all again, have the rush of grief overwhelm him as he watched Sera and Alistair crumble.

He let out a sigh and stood. There was a flash in the sky. "What in Eraphon's name?"

A flaming projectile arched toward the center of the Citadel. He couldn't look away from the ball of flame. When it hit the barrier the coven guardians kept around the city, it burst into sizzling sparks that poured over the warded dome.

Chapter Forty

Seraphina

It was the perfect late spring day. The sky was a clear blue, the clouds were white and fluffy, and Sera had created a lie so terrible, she was sure her soul would be damned for eternity never to enter the Shadow realm.

The lie she'd told Al was... runny shits.

"We're going to work with... what did you call it? Death fog?"

Sera rolled her eyes. "Sorry the vernacular wasn't correct."

Vasso smiled at the sky before landing his gaze on hers. "Well, what have you accomplished so far with this *death fog?*"

Their steps crunched as they crossed the meadow to the center of the training circle. Sera had thought all night about what she was going to ask him. She wondered how her magic worked within her to begin with, but the worst of it was the voice's assurance that she'd hurt Al. She'd never been so close to doing so as when he'd called her a Jedan witch.

There was nothing wrong with Jedan's members. It seemed the prejudices of the Citadel had followed her even here.

"It kind of just falls out of me. It only takes shape to surround me in a form of protection. It's... almost sentient."

The corner of his lip twitched.

She hoped he wouldn't ask what she was being protected from. She didn't want to have to admit that she'd been curled in a ball, having a nervous breakdown. He didn't need those details.

Vasso released some of his mist, and Sera instantly heated. Her darkness thrashed inside her, ready to play.

"You can manipulate it as you would your arm." His magic took shape, snaking forward, forming a claw, and delicately picking up a strand of her hair. "Think of it as an extension of yourself. It's connected to you, but if it's broken, you will lose your ability to manipulate it."

"How would it break?"

"Run your hand through it," Vasso quipped. There was a lightness about him today. She couldn't put her finger on what it was exactly. Maybe it was the smooth way he held himself, or the slight sparkle in his eye. Regardless, she'd rather have this Vasso around than the one she'd dealt with yesterday.

She swiped at the claw, and it dissipated. "That doesn't seem very useful, if anyone can break the connection."

"No?" he asked with a smirk.

Something flicked her ear. Sera swatted the shadowy mist away, but just as one tendril disappeared, another flicked her other ear.

"Hey!" A prodding at her cheek had her swiping again, only to be jabbed in the ribs. Sera waved her arms around her body when her feet were swept out from under her and she was hauled upward. Her face was even with his, and she couldn't look away from his amusement.

And that laugh—it was like sunlight, like air.

"Are you going to let me down?" Her voice was nasally from hanging.

"Let yourself down." His eyes danced all over her. She must look ridiculous hanging there, at least six feet off the ground.

Sera reached for her magic, which happily obliged, unfortunately not in a helpful way. Surrounded by a curtain of black fog, she could barely hear

Vasso's snickering above the hum of it. The fog just kept falling, and deep in her mind, her darkness laughed too.

Sera's cheeks were heavy with a rush of blood, so she bent up and swatted her ankle. Her finger had barely brushed Vasso's magic when she realized her error and fell.

"Whoa," Vasso blurted out before she landed directly in his arms. She could feel his heart pounding. The smell of fresh air and his scent filled her lungs with each inhale. Sera couldn't stop the heat blooming across her cheeks. Nor could she look away.

Vasso raised a brow and grinned wider at her. "My my. If I'd known it was this easy to get you to fall into my arms, I would have strung you up outside Crowpass."

Sera slapped his chest, and Vasso only seemed more pleased with himself. "Let me down, you fool." He lowered her feet to the ground, and she made quick work of putting some distance between them.

"Okay, teach me."

He squinted at her, but his smile was playful. Vasso crossed his arms. "It's not easy. Could take you years to develop."

"Believe it or not, *Lord Vasso*, but I'm a very quick learner, and as much as I'm sure you'd love to teach me for decades, I don't have time."

Vasso's smile dropped. "Well, let's not keep you waiting, then. Let it flow."

Sera released her power. It crept from her feet, surrounding the entire training circle with mist and shadow. Her stomach lurched at the sight. It looked exactly the same as when it manifested before, only instead of a field, it had been homes, then flames.

"Well, you've got good reach. Start with something small. Visualize a tendril. It can be as thin as a lock of hair."

Envisioning the natural curl of her hair, she imagined a wisp of mist reaching out in a coil. Tiny tendrils began to rise from below, only to be reabsorbed into the brume below it.

She concentrated again, and again. Vasso stood still in the knee-high fog, his arms crossed but silent. Sera held out her hand.

Vasso hadn't needed his hands to manipulate the magic, nor words...

But Vasso isn't a witch, her magic called back.

"*Vatera,*" Sera whispered. With the turn of her hand, the darkness took shape, reaching up to her palm. She had no idea why that word slipped naturally from her tongue.

"Good. Now try and move it."

Curving her fingers into claws, she visualized the mass as it moved. Microsensations racked her body; blades of grass scratched under her palms. She felt the wind, even the leather of her and Vasso's boots.

"You can feel what it touches?"

Vasso nodded. "I'm going to assume that you were probably petrified and didn't notice. It's an extension of you." A wisp rose out of the mass, caressing her cheek. Her darkness climbed his in a dizzying spiral that set her stomach fluttering.

Sera curled her finger and pointed at him. He didn't flinch when the dark tendril slammed into his cheek. A whisper of warmth glided along the pads of her fingertips. She could feel the smooth skin up the line of his jaw, over his cheek and temple. Lastly, she raked her magic through his hair.

Mesmerized by the sensations, Sera took a moment to notice the rakish grin plastered across Vasso's face. An electrical current aimed straight for her core had her sucking in breath when he waved her magic away.

"I want to try something," he said.

Sera took a step back. "We aren't going to kill something again, are we?"

"You don't trust me, Subdina?"

"No."

Vasso gave her an exaggerated sigh. "Hold it in front of you."

Sera huffed. "*Vatera,*" she said and pulled her darkness into a pillar of blackened smoke.

"Keep it there," he said, and released his own. It changed from something opaque and foggy to a pillar of solid night. It turned and twirled until it was something she could identify—a trunk, then branches, and lastly buds of leaves. Each individual leaf had such perfect likeness that she could recognize each ridge and vein.

Pulling deep from her well, she fed his creation, urging him on. "Keep going," she whispered. The smoky tree soared, mimicking the ironoak trees surrounding them. With each passing second, the canopy grew thicker, blocking out the sun except for speckled rays of light twinkling around her.

Another surge, and she took a deep breath against the buzzing of her skin, relishing the warmth radiating through her. This was what euphoria felt like. This was... living.

Vasso circled their creation, his grin lighting up every inch of his face as the branches and leaves formed—hundreds of years of growth in the matter of minutes.

Sera dared to glance at him again, watching him squint in concentration, and below that straight, regal nose, his lips pulled to the side as he focused.

"Look," he said and pointed up.

Black buds covered the branches. One by one, they unfurled into blossoms grouped into clusters of dark inflorescence. A mighty tree made of mist, fog—shadow.

Sera didn't realize she'd stopped feeding Vasso her magic, and one by one, the blossoms rained around them. Her heart pounded in her ears—they were smoky gray, the color of his eyes. Ash. Darkness.

Her head was fuzzy. Too much magic, she thought. Or was it the natural pull she had to him?

Vasso regarded her as well; amusement danced across his features, melting into curiosity. As the blossoms and petals showered around them, each touch was a tap in her palm.

"I've never done that before," he said quietly.

"Made a tree?"

He shook his head. "Mixed magic, or at least made something with it." His voice dropped. "I didn't know it was possible."

Sera smiled. For so long, she'd wished to be accepted. Not to be the poor sister whose mother had to get her out of Jedan. The one who needed to use her brain instead of her power to navigate the world.

But this had been beautiful. Not destruction. Not death disguised as a mercy. It was life.

The layers of darkness were gone. He took a step toward her, so close she could touch him. Something snapped tight within her, right in the center of her chest. She gasped, holding her finger there, and on his face was a silent question. What was it about him?

She was a fool. A fool who, for a moment, didn't feel alone or defective. Who'd watched a man make something beautiful out of a power she'd only ever feared. It was a contradiction.

He was a contradiction.

Sera took a step back, but Vasso reached for her.

"What are you doing?"

He pulled a piece of dried grass from her hair.

"Oh." She let out a breath.

"Relax, Subdina."

"What does *Subdina* mean?" The word was awkward on her tongue. In her years of studies, she'd only read portions of the old language. Asking Al would be the next logical thing, but something told her she wanted to hear it from Vasso's lips.

Vasso placed his hands in his pockets, his dark brows pinched together as if he was deciding whether he should tell her. Instead, he smirked and said, "I'll tell you one day." Then he turned toward the manor.

Sera followed him.

His shoulders swayed with each step. An effortless swagger that he probably didn't even realize he had, but with each run of a hand through his hair... What wasn't he telling her? Vasso walked into the dark cave tunnel.

More. She needed to train more, but knew better to demand it this time. Her darkness's laugh echoed through her head.

Back in the tunnel, waiting for her eyes to adjust, she could sense him mere inches away. His magic flowed off him and over her like an exhale, and she couldn't deny that she craved the feel of it mixing with hers, along with the lingering smell of him that seemed to follow her wherever she went. A clench in her chest made her heart beat faster. She wanted to touch him, get that sensation back. The blooming in her chest, the unfurling of leaves...

Slowly, his face became clear. She wondered if the cut of his jaw would feel the same under her fingertips as it had felt under her magic. Sera raised her hand.

"Don't." His breath shuddered. His dark brows were pinched tight in confusion... or was it horror?

"But..."

"Please," he begged and left her in the dark.

Chapter Forty-One

Seraphina

He had left her there. Alone. In the dark, with her breathing so loudly, she wanted to scream. She had been a fool to think he would accept her advance.

Had it been an advance? She didn't even know. All she had wanted was to experience that rush of their magic mixing.

And to feel his jaw and throat.

"I'm fully capable of embarrassing myself. I don't need you to remind me."

Her magic laughed at her before thankfully going silent.

Sera pushed her hair off her shoulders and finally moved. It was getting late, dinner was expected, and...

Her stomach dropped. Why couldn't she hate him? He obviously didn't want anything to do with her. But today, she hadn't put a small fox out of its misery. She hadn't lit things on fire. No, today they'd made something beautiful.

She could still picture what he looked like in the rays of light peeking through the canopy of shadow above them. The light had settled on the dark hair of his brows, down his straight, regal nose, across the full pink lips of his smile, against his fair skin.

Sera shook the thought away. Fool, fool, fool.

As Sera crossed through the mirrored pool chamber on the way back to her room, Ophelia called out, "Seraphina, don't worry about changing for dinner. It will be casual." The oracle turned back to her threads, and the blue glow on the far side of the lake pulsed with each movement of the witch's hand.

Casual.

She was pretty sure she was living inside a bad joke. A demon lord who sings to her magic, an all-seeing oracle who speaks in riddles, and a warlock she could potentially kill with a touch walk into a tavern.

A terrible joke. One that was becoming so entangled she had no idea how to get herself out of it.

Nora.

That was her true north. She needed a doorway. No more shadow trees or wasting time; she needed Vasso to teach her control. How stupid could she have been... She hadn't even asked him. Sera groaned, then entered her room and immediately stripped out of her black leathers into brown trousers, boots, and her Legion tunic. She let her hair fall in clustered curls around her. Eventually, she'd need some cream to help with the frizz, but one more night wouldn't hurt.

What was far more pressing was figuring out what lie she'd tell Alistair next so she could train again tomorrow. She was sure an upset stomach would only work for so long.

Sera pressed the heels of her palms hard into her eyes and rubbed. She hoped she looked like she'd been sleeping most of the day. She'd be screwed if Alistair had actually gone into her room to check up on her. Well, let him call her bluff.

Vasso's words drifted over her. *Why don't you ask your captain what happened to his clan?* Dread slithered through her like an eel. She had a feeling she wasn't going to like what he had to say about it.

Sera knocked on Alistair's door. Nothing. She knocked again, and silence was the only response. After a few moments, she turned the handle and peeked inside.

The room was organized. His bed was made with folded corners despite the thick, elaborate duvet, and his weapons were laid out in a perfect line.

Not a single thing was out of place.

Tempted to turn one of the swords slightly askew to see if he would notice, she plopped on his bed, unbothered by the creases she created, and burrowed her face in his pillow.

How did she get here? All desperate and longing? *A stupid crush from childhood, that's how.*

A clattering in the bathing room had her jolt upright, and the door swung open.

Alistair walked into the room, running a towel over his face, the rest of his glorious body on display. Sera covered her eyes with a yelp when the image of his massive member seared itself into her retinas.

He really is built to inflict damage.

"Fuck, Sera!" he yelled. She peeked through her fingers while he wrapped the towel low around his hips. "What are you doing in here?"

It wasn't only the black blood across the front of the towel that gave her pause; it was the smell. Ash mixed with iron, and the metal tang hit her tongue as she looked at Alistair.

His hair wasn't wet. He hadn't just finished bathing. Undressed, yes... but covered in blood. Welts spanned his arms and face. And she couldn't help but wonder for a second if her blood would do the same. "Why are you covered in demon blood, Alistair?" The heat from her cheeks faded.

"What are you doing in my room?" His voice was a low growl.

"I came to walk with you to dinner. Why is there blood all over you?" She pointed to his arm, which was now covered with nasty red splotches underneath the black blood. "I thought you were still injured and couldn't travel?" She rose from the bed.

Why don't you ask your captain what happened to his clan? Again, Vasso's voice rattled through her. Her mouth went dry.

"You should have knocked," he said, crossing the room and gathering his clean uniform.

"I did. You didn't answer, but that isn't my question, is it? Where the fuck were you, Al?" His face was set in a hard line. "You traveled, didn't you?"

Al glared at her, his knuckles turning white around the Legion uniform in his hand. He closed his eyes and sighed.

"How long?" she asked.

"Minnow." He took a step toward her. Sera reared back.

"Do not Minnow me. You've been breathing down my neck, asking me where I've been, what I've been doing. I think I deserve an answer."

"I'm not the one in danger here." His lip curled.

She raised her chin to meet his eye. "That parasite might have said otherwise. The burnout... Those marks." Sera pointed to his face.

"A few days." He scratched the purpling welt on his cheek. "I've only been practicing."

"Do not fucking lie to me right now," she said. "You don't get covered in blood by practicing traveling. What happened to Snik's clan?"

Alistair threw the coven-blue uniform to the floor and crossed his arms. The cords in his neck stood out, his face deadly still. "Who told you to ask me that?"

"It doesn't matter." Sera backed up a step.

"Did *Lord Vasso*?"

She wouldn't give him up. Obviously, Al was hiding something. "Just tell me!"

"They were slain! The woodland goblins were ordered to be executed by the Council. I had nothing to do with it; it was Crag and his company."

Sera raised a shaking hand to her mouth. "They are innocent," she whispered. "You know they do no harm."

"They were orders, Seraphina. The Council wants demons dead... so we kill them. The goblins might not have been able to retaliate, but you know others would. They've been slaughtering us for centuries."

Her stomach dropped. She could understand his reasoning, she supposed. Her family had been so far removed from the Legion's casualty list since her father had died. But Snik was just a small creature. And his kind lived in burrows and glens.

She could almost smell their burning flesh. But when she closed her eyes, willing the phantom stench away, it wasn't small goblins she saw; it was the bodies of those humans in the village of Feybury. The feel of the people who'd been caught in her blaze in the tavern.

"Oh, and by the way," Alistair said in an almost sneer. "The ceasefire has ended. We're back at war."

The room spun. War. She swallowed against the burning at the back of her throat. "When?"

"Can we talk about this after I wash?" He pointed to the welts turning indigo on his arms. They looked painful, but he didn't seem to be bleeding anywhere. Still, he stood there, waiting for permission, with every dip and swell of muscle on display. How many times had she thought about running her hands over him? And now?

Bile threatened to come up.

Sera nodded. She didn't watch him reenter the bathing room chamber, but the sound of splashing water reached her ears; at least she knew he was still there.

Her darkness rumbled through her. Sera let her fingernails bite into her palm, sure to leave half crescents in their wake.

Snik. Poor Snik. His clan slaughtered for nothing. Did he have kin? A mate? Sera glanced at her palms, at the death magic that lay within them.

Thump. Her darkness raged.

Thump. They were back at war.

It was inevitable, her magic hissed. *The threads are pulled.*

War or not, the Council members were monsters for ordering the wood-land goblins' slaughter. She remembered the stench of Crag and his company, the stains of blood on their knees and across their torsos.

Al returned, fully clothed this time. His damp dark hair brushed back in waves, the sides of his mouth drooping in a frown.

"Sit. What I'm about to tell you is confidential. Do you understand?"

Sera lowered herself slowly to the edge of the bed, unsure if it would burst into flames at her touch. Taking a deep breath, she crossed her arms and listened.

"Two nights before we departed from the Citadel's walls, the ceasefire ended."

"That was the day before Nora was taken… They'd delayed the trial. Why wasn't the coven alerted then?" she asked.

"That's the Council's business." He sat in the small writing desk's chair. The wood screamed under his muscled weight.

"So you're telling me that the Solarni coven has been at war since we left the Citadel two weeks ago? And we happen to be holed up in the underground manor with one of the most powerful beings on the planet… who is our active enemy?"

Al swallowed hard. "It would seem so." He leaned forward, forearms settling atop his knees, the brown trousers bunching beneath his elbows.

"And you're just telling me all this now?" Her voice was down to a deadly whisper. The vatra within her turned into a tumultuous violence, roaring in her ears, raging through her veins. Sera shook with restraint.

"It was confidential. I wanted to tell you! Shit, I wanted to, Sera, but I was sworn to secrecy."

"And now that I've caught you, you have no choice but to tell me? Is that what this is?" Sera closed her eyes, willing her magic to calm. It just laughed at her. They needed to get to dinner; they were expected. "I'll meet you in the dining room."

Alistair reached out to grab her hand. Sera snatched it back before he could touch her. With every second she looked at the warlock, a pounding pressure built in her temples.

"Sera, there is more I need to tell you." Those broad shoulders dropped. Whatever he needed to tell her wasn't good. After Snik... knowing they were back at war, her chest already felt tight.

"Tell me later," she said through gritted teeth.

Al shot back in his chair. "Sera—your eyes."

Sera didn't wait to hear whatever bullshit he had to say about her eyes and walked out the door.

She fumed the entire way to the dining room. It didn't help that her magic was humming an unfamiliar tune in her mind.

"Will you stop that? You're making me look insane."

It laughed, but finally shut up.

The dining room chandeliers swayed in their nightly waltz, casting dancing shadows along the walls and floor. The constant light interruption was making her headache worse with every step toward the finely set table.

Ophelia was at her place setting. "Sit next to me, dear. You seem ruffled."

Sera didn't object and waited for the lesser demons to change around her plates and cutlery. The lesser demons looked so much like goblins. Their ears weren't nearly as large as Snik's, and they were black with fur, but she couldn't stop picturing their bodies strewed... their homes burning. She blinked back tears.

War had taken her father. It had taken mothers, brothers, and daughters. Would either side give up? Or would the result be the complete annihilation of the dark ones?

Dominick's last message had said that aliato were in the Citadel. Sera gripped her raven pendant and slid it back and forth on its cord.

An alliance. That could be the only reason both races would be communicating with the Council. But did her companions know? Alistair must have been traveling back and forth with information much longer than he'd admitted. They'd been apart enough that he could go without her noticing. Sera pursed her lips and glanced at Ophelia. Did the oracle know? Did Vasso?

Around and around the shadows danced. She swore that out of the corner of her vision, she could see sprites among them, twirling with their wings flitting.

"Come, sit, dear." Ophelia motioned to the seat beside her.

Sera obeyed and plopped down, still zipping her pendant back and forth. If the Council was willing to kill off an entire clan of goblins, what was to stop them from trying to eradicate other gentle dark ones, like the domovoi? And where was the goddess in this mess?

Shadow had been the champion of the world. She was supposed to protect the dark ones, protect Eraphon herself.

Shadow was locked away... waiting to be awoken.

"The world feels a bit darker today, doesn't it?" Ophelia said. The oracle brought a glass of water to her lips. The lines in her face seemed deeper.

"I suppose so, yes." Sera rubbed her temples.

The far door swung open as Vasso strode to his place at the head of the table. His easy smile from earlier was gone, replaced by a jaw clenched tight and a constant rubbing of his brow. His black dinner jacket was unbuttoned, along with the top of his shirt. Reddened bags were under his eyes, as if he'd been sleeping.

Yet no matter how many times she glanced at him, he didn't look up.

"Lord Vasso," Ophelia said with a smile.

"Ophelia," he grunted back.

Alistair filed in next. His hair was still damp, his steps rigid as he took the seat nearest Vasso, clearing his throat.

Silence was thick in the air until the first course was served, and Ophelia popped open a bottle of wine.

"You simply must try this, Lord Vasso. You, too, Alistair and Seraphina. I think you'll all find it delightful." She poured the wine, her blue robes draping elegantly across the table as she decanted it into the goblets.

The deep red sloshing in the crystal reminded Sera of blood.

"My dear?" Ophelia asked.

"Not right now, thank you." Sera swallowed, watching Vasso and Al under lowered lashes, trying to figure out if everyone in this room had been lying to her.

They have.

Sera winced at the tinks and scrapes of polite dining. Each clink grated as she tried to untie the knot of information Al had given her. She fully understood why Ophelia hated the chandeliers. The constant sway of light was making her agitated.

"Do you need anything replenished in your rooms?" Vasso hid a yawn behind the back of his hand.

"I'm fine," she said. Alistair continued to stare at her and emptied the wineglass in one go. Vasso drained his and tapped his fingers on the table.

He was nervous...

"Well, the conversation is delightful this evening," Ophelia said. "Since no one else will speak, I will inform you of my intentions for the next few days before we are due to leave." She took another sip of water. "I hid my prophecy grimoire a few years ago and plan on retrieving it. Seraphina, do you think you'd like to help me?"

She was running out of time. The pressure in her chest increased with each beat of her heart. She needed a doorway. "Sure, I'll help."

Alistair's face slammed into his first course. Pink seafood bisque splattered all over the white tablecloth.

"Al!" Sera leaped from her chair.

As soon as his name was out of her mouth, Vasso slid to the side, knocked out cold on the floor.

"Finally," Ophelia said, rising from her place.

"What happened to them?"

"I thought you and I should have some time together." The oracle raised her brow at Alistair and Vasso. "The men get in the way."

"You drugged them?"

Gurgling bubbles splattered around Alistair's mouth and nose.

"A witch never tells. Come, Seraphina."

As frustrated as she was at the pair of them, she wasn't sure drugging was the solution. Sera crossed the room, lifted Al's head, placed it on the table so he wasn't breathing in soup, and reluctantly followed Ophelia.

CHAPTER FORTY-TWO

SERAPHINA

The carved dark hallways brought her to a part of the manor she'd never seen before. There was a slight incline to the tunnel, and the air smelled more like soil here.

"Where are we going?"

"To get my grimoire. Didn't you listen to me?" Ophelia said. Rounding a bend, they approached a doorway that Sera guessed must lead to the surface.

"Right now?" As if she didn't have enough to deal with.

Ophelia gave her an exasperated sigh. "You might also find what you're looking for."

"The doorways?"

The oracle didn't respond; she just pushed open the wooden door, revealing what appeared to be a makeshift stable that had been created in the mouth of a cave. The aroma of hay and droppings overpowered the earthy scent of the tunnels. Wooden stalls separated the horses; two out of twenty were occupied.

Ophelia stopped before a chestnut mare. "You take Ponic." She pointed to the end stall.

Sera approached the black horse Vasso had ridden when they'd first met. "You planned this." Ponic's nostrils flared at her raised hand, breathing in her scent.

"Of course I planned this." Ophelia pulled the mare from the stable, leading her outside. "Do you want your answers or not?"

She did. More than anything. The insanity of the last few months had been exhausting. She wished she could go back to normal—be normal.

You didn't ask for normal. You asked for power, her magic whispered.

"Oh shut up," Sera said back.

"What was that?" Ophelia called to her from outside the cave entrance.

"Nothing!" Sera opened the stall door and approached the massive horse slowly. "All right, boy. Please don't bite or kick me." He snorted in what she hoped was more of a laugh and less of a promise.

She led the stallion to the dirt path where Ophelia was sitting atop the mare against a twilight sky. Above the ironoak branches floated clouds in deep plums and dark blues, almost the color of the night sky. Sera hoisted her leg over Ponic's broad back and settled in the saddle, her feet barely reaching the stirrups. He was massive, and she hadn't ridden in a long time.

Riding lessons were only for Daedeth or Legion members. It had been her mother's placement that allowed her to learn as a child. Basics. Lavinia always wanted her daughters to learn the basics of everything. Sera supposed she should be grateful for that in this moment.

Ponic instinctively walked to the mare's side.

"There are demons out here. The agbris. Are you sure we should go out there alone?" Sera asked.

"The exact question I was about to ask myself..."

Sera froze. Ophelia's grin dropped to a straight line. A thick fog sprang forward, tendrils reaching for the horse's reins.

"How are you awake? I put enough belldon in that wine to put down an elken," Ophelia said, carefully rearranging her robes in front of her.

Vasso emerged from the shadows behind them. "You think simple alchemy could keep me out for long enough to steal my horse and escape my grounds?" There was a menacing tone to his voice and a rigidity to him like a cat ready to pounce.

"We have things we must see to, my lord. You can either let us be or come along, but I will not have you keeping me from my grimoire."

"You are getting bold, witch." Vasso stalked closer, his eyes glowing a brighter red as he neared Sera.

Sera wished a hole would open beneath her and Ponic. Shadow, she'd take a hole big enough to swallow the continent right about now. Releasing Ponic's reins, she let Vasso's magic take them. "I'd like to say that I had nothing to do with this..."

"Oh, hush, witchling," Ophelia hissed.

Moons, Ophelia had a death wish. Based on the violence promised in the demon lord's gaze and the way he rubbed his temple, she was sure Vasso didn't appreciate being drugged at his own table.

Before Sera could dismount, Vasso rushed forward, kicked his foot into Ponic's stirrup, and was behind her.

She hadn't been ready for his touch, the blazing heat of his chest at her back. Sera leaned forward, attempting to put some distance between them.

"Saddle me another horse. I don't need to ride with you."

Vasso looped his arm around her middle, pulling her tight to him. He was solid, and the power flowing off him surrounded her like a warm blanket. His thighs cradling hers, his scent awakening something eager. "You're staying right here."

That warmth that had wrapped around her went straight to her core, then lower.

"I'd prefer it." Her voice was breathy. Not that she had meant it to be, but now that he had her in his arms...

"Do not move." His words hot on her ear, his grip flexing around her side. "I have only the two horses."

This was more than she had anticipated for the evening. After he'd left her alone in the darkness of the cave, Sera had thought herself daft for wanting to touch him. But now that a good portion of her was, she didn't know what to do with the sensation. Her magic was... calm. It always seemed to be when she was around him. And that burning tug deep in her chest had gone slack.

"Are we ready, then?" Ophelia looked mighty pleased with herself.

Vasso let out a frustrated sigh that tickled her hair. She turned around to glance at the lord, who continued to rub his brow.

"Aha!" Ophelia's face cracked into smile lines and crow's feet. "I knew the belldon was still affecting you." She preened, then gave her mare a small kick and took off.

"Hold the reins." His hand brushed hers as she took them. Vasso let go of her middle, and she instantly missed his touch. Foolish, foolish witch. Ponic picked up to a trot after Ophelia and her mare. "I don't think I need to explain the dangers in these woods for you, do I?"

"Ophelia was granting me answers. Ones that I had asked you for, by the way."

"Ah, so you're stubborn and reckless. Good to know."

Ponic's trotting set them in a steady movement that was wonderful and terrifying at the same time. "This wasn't my idea!"

Vasso ripped the buttons from his cuffs and forcibly rolled his sleeves above his elbows. "You are on this horse." He pulled her flush to him again. "Therefore, you are just as guilty as she."

"You can be such an ass, you know that."

Vasso leaned over, and the curve of his cheek met hers. "I am so much more than a piece of ass, Subdina."

Sera reared back her elbow with the intention of bruising at least one of his ribs, but before she could do any damage, Vasso kicked Ponic into a full gallop.

"Oh no, no no no…" Sera lurched forward, gripping the saddle horn for dear life. Dying today would be unfortunate, more so if she was kicked off a horse rather than, say, slashed to death by a demonic creature.

"I've got you." Vasso's voice was low, his arm steady around her waist.

"A minute ago, you wanted to kill me."

His chuckle hummed through her. "As I told you before, if I wanted to kill you, I would have done it the day you walked into my woods."

Branches and trees rushed past at a dizzying speed. In an even worse move, she glanced down at the ground, watching Ponic's hooves beat the dirt path into submission.

"I won't let harm come to you, Seraphina."

"I think I'm okay right here," she yelled back to him. Her mouth flooded with saliva, and she choked down the little bit of dinner she had eaten.

A powerful arm slithered up between her breasts and gripped the curve of her shoulder and neck. With one powerful jolt, she was upright again.

"I said, I've got you."

The strength of his arm across her body had her gasping. The way he clung to her as if she were something precious sprouted a dangerous feeling in her chest. They did not belong. Despite their magic or the unspoken understanding between them, this would never… could never…

Subdina, her magic said in answer. If she hadn't practically been sitting in Vasso's lap, she would have demanded that voice tell her what it meant. Clearly, Vasso and their magic were in some sort of alliance that she knew nothing about, and Sera was getting sick of it.

Ponic leaped over a fallen branch. She screamed and clamped her hands around Vasso's forearm. He pulled her tighter to him, settling her head against his chest, just below his collarbone. The muscle beneath flexed as he gripped the reins, steering the beast below them nimbly through the trees.

"If your nails weren't sinking into my arm, I'd guess that you rather enjoyed this."

"Nothing like being held hostage to really put a witch at ease."

Vasso barked a laugh, and she couldn't help the corners of her mouth tilting upward.

He stroked his thumb against the hollow of her throat. She knew, deep in her bones, that he was only trying to comfort her, but... every swipe of the pad of his thumb against her skin was another hitch in her breath.

Another shiver down her spine.

Another pulse at the apex of her thighs.

When was the last time she'd been caressed? Shadow, when was the last time she'd lain naked against a man, letting him trail fingers over her goosefleshed skin? She and Alistair had kissed, which had turned into burns covering his lips, but before that... it had been a long time.

Letting out a silent sigh, Sera closed her eyes and just... felt.

Her magic danced within her, and she wondered if that was why Vasso was so warm against her back. Was his magic flitting in the same way? Did it hum in tune to a song she didn't know? She wanted to know it. Wanted his fingers to trail lower. Wanted her heart to beat faster.

After a few moments, the stiffness in Vasso's shoulder softened, and he stopped his thumb but didn't raise his hand from the bow of her neck.

They'd finally caught up to Ophelia, who was racing at reckless speed. Her blue robes whipped behind her like a flag on one of the human ships that sailed around the Citadel's peninsula.

With each passing second, the forest grew darker. Ophelia threw a mage light into the air, illuminating the path between the trees.

They had headed west when they left Vasso's manor. It was hard for her to determine how far they'd traveled without her map; she would have to estimate it, if a doorway was truly there.

Ophelia slowed, turning at a stone marker. Above them, the three moons of Eraphon were cresting the trees, drenching the branches in a pale radiance.

"We're here," Ophelia said with a grin. Her blond-white hair was wild about her, but the blue of her eyes almost glowed in the dark.

Vasso dismounted, leaving Sera to shudder at the absence of his warmth.

"I can get down on my own." She swatted his hands away.

"Stubborn." He shrugged and left her to her own devices.

Sera swung her leg over Ponic's rump, miscalculating the clearance she needed, and the back of her knee caught the edge of the saddle. Somehow, she saved herself from landing on her ass in the dirt. Thankfully, Vasso wasn't watching.

"Is this..."

"A pile of rocks that used to be a castle? Yes." Vasso crossed his arms.

Ophelia was already far in the ruins. The dim glow of the light above her stood out like a beacon. At least she wouldn't be lost easily.

"We're on the border of the Emerald Glade, aren't we?"

He raised a brow at her. "We're close. You're informed for a Solarni witch. At least more than I'd expected."

"Ophelia was once a Solarni witch. Are you calling her dim?"

Vasso put his hands on his hips and gave her an incredulous look. She decided to put her attention elsewhere.

Ancient stone slabs emerged from the ground, and on them the rough shape of a building. Sera recognized where the round turrets once were. Following the crumbling stone walls, she could make out where the gate had been. Divots from centuries of wagon wheels that led into the dilapidated castle were now filled with soft grass.

Sera turned to Vasso and halted.

The moons' rays washed over him. It looked like he'd been born from their essence. As if the largest one, Nubenia, had floated him down on one of her moonbeams as a gift to Eraphon. Vasso's gaze met hers, and he smirked. "Like what you see?"

"You're just... so pale."

Vasso scoffed.

"Are those rock guardians?"

Erected at each corner, bodies of giant beasts with scales and claws wrapped the wall in stone limbs. Most of their vicious heads had crumbled away as the rest of the castle had. But Sera remembered seeing their snarling reptilian faces in tomes throughout the archives.

The rock guardians alone dated this castle back five thousand years. Possibly older.

"Aah, the famed beasts of Shadow. They say when the goddess awakens, the guardians will come back to life." He placed his hands in his pockets, taking the stone beasts in.

"That's ridiculous. Nothing could live inside stone."

Vasso shrugged, unbothered by the looming presence of the castle. "If I had to guess," he started in his mocking tone, "I bet your Citadel's libraries are probably lacking in the ancient lore of our peoples. Not only about the war, but of the traditions themselves. You probably don't even know what Shadow's gates look like."

"You do?"

"I've seen them from afar. They are connected to Gehenna, after all."

"Could you—I mean, do you have a painting of them? Back in your manor?" To see the gates of the afterlife would be a dream. He was right: They had no renditions of the gates listed in the archives. At least from what Sera could gather.

"And what would you give me if I did?" That smirk was once again plastered on his face, making his jaw sharper and his features more devious.

"Nothing," she gritted. "No more bargains." Sera huffed and walked through the arched entry, trying to make out the rest of the buildings and their condition in the glow of Ophelia's mage light on the other side of the castle. The oracle was pacing back and forth, searching for something.

"Watch your step." Vasso pointed out a barely visible crack in the foundation of the stone staircase.

"I'm perfectly capable of watching where I'm going."

"You could really be more pleasant, you know that?" Vasso said.

Sera hopped to the top of the crumbling staircase just to prove her point. "Just because you're teaching me how to use my magic doesn't mean I have to be *pleasant* to you."

"I'd sure like to meet the person who taught you *manners*," Vasso grumbled and climbed the steps behind her.

And wouldn't that be a recipe for disaster? Her mother prying into his mind, and Vasso, no doubt, ripping her apart with his vatra. Sera twisted her long hair around her wrist and threw it over her shoulder.

Oh, how she had wished Ophelia's potion had worked. Then maybe she wouldn't feel so...

Flustered?

Sera ignored her magic's whispering and followed Ophelia to the far corner of the crumbling courtyard. An orb of blue light lifted from Ophelia's fingers, and the oracle whispered her spell. Ivy curled back from a rotten wooden door in the floor.

"Help me with this, won't you? I'm not as strong as I once was."

Sera lifted the iron handle. A stench of rot and mildew emerged from the hole below. "Oh, Shadow, that's vile." Ophelia dropped her mage light into the space below, revealing a rope ladder. "That doesn't look safe," Sera said as she eyed the fraying knots.

"It's an adventure, remember? Sometimes you've got to take risks."

"I've got to admit that I agree with Seraphina," Vasso said.

"You weren't supposed to be here." Ophelia pulled her long blond hair together, tucking it into the back of her robe. Before anyone else could interject, she lowered herself down.

Sera whispered a prayer and threw a kernel of power to Shadow, then gingerly followed the oracle into the dark.

CHAPTER FORTY-THREE

SERAPHINA

Sera's feet sank into moss and fungi when she dropped from the bottom rung. The smell wasn't exactly worse, but there was an underlying scent of something sweet had her suspicious that it was a tomb.

"Are you sure your grimoire is going to be readable?" She waved her hand before her nose, looking up to see a grimacing Vasso. "The mildew alone has probably ruined the pages, Ophelia."

"I'm not an idiot. I placed a preservation spell around it." Ophelia waved away her question, and Sera wondered if she also had a spell that made her unaffected by the stench.

Vasso landed hard beside her, causing spores and dust to plume into the air.

Sera plugged her nose. "And I thought it couldn't get any worse."

He hunched over to keep his head from scraping the ceiling. "What have you brought us into, Ophelia?"

"Mind the spiders. They're more helpful than you think," Ophelia said and marched forward.

Sera frowned.

"Seraphina," Ophelia's voice chimed. "What do you know of Lavinia's family?"

"Considering that Lavinia is my mother... it would be my family as well. But I know that my grandmother died when my mother was my age."

"Did she have any siblings?"

"No, just her."

"Hmm..." Ophelia ducked in front of her, and Sera got a faceful of web.

"Damn it!" she screamed and swiped in frantic slaps. Vasso snickered behind her.

"I told you to mind the spiders."

Vasso's low baritone filled the damp tunnel. "Ophelia, why did you hide your grimoire down here?"

"Can't let the universe's secrets get in the wrong hands, can I?"

Underground, the decline was slight. There'd been no turns, just a straight shot to... somewhere. As the minutes drudged on, Sera noticed a heaviness to the air. Everything was damp. Her cheeks, the walls—

Sera's feet slipped on the wet stone, and she was falling... straight into Vasso's arms.

"I've got you."

Her heart slammed into his chest before he stood her upright. "Thank you," Sera said, straightening her tunic.

"So you do have manners... You're welcome. See, I can be pleasant too."

"Moons, you're insufferable."

Vasso chuckled, and she made sure to be more cautious with future steps.

"Here we are! Let us have some more light." Ophelia clapped her hands, and thousands of candles perched on stone ledges flared to life.

The cavern held—no surprise, this being Ophelia—another pool of water. It was smaller than the one in Vasso's manor, and the candlelight reflected off the surface. Deep limestone caverns housed minerals that had crystallized on the walls, creating a delicate yet symmetrical garden of rocky blooms.

"You like that trick, don't you?" Sera asked, admiring the crystals beneath the water.

Ophelia had used that same movement to light the same type of candles when Sera and Alistair had fallen through the stone. Her cheeks grew warm at the thought of his lips on hers, then cooled with another reminder of betrayal. He had known, this entire time, that they were at war.

And Nora was in the underworld. With the enemy.

Sera's stomach rolled, and she coughed to cover the sound of her gag. The likelihood she'd reach her sister before demons killed her was worse now than it had been. Sera had been so stupid.

But... but... her mother.

Sera rubbed her forehead. Her mother had known. She was a master mastria, a shoo-in to become the next Council member, and she'd sent Sera on a suicide mission. What if her mother didn't want her to return?

"Calm your mind, Seraphina," Ophelia said.

"Are you a mastria now too?"

"No, my dear, but I can see the agony on your face. It isn't worth it." Ophelia's hands shot over the pool and called, "*Konac laz blizt.*"

Sera glanced at Vasso, who was in the corner of the room, studying the wall. Sera swallowed the lump in her throat that had lodged itself with her thoughts of Nora and her mother. There had to be an explanation. Her mother wasn't *that* cruel.

Deep from the depths of the pool, threads swam to the surface like golden eels in a school of past and future.

"Ophelia, before you start whatever this is"—Sera motioned to the golden strands—"please, could you pull my sister's? I have to know she's okay."

The oracle's normally sharp gaze softened a touch. Ophelia rolled her eyes back, and forward came a blue strand. With a twirl of her wrist, a projected image flickered to life. It was Nora. Sitting on a bed, a little pale but whole and unharmed.

Sera took a step toward the image. "When was this?"

"Seconds ago."

Sera dropped to her knees. Her breath came out like broken moth wings, and tears burned her eyes so fiercely that she winced. "Thank the goddess she's all right." She didn't care that her face was swamped with tears, that her knees were soaked with whatever standing water had been left in this godsforsaken place. Her sister was alive. "Can you show me more?"

Ophelia approached her, squatted, and took her hands. "This I can promise you: Honora Wildrick does not die belowground."

"Oh gods. Thank you," Sera cried out again, letting a new stream of tears break their dam.

"Now let's get you up. Tonight was for my grimoire, but I promised you some answers."

Sera nodded, and Ophelia helped her to her feet.

She could feel Vasso's eyes on her. That hum of calm rushing through her soul, but she didn't want to acknowledge it, whatever it was.

"You've been busy," Ophelia said.

Black bands wrapped around countless golden threads now, so many more than before. "If I'd known it was called vatra magic, I would have asked my mother to find a tutor." Sera dried her eyes.

"Your mother cannot help you." Ophelia's voice was cold.

Sera frowned. She'd wanted to believe her mother had her best interests at heart, but Lavinia's motivations were not always clear.

"Soon," Ophelia started. "You will have choices to make. The world as we know it hangs in the balance. The prophecy has been pulled."

"What is this prophecy?" She crossed her arms.

"More like... which prophecy?" Vasso said, now at her side.

The oracle gave them a half smile. "Tell me, witchling, have you ever wondered why I was shunned?" Ophelia's lilting voice ricocheted off the damp walls of the cavern. "Do you know why they fear me?"

Fear? Sera shifted on her feet. Chair Renata had wanted her back, which she assumed was due to her skill in making accurate predictions. Ophelia claimed she could see much further into the future than any other oracle she knew of. Probably further than Chair Renata herself.

"No."

"They shunned me not because of my power but because of the knowledge I kept from them—the truth. I could alter the very existence of realms on Eraphon. I was surprised they let me live when they found my journals. That is, until you appeared in my threads." Ophelia turned back to the water. "You were made for more."

The golden threads in the pool danced across the water, organizing themselves in a line. The bands of darkness turned to solid strands of black. The only hints of gold were at the tops and bottoms of the strands. "Some of these are almost wholly black." She could hear Vasso shift uncomfortably beside her, but she gave him no mind.

"It indicates your current standing on the path to come."

Sera zipped her raven on the cord around her neck. "You say this is the path I'm leaning? More death?"

"Just because it's black doesn't mean it's death," Vasso said.

"Precisely." Ophelia maneuvered the threads with black bands forward.

"My magic has caused death and destruction. That bit of mercy still involved death. It only functions how I want it to if Vasso is near." Sera looked at him then. His brows scrunched in concentration, his eyes glued to the floor. "I just don't know why this is happening, or what I'm supposed to do with it."

One lonely thread snapped taut from the water to the ceiling and glided forward. Ophelia pulled at the purple line, and a projected image appeared on the wall where she'd just seen her sister's face.

A woman was giving birth atop a heap of blankets with a man beside her. They were sitting on a wooden floor, with simple furniture scattered around the room. A table covered in plants and potions. Flora hanging from the perlin beams.

The memory came into focus, and she recognized her mother's face. Slick with sweat, writhing in pain, with a swollen belly and knees spread wide. Her hair was free from its braids, long and spiraling, just like her own. She'd never seen her mother's hair down like that before, never known her mother to dabble with potions either.

"Is this my birth?"

Ophelia nodded once.

"But that isn't my father," she said, to herself more than Ophelia. She watched as her mother pushed. Saw the head crown, and her body expelled. The pale man lifted her and placed a single kiss atop her head.

"Darius?" Vasso whispered.

The man's face held so much pride it made her heart clench. Sera touched the top of her head as if she could feel the kiss he'd placed almost twenty-four years ago. "You knew him?" she asked Vasso, who wouldn't look away from the projection.

"I did…" Vasso whispered.

The man in the projection kissed her mother then, and she noticed his eyes. They were green, like hers, and around his neck was the same stone raven she wore. Sera gripped it in her hands.

"Are you saying this is my father?" She turned to Ophelia.

"You needed to see something true." Caution was laced in Ophelia's words. "Much of your life has been a lie, Seraphina."

Vasso was silent, as if what he was seeing was just as shocking as it was for her.

Sera swung on Ophelia. "If he's alive, you need to show me." She pointed to the golden column standing tall above the water. Those threads were the future, or at least one possible version of it. If he was in one of those outcomes, she needed to see it.

"I will not show you everything you want to know. Some secrets you need to discover on your own."

"Ophelia, please," she begged. "You don't understand what it's been like. I thought that relic in Feybury did this to me." Sera let plumes of darkness fall from her hands, dripping like ink into water. "But if the man I thought was my father isn't..." In the image, the green-eyed man looked at her mother so lovingly that it nearly broke her.

No one knew what it was like to have to earn every ounce of affection. Transactional, that's what her life had been under the care of her mother. If he was out there, maybe he could teach her how to use this magic. Maybe he'd understand her. "I'll beg. I'll bargain. Whatever you want—please." She didn't feel the stone as she fell to her knees. Nor the heavy tears falling down her cheeks, only the mixture of hope and desperation clenching and releasing in her chest. He had to be alive.

Ophelia took a step back.

"Show me the future, Ophelia!" Sera cried.

The rock beneath her trembled. Ripples broke the smooth surface of the pool. Her darkness filled the chamber, clawing its way up the walls, dimming the candles, reaching out with a mind of its own.

"Seraphina," Vasso called to her, but she wouldn't hear it.

"*Now*, Ophelia."

Ophelia's eyes rolled into the back of her head, her arms stiff over the water, and thread after thread pulled forward, twisting and turning around each other, before the images began to flash.

At first, Sera didn't know what she was looking at. The moments of her future blinked by until she realized it was one face. Over and over.

"You need to stop this," Vasso said.

She'd never heard his voice so soft. Flash after flash, she saw him. White hair, strong dark brows, that smile that hurt to look at.

But it wasn't just the images of him; it was the *way* he looked at her. First exasperation, an expression she was used to seeing, but then kindness and laughter. His head tilted back with his eyes closed. Then he was panting hard above her, covered in blood. In these images, Vasso was looking at her like that man—her father—had looked at her mother, tenderness traced in every line. Image after image.

Sera glanced at Vasso, who stood there, that sharp jaw grinding, his eyes watching the same scenes she was.

It wasn't just laughter and tenderness in these projections. There was anger. His red eyes bore into hers, but underneath it was concern, not hate.

"Seraphina, stop it," Vasso gritted out.

"I'm not doing this," Sera said. She didn't want to look away. They rode on horseback together, sat in bedrooms and in throne rooms. She recognized the white walls of the Citadel in one image where his features were lined in panic.

In the flashes of further images, he was talking to her like she was an old friend, like they were whispering secrets with one another, and then it turned to them writhing in the throes of ecstasy.

Vasso grabbed her upper arm and turned her toward him. "You're not doing it on purpose, but you need to let her go." His throat bobbed. His shoulders had dropped like the corners of his mouth.

"What is this?" she whispered to him.

"Let her go."

Sera let out a shuddering breath. *Release,* she thought. And the flashing projections stopped. Vasso was running to Ophelia, and all Sera could do was gasp.

The last thread, displaying its future memory, was of Vasso, but there was no life there. He was pale. Black blood trailed from his mouth. His beautiful gray eyes were unseeing. She knew those hands cradling his face. She lifted her hand to see the scar Nora had given her when they were children, side by side with the one pressed against Vasso's dead cheek.

CHAPTER FORTY-FOUR

SERAPHINA

"I didn't mean to show her." Vasso was holding Ophelia's elbow, keeping her upright. In the flickering candlelight, the oracle looked like she'd aged fifty years.

"You knew about this?" Sera pointed to Vasso's dead face hovering above the water. "Both of you knew this could happen?"

Her magic dissipated with the shattering of her heart. They were linked, she and Vasso. More than she realized. More than the magic they shared.

"There is still free will," Ophelia said. "You can choose not to indulge."

Sera glanced at the demon lord, who was making a point not to look at her. "Vasso?"

He was silent.

"You—you're dead, and those are my hands." Sera raised her palm to show him the scar. "And my father? You knew him too?"

Vasso's head snapped up. "I had no idea he was your father."

"But you knew him!"

One nod was all he gave her.

"And am I to believe that the reason you knew him was because he's a demon? A friend of yours?"

With Ophelia steadied on her feet, Vasso let go of her. He redirected his attention toward Sera, his lips pressed together in a firm line. "Is he a demon? Yes. I knew him through the circles, nothing more. He's been missing for a century."

"Well, he was obviously near the Citadel having relations with my mother, otherwise I wouldn't be here." She needed to get out of there before the walls caved in. Spots already invaded the edges of her vision, and she just wanted to take a deep breath that didn't involve mold and rot and death. Quick steps into the dark tunnel, then onward to the entrance. That was all she could do.

"Seraphina, come back," Vasso said.

She didn't stop. She didn't care that it was pitch black and she couldn't see an inch in front of her face. It was straight to the surface, and she needed to get out. The rotten air choked her. Her darkness whirled in a fury of all the lies she'd had to unravel, but it was the image of Vasso dead in her hands that made her stomach roll.

Those projections... He'd been so happy. There was love there. Deep and unwavering. Something she'd wished for her entire life.

Sera put out a hand to follow the wall, barely feeling the slime and moss under her fingertips.

How was her father a demon? Which made her half demon. Which made her mother... What, an enemy of the state? The coven had been in open war with demons when she was born. Did the Council know?

Does it matter now?

"Ugh, I don't need to listen to you too," she said back to that phantom voice.

Vasso... he...

He is an option.

Sera huffed. "By the way he looked at me, I'd say he's the only option." Her heart pounded. "No one has ever looked at me like that. Not Alistair... no one."

Moonslight shining into the shaft lit the rest of the way forward. On leaden legs, she ran. Up the ladder and out around the ruins to a small cluster of rock she imagined used to be a well.

"This is such a mess."

Life is rarely easy.

"I'm talking to a fucking voice in my head." Sera ran her hand down her face.

Her magic scoffed. *I don't much like being in here either.*

"Why are you here, then?"

The voice was silent.

"Not even you know."

Taking inventory of the things she'd learned, she focused first on her sister. Nora was alive. At this very moment, her little sister sat on a bed that seemed covered in fine textiles underground.

Her father was a demon.

Her mother— She didn't want to think about Lavinia right now.

Vasso.

A tug pulled at her chest at the thought of him. Dangerous territory. The involuntary shivers her body made when they touched. The way her magic calmed, the way her core heated.

They were tied together somehow. To have that many future moments couldn't be a coincidence.

A crunch of gravel had her looking up.

Vasso strode toward her. His face was unreadable. When they locked eyes, he paused, then let out a breath. "I thought you were a vuk for a second."

"Nope, just a demon witch sitting in the grass." She didn't mean to sound defeated. "Were you ever going to tell me about us?"

Vasso ran his hand through his hair. "If it came up..."

Sera scoffed.

"I want to show you something."

"I don't want to play games with you, Vasso."

The demon lord lowered to his haunches. "You told me once that there was only one way I could earn your forgiveness. Will you let me try?" He held out his hand.

A doorway.

He was going to show her where a doorway was. Sera glared at his outstretched hand. "No bargains," she said.

"Just trying to help you out of the grass."

"All right." His hand was warm, firm in hers. As soon as she was up, she let it go, ignoring the electric sensations bringing her to life. Why did she have to see those images? Why couldn't she have stayed dumb and stupid about that future? "I guess I enthralled Ophelia, didn't I?"

"Yes."

"I'm such a fucking mess." Sera held herself as they walked. The grass swatted at her shins as they trudged farther into the field.

"You're not any more of a mess than the rest of us," he said.

Insects sang in the night, the chirping a peaceful lullaby to the slumbering birds.

"How long have you known? About that future of us?"

Vasso fisted his hand, then released. "I met Ophelia sixty years ago. She was stubborn. Going on and on about prophecies and the future. I didn't believe her, thought she was some insane witch who'd been shunned by the Citadel due to her instability." He glanced at her sidelong. "Until she showed me a few future threads... and I saw you."

"What was I doing?"

He smirked. "I'll tell you when I see it."

He stopped, pointed his chin to the sky, and sniffed. She could smell it too. Ash on the breeze.

"We're close," he said.

They'd reached the edge of the forest. Vasso stepped into the dark shadows under the tree branches, and she followed.

"Vuk. I've seen that before. In a sketchbook that was brought to the Citadel. It looks like a wolf."

"Vicious creatures. I was once obsessed with them. I've never seen one in real life, and no one I know has either. I hovered over their forms in books while perusing Gehenna's libraries. When you were sitting there in the shadows, your eyes were glowing such bright green I thought you might have been one." He slowed his pace. "We're here."

There was a clearing in the trees. A massive boulder stood in the center of a circle of trees, awash in a pale glow. "This is a doorway?" she asked.

Vasso held out his palm. "*Ovarati vas rata, Gehenna.*"

A low hum came from the rock, and with it, the dark outline of a door pushed forward. The moonslight didn't touch the magic along the surface. Skulls, eels, demonic faces, and wings adorned the frame. The ominous hum stopped with a crack. Then a woosh of air pulled her forward, and it was open.

Sera peered in. Stairs led deep into the ground. "How did you know it was here?"

"The chamber we were in is below our feet. I could hear something through the wall. Feel it. Now, are you going to tell me why?"

She wanted to let the words run from her lips. Tell him that the Council of Elders needed to know where they were, how to access them. That it was their terms for sending a band of Legion warriors to save her sister. "My reasons are my own."

He scoffed. "Throwing my words back at me?"

She smirked at him.

"*Zatvori,*" Vasso said, and that humming rang through the stone. A second later, the hole closed, and the doorway was again camouflaged as rock. "Will you forgive me now?"

"For which part? You forcing me to kill that fox, or lying to me about our *loving* futures?"

He stiffened. "The fox. If you do not wish for that future to come to pass, it will not. I won't apologize for instances that haven't happened yet." There was bite to those words. Vasso turned from her, and she grabbed his hand.

"I forgive you, for the fox I mean," she said.

He stared at their joined hands. "It was a surprise to me too."

"What was?"

His eyes locked with hers. They looked like moons themselves when they weren't blazing red. "How happy I was in those images... the *way* I was looking at you," he whispered.

Each throb of her heartbeat banged like a drum in the still moment. The confusion and apprehension she felt were also painted on his face.

It couldn't work. She needed to go to the Citadel to save Nora. She needed to be there for Dominick and the witches and warlocks of Jedan. She wondered how Galene was faring and what new treasures she'd found. None of that would happen if she lived out this fairy tale. Sera let go of his hand.

"Well, it seems we both received some unpleasant truths, then." She walked past him back toward the ruins and Ponic.

CHAPTER FORTY-FIVE

DOMINICK

The Legion's presence throughout the fortress had increased. Projectiles regularly showered the city's barrier, fizzling on the coven guardian's wards. News had surfaced that the demon army was amassed outside Egerton, a mere five-day march from the Citadel. The Council remained silent, withholding further information, and coven members buzzed with rumors.

Theo had continued to record the number of lives lost, comparing it to the posted figures, and the discrepancy was staggering.

Dominick scratched at the stubble on his neck as he crossed the threshold of the Ogdelo. After burning Colton a few days ago, he no longer saw the point in shaving or maintaining appearances, not if everyone he loved would die anyway.

Chimes rang out across the speakers, and Chair Renata addressed her people. "Attention coven members, please report to the Menage immediately."

The pool chambers emptied around him. Rising to the tips of his toes, he searched through the sea of heads for Theo. When he spotted him, Dom snuck behind and grabbed his hand.

Theo ripped it away. A grin tightened Dom's cheeks.

"First smirk in days, and of course it's because you're fucking with me."

"Oh, I'll fuck with you. All you have to do is ask."

"Ass." Theo bumped his shoulder.

"Precisely." The teasing didn't feel quite right, but he wanted to be normal for a while. He couldn't take his eyes away from Theo's pinkening cheeks and sly smile. The only thing that made him feel alive right now was the warlock beside him. "This is going to take forever."

"Calling the entire coven on such short notice for an assembly is unheard of. What do you think it means?" Theo asked.

"Nothing good."

After hours of standing and slowly shuffling into the Menage, Dominick and Theo took their seats in the upper decks of Daedeth level. Every bench was taken, from the high boxes to the floor. Some younglings had to share the standing space on the ground with Jedan members.

A marble platform had been erected in the center with the five thrones evenly spaced. Four of the Council members were seated, leaving one empty.

Council Elder Briar was missing.

Chair Renata stood from her throne and amplified her voice for the crowd. "Witches and warlocks of Solarni coven, on behalf of the Council of Elders, I thank you for your patience and cooperation in attending this last-minute gathering. There are a few pieces of business that we must attend to."

The crowd murmured, interrupted by another flaming projectile fizzling overhead. They had become so common that Dominick no longer flinched. Still, he couldn't look away from the sizzling embers every time they rained and crackled on the invisible dome above.

"First and foremost," Chair Renata continued, "it is with great sadness that Chair Briar has chosen to step down from the Council."

Frantic whispers erupted around Dominick, circling every level of the arena. It was rare for a Council member to step down. Though he supposed the old witch had been governing for some time.

"Has that happened before?" Theo asked.

"Not that I recall, no. Sera would know better, but Briar was ancient."

Theo's face matched his own. His gut sank.

Chair Renata hushed the crowd. "Please settle down. It has been decided that a new member should be appointed directly, and by unanimous vote, we present you with your new Council elder: Lavinia Wildrick."

Sera's mother crested the back stairs of the platform. Her signature black robes framed a coven-blue dress beneath. Her full, round lips were cut in a diplomatic smile, showcasing perfectly white teeth. There was no question where Sera and Nora got their beauty from. Cheers exploded through the crowd as she waved.

Theo scoffed. "She's smiling while both her daughters are in danger?"

"Clearly you've never met Lavinia Wildrick. It wouldn't matter to her if Sera were strung up and rotting, being picked apart by crows. She'd hesitate for Nora—it's no secret she has a favorite daughter. But Lavinia has aimed for this seat her entire life." Dominick watched as Sera's mother scanned the crowd. He could have sworn she looked directly at him and pursed her lips. "She's bloody powerful too."

Lavinia amplified her voice, and the crowd hushed. "I am humbled by the Council's decision and plan to utilize every resource I have to earn your trust during this tumultuous time." The crowd exploded again, and Lavinia bowed. Her long braids almost touched the floor before she sat on the empty throne.

Chair Renata nodded to Chair Lavinia, then addressed the crowd once more. "Our next order of business involves the war." The coven grew quiet. "As you know, our feud with the demon realm has caused catastrophic losses to our coven over the last two thousand years. Our ancestors, who had been persecuted, tortured, and killed, escaped the tyrants to create our haven here, in the Citadel fortress. Your Council has been negotiating, and we have secured new allies to help us in this fight."

A pair of aliato, their glittering white wings high and broad, along with a pair of humans who seemed to be of some wealth, walked to the center of the platform.

"You've already become familiar with our friends the aliato. But now the humans will join us in destroying the demons once and for all." The coven unleashed a near-deafening roar. Renata gave them a smug smile and raised her hands, motioning for the crowd to settle. "We are honored to have them here today. You will see more of both allies around the fortress. Your Council requests that you be courteous and accommodate our new friends."

Dominick wiped his hands on his knees.

Chair Blackwell stood and crossed the platform. The pairs of aliato and humans retreated behind the thrones as Blackwell took center stage.

Chains clinking against stone steps hushed the members of the coven. A warlock climbed the stairs, and behind him, holding the chain, was a giant aliato. It was the same one Dom had seen in Lavinia's house. His gold armor was blinding in the sun.

A metal collar had been welded around the warlock's neck with a thick chain hanging from its center. Additional links branched off the chain to shackle each hand and foot. The warlock tripped going up the stairs, but the winged warrior behind him roughly pulled him to his feet.

The Menage stayed silent.

"We are at war," Chair Blackwell bellowed. "This is no secret to any of you. This Council has been patient, negotiating a ceasefire and potential peace for the last twenty years. But the demon spawn will not accept our emancipation. They have planted spies among us!" The crowd gasped—unease built in Dominick's chest. Blackwell pointed to the warlock in chains. "They will not be allowed to share our secrets."

The aliato shoved the warlock to his knees. With his shackles, he was barely able to brace himself.

Dom glanced at Theo. He was pale. Dominick took his lover's hand in his.

"We have brought this filth here to show you that collusion with the enemy will not be tolerated."

Terror climbed its way up Dominick's throat. He didn't recognize this warlock. He was gaunt and filthy. His clothing was worn to rags and soiled with not only blood but also excrement. How long had he been in the tower? Years?

"Typically," Blackwell continued, "executions are completed in front of a small audience and with magic. However, considering the circumstances, the Council of Elders had decided a public execution is necessary. To be a warning for any of those who might be tempted to sell our secrets."

Another crash of fire exploded on the warded dome high above the Citadel fortress.

The aliato raised his hand to the sky, and with a crack of lightning a sword appeared gripped in his hand. With a touch, it ignited in an iridescent flame.

The blood drained from Dominick's face. This wasn't the way. The Council didn't allow foreign beings, allied or not, to execute their kind.

Murmured whisperings and hushed concern swept through the arena like a wave.

"In celebration of our new alliance, we have granted the honor to our allies."

The warlock sobbed on his knees, a large dark puddle forming beneath his legs as he let out a rasped plea that Dom couldn't understand.

"They cut out his tongue," Theo whispered.

Blackwell's eyes were glassy, almost crazed. Chair Thorne looked grim, pained even. Lavinia, Renata, and Corbin were seemingly unbothered by what was about to happen.

"You may proceed, Raphael," Blackwell finished, then took his seat.

Raphael pointed his flaming sword at the sky. Just as his arm was fully extended, a barrage of fireballs collided with the barrier above them.

An omen.

Raphael stood with his white-and-golden wings stretched wide on display. Holding his sword with both hands, in one sweeping motion, he connected with the warlock's neck.

The prisoner's head rolled off the marble platform onto the screaming younglings and Jedan members below. The open neck gushed blood down the white marble stage and splattered vibrant red across Raphael's face and wings.

Screams erupted from the coven, and a flurry of movement broke out. Some vomited in the aisles, causing others to slip and fall while trying to escape. Jedan's members attempted to shield the younglings from the blood that was dripping around them. The youngest class down there was aged only seven.

"They've lost their minds." Theo gagged, holding his hand to his mouth.

"We need to get out of here," Dominick yelled over the panic. He pulled Theo to his feet. Dom stared straight at the marble platform, at his Council, and none of them showed emotion when Raphael licked his sword clean.

CHAPTER FORTY-SIX

SERAPHINA

It had been two days since she'd learned about her father.

Two days since witnessing looks of adoration in Vasso's future gaze.

And Alistair was still asleep from the belldon Ophelia had drugged him with.

Ophelia had assured her that he would wake the next day, pulling his threads to prove her point, and Sera finally stopped berating the oracle for what she'd done. She hadn't worked up the courage to apologize to the witch.

She was so angry. About her father, the lies her mother had told, the look on Vasso's face when they were definitely having future sex. That in itself brought on a slew of emotions she didn't want to unravel right now. It didn't help that Vasso had left her in the training circle the day before with a simple instruction to burn targets, and left.

Sera cocooned herself deep into the feather pillows of her bed, soaking in every inch of the gray silk nightclothes the domovoi had given her. They were big but much more comfortable than her trousers and tunic.

Snik snored beside her.

"So I'm half demon," she said to her magic.

A little more than half, but yes.

"And is that where you come from? Do all demons have random voices in their head?"

Her magic giggled but didn't answer.

Sera unclasped the necklace her father had left her, turning the stone raven between her fingers. On the ride back from the ruins, she'd asked Vasso to tell her everything about her father. He'd told her his name was Darius, and that he'd been an adviser to the previous demon king. His most trusted, according to Vasso.

Darius was at least eight hundred years old if he were still alive. A war general with a keen eye for battle strategy, was what Vasso had said. But after the last battle of Okaterth, he disappeared.

She remembered studying that battle. It was a bloody one for both sides. The ground had been burned so badly that nothing grew there, as if that small outcropping was an island made of Deadlands.

This entire time, her mother had lied. About who her father was. What she was. Her darkness. Had Lavinia known about it from the beginning? She had to have. Her mother was too calculated, too motivated... too fucking powerful.

Sera turned the necklace over again, and the pad of her thumb caught on the beak.

"Oww," she said, sucking the blood from the prick.

Crack. The pendant turned hot as an ember in her palm. Sera gasped with the pain and threw it to the ground.

"Eeeeech?" Snik cooed at her.

"I don't know," she said. The stone cracked again. Blinding light seeped from the fractures of the bird, and in a snap of magic, a black raven half her height appeared, releasing a mighty caw.

"Oh, Shadow. Ophelia? Vasso!" she yelled.

Snik was on all fours, snarling at the thing, then talking to it in his little animal language. The bird only stretched out its wings and flapped.

Her bedroom door crashed open. Vasso stood there panting as if he'd run to her from the other side of the manor. His eyes blazed bloodred. "Seraphina?" She couldn't say anything and just pointed to the massive bird. Vasso let out a breath. "What is it?"

"I don't know! Will you get Ophelia?"

"One moment," he said.

The raven croaked, then trilled so loud she covered her ears. What on Eraphon was this? She'd never seen a raven so big before. Its beady black eyes bore into her as it tilted its head from side to side. Snik took a swipe, but Sera grabbed him by the middle and pulled him to her chest.

"Oh my." Ophelia's smooth voice descended over the room. Vasso was behind her, shaking his head with an exasperated look.

"What is it?" Sera asked.

"Well, I believe it's a familiar." Ophelia stepped closer, holding out her hand. "I never thought I'd see one."

"A familiar? I thought they'd left the witches? One hasn't been bonded in thousands of years."

"May I?" The oracle motioned to the bed, and Sera nodded.

"I'll leave you two to discuss." Vasso closed the door and left.

Ophelia sat at the foot of the bed. She was dressed in gray robes today. Sera's heart ached for Dominick. If she and the oracle were on better terms, she would ask Ophelia to pull his thread so she could get a glimpse of him.

"It seems your father has left you quite a gift," Ophelia said.

"It's not very inconspicuous. I'm pretty sure I could ride on the back of it." In a flash of light, the raven shrank to a normal size.

Ophelia clapped her hands in delight. "How did it break free?" She turned her sky blue gaze to Sera.

"I was just playing with my necklace. I never realized how sharp the beak was. My thumb caught, and a drop of my blood touched the stone. Next thing you know, it appeared."

"Fascinating."

She supposed it was. The only thing that Sera couldn't figure out was why her father—a demon—had access to something only witches were supposed to bond to. "Do you know how to bond it to me?"

Ophelia adjusted her robes and stroked the bird's head. "If I had to guess, I think the drop of blood took care of that."

"Ophelia, I wanted to say I'm sorry. For enthralling you, and for badgering about Al."

The oracle raised a white-blond brow at her. "I apologize for revealing something that you should have learned on your own."

It *had* changed something between them. She and Vasso both, judging from the way he looked at her in those images. Knowing what it could be. But then his dead face in her hands—it made her want to run in the other direction. "I just—so much is happening right now. The war is picking back up, Nora kidnapped, my powers, Vasso..."

"Hmm, how do you feel about him?"

"Vasso?" She had no idea, really. Somewhere between lust and annoyance, she supposed. "I don't know enough about him to make any sort of opinion. Other than he can be vicious at times, but I think..." She thought that deep down there was a reason for it. That he hadn't had an easy life, and maybe, like her, he was missing bit of kindness. He cared. For the beings of the forest, for Snik, for the domovoi. Even the fox. She knew now that he had taken away its pain, pouring it into her, so she could learn. "I don't know what I think."

"The prophecy spoke of a witch with the power to bring the covens back under demon rule. That she would change all life on Eraphon." Ophelia took Sera's hand. "Seraphina, I think that witch is you."

Her mouth went dry. "Even if I wanted that, I don't have that kind of power. The Council of Elders would never listen to me. They've been fighting this war for two thousand years. Not to mention our ancestors rebelled for a reason. I'm only one witch."

Ophelia sighed. "But you're not just a witch, are you?"

Her familiar hopped onto the bed and balanced itself on Sera's knee. Snik whined.

"Do not eat it."

The goblin harrumphed, and she let him go.

"What good would it do, anyway?" she asked the oracle. "Even if the Solarni coven did surrender and go belowground, I imagine they'd try to rebel again."

Ophelia stood. "I know you're managing a lot. But only the strongest will endure. Have faith."

"In Shadow?"

The oracle gave her a soft smile before opening the door to leave. "In yourself."

CHAPTER FORTY-SEVEN

SERAPHINA

Clouds built in the atmosphere, obscuring the brilliance of the blue sky. A slight breeze rustled the tops of the ironoak trees. Sera had dressed in her training leathers, intending to take advantage of Al's state of unconsciousness.

Running her fingers through her hair, she thought of the image Ophelia had shown her of her birth.

It wasn't how her mother had described it at all. Lavinia had mentioned more than once that Sera had been a difficult delivery and had teased her about how she'd needed a healer's assistance.

There hadn't been healers in that cottage, and the birth didn't *seem* difficult. Sera pulled her hair back and began to braid. After knotting off the end of her plait, she wiped her hands across her face.

Her father wasn't the warlock with kind brown eyes and a full laugh, who balanced her on his knee.

It was bittersweet. Almost. That she had been blessed with time, and Nora hadn't.

Sera rolled out her shoulders in the middle of the training circle and warmed up with a series of motions Vasso had taught her. Centering herself, she called to her well of darkness and let that death fog fall around her. It bubbled and churned.

Sera envisioned it taking shape. Miniature trees, weapons, buildings—anything she could think of, and the mist transformed while she stretched. Sera grabbed the cracked pendant at her throat, and her new familiar cawed long and loud through the forest.

How long had her familiar been trapped in stone? It must have felt wonderful to stretch its wings, to feel the wind in its feathers.

Sera lunged again and reached her hands high above her head when a screeching bugle echoed through the woods.

"Snik?" she called out, her magic dissipating. The goblin was out hunting hares and rodents.

Another screech had her sprinting toward the south side of the forest. A fury of cries, roars, and mauling sounds continued as she leaped over logs and stones. Her heart was in her throat. If one of the agbris had him...

She'd light the entire forest on fire.

The sounds grew louder. Sera halted, finding low bushes, and crouched behind them, heaving in desperate breaths. A creature with great antlers extending from its head bellowed at the agbris surrounding it.

Sera swallowed her gasp.

An elken. A mighty one. The animal was massive. From hoof to antler tip, it was over twice her height.

The elken swung his head low, aiming its tines at the agbris' bodies. Blood was smeared over its chest, dripping down one leg.

The demons in their robes and swiping claws had it backed up against one of the massive tree trunks. Seven of them surrounded it. Saliva poured from below their skull masks as they waited for the kill.

The animal looked at her, panic in its golden eyes. Sera pulled her flames into her palms, taking note of the dry dead leaves scattered across the forest floor. One of the agbris lunged, and the elken cried out in pain.

"Fuck it," she said and jumped out from her cover, blasting three of the seven.

Their tattered cloaks caught fire. The agbris' screams were louder than the elken's bugles as they fled deeper into the forest.

The other four turned toward her.

The mighty white beast's massive antlers glided past the low branches as it ran.

Click, click, click.

Sera suppressed a shiver. The clicking and screams were half the reason she was terrified of the monsters. The other half was the magic-eating parasite underneath its claws. Her pulse drummed in her ears. She wished she had a dagger.

Four agbris lowered on their haunches. With every low growl and snap of teeth, her darkness pulsed in her veins.

Show them, her magic said. *Show them what you can do.*

Her body warmed, and Sera lifted the lid on that well of magic. Black flames flared from her palms. Sera aimed and let go. Power ripped through her like raging whitecaps.

The beasts dodged and ducked.

They gnashed at her. The animal-skull masks flapped like loose teeth with each click of their jaws. Sera aimed again, and the beasts evaded.

One lunged.

"*Barijara.*" Her barrier coated her like a skin of blue steel.

She aimed her flames again. This time, she hit her mark.

An awful high-pitched sound escaped two of the beasts as black flames wrapped them. The odor of burning, rotten flesh wafted through the air.

Every hair on the back of her neck rose as the remaining two beasts growled.

Run, her magic screamed.

Sera ran toward the manor entrance, pumping her legs at a furious speed. As she ducked under a low-hanging branch, a stick snagged her cheek, and hot blood dripped down to her chin.

She couldn't stop.

They were going to tear her apart, or worse, get their parasites under her skin to eat her from the inside out. A burning ache radiated from her sternum through her chest. She felt like she was choking or being smothered; she couldn't decide which was worse.

Sera dared to glance over her shoulder. The agbris were closing in. Another ear-piercing roar echoed through the trees.

Two of the demons she had downed were now racing toward her. The smoke billowing from their burning robes made them look like moving pyres.

They regenerate.

That's what Alistair had said the last time she was running for her life. She was a fool for even thinking she had a chance against them.

Her lungs screamed for air.

Two of the agbris had caught up with her, flanking her as they crossed the south meadow. She could make out the glow of their red eyes through the socket holes of the animal skulls. Another two herded her away from the manor's entrance.

A giant raven dove from the sky, snatching the one to her right. Her familiar buried its talons into fabric, then flesh and bone, ripping the beast high into the air.

The agbris screamed, a sound so sharp she was sure it pierced her eardrum.

As she burst into a sprint, her palms tingled.

Taking as deep a breath as she could, Sera stopped short, turned, and slammed a stream of black flames at the two beasts directly behind her. They immediately dropped to ash.

Hands on her knees, she sucked in great gulps. A dark cloud rose through the canopy, polluting the sky above.

"No!" she breathed. The mighty ironoaks were burning.

Her blue second skin flickered. The remaining two demons circled her, claws extended, fangs out.

One of them howled, and Sera froze... for what sounded like a chorus of hundreds howled back.

"Oh gods." She'd been utterly stupid to come out here alone. Flames in each hand, Sera sidestepped in a circle to keep the two she could see in front of her.

The ground shook as a stampede of agbris broke from the trees. Their white skulls, all antlers and teeth, moved like they were braying as the demons surrounded her in the open field.

"Any suggestions?" she asked her magic between gulps of breath.

It did not respond.

Her heart pounded in her chest, and the tightness in her ribs wasn't helping as she gasped for more air.

This was how she would die.

She'd never make it to Nora. She'd never see Dominick again, or Alistair, or Vasso. Sera winced as a single tear rolled into the cut on her cheek.

Taking a deep breath, she pulled for more vatra. A thick layer of black fog saturated the ground around them. Sweat rolled down her back. Shadow, she was hot. Her veins cooked under her skin, but still, that well ran deep. Not even close to burning out.

Two agbris lunged. She blocked one, sending flame into its gut, then the other. Alistair's training rang clear in her head. *You're small. Learn how to fight at close quarters.*

Well, she would fight close as long as her barrier stayed intact.

The next one came at her, and she drove her elbow into its guts before spinning and gripping its neck. She screamed. Mist swirled around the demon, who hissed and snapped at her. Her magic twisted around and around like a constrictor, squeezing the life from it, and when she let go, that twisted fog blazed into hot flame, reducing the thing to ash at her feet.

Yes... she liked this. Liked the roll of her magic flowing through her without a thought.

Another beast lurched from the horde circling her. It sliced its poisoned claw at her middle, and her barrier fell.

"Shit," she hissed and jumped back.

Thump, thump, thump, thump, thump. Her heart beat like frantic bird wings. She took a few steps back, her hands up in defense, as the crackle of burning timber broke through the demons' cries.

The agbris in front of her raked its parasite-infested claws in the dirt, snarling and clicking, while the rest of the horde stayed in place.

This one had claimed her.

A flash of red behind that mask of some dog or fox skull had her swallowing hard.

It would kill her.

Sera took a deep breath and pulled the flames to her again. The agbris inched closer. Its tattered, rotten robe dragged in the grass.

A bugle shrieked in the distance.

Well, at least the elken had lived. She wasn't so sure she could say the same of herself for much longer.

Then a flash of movement caught her eye. The mighty white elken was charging through the horde straight for her, smashing the agbris out of the way. The animal slid to a stop, bowing on its front legs.

"Fucking miracle." Sera didn't hesitate.

She threw herself across its massive shoulders, barely managing to get her leg over its neck, and grabbed the antlers before it took off. The haze of smoke stung her eyes as they galloped across the field.

A trilling caw rang out high above her, and then her familiar was beating its massive black wings at her side. It had helped her, ripped that demon into the sky.

The agbris swiped at the elken's legs as they ran, snarling and clicking behind them. The entire horde was chasing them.

Sera threw a wide arc of flame behind her. Few fell. She slammed her hand into her chest as a sharp pain cracked through her. "Fuck..." She winced.

It was pain, and fear, and terror wrapping itself around every one of her ribs. The closer they galloped toward the training field, the more of a pull she felt.

Sera gasped. Was this what it felt like to burn out? She'd imagined it would be closer to melting, the magic burning you from the inside out, but this felt like heartbreak... terror and rage all mixed into one.

Cresting the hill, a thundercloud of black shadow raged toward them. It rushed past her and the elken, blotting out the sun. As if she and the white beast were a singular rock standing firm against the battering sea.

In the midst of it all was Vasso, sprinting straight for her.

The pull. That thread in her chest gave way to relief, and she sobbed as his white hair flashed among the black of his vatra.

Her mount continued forward, but Vasso rushed past them.

"Vasso!" she screamed. Sera grunted, pulling on the elken's antlers. The beast bellowed beneath her and slowly came to a stop.

Sera fell to the ground and ran.

They'd kill him. It was too many. He couldn't survive. Maybe—maybe if she gave him her magic, he could put them down. She reached the top of the hill.

The landscape had changed.

Black shadow expanded deep into the forest. He was stanching her inferno. The vibration of his magic soothing hers was more relief than pleasure.

But the horde stood there. Waiting.

"Vasso," she whispered between heaving breaths. "There are too many."

He glanced at her. His eyes blazed red with a promise of death.

"Here, take my magic." She held out her hand. Tendrils of smoke swept up her back, over her arms, before grazing her cheek. He was soothing her. She leaned into his magic and released a breath. She was safe. "Vasso…"

Vasso unleashed his power.

The horde disintegrated.

Ash fell in mounds. Not one body was left, only ashes swept on a high wind, which carried the remains into the forest, dusting the trees in an unnatural soot.

"The flames in the forest?"

"It's fine." Vasso turned to her, taking her hands in his. He turned each one over and kissed the center of them. Sera shivered at the sensation.

"You saved me."

"No," he said, releasing her hands. "He saved you." The elken snorted behind her.

Her raven, back to its regular size, was perched on its highest antler.

"Thank you, old friend. Seraphina, meet the elken king. His kind have lived many years in these woods. I've made sure to protect them when he cannot." Vasso reached over her shoulder and scratched the beast's chin. "He's thankful you offered to save him."

Despite Vasso's kind words, he held his mouth in a hard line.

"Thank you, Your Majesty." The elken's white fur was silken under her fingers. She was careful not to touch the gashes in his chest. "Will he be okay? The parasite—"

"As majestic as they are, they aren't magical. There is nothing for it to feed off." Vasso stepped closer, hovering his hand over the gashes. Black mist circled the wound, and when he pulled back, the wound had closed.

The king tousled his head and perked his ears. With a grunt, he cantered into the forest. Her familiar croaked and settled in the grass, pecking at the ground.

"How did you find me?" she asked.

"I felt you." He rubbed his chest. "I felt your panic—your terror."

"Is that one of your powers?" Her words were breathy, from the loss of adrenaline or how he looked at her. "Is that part of being a demon lord? You can feel terror?" She had no idea why she asked. Only that she needed the fill the silence between them.

They'd barely said two words to each other since returning to the manor. After the doorway, after those images.

Vasso's intense stare pierced her, "No, Seraphina. It's not a demon thing."

She swallowed at the sound of her name on his lips.

"It's not a lord thing." His voice lowered to a husky whisper. "It's a *you* thing."

Her magic coaxed her forward, but she stood her ground. "So, this isn't normal?" she asked, staring at those full lips.

"Not for me," he said.

Sera tilted her head to look at him. Her gaze roamed over his perfect face.

He did the same to her.

She was bare to him. He'd had that power over her since the moment she saw him astride Ponic in Crowpass. "Vasso—"

"You need more training if you're going to be out here alone."

"That's all you have to say?"

His shoulders bunched. Ash floated around them in flurries. "What do you want to hear?" he snarled. "That I would beg, here in the ashes of my wards, on my hands and fucking knees, for your forgiveness, because I didn't get to you sooner? That I should have ripped each one of them to pieces before burning them for that scratch on your cheek? That I— No."

He turned his back on her.

"So your solution is to—what? Rage and be pissy? You've already done that!" She wanted to throttle him. Kill him. She had no idea why, but her chest was burning with rage and... fear. "Why won't you talk to me? You're the only one who understands this, and yet... and yet you leave me with it, to figure it out." She was spinning.

Those future looks from him flashed in her mind. His smile, the way he bit his lip, the stern look lined with a smirk, but then—pallor, death.

"Why have you been so quiet?" she asked.

He marched toward her, his eyes darkening, his lips parting. Vasso tilted her chin higher. She shivered under his touch as his gaze dropped to her lips.

"So I wouldn't do this."

For a moment, time stood still.

There was no wind.

No sounds of insects or birds singing.

There was nothing but his lips on hers. His mouth—warm and firm. She whimpered when his tongue asked for permission to taste her.

She let him.

It wasn't just a kiss. He was all-consuming. Inside and out. Their magic swirled in a chaotic dance around them. Heat pooled between her thighs, and Vasso's hand traced down her throat, then her side, gripping her waist.

Each inhale had her breasts brushing against his chest. Vasso wrapped her braid around his wrist, pulling in an unhurried tug, deepening his access, his tongue taunting hers.

She breathed him in, sandalwood wrapping her senses. That smell had been burned into her since that day in the market. His taste was divine, but the way he kissed her, slow, deliberate, was a promise of what else he could do.

And she wanted it. She wanted it all.

Sera pushed her hips into his, seeking sweet, sweet friction. He groaned. The rumble vibrated through her, setting her alight all over again. This was everything. No other kiss had been this compelling, obsessive, or intoxicating. It filled her up, wrung her out. That missing piece clicked into place.

It was him.

There was no other way to describe it.

He moved from her mouth, kissing her jaw, running his tongue across the soft skin below her ear.

"Shadow," she whispered.

He froze, took one step, then two. "I'm sorry..." A pained look crossed his face before he turned toward the manor.

"Vasso?"

He didn't respond.

"You're leaving?"

He stilled, fists balled tight, but didn't face her. "If I don't walk away right now, I'd make a decision I'd regret."

Her breath caught in her throat. Magic, dark and pulsing, raged through her veins. How dare he? That kiss was everything. That link snapping tight between them. And Shadow help her, she knew it would never be the same.

There was only his lips.

His scent filling her lungs.

His tongue and teeth and hands pulling her braid.

Vasso was at the manor entrance. She started walking. He watched her with a stern mask in place, and when she got to the center of the training circle, he entered the manor, leaving her alone with nothing but the wind and ash speckling her cheeks.

Chapter Forty-Eight

Dominick

Neither of them had slept much. The first thing Dominick wanted to do when he woke was go to Sera's boarding room and check that the journal was still under her mattress. So that was where he and Theo were headed.

The events in the Menage the evening before had the entire Citadel in pandemonium.

Coven members from every class had rushed to their homes and bolted their doors. The aliato, however, had practically invaded the fortress city. The winged soldiers were on every street, including those of Daedeth Quarter. Patrolling. Surveying.

Dominick entered the boardinghouse, took Sera's spare key from his pocket, and opened her bedroom door. It was...

Fine. Nothing was out of place, or at least there was no indication that the room had been searched. He crossed the floor, lifted the mattress, and exhaled a sigh of relief.

"It's still here?" Theo asked.

"It is." Dominick picked up the small notebook. "I think we should burn it."

"No."

"What do you mean, no? You saw that warlock yesterday. He was pissing blood... Theo, they had cut out his tongue!"

Theo held his hands wide. "*Teesina*," he cast, placing their sound barrier in place. "The Council of Elders is obviously hiding things. Which means the records the master oracle is keeping are false."

"And if we get caught with these, what would that make us?" Dominick asked, straightening his robes before sitting on Sera's bed.

Theo didn't answer.

"Enemies... and what does the Council do to their enemies? Kill them."

"I won't be complicit in lies. Dominick, they're changing our very history." Theo paced back and forth across the wide wooden floorboards. "The outbreak of this war is already killing our people by the hundreds."

"And what if they come for you?" Dominick said. He dropped his head in his hands. "I don't think I would ever forgive myself if they did to you what they did to that warlock."

Theo stopped his pacing. His shoulders sagged, and he sat on the bed beside Dominick. "Then we work to protect ourselves."

"How?"

"We build barriers in our minds, we come up with a code, we learn more complex illusion spells." Theo crossed his legs on the bed. "We'll start with the barrier."

Dominick stared at Theo, his earnest ocean eyes.

He'd meant it when he said he wouldn't be able to forgive himself. It was the closest he'd gotten to an admission of how he felt, but it was true. He'd be ruined if Theo was taken, especially over something stupid like miscalculated deaths.

But he also didn't want to extinguish that passion in his lover's eye. So Dominick turned to face Theo in a dirty boardinghouse in the middle of Jedan Quarter, and practiced.

Chapter Forty-Nine

Seraphina

Sera awoke to a knocking at her door. She opened it, and Alistair stood, his face grim, dark circles around his eyes.

"Al," she said and ushered him in. "Come in, how are you feeling?"

He took stiff steps to the bed and sat upon it. "I feel like I was placed in a bag and trampled by a company of horses," he said, rubbing his eyes. "How long was I out?"

Lying was bad, but she'd decided after the first day he hadn't woken that it would be better to fib than be barraged with questions about what had happened in those days. "Just a day."

"I think I pissed for two minutes straight when I got up."

"Bad wine. Vasso and Ophelia were in the same condition," she said.

"What's with the bird?" He pointed to Raven, perched on the corner of her bedpost.

"Funny story that. Apparently, I have a familiar." The bird made a knocking noise and flapped its wings.

Alistair rubbed his forehead. "I don't even want to unpack that right now."

"Let me get you some water." Sera walked to the basin and poured him a glass.

He grunted, then took a deep breath. "I know I didn't tell you about the coven being at war."

"Or the fact that you're the Mesar."

He nodded. "And that. But, Sera, there have been casualties."

Her heart slowed. She lowered herself onto the small desk chair and gripped her knees. Al let out a shuddering breath, his eyes growing damp.

"Who?"

"Colton," he whispered.

The only thing she could hear was her own beating heart in her ears before she ran to the bathing room and emptied the contents of her stomach. Dominick was alone in the Citadel, and Colton was dead—Colton, good and strong Colton.

When she emerged, Alistair was unraveling. Face in hands, his shoulders shaking under a great weight as he wept for his best friend. Sera pulled his gloved hands away and let his cheek fall to her shoulder.

Poor Alistair.

Poor Dominick and their parents. It was too soon. How had this happened?

Careful not to let her bare skin touch his, she wrapped her arms around his chest and let him grieve.

"Shh, shh, shh, it's all right." She rubbed his back in long strokes, doing her best to keep her tears at bay. Al was strong, unbothered, a professional warrior, but Colton was his best friend. "When?" she choked out.

After a few moments, when his breathing became steady, he spoke. "Not long after we left," he said, letting her go. He wiped his face in the crook of his elbow.

"I am so sorry. I loved Colton, too, but wasn't nearly as close as you two were. You held on to this the whole time?"

He nodded. "The Council stated there were minimal casualties. But apparently, they had instructed the head generals to move the battalion a few days early. They were in position, ready to strike. I don't know all the details, only that it was supposed to be a surprise attack. But the demons were ready."

Sera's twenty-three years of life had been relatively peaceful. They'd been in a ceasefire for most of it. She, Dominick, and Nora were all too young to have been affected by the early skirmishes. But Colton and Al had lived through them.

"Thank you for telling me." Her voice trembled. "Can you take a message to Dom for me? Bring me home so I can see him?" Dominick must have been devastated.

"I can't go back without Ophelia," he said, sniffling. "Renata was adamant she didn't want me within the walls without the oracle in tow."

Sera nodded.

Their time was dwindling, and there was still so much she didn't know. "Lie down." She motioned for him to move, and he did. Curling her hands into her chest, she faced him, her hair spread wide on the pillowcase. "Tell me of a memory. One of you and Colton."

Al pressed his thumb and pointer finger hard across his eyes. "I, uh, I don't think I can right now, Minnow."

"Then I'll tell you one..."

She began. Sometimes her stories involved Al, sometimes they didn't, and when she couldn't think of anything else, she lay there in the silence of their grief until Alistair's breathing grew heavy. Silently, she cried for Dominick. Her longing to be back in the Citadel's walls had never been so strong. She wanted to tell him it would be all right, to hold his hand at the burning.

But if she didn't get to Nora soon, she'd be doing the same thing.

CHAPTER FIFTY

SERAPHINA

Sera snuck from her room and walked the halls to find Vasso. She needed a plan. One that didn't rely on the Council of Elders. She'd done what they asked, found a doorway, and written a note, doing her best to render phonetically the sounds of the words Vasso had used to open it.

The task was complete. The only problem was that the Council could choose to go back on their word, and, well, a demon lord could not.

Ophelia was pulling threads in rapid succession from the center of the pool. It was late... or early. Sera had fallen asleep beside Alistair and had no idea what time it was.

"Do you know where Vasso is?" she asked, rubbing her eyes with the heels of her hands.

"In the training field, I believe," Ophelia said over her shoulder, but when she caught sight of Sera, she paused. "Seraphina, are you all right?"

"I'll be fine." And wasn't that the biggest lie she could tell herself? Nothing was fine.

Waving Ophelia off, she trudged to the entryway that led outside. The stone door was open, and the dawn light trickled in. What she needed to figure out, preferably before she set foot in front of him, was what Vasso wanted. They were at war. She was his enemy, and he had agreed to a bargain to teach her how to wield magic. Why?

Reasons, her magic said to her.

Nothing of use, per usual.

There must have been a book in the archives that could explain the two of them. She didn't think that a witch and a warlock with the same magic would experience this. In fact, she was positive they wouldn't. Otherwise, surely Dominick would have been exclusively with other oracles.

An ache formed in the center of her chest, and she rubbed at it absently, scanning the training circle for Vasso. His lean figure was nowhere to be seen, but a butterfly made of shadow, leashed by a wisp of black mist, landed on the tip of her nose.

She smiled to herself and followed it into the woods.

Ironoak Forest was waking around her. When the butterfly's silhouette vanished into the thinning trees, she saw Vasso atop a boulder overlooking the valley. He had a book in his lap and graphite in his left hand, shoulders slumped and white hair in disarray.

Her heart lurched when he looked at her. Moons, he was stunning. Unnaturally so—otherworldly, even, if she had to guess.

"Am I interrupting you?" He seemed so serene, sketching on his pad, she felt a little guilty.

"No."

The boulder's rough surface ripped at her palms when she climbed up beside him. There was a sheer drop off the ledge below, and she realized that she and Alistair had almost died at the bottom of this slab of granite. But up here, with the sun rising over the Lanac mountain range, where the clouds burned with orange, rose, and lavender dawn, she wished her heart didn't feel so heavy. The beauty of the sunrise was mocking her grief as she thought of Colton and Dominick.

"She's beautiful, isn't she?"

"Who?" Sera asked.

"Plaranina." Vasso pointed to the highest peak with his stained fingers. "Even so close to solstice, she is still capped with ice and snow."

"I didn't realize she had a name. We just referred to it as the Lanac Mountains."

"You've been above ground for too long," he said and rubbed at his chest. "You've been crying." He scanned her face, then her body with a pinch of panic she'd never witnessed from him. He was usually so cool and unconcerned. "Would you like me to maim him for you?"

Sera huffed a laugh. "No, he didn't do anything. Well, he did, but it wasn't his fault." She sighed, thinking of how hard Alistair had cried when she held him. "I know that we're at war now. I know our realms are fighting each other for power."

"Supay seems to be hungry for it."

"Is he the one who took Nora?" she asked.

"Yes. He's unstable, to say the least. Making desperate decisions that don't benefit the realm." He ran his hand through his hair. He was wearing his signature black outfit with the sleeves rolled up and the top two buttons undone.

"How long have you been out here?" she asked.

"A few hours. I enjoy the air. Sleep comes difficult to me. Where'd you get these?" he pinched a piece of gray silky fabric from her sleeve. "I saw you wearing them the other day when we met your familiar."

"The domovoi brought them to me. Figured you wouldn't mind, with how accommodating you've been lately."

Vasso scoffed.

Sera hesitated, but took a deep breath before asking, "Are we going to talk about yesterday?"

"It's been a lot to take in." Vasso worked his jaw and stared back out at Plaranina, his voice deepening. "But I like the way my clothes look on you."

Heat blazed up her neck and across her cheeks. Of course they were his. They were the color of his eyes.

"Why do you keep braiding your hair?" he asked and pulled her braid from behind her back, laying it on her shoulder.

All she could think about was the way he had tugged it. How deeply he had kissed her, how much she wanted his hands on her even now. "I need some hair creams from the Citadel. It's a mess if I don't moisturize it." Losing her nerve to bring up their kiss again, she said, "I didn't know you liked to sketch," motioning for him to hand his book over so she could inspect it more closely.

He raised one brow at her but relented.

The sketch was of the mountains. The peaks and valleys had just enough shading that the empty paper appeared to be white snow. "It's exquisite," she said. Vasso didn't say anything, just continued looking toward the rising sun, deep in contemplation.

She flipped back a page, and there was Snik, seated, his head tilted, ears out wide. The resemblance was uncanny. She could feel the curiosity coming off the page as the goblin looked forward.

Then further back again, and there was a bird in three phases of flight. Then a vuk. "How long have you been drawing?"

"For as long as I can remember."

Sera turned the book over, taking in the type of leather it was bound with. "I've seen these before. Have you lost a few of these sketch pads?"

Vasso shrugged. "Most definitely throughout the years. What did it have in it?"

"A wolf, or vuk, like this one. Three birds in phases of flight. There was an aliato..." She flipped the page again, and there, in much more detail than the crude drawing she remembered, was the elken.

One more turn and Sera held her breath. Everything around her grew silent as she stared at a perfect rendition of her face on the page. He'd drawn her, captured her flawlessly. Her hair was wild, her brows scrunched in concentration, and her chin set firm as if she was determined to make something work. She should've been embarrassed by the face she was making, but it was so expertly captured that she could only behold it in awe.

"It was yours," she whispered.

"What was?" He glanced at her then. "Aah, you weren't supposed to see that one." Vasso closed the sketchbook and placed it on his other side.

"You drew those pictures. The one I was cataloging before I left the Citadel."

"I don't know how I feel about the Citadel having renditions of my work." He lowered his voice. "But if it was you who preserved them, then I guess I can live with that."

He gave her a half smile, and a fluttering exploded in her chest. Somehow this felt like a quiet apology.

They sat silent together until the sun had crested the highest peak. Sera curled her knees to her chest and rested her chin atop one. "How do you really feel about what we saw at the ruins?"

She didn't know why she asked. Probably to get the disappointment over with. That, and to avoid the topic of their kiss. He was already pulling away from her, not that they had been close to begin with, but there had been contact between them. And yet Sera couldn't stop thinking about his lips. The undiluted joy in some of the images. And although she was seeing Vasso through her own eyes, she knew that if she could have seen her face in those moments, the looks would be reflections of each other.

Sera felt the heat of his gaze along her cheek but refused to look at him, not wanting him to read desperation on her face.

"That's a complicated question," he said.

"Why?"

"I have lived a long life." Vasso cleared his throat. He rubbed at the callus along the inside of his palm over and over. "Your—our vatra magic isn't common among my kind. The fact that we can wield it together…"

Sera let a trickle of her mist leave her hand. Thinking of her familiar, she manipulated the fog to form the raven.

Vasso chuckled. "You and birds." He pushed his magic into hers.

A chill ran through her, followed by a rush of warmth, and slowly her mist raven flapped its wings. It was Vasso who made it move—made it better.

"I need to ask you a favor," she blurted out.

He tilted his head toward her. "A favor? I thought you said no more bargains."

She smiled and nudged his shoulder with hers. A slight breeze had a few stray strands of hair tickling her cheeks and neck. "Alistair needs to take Ophelia within the next day or two. He will return for me... but..." She swallowed. She prayed Dom would forgive her. "I can't go back."

Vasso raised his brows.

"The Citadel is in full war mode. They aren't going to spare a team to save Nora," she said.

"You know this for certain?"

"I don't, but they were already reluctant. They won't give me a team if it means more demons can be slain in this war." The sun burned bright ahead of them now, washing away the purples and pinks of the morning, painting the sky solid blue. "I need you to take me."

"Shit," he hissed.

"What?"

"So you want me to march you into the underworld and do what with you? Seraphina, they'll rip you apart."

"I plan to ask for a trade. Me for her. I'll sacrifice myself if I have to, whatever it takes. Barter me... I don't care, just help me. Please."

He bared his teeth and looked away.

It was a death wish. She knew that was what he was thinking, because she felt it too. It was the least she could do for her sister. Somehow Nora had escaped death, but Sera knew it wouldn't be for long, and that was one thing she wasn't willing to let happen. Sure, Ophelia had said Nora wouldn't perish underground, but the witch also went on and on about free will.

"And what do I get in return?" he asked. There was no lilt to his voice, no smirk or sarcasm.

"Anything you want," she whispered.

His gaze danced along her forehead, across her eyes, before settling on her lips. She parted them, dragging in a shallow breath. Was that what he wanted? Her?

"I'll think about it," he grumbled, and he slid off the boulder.

"Vasso, I don't have much time."

He started to walk away, but stopped. "Nothing will bother you. Follow the butterfly if you get lost."

The mist insect floated in the air, and he departed without another word.

CHAPTER FIFTY-ONE

DOMINICK

It hurt him to see his mother suffering. She refused to attend her position in the arcana wing, and Dom was terrified the aliato would take her for insubordination. He was relatively sure that the only reason she hadn't been interrogated was that she was in Daedeth.

Every day, the death toll increased. Few families had been affected by the carnage, but still, Theo would come home and tell him of discrepancies. They were losing too many Legion fighters for this war to make sense. Theo was sure they would start conscripting Jedan into service just to increase the body count.

Directions from the Council stated that Legion forces combined with the aliato had pushed the demon army from Egerton. Since then, both sides had obtained reinforcements.

The flaming projectiles crashing into the warded barrier above the Citadel had ceased for now, giving some credibility to the information the Council was releasing. But so much more was going wrong inside the walls.

Mastrias were now assigned to the light-bringers. They were always watching the coven populace, ripping through their minds. Searching for traitors. Theo had trained Dom to keep his walls up. He made sure to let a memory or two slip through so it wouldn't be so obvious they'd learned to keep the mastrias out.

Dom was rather proud of himself when a mastria threw a coughing fit as he walked by. He'd purposely thought of the first night he had sunk to his knees before Theo. Even now, he smiled at that.

It was overcast. Dark clouds grew over the ocean, headed toward the mainland. Strange to have a storm coming in now when usually the wind swept in the other direction at that time of year. Trudging toward the Ogdelo, Dom itched the hollow below his ear and wished he had heard back from Sera.

Theo had left hours earlier to collect information about the war before the other oracles arrived. It was risky. But Dom had agreed to let his lover continue with his mission. Someone needed to record the truth.

Dom smiled to himself, looking forward to calling Theo something other than *lover*. Though he was a proficient one, he was more than that now.

Careful not to trip on his gray robes, Dom climbed the main stairs to the Ogdelo.

"Oracle Benero," the master oracle called to him.

"Master?" Dom bowed. "How may I be of service?"

"I'm moving you. Congratulations. Consider it a promotion." The master was already searching for another face among the crowd. Dark bags sagged beneath the old warlock's eyes.

"Sir?"

"You're being moved to lifelines. Please report to Oracle Hanu; she's waiting for you inside."

Before he could ask any questions, the master oracle approached another junior.

Changing placements wasn't expected until the new year. Six months away.

He walked into the lifelines pool, admiring the expansive layout that he got to play in now. Multiple platforms extended throughout the body of water. Oracles pulled threads in bright sheets of color, some of them disintegrating before they reached their fingertips. On the far side were the Legion oracles, dressed in their uniforms instead of robes.

Which one of them had pulled Colton's lifeline before he died? An ache grew in Dom's chest.

A petite witch approached him. "Dominick Benero?"

"Oracle Hanu, I presume?"

"You presume accurately," she smiled. She was pretty and had every oracle's light eye and hair coloring. Her blue eyes were hooded and angular. and The witch's blond hair was pin-straight to her waist, framing full, round cheeks. "We'll start your training soon. The master wishes to speak to a few of us. Then I'll be right over."

He gave her a mock bow, and she smiled with her rosy lips before leaving him alone again. Scanning the pools and streams of gray robes, he searched for Theo. Dom remembered him saying something about a mandatory meeting today. Most likely the same one that Hanu was reporting to. If there was a rank change, Theo would most likely be promoted as well. Maybe even get the training roll he'd been so eager for.

A surge of warmth flitted through Dom as he thought about this evening. He couldn't help the slight smile spreading across his face. Tonight he was going to ask Theo to be official. It had been almost a month since they'd made out in the alley behind Radost, and he didn't want it to end.

He didn't think they'd be life partners. Shadow knew he didn't want to think that far ahead. But right now, he didn't want anyone else.

It was a step. The biggest one he'd ever taken.

More oracles filed into the great pool chamber. Many of them looked him up and down, "like an ancient relic," as Sera used to say.

Dom sighed. He still needed to get with Galene. Find out what she knew about the aliato.

"Dominick, please join me over here." He joined Hanu on the platform in a quiet corner of the pool. "We'll be conducting some preliminary tests, and depending on how well you do, we will have you pulling threads by the end of the week. For now, I want you to focus on people you know, such as loved ones, family, and friends. Those we are connected to will appear the strongest at first. Others will call to you in time, but for today, I want you to call your family."

"All right, how do I call? Is it the same as weather patterns and crop yields?" He winked at Hanu.

She giggled, and a pretty blush spread across her cheeks. "With enough practice, you will be able to just call them by name, but for now, please close your eyes and think of them. Think of their face and how they make you feel."

He thought for a second about calling Theo's, but shook his head.

Instead, he pictured his beautiful mother. He envisioned her sitting at the table, her face gaunt, holding a cup of undrunk tea. The bags under her eyes hadn't left since they'd received the news of Colton's death. Her strawberry blond hair was pulled back beneath a scarf, where a few ringlets peeked out at the temples.

"That's it!" Hanu said. Dominick opened his eyes, and a red thread skated along the water's surface to him. Its top touched the ceiling; then it sank far into the water below. "You were thinking of your mother?"

"How could you tell?"

Hanu touched the thread. An image of his mother appeared before them, the same he'd just pictured in his mind. Her blank stare was haunting, her mouth now etched with deep lines that seemed permanent.

"She looks sad," Hanu said.

"She is." And Dominick wiped the image from his mind.

Chapter Fifty-Two

Seraphina

Sera had sunned herself for a few hours atop the boulder, looking out over the ravine and onto the Lanac Mountains. It'd felt glorious. When she got back to her room, she was met with a note from Alistair saying he had some business to attend to.

Apparently, he wasn't keeping the traveling a secret anymore. She should be relieved, but Sera didn't know if she could handle another instance where he came back covered in blood again. A piece of her grieved for him. Not because Colton was gone, but because of what she and Al could have been together.

That kiss had been rushed, yes, and at the time Sera thought she had everything she'd ever wanted.

But Alistair wasn't Vasso...

Heat crept up Sera's neck and across her cheeks as she thought of their kiss. The way his mouth fit hers.

Sera sighed and went to find something to distract herself.

After a few hours, she found a tome in one of the seating areas within the manor. It was a catalog similar to the codex, and she admired the various pieces of art labeled in it as she tried to distract herself from Vasso.

All she wanted was to be near him again. Swim in the depths of his eyes, breathe in his scent. He was intoxicating. And that picture he'd drawn...

Had it been fate? That she had been the one commissioned to preserve his sketch pad, then to be stopped outside of Crowpass?

A tap on the door had her opening it.

Her familiar flew in, taking its usual perch on the bedpost. Behind the bird, a blue velvet bag held by a wisp of shadow floated in.

She waved her hand through the smokiness, her vatra rippling within her, and the bag plopped to the floor. She peeked inside, then squealed and ran to the bathing room.

Small bottles of fragrance, oils, butters, and creams for her body and hair were wrapped in a silk scarf. She smelled each of them, choosing one that reminded her of the ocean and sunshine.

Summer in a bottle.

Sera soaked in the hot water while methodically using the cream to separate her curls into some semblance of a shape. It would take more than one application for her curls to be back to normal, but she didn't care. Laying her head on the rigid rim of the tub, she smiled. He couldn't have gotten this from the Citadel, but knowing he'd gotten it for her at all had her blushing.

She hadn't felt herself in ages, and this little kindness made the fluttering in her stomach beat harder. She should be petrified. It was clear Vasso was hiding something. Obviously his feelings about her, but she couldn't help but think there was something else.

Sera lifted herself from the tub and stepped into a clean towel.

Snik was now sitting on her bed in animated conversation with Raven, who flapped its wings and croaked in response. Hanging on the mirror was another beautiful black gown.

"You two aren't very good guards, are you?"

Raven and Snik made a noise that sounded like a huff.

The dress was stunning. Dainty straps held on to her shoulders. The bodice was simple and cut low enough to tease a bit of cleavage without being immodest. The skirt was full, cut in ripples and waves of black tulle.

It was a little much for dinner, but she couldn't deny that she looked beautiful in it.

Sera beheld herself in the mirror, transfixed by the eye color she shared with her father—a swirling mix of emerald and sage.

A knock at the door had her giddy. He'd come to see his handiwork. Skin smoothed and softened, her hair with its natural curl back, albeit damp. She opened the door with a smile, then stopped short when she saw Alistair.

His gaze danced over her, from her face down the bodice of her dress and back up. He inhaled, closing his eyes.

"Are you smelling me?" she asked.

Red streaked his cheeks, and he cleared his throat. "We need to talk."

Sera swallowed. "I don't think I can take any more bad news, Al."

"I know you've been sneaking off with *him*." He walked past her, glaring at Snik and Raven.

"You don't know anything." She closed the door.

"*Mesar*, remember? You're covered in his power. I can feel it coming off you in waves."

The dagger at her spine pulsed in warning. Their bargain was that he couldn't know Vasso was training her. Technically, if he found out she had the same power, it wouldn't break her bargain with the lord. Not that she wanted Alistair to find out at all.

"And you fucking lied to me—I was out for three days!"

Sera scoffed. "You've got a lot of nerve calling me a liar," she said. "You've lied to me since we left the Citadel."

"The difference is that *I* do it to keep you safe."

Another knock on the door had her stomach rolling. She hoped it wasn't Vasso. Swinging it wide, she exhaled to find Ophelia there.

"Would you both please meet me in the parlor for dinner? Lord Vasso will not be joining us this evening, and I cannot stand the swinging chandeliers. He's the only one who can make them stop." Ophelia huffed and led them through the manor.

Underneath her frustration at Alistair was a wave a disappointment. She was sure Vasso would've wanted to see her transformation. Shadow, *she* wanted him to see how beautiful she looked. A gifted set of creams and a gown that was made with her measurements in mind, and the lord wouldn't see his altruism?

Alistair stomped behind her like a cave troll as they made their way to a cozier area of the caverns. An intimate table, set for three, and the first course was already plated. Alistair held out her chair, and Sera huffed before taking a seat.

"Now, let's discuss logistics, shall we?" Ophelia said. Al raised his brows at her. "Don't be so naive. I know you're biding your time with this one." Ophelia held her wine and pointed her finger at Sera. "Before you take me to my doom, of course."

Al choked.

"Your doom?" Sera asked. "The Council doesn't plan to kill her, do they?"

Alistair didn't meet her eye, just sucked down water.

"They most certainly do," Ophelia responded. "Isn't that right, Alistair?"

"I'm not privy to the Council's plans. My instructions are to deliver you to them." He took a bite of his greens.

"Al, we can't bring her back if they mean to kill her."

"He will, and he must," Ophelia said as if they were discussing a bout of bad weather and not her death. "I have made my peace with Eraphon and fate."

"We aren't bringing her back." Steel slid into Sera's voice as she glared at Alistair. She wouldn't be an accessory to her murder. A slaying for what? Knowledge? Or just because she was a better reader than Chair Renata?

"I don't have a choice, Sera. My orders are to deliver her." He pinched the bridge of his nose. "I have to."

Ophelia filled her wineglass again and sipped. Her face was smug as she stared at Al. "Are you going to tell her the rest?"

Sera glared at him. His jaw was tight, staring daggers at Ophelia.

"What else is there?"

"Go on, tell her," Ophelia said.

Alistair slammed his fist on the table. The clattering of glassware and utensils made Sera jump. She was surprised the table hadn't split.

Ophelia kept her feline smile planted on her face. "You're not going to tell her, are you? Coward."

"Tell me," Sera gritted out. Her magic drew back like a bow, ready to send an arrow flying should she demand it.

"There's nothing to discuss." Alistair stood, avoiding her gaze.

"Sit," Sera said. She was tempted to tie him to the chair with her magic if he didn't answer, which would put her into a world of trouble, but she was so damn sick of his lies. Alistair turned to leave.

"She said sit!" Ophelia threw a blast of air at the warlock, pushing him back into his chair.

"I have no idea what you're talking about," he snarled.

"The Council told you to leave her. Take the map of the doorways and discard her in the forest."

Sera gasped.

Pure, unabashed rage lined Al's features.

"Tell me it isn't true," Sera said.

"I was going to sneak you in," he said.

Ophelia laughed. "You think Blackwell wouldn't have felt her through the wards?"

"But why?" Sera asked.

"They didn't give me a reason. It doesn't matter. I'm not leaving you. I won't lose you too."

She couldn't believe what she was hearing. He had planned to leave her discarded in the forest? What did that mean? Did the Council want her dead?

"I will come with you willingly, but do not be fooled by their words; they will kill me. And I am prepared to die, but you must not pursue this." Ophelia pointed to the two of them. "You leave her here, with Lord Vasso."

The chair behind her thudded on the carpet as Sera launched to her feet. "Don't I get any say?"

"Sera," Al called to her.

She was already out of the room. Any guilt that had crawled through her earlier was now gone. He was never going to bring her back, and maybe she was wrong for not planning to return anyway, but he hadn't known that. It was the fact that they were making decisions for her.

Her feet carried her through the manor as she stewed.

With each step, a tug in her chest pulled tighter and tighter until she reached the door to Vasso's study. She burst through to find Vasso sitting at his desk.

"Seraphina?"

"That motherfucker!" she screamed. Vasso's mouth twitched at the corners. "Don't you laugh."

A deep chuckle escaped before he reeled himself in.

She couldn't control her swirling emotions. Al had been ordered to discard her in the woods. They were never going to give her a team of Legion soldiers. They were never going to let her try and save Nora.

A sickening nausea curled within her, then a blast of mist enveloped the room.

"Subdina." Vasso's low voice soothed her. A brush of his fingers against her cheek had her leaning into his palm. The only thing she could see within her own darkness was bright red irises glowing at her.

He was so close, and she had shrouded the room in darkness.

"You seem awfully angry for a witch dressed so beautifully."

She stiffened, pulling away from his hand. "I didn't realize they needed to be mutually exclusive."

"Are you done hiding in the dark?"

"If I could pull it back, I would have already." She waved her hand in front of her face to try and dissipate the inky fog.

Vasso snapped his fingers, and his magic flowed. Goose bumps coated her in a moment of seductive frisson. Her breath hitched in her throat with an involuntary moan.

"Don't go making noises like that," he said, his eyes darkening, "I'll never let you leave."

She wanted to bathe in his words, linger, and ask him if he meant it. Whether that was something they could try, just once, to see if maybe their future together did make sense. But then she remembered what Alistair had been ordered.

"It seems I don't have a choice in the matter."

Vasso quirked his dark brow at her.

"Why weren't you at dinner?" Sera plopped into the chair opposite his desk. The tulle of her skirt fluffed around her in a ridiculous display.

"Something came up." He rubbed his brow, then flashed her a rakish grin. "Did you miss me?"

"I figured you would have liked to see your handiwork." She ran her hand down the length of her body, showcasing her curls and dress.

Vasso steepled his fingers and stared. "You *are* exquisite, if you're fishing for a compliment. Smell quite delicious as well. I was hoping that would be the one you chose." He cleared his throat. "But providing you with basic necessities and decent clothing doesn't entitle me to admire you as an object, Seraphina. I wanted you to feel comfortable, whether I'm in the room or not."

Her jaw went slack.

Vasso smirked at her. Sent a tendril of mist down her arm. "Unless you *want* me to treat you like an object. Do you want to be my plaything, Subdina?"

His velvet voice caressed her like an exposed nerve.

Shuddering.

Electric.

An intensity teetering somewhere between pain and pleasure.

Their kiss had awoken something within her. As much as she wanted to take him up on his words that very moment—on that desk, in that chair, on the damn floor—she needed to figure out the situation with Nora. "I'm afraid what I want doesn't seem to matter to anyone. Alistair is making it increasingly difficult—"

Vasso's teasing smile fell. "As much as I enjoy your company, did you need me for something?"

"Yes. Will you take me to the underworld or not?"

Vasso closed the ledger he was working in, sighed, and sat back.

"You didn't think I would forget, would you? They're leaving tomorrow, and I need to know. I'm going, with or without you." She tapped her fingers on the velvet chair arm.

"That would be unwise, to attempt to breach Gehenna alone."

"Well, I'm out of options," she said.

The candlelight from the sconces along the far wall scattered shadows along the shelves behind him. In those shadows, she swore she could make out wings.

"Your offer is still whatever I want?" he asked.

She gulped. This was dangerous, stupid, positively idiotic. "Yes."

"I'll bring you to the underworld only if you follow your destiny."

Sera scrunched her brows. "I don't understand."

He held out his hand. "We all have been destined by fate. Ophelia has her assumptions, I have mine. Regardless of what they are, I want you to follow them."

"If it's destiny or fate or whatever, wouldn't I do it anyway?" she asked.

"Ophelia insists there is free will. I suppose if you were face-to-face with your destiny and decided to walk the other way, you could."

"And if you break yours? If you don't take me into the underworld, then what?"

"Then I suppose that you'd be free to do what you want and I'd be in your debt."

There was a loophole, something she was missing. There had to be. She thought of Nora on that bed, pale and disassociated. She thought of her mother with her head planted on the Council chambers floor in complete submission, begging them to let her go. Then Dominick in front of Colton, on a burning pyre.

"Okay." She stood and grabbed his hand.

"Oh, fucking tits." He hissed and jerked. On the inside of his forearm was a brand, already raised and red. Sera grabbed his wrist to inspect the mark. An insignia of a raven was seared into his pale skin. "Shit, that hurts." He blew on the brand.

"Is that what I think it is?"

"A bargain brand? Yes. Though I've never been stupid enough to be on the receiving side." Vasso ran his hand through his hair and stood, crossed the room, and opened the door for her.

Before she exited his study, she asked, "You'll be ready tomorrow?"

He nodded. "I'll be ready."

CHAPTER FIFTY-THREE

DOMINICK

Dominick's eyes throbbed. He strained to keep them open as he pulled on the heavy door to Dobro level in Darine Hall. Following the sign to the keepers' wing, he almost missed the door that used to have Sera's name printed across it. Now only scrape marks were left.

He knocked before letting himself in and heard a shuffling in the back of the stacks and a muttering of curses. Following the sound, he spotted Galene teetering on the top rung of a stool, reaching for what looked like a cup of some kind, and cleared his throat.

"Goddess Shadow!" Galene squealed. Dom rushed to catch the stout witch, barely getting under her before she hit the ground. She threw her magic at the dirty cup instead of saving herself. "What are you doing in my office?"

Galene shuffled toward the levitating dish, fuming. Her gloved hands lifted it from the bottom and placed it on a cart.

"I, um, I'm Dominick." He got to his feet.

"Am I supposed to know who you are?"

"Sera told me to find you."

She quirked her silver brow at him, then crossed the space and locked the door. "*Teesina*," she said. "What do you know of Seraphina Wildrick?"

He couldn't stop his snicker. "I know just about everything there is to know about her."

Galene pursed her lips, and Dom saw exactly what Sera had always described—she did look like a gnome.

"They scraped her name off yesterday." Galene wrung her hands over and over. "I don't think they plan on her coming back."

He suddenly became overheated. "Who's they?"

"The master keeper. I thought her mother might prevent it, since she's a chair now, but these aliato have been too close."

"That's what Sera told me to ask you about." Dominick pulled the journal from his robes and handed it to the witch.

Galene let out a breath. "Thank Shadow," she said. "I would recognize that irksome looped handwriting anywhere. I was sure they killed her."

"Not quite." He took a seat behind one of the worktables and rubbed his eyes. As much as he appreciated the promotion, lifelines was constant staring. "The Council sent her on a quest before they would help her retrieve Nora. The aliato... Sera told me to find out more from you."

"Aliato, the winged soldiers of their maker. *Angels*, in the old language." She stepped closer. "The world needs balance. Light and dark. Angel and demon. Where we went wrong was when our founders defected." Galene ripped off her gloves, pushed back a scraggly lock of hair from her forehead. "Minimal texts are left that share our turbulent history with the aliato. Many died for the knowledge to be secured."

Galene slipped on a new set of pristine gloves and motioned for him to follow her back into the stacks.

Books, artifacts. He swore he saw a pair of boots inside a glass case. All of it was old and obsolete. He sneezed, and Galene glared over her shoulder. The old witch unlocked a case that lined the back wall with a small golden key. She pulled out a heavy tome and carefully turned the pages until she found what she was looking for.

Placing the tome on a stand, she pointed. "Look for yourself."

The book was old. Older than anything he'd ever seen before. In the center of the page was an image he couldn't quite make out: a red circle with a simple black figure emerging. On the page beside it was the outline of a woman. "I don't understand."

"It is the birth of Shadow."

"The goddess was birthed?"

"She wasn't a goddess at that time. She was a champion." Galene flipped the page to a picture of the world. "The Dark Ones were born for the sake of Eraphon. We are the dark. The protectors."

Dom's brows reached his hairline. He wasn't one for religion; he prayed to the goddess only when he needed a bit of luck. Come to think of it, that was all most of the coven members did. An old temple existed somewhere within the fortress, but he didn't know anyone who went there.

"What happens," Galene continued, "when a portion of that race aligns itself with the light?" Galene closed the book and put it back on the shelf, locking the cabinet and hiding the key around her neck. "Nothing good can come of it."

She seemed paranoid, unhinged even. But the story was that witches and warlocks had been made from demons. To protect the planet from what?

"Thank you," he said to the keeper.

"Tell Seraphina not to come here." Galene hesitated. "She isn't safe." With a wave of her hand, the sound barrier lifted.

Dom could only nod, unlock the door, and head to his flat.

Chapter Fifty-Four

Seraphina

Sera sat on the central platform of the mirroring pool, waiting for Ophelia, the water tepid on her toes. She watched as the colored threads avoided her skin. She wanted to ask the oracle a few more questions, but when she'd gone back to the parlor, it was empty.

Snik whined at the beginning of the walkway, petrified of the pool as she kicked at the water.

Instead of her face on the pool's surface, it was Nora's that flashed. Nora screaming for their mother as Supay dragged her away.

She was letting her sister down. All this was taking too long.

Alistair's lumbering frame appeared behind her in the water's reflection. Always watching. Ever the protector.

"You knew from the beginning, didn't you?" Sera kicked at the water, sending ripples across the surface.

"I wasn't certain they'd kill Ophelia, no."

"So much death," she whispered. Al removed his boots and dipped his feet beside her. Colton, Ophelia, how many hundreds more would be erased? How many piles of dust would line battlefields?

"It's war."

Sera hated it. She knew if the safety of the coven was of the greatest concern, then it would have to be done. She'd kill anyone who'd hurt the people she loved. But this seemed senseless.

Pulling her dripping toes from the water, she hugged her knees. The tulle from her gown puddled around her.

"I've really fucked up, haven't I?"

She didn't know what to say. His blue gaze bore into her.

It had been... They could have been... She didn't know anymore. Only that it was never going to happen. Not if she was half demon.

"I haven't been truthful," he continued quietly.

Sera sighed. Trust was a fickle thing for her, one she didn't give lightly. "No, you haven't. But I could have been better too."

"Forgive me?" Hunched over his knees, he didn't look at her. No hint of dimples, just sadness. This was Alistair, the warlock she had grown up with. But what of the captain of the Legion? What was he thinking about? Or the Mesar? All of them had separate agendas.

He was the most loyal person she knew, and even though she wished that he could see he was a pawn for the Council, she didn't think he'd change.

"I need you to take care of Dominick for me." She hoped Dom would understand. Her heart ached at the thought of leaving him behind, possibly never seeing him again. But, as Al had so eloquently put it, this was war.

He sat up straight. "I'm not leaving you here. I'm coming back for you."

"Al, it might be better for everyone if you did leave me. Vasso won't harm me."

"Back to this again. If I didn't know better, I'd think that demon put a fucking spell on you." He put his sock on, then a boot.

"That's not fair."

"Isn't it?" he bit back at her. "Sera, we had something until we set foot in this place."

"One kiss doesn't mean anything," she said. He looked like she had punched him.

"That's a lie. I know you felt it." He slipped on a second sock and boot. The glow from the other side of the pool painted his face blue, cutting into the harsh lines and furrowed brow.

"Regardless of what I felt, I'm not putting you or anyone else in danger because you want to play hero and bring me back to where I'm not wanted."

"I want you there."

"But your Council doesn't!" She stood to face him, raising her chin in defiance.

Alistair crossed his arms. "And what if I don't give you a choice?"

There it was, that prideful warlock bullshit. Not pity, not understanding, but control.

Picking up her boots, she leaned toward him, her voice low. "If you try to take me, Alistair, I promise it will be the last thing you do."

Those crystal-blue eyes of his seemed to bulge at her threat. Sera left him in the center of the platform, not willing to continue the conversation. Rage ran through her. Sera's magic snapped tight, and she rubbed at the pain in her chest.

The audacity to imply he could force her, take her against her will. She almost laughed at how far off the mark he was. She could kill him with a thought. The amount of darkness she could wrap him in, and the fact that he couldn't heal properly from it...

Snik whined, chasing after her as she rounded the corner toward her bedroom.

"Snik, I need some time alone." He gave a cry. She softened her tone. "I'm sorry, boy, I just need some time."

Her friend bowed in understanding and trotted down the hall.

Sera closed the door and rested her forehead on it, pressing into the ache radiating from her sternum. She wanted to scream—cry.

"Are you all right?" His voice, like smoke, caressed her spine. Tendrils of mist and fog surrounded her, brushed against her rib cage and the length of her neck. She shivered. "I felt you again."

"I'm fine." She turned, leaning her back against the door. Vasso stood in the shadowed corner of the room. His cool mask was in place, but she noticed the shudder in his jaw, the way he instructed his magic to caress her arms, her cheek, to soothe her.

Guiding a tendril of her own, she envisioned herself stroking his temple. Vasso jumped, clearly not used to being the recipient of misty caresses, then closed his eyes. She ran her smoky fingers across his forehead, around his ear, and down his corded throat.

Her magic passed over the folds of his shirtsleeves, flattening every wrinkle of fabric under her phantom fingertips before grasping his warm hands. She wished it were something as simple as a spell. But she knew by the way he looked at her that it wasn't.

He was just as tortured. Just as hesitant to let this knowing between them happen. A wave of heat radiated from him as he crossed the room. His magic poured over her, setting her insides alight. Shadow, they weren't even touching, and she was breathless.

"Tell me the truth." She hated that she had to ask him. Hated that Alistair's lies had burrowed their way into her. "Why weren't you at dinner?"

Vasso caged her between his arms, put his mouth to her ear, and whispered, "Because I couldn't stand to see you near him. *Him* looking at you..." She couldn't stop the pull, the primal want of her body to be molded to his. "I think about you all day and night, for every second you've been under my roof. It's only gotten worse since we saw those moments with Ophelia." His eyes were on her lips now. She parted them. "What have you done to me?"

"Vasso..."

He closed his eyes and took a deep, savoring breath. As if the sound of his name on her lips were a prayer, a call to the almighty goddess, and Sera was his salvation. Her heart pounded.

Power.

She had power over him. And Shadow save her, she wanted to abuse it.

"Seraphina." He looked at the ceiling. She watched his throat bob before he met her eyes again. "Just say the word…"

"To continue? Or to stop?"

He didn't move. He didn't breathe.

Inching closer, she stared at the demon lord. So many times she'd thought of his kind as monsters. This man was anything but.

Stretching to the tips of her toes, Sera brushed her lips against his. Vasso stood so still she wondered if he was drawing in air.

Then, on a shaky exhale, he said against her mouth, "You'll be the death of me."

Sera devoured him. She gripped his shoulders, and he practically purred when her nails sank into his skin. He lifted her from the floor, guiding her legs around his waist.

She gasped.

He held her firm with one arm steady against her spine, his other hand gripping her inner thigh, all while he teased her tongue with his. Closer and closer his fingers inched toward the apex of her thighs.

She needed him. Now.

His kiss moved to her neck, and she moaned.

Sera couldn't remember the last time she'd ached for someone. Didn't want to remember.

He carried her to the bed and knelt on the mattress. "I've wanted you from the moment I saw you." His breath was hot on the hollow of her neck. "Since I knew you were mine."

Sera bit her lip as Vasso brushed the strap of her dress down. He scraped his teeth against her shoulder, leaving a wake of molten ache pulsing lower and lower. With her breast exposed, she arched her back, and Vasso took her nipple in his mouth.

Her world was obliterated. Somewhere deep down, she'd known it would be like this. Maybe from that moment in the woods when she'd given him that scar on his cheek.

She needed him lower, but he stayed right there, licking, sucking, grazing with his teeth. Heat pooled between her legs as Vasso pushed her skirt higher on her hips.

A pounding on the door had her jolting upright.

"If that's him, he's dead." A guttural tone of violence rolled from the back of Vasso's throat. He didn't let her go, and Sera was pretty sure his words alone would push her over the edge at any moment.

"Seraphina? You wished to speak to me?" Ophelia's voice floated into the room.

"I'll be right out," she said, trying to keep her voice steady. She slid from beneath Vasso and righted her dress. Vasso crossed the room, desire lacing in his red eyes.

"We're not done," he whispered, then kissed her forehead.

She gave him a sly grin. "We'll see."

He tilted his head to the side and disappeared into a pool of mist. Once they'd relieved some tension, she'd have him teach her that little trick.

"Ophelia." She opened the door with a breathless smile. "I was looking for you."

"Not very hard, I see." Ophelia raised a brow at Sera and turned down the hallway. "I'm leaving you my grimoire."

Sera wanted to protest and demand that Ophelia keep her beloved book of prophecies, but she knew that the oracle wouldn't need it within the Citadel walls. Life was cruel. That was a lesson she'd learned long ago.

"Come," Ophelia said more softly. "Ask me your questions, for we don't have much time left."

Sera settled into the plush pillows on one of the ruby-red sofas in the small seating area off the main chamber. On a low table, a complete tea set with baked goods awaited them. She hadn't realized how hungry she was and grabbed one.

"You said that you think I'm the witch from the prophecy. To unite the coven under the Gehenna banner once again?"

Ophelia nodded.

"If I'm that witch, would that make it my destiny?" She had to know. Her brand was already on Vasso's forearm, and if that was her destiny, then she needed information. She needed to know about Supay and the levels of Gehenna.

"Destiny and fate are often interchanged. Everything is up to interpretation, of course. We have power, and destiny is our potential. You choose your destination. But fate..." Ophelia nibbled at a pastry. "Fate is pulled by a force we have no control over. It stays the same no matter what threads we pull."

"Supay is the leader of the underworld."

"Shadow, no. If he were, we would have lost this world long ago. He is the steward. A placeholder for when the heir comes into full power. Supay must still abide by the heir's wishes. Well, he's supposed to."

"Our texts didn't mention a new ruler coming into power. That would be a severe oversight." A change of power in Gehenna would be felt throughout the world. Magic would react in a way no one could predict. The last time there'd been a new ruler was over six hundred years ago. The texts said Eraphon shook with such force that it caused the Lanac mountain range to split.

Ophelia shrugged. "I don't know much else. Vasso would know better, being part of the high court."

"What's happening in the Citadel?"

"Ahh, now there is a question," Ophelia said as she poured out two steaming cups to the brim. "Alistair hasn't been forthcoming with information?"

Sera rubbed absently at the middle of her chest. Ophelia's eyes tracked the movement. She couldn't call it pain, exactly. It was a current. Always pulling from her, a tether linking her to an unknown.

"I'm asking you. Not Alistair." Sera brought a teacup to her lips. The steam tickled her nose, and she blew it away.

"The Citadel has put itself in a precarious situation. Alliances have been made with humans and the aliato, a move even I did not see coming."

It was dangerous. So much talk of balance between light and dark. Now it seemed the scales were tipping. Sera furrowed her brow and set down her cup right before Raven landed on the sofa beside her.

Ophelia smiled brilliantly at her familiar.

All oracles had a beauty to them, with their light hair and eyes, but Ophelia seemed transcendent when she smiled. Sera pictured her as a goddess bathed in light instead of darkness.

"The city is frightened. The light-bringers are a vicious race, and the coven is witnessing that firsthand."

"What about my friend Dominick?"

"He is well. You don't need to worry for him."

Sera slumped deeper into the sofa, a weight lifted. "Can you tell me about the process of regeneration? For demons?"

"You'll have to discuss that with Vasso."

Sera rubbed her chest again. "What about this pulling?"

The oracle looked stunned. "A pulling, you say? Where does it pull you?"

"Does that matter?"

"Very much so, Seraphina." Ophelia sipped her tea, eyeing her over the cup's rim. "A fate tether can lead you to love or demise. Fate never shares. We have little knowledge of those tethered of the heart."

Another cryptic message. Fate. Love or demise. Riddles forever burrowing themselves into Sera's brain from this blasted oracle. "Can you tell me where Vasso is?"

A lupine smile crossed Ophelia's face. "He's in his study. I think you're familiar with the area."

Sera stood. "Thank you, Ophelia, for taking this time with me. I wish it were different. I wish I could have known you long before any of this happened." The thought of Ophelia at the hands of the Council made her sick. If she could change it, she would, but what could she do?

The oracle looked torn. "Seraphina. About your father... I wanted to tell you that he's alive, but you must know that he isn't... He's being blocked somehow. His strings, I cannot pull them." Ophelia put her teacup down on the tray. "Yours are golden, which means someone is protecting you within the Citadel walls. But his are gray."

"But he's alive?"

Ophelia grimaced, like maybe he shouldn't be.

"Thank you, Ophelia. It's at least good to know." She had a father, and he was out there. Waiting for her. Ophelia spoke in riddles. Being blocked could mean many things, but that was secondary to saving Nora.

She needed to get her sister back.

Then she'd find her father.

CHAPTER FIFTY-FIVE

SERAPHINA

Sera made her way through the underground manor, past the dining room and down the stone halls bathed in candlelight. She didn't know how she was going to bring up her questions. She'd barely figured out what questions she wanted to ask.

As she stood in silence, watching him through the crack of the door, a warm glow came over her.

His hair flopped forward, and he was scrawling something into his ledger, quill in hand. She thought of the tether between them. A fate tether, Ophelia had said. Something that tied them together, no matter the cost. Vasso's dead face against her hand flashed in her mind.

She gave the tether a yank. Vasso rubbed his chest, then looked right at her.

He gave her a wry smile. "Sneaky witch." He left his desk, pulled her into his study, and closed the door. "Are you back for more?" he said against her lips, locking them with hers. She wanted to melt into him, forget everything for a while, and just... feel.

"Wait," she said. "I have some questions."

He straightened for a second but didn't let her go. "Go ahead."

"In the forest, when I saved the elken king, I lit two of the agbris on fire. They were down and burning—" Vasso dropped his hands from her waist;

the flirtatious look was replaced by a neutral mask. "Al explained to me that demons can regenerate."

Vasso stepped back, circling the desk, and took a seat in his chair. This didn't seem to be going well. She should have known that by mentioning Alistair, she'd get some sort of reaction. That had been stupid. But all she wanted was to keep herself safe, and if there was a certain number of repeated kills she needed to reach in a fight, the more prepared she was, the better.

Sera perched herself at the edge of the velvet chair across from him.

"So you're asking me to reveal demon secrets."

"I guess so. I mean, apparently I'm half demon, so it would affect me too." She hadn't even thought about what that meant for her, but didn't plan on trying the theory.

"Do you think me naive, Seraphina?" The light cast sharp shadows across his face. "I've been alive a long time, and if you think I'd share one of demonkind's most valuable secrets, you're mistaken."

"But—"

"No." He pushed up his shirtsleeves, revealing her raven brand on his forearm. "Just because I'm dying to bed you doesn't mean I will lay down my secrets."

Lust. She wanted him without care or consequence, despite what that might mean for her.

"I'm assuming you know a bit more now about this fate tether?" Vasso pointed between them. Sera touched her chest. "That's a yes, then."

"Yes, her cryptic bullshit about love or demise." Sera stood, already tired of the turn this conversation was taking.

"Perfect," he said and escorted her to the door.

"It's like you fear me."

"I fear what you could tell your precious bodyguard." He sneered.

Sera froze. He thought she was going to tell Al. Give away their biggest secret for an advantage. Her voice shook. "I can't believe you."

"Why not? He still hovers around you like you're his to keep. I'm sure he'd love some extra information about how to defeat us that he could feed to your Council."

"So that's it? You think I'm going to cause your downfall by revealing secrets?" She fisted her hands. Her magic raged within her as she glared at his perfect face.

"Did you forget that I lay dead in *your* hands?"

"You're a demon lord! You could ruin me without a thought!"

Vasso let out a breath and took a step back. She held herself, not moving, only watching him pace across the dark carpet, one, two, three times. Then he was back. Close enough to breathe in, close enough to kiss. "I could ruin you in more ways than one, Subdina."

Sera scoffed. She didn't do what she wanted to: curse him, scream, point out that the scar on his cheek was from her. Getting into Gehenna was more important, and she wouldn't be able to do it without him.

He towered over her. "I would burn and rebuild the world with you at its center. I would end every life on Eraphon, maiming and killing any being who would think to take you from me. Burn them with the vatra we share—and it makes no sense." He caught a piece of her hair between his fingers and twirled, seemingly hypnotized by the feel of it. "We barely know each other." He pursed his lips. "I've waited three hundred and fifty years—"

"You're *how* old?"

He sighed and pinched the bridge of his nose. "Fate has decided we are tied together. We both saw how I ended. I'd be a fool to tell you my realm's secrets in hopes that whenever I die, you'll forget your promises to me and share them with your coven."

Metaphysical bullshit. Fate bullshit. Every second of her life felt like it was layered in a thin coating of shit.

"And what do you choose, Vasso? Love, or should we kill each other? That's what demise means, after all."

His brows scrunched as if he couldn't believe what she was asking. "There was never a choice for me."

Her heart pounded. The tether between them grew thicker, from a single strand to a braid, all while she was staring daggers at him.

She wanted to believe that they could be together, but what could be given could be taken away. Sera knew the transactions involved in "love" well.

"I don't want to fight with you. I just can't trust you yet," he said, and Shadow help her, he sounded genuine.

"You seem to trust me enough to be your naughty little plaything."

His mouth broke into a wicked grin that had her closing her thighs tight. "I want you to be my plaything, oh, I do." He grabbed her chin. "I could be yours too," he whispered against her lips. "Give you that power... let you control me."

Dangerous thoughts rushed through her mind. First, her on her knees, taking him in her palm. She imagined him tied to a bed, his eyes blazing. Then pushing his head between her legs...

But if he didn't trust her, then none of it mattered.

Sera pulled her chin from his hand. She went to the desk, ripped a piece of paper from his pad, and scribbled a quick note. "I'm going to rest," she said. "Tomorrow is a big day."

"Seraphina—"

"I don't know what you're going to say, but don't."

Sera ripped open the door and marched back to her room. She clutched her raven pendant, and a moment later her familiar soared through the dark halls to land on her shoulder. "You're connected to me, right?" she asked it.

The bird made a noise that sounded like a knock. She held up the rolled note. "I'm taking that as a yes. Bring this to Dominick in the Citadel fortress. He's an oracle and a smart-ass. You can't miss him."

Her familiar grabbed the note with its beak and took off through the tunnels.

Chapter Fifty-Six

Alistair

Alistair awoke early, packed his bag, and prepared to return to the Citadel. He checked in on Sera while she slept. Her dark eyelashes cast a shadow across her light brown skin as she held Snik close to her stomach. Even in sleep, they were inseparable. He couldn't say the same for the raven.

He was happy the bird wasn't perched in her room. He hated birds.

Alistair swallowed hard. It had all gone wrong.

When he learned that she'd accompany him on this mission, he'd almost told Chair Renata to demote him. Sera was stubborn, rude, and so fucking beautiful. By some miracle, she'd warmed up to him.

He still thought about their first night in the tavern. Sera twirling under his arm in that oversize purple dress he'd bought off a washerwoman. The way her hair bounced when she danced, her smile brilliant in the middle of the tavern floor. She looked free. At that moment, his heart opened to her, to the possibility that this mission might bring him something more than a job well done.

When he saw that human in their room in Ironoak, Sera scared out of her mind and wielding his dagger, he'd lost every ounce of control he'd attained as a Legion captain. When he traveled that human to the clearing, he'd gripped the bastard's throat until his face turned purple. He'd let one breath fill his lungs, then seared him from the inside out. He'd felt his magic rip through every one of the human's blood vessels and watched him writhe in agony. Just before he was about to die, Alistair had snapped his neck.

Then he'd traveled back to her.

Seraphina.

Now, Al went to look for the oracle to make sure she hadn't escaped in the night—hadn't changed her mind, causing more chaos. But when he went to the mirroring pool, she was there.

"Warlock, is it time?" she asked without turning away from the water.

"It is."

"Wish to sneak me away without her knowing?"

Alistair cleared his throat. "I wouldn't do that. I'll let her say goodbye."

Ophelia was eyeing him suspiciously, but he didn't care what she thought of him. She would be the Council of Elders' problem soon, and he could move on to something else. Perhaps he'd travel back here, kill Vasso himself.

"You're torn." She smirked. "Maybe *torn* is the wrong word. I think a better term is *feeling guilty*."

"I have no guilt. I do what must be done, is all."

"That is not all. Everything hangs in the balance." The oracle seethed at him.

"You and all this mystic bullshit. You go on and on about the world but share nothing of use. It amazes me this demon kept you for so long."

"Showing your fangs, warlock?" Her voice was sly. The feline grin crossing her features turned into something feral. "Tell me what I am." Ophelia flung her arms wide, and image after image came from the threads that shot out of the water.

In the projections, he watched a spear pierce his heart. Next, he was alight with black flames. Another had him holding Sera limp in his arms, Dominick dead at his feet.

Image after image flashed before him. Hundreds of ways he would die. A sickening unease built in his gut.

"We have free will, yes," Ophelia told him, more images flashing. "But what is free will if it all ends in disaster? These are all the ways you will die if you take her with you on this day. Only one may come true, but the possibilities are endless. I am warning you one more time, warlock. Leave her."

He tried to swallow his nausea. "How do I know you're not manipulating me?"

"Of course I'm manipulating you, but only for the good of Eraphon. For if you take her, you aren't the only one who will die." The oracle swung her arms again, and images of Seraphina and Dominick appeared. Sera was beheaded and hanged. Dominick was buried and burned. He watched as they screamed over and over again. He watched Sera covered in blood, howling his name.

"Stop it," he choked. The oracle dropped her arms, and the images and the threads from which they came disappeared. "Swear it, swear on Shadow this will happen if I take her back."

Ophelia left the center of the pool and walked toward him. "One of these events will happen. I swear on Shadow." She placed her hand over her heart. "On Eraphon." And bowed.

The sinking feeling in his gut did not cease with her promise. "Get whatever you need together," he instructed, and went to wake up Sera.

Outside the door, he gathered himself. He took a deep breath, then knocked. Sera answered, her hair half up, Snik beside her.

Her pack wasn't on her shoulder where he wished it was; it was lying against the far wall.

"Ready?" she asked.

He nodded.

"Al, I want you to know, I'm not mad at you. I know you meant well, all of it, and I'm sorry."

"You have nothing to be sorry for." He pushed into her room, pulled two daggers from the back of his waistband, and set them on the bed.

"Al?"

"These are for you. Carry them with you everywhere," he said, then reached into his pocket and pulled out two quartz spheres. "Open your hand."

She did, and he dropped the stones in her outstretched palm.

"These are summoning stones. They're enchanted. You break one and I'll know exactly where you are."

Silver lined those beautiful green eyes.

"Anything…" His voice caught. "If you need me for anything, you throw that on the ground and crack it, and I will come for you."

She didn't say anything for a long moment, and every second her eyes bore into his broke him. He would come for her if she needed him. He could give her that in atonement for all the secrets he kept from her.

Barely above a whisper, she said, "I'm sorry for what we could have been. I think"—she wiped her nose on her sleeve—"I think we both know it wouldn't have ended well for us."

Her breath hitched, and it felt like a knife piercing his heart. He didn't need to watch it in the images from Ophelia's threads. He felt it here, in her words.

"Come on, we're wasting time," he said and left her room.

Every step closer to the mirroring pool was a step farther from her. Chair Renata had been adamant that he bring the oracle back today. The last time he'd been there, the Citadel had been playing on the offensive, or at least trying to, and he didn't want to push his luck.

Vasso walked into the room, and Al straightened. The witches were saying their goodbyes. He approached the demon lord.

"I don't like you," he said in a whispered warning. "I don't trust you with her." Vasso's eyes blazed red, but he kept the smirk on his face as if

Al wasn't a threat. "But I'm not blind. Something is going on, and I want assurance you'll not harm her."

"Your loyalty is admirable. I will promise you that no harm will come to Seraphina while I am near."

Seraphina and Ophelia were whispering to each other. He only had a few more seconds, and this was going to hurt, but... "I want to make a bargain." Vasso raised his brows. "I want your word that you'll protect her with your life."

"What do I get in return?"

"What do you want?"

Vasso's eyes shifted from him to Sera and back. "I want the same. You'll need to protect Seraphina with your life, if it ever comes to it."

Alistair slid his glove off his hand and held it out to the lord. Vasso took it. His palm felt like a hot coal. That sensation raced up his arm, over his shoulder and onto his ribs. Then searing, blinding pain.

Al bit down so hard he thought his teeth would crack to prevent himself from crying out. She'd hate him even more for doing this, but he couldn't help it. He wouldn't chance her being harmed by him.

Vasso breezed by him. "Leaving without saying goodbye? How rude." Ophelia walked to the demon, her hands extended to him.

Alistair only saw Sera.

He took her in—her raven hair and tawny skin. Those sage-and-emerald eyes were brilliant against the tears spilling down her cheeks. She was wearing the Legion tunic, one that she was never meant to wear but willingly had to save Nora. She'd jumped into this quest without training, experience, or knowledge of the outside world. She was the bravest witch he knew.

He swallowed.

Sera locked eyes with him then, and he approached. He held out his arms, a prayer, a sign of forgiveness for doing the unforgivable. She stepped forward and hugged him back. He breathed in that nutty smell of sea air, savoring every moment of her in his arms.

It was the way it should have been if he hadn't been so damned stupid. He didn't want to let her go, but she broke the embrace.

"Promise me that you'll take care of Dom?" she asked.

"I promise, Minnow."

Her lip quivered, and he took a step back. He didn't want to break in front of them, in front of her. Al looked at Vasso. The demon's face revealed a deadly assessment of him. It seemed he wasn't the only one who'd fallen for her.

He gave the demon lord a nod of understanding. Vasso gave him one back.

Look at her—just one more time.

He didn't want to know what she was thinking. He didn't deserve to know, and it killed him to leave her here. But if one of those outcomes came true, if he was the reason for her death, he'd never live with himself. He'd lost his father, his mother, and Colton. Now, the only hope he had of love again stared back at him with a sad smile and tears streaming down her cheeks.

Alistair crossed the room, grabbed the oracle's hand, and was gone.

CHAPTER FIFTY-SEVEN

DOMINICK

Pink slivers of light were breaking across his floor when he decided he needed to leave. Dom walked the streets of the Citadel complex looking for Theo. He hadn't shown up last night. They had made plans; Theo knew it was important. Dom's hands shook within his robes as he stepped onto the white stone of Daedeth's streets.

Bakers and merchants were setting up their stalls and unlocking their doors as he raced to Theo's flat. Dom pounded on the door again and again, yelling his name.

There was no answer.

So he turned to the only place he had left.

"Have either of you seen Theo?" He was frantic. His parents looked at him as if he were drunk. He wished he were. Wished that in a few hours, he'd snap out of his stupor.

"What is wrong with you?" His father's clipped voice shot through him. "Your mother is a wreck, and you charge in acting a fool?"

"He's gone," Dom whispered.

His mother set her teacup down with a delicate clink. "When did you last see him?"

"Yesterday morning. He left early for the pools." Dom collapsed into the kitchen chair. "They were closed when I tried to return... when I realized he wasn't home."

"We'll find him," his mother said.

Tristan Benero nodded and swung his red cloak around his shoulders. "He must be somewhere within the walls."

Desperate for help, he followed his father from the row house. His stomach was sour from stress and lack of food, but the thought of eating something made it worse. He had to find Theo.

"You sure he's not visiting a friend or something?" his father asked.

"No, it was..." Dominick hesitated. It didn't matter what his father thought. Theo mattered more. "It was an important night. He knew it was important. Theo wouldn't have missed it."

"Dominick." His father stopped. Dom noticed for the first time the gray hairs in his father's goatee. The lines around his eyes. He'd aged years, it seemed, since Colton. "You and Theodore are good for each other. We'll find him, bring him home for a hot meal, and all will be right."

Something in his chest snapped. Instead of shame flooding in, it felt something like relief. Relief that his father saw him for who he truly was and, in his way, had given permission for Dom to be himself.

Dom wiped his nose on his sleeve. "Thank you, Father."

"Come on. You recheck the pools, and I'll go to the dining hall and common areas in Darine Hall."

Dom raced up the front steps of the Ogdelo, ignoring the mastria and the aliato posted at the entrance. He kept the wall tight around his mind, not bothering to give them a memory to latch onto.

The pool was quiet. A few oracles were on platforms, starting their day's quota. Throwing his hands out, he pulled for Theo. A string of blue wobbled, then pulled tight, racing for him. It didn't fall apart or crumble; he was still alive. He wished he had gotten far enough in his training to pull the image, but this was enough; it had to be. Theo was alive. But where was he?

Too many were disappearing. Too many had been executed by Raphael's blade over the past week. He wouldn't let it happen to Theo.

Dom raced down the steps to meet his father in the Darine courtyard.

Tears spilled down his cheeks. Gone. Gone. Gone.

Theo was fucking gone.

Colton, Nora, Sera... Theo.

Heavy arms wrapped around him. His father pulled him to his chest, and Dom broke. "I'll take you home, son."

They left the courtyard. His father hugged his shoulders tight in one arm and guided him through Daedeth Quarter's streets back to his childhood home. His father didn't let go until he sat him down in a chair facing the bronze clock in his parents' sitting room.

He had to keep hope. Had to.

A high-pitched ringing in his ears drowned out the sound of his parents whispering in the other room. Quiet. Numb. Nothing but the clock ticking away in time with his heart.

"Dominick!" his mother screamed as she ran into the room and threw him to the floor.

A second later, his father was above them... and the walls caved in.

CHAPTER FIFTY-EIGHT

SERAPHINA

Sera wiped the tears from her face. Alistair was gone, and the emotion rocked her much harder than she'd anticipated. That stubborn warlock had been her safety net. All she could think about was what she'd said to him. How sorry she was, and that this was the way things had to end between them.

He was gone, and Ophelia...

She didn't want to think about what the oracle was about to face. All Sera knew was that it was time to save Nora.

"We need to leave," she said to Vasso.

"Your belongings and Snik are already waiting for us in the main chamber. Though I don't know where your familiar is."

"Raven will find us," she said. Sera went to walk past him, but his fingers brushed hers, halting her.

"Are you all right?" he asked.

Her gaze met his. She saw it then, for the first time—pain lingering in the lines around his mouth. Vasso's shoulders were wound tight, and her chest began to ache.

Everything was a damned mess, but after all of it, she was here with him. The connection between them ate at her. He didn't trust her, and she shouldn't trust him. She should walk away, let herself process losing Al in her own way, in her own time, alone. It was how she'd always done things.

You are fated, her magic said. *Can't you feel it? He hurts because you hurt.*

Sera let out a shaky breath and embraced him. She buried her nose in his chest and breathed him in. How could a person feel so lost but found at the same time?

Vasso wrapped his arms around her. The tension melted from the planes of his back as he pulled her tight like his life depended on it. She wondered if it did.

"Are you?" she finally asked. "All right, I mean?" Those eyes. Gray with flecks of silver and black.

"Better now," he said, giving her a sorry smile that made him look boyish.

"We'd better get going."

Vasso took her hand and led her to the main chamber. Sera looked around, taking in the rock formations, the tapestries along the walls, and flits of shadows across the lush furnishings.

Snik yipped, dragging her pack across the floor behind him. "You ready for another adventure, buddy?"

"Eeeeeeck," the goblin squealed.

Sera checked her pack. The daggers that Al had given her and the summoning stones were in there, along with the remaining bottles of her sleeping elixir. Sera huffed a laugh.

"What's funny?" Vasso asked.

She held up the glass bottle. "I just realized I haven't needed one of these since I've been here."

"Subdina, if there was something you needed, you should have told me."

"No, no... It's all right." Sera swung her Legion pack onto her shoulder.

"You're not wearing that."

"Not fancy enough for you?" She glanced down at her Legion uniform.

"Do you think it's wise to be riding into the Deadlands with that uniform on?"

Well, when he put it like that. "All right," she said with a huff. Vasso put his finger to his chin and eyed her up and down. The glint in his eye made her a tad wary of what he intended next. Her brown boots and trousers turned black with a snap of his fingers. Her long blue tunic became a formfitting bustier, barely reaching her navel.

"You're not serious."

"It's basically summer. I thought you might like the breeze." He tried not to smile but failed miserably.

"My tits are to my chin, Vasso."

His gaze explored her, that smirk turning sly.

"A full shirt, please," she said.

Vasso sighed and snapped again. A sleeveless black cotton shirt formed around her, covering her entire midriff. He'd even included a supportive bralette beneath. "Thank you."

"The stables." He pointed. She followed.

Ponic was in the far stall. Sera clicked her tongue at the horse, who nuzzled his black velvet nose in her hand.

"Cheating on me, boy?" Vasso said and saddled him. "Yours is over there."

A black mare with a white diamond on her muzzle stepped toward her. "She's beautiful."

"She's yours. Though Ponic seems quite taken with her."

"Mine?"

He nodded. "I purchased her the first time you asked for my help."

A flush of adrenaline tingled through her; she beamed at him. "You were always going to take me, weren't you?"

Vasso cleared his throat, obviously avoiding her question, and focused on fitting the bit into Ponic's mouth. A strand of hair had fallen into his eyes again. His veined forearms flexed with the passing of the crown over Ponic's ears. He worked efficiently, as if he had done this a million times before.

"Her name is Navine," he said.

"Navine, you're stunning."

"A stunning horse for a stunning witch." Vasso smirked and led Ponic from his stall.

"Such a charmer, aren't you?"

Once Ponic was secured outside, Vasso set to saddle Navine and instructed Sera to mount. She climbed up and waited. "You're next, little one." Vasso lifted Snik to sit in front of her.

His hand rested on her thigh. A question lay blatantly across his face, but the words that came out didn't match. "Yes, I was always going to bring you."

"You don't seem too happy about it."

He squeezed her leg. "I wouldn't bring you within an inch of Gehenna if I could." Vasso let her go and mounted Ponic.

Sera had a sinking feeling there was something he wasn't telling her. It was too late for that now. "Where are we headed?"

"Port Sidnah. There's a gateway there, a lesser-known one. Plus, I want to show you something," Vasso said.

Navine brought herself next to Ponic, and they began trotting into the warm wind from the southeast.

CHAPTER FIFTY-NINE

ALISTAIR

The fold between space brought them to the Citadel. His boots hit the marble steps outside the Council chambers, but around them was chaos. Ophelia held herself together well enough. She looked pale, but at least she didn't vomit.

Projectiles flew through the air, some aflame, others not. But all crashed into buildings, streets, and coven members between the walls. Black smoke rose from every quarter.

Rage ripped through him. These fucking demons. He needed to get to a higher vantage point and figure out where the Legion was stationed. The barracks were still standing, from what he could tell.

He pulled a wide-eyed but silent Ophelia through the entrance of the Council chambers. Apparently, she hadn't seen this coming either.

Two guards positioned themselves in front of the carved doors at the end of the main hall, and by the looks they were giving him, they weren't about to let him through.

"I'm here on Council business," he said, pulling Ophelia closer. He lightened his grip on her wrist a touch, not realizing he'd been holding her so tight.

"Council of Elders isn't to be interrupted."

Alistair pushed the guard hard against the wall with his free hand, pinning him by the neck with his forearm. "Let. Me. In," he snarled.

The guard's eyes bulged. His hands scrambled for purchase on Al's arm, but Al didn't budge. His people were dying.

The second guard clicked open the door, Alistair released the first and entered.

Raised voices sounded ahead, but when Al burst into the space, everyone went silent. He bowed before four of the Council members and presented his task. "I bring you Ophelia Fray." Al pulled Sera's map from his back pocket and threw it on the table between them. "And the doorways."

"You fool," Chair Renata snapped, raising her hands for an attack. "You brought her unshackled?"

Ophelia laughed eerily. "Relax, Renata. I promised complete cooperation. And I keep my promises."

A guard stepped forward, holding out a pair of onyx manacles. Ophelia didn't flinch when the stone inlays touched her wrists, but he could see where her skin was already turning red. He had to admit, she had grit.

"Guards, take her to the holding cells," Renata called out.

Alistair didn't bother to watch her leave. He dipped his chin to the Council members, awaiting his next assignment. Beyond their thrones, the expanse of the sea was serene, at odds with the chaos that was raining down around them. Vibrations from projectiles shook the glass.

"You will wait to be dismissed," a cool voice said. The secret panel was ajar, and Lavinia Wildrick, master mastria, Seraphina's mother, watched him from the doorway, carrying a cup of tea in her hands. "Where is my daughter?"

He was sure she already knew the answer and was asking only for the benefit of the other chairs. She'd already picked his mind clean.

"I was told to leave her, so I did," he said.

"Hmm." She pondered, one brow arched. Her amber eyes seemed to glow against her dark skin. Alistair glanced around at the other chairs. They just stood there, silent, breathing, and staring into space. Lavinia smiled.

A boom in the distance shook the building. He needed to leave, now. Somewhere in the fortress, coven members were dying, and this bitch wanted to talk semantics. Lavinia's eyes flared. He probably shouldn't have thought that.

"What have you done to them?" he asked. None of them had moved an inch. "They are your leaders."

"That's where you're wrong. A lot has happened since you've been away. I'm a chair now." She smirked and looked at the other Council members. "And how wonderful it is to have control over everyone."

Another shudder went through the building. "You're going to let it burn?"

"No, I won't burn it down. Just rough it up enough to get the coven a little angry." Lavinia placed her teacup in the middle of the city map that was laid out on the table. Chair Thorne and Blackwell were leaning over it, frozen. "Now," she said, crossing her arms. "You're going to bring my daughter back."

"The Council ordered her to be left before you were appointed. Why would I?"

"I'll take care of them, don't worry. Do I make myself clear?"

Hope surged through him. If she could control Blackwell, then neither he nor the guardians would care that she was within the walls again. Then those actions Ophelia showed him, the ones where Sera was being killed over and over, wouldn't happen. He could get her, bring her home. "Clear as the wards above the city," Alistair said.

At once, the Council members began moving again. "Alistair, why are you still here? Did you travel and bring Seraphina back?" Chair Renata asked.

Lavinia's face was stone.

"I'll be retrieving her soon." He bowed to his rulers and left the chambers as fast as he could without being beheaded.

***

Alistair sprinted into the city. He had to find Dominick first. He'd made a promise to Sera.

Daedeth Quarter was mostly standing. He rounded the corner, but where the Benero row house should be was an empty space. His heart pounded in his ears, and Al leaped into the rubble. Straining under large chunks of travertine, he pulled what he could from the foundation. They couldn't be in there. They had to be at their occupations.

Alistair heaved another heavy slab of stone out of the way, grunting under the weight. He couldn't deal with burning another set of parents. Because that's what Tristan and Mauve had been to him since his father had died.

"Mr. Benero? Dominick? Are you in there?"

A surge of power followed a muffled response deep in the rubble. Alistair traveled to the sound, barely fitting into the space where Colton's father held a domed barrier above his wife and son. The weight of the stone row house was crushing against the slowly cracking barrier, which was barely big enough to hold the four of them.

"Oh, thank Shadow," Dominick said, pushing his mother forward.

Colton's father's expression was fixed in a painful grimace. "Get them out!"

Alistair grabbed Mrs. Benero first, traveling her to safety. Dominick was next, and lastly, a split second before his barrier fell, he got Mr. Benero out.

"Oh, my boy." Mauve grasped him hard around the middle. "I am so glad you are home."

"I'm so sorry about Colton, that I couldn't be here..." He did his best to keep his composure. Tristan wrapped his arms around him, and his heart broke for the warlock.

"Where is Sera?" Dom asked, wringing his hands. He looked a wreck. A fine layer of dust coated each of them.

"She's safe for now," he said. "Not here."

Dominick nodded. "You still have clearance to get into the dungeons?"

"As far as I know. What's going on?" he asked and released Dom's parents.

"I'll tell you on the way."

"Dom, I need to get to the barracks, report to my post."

Dominick seethed at him, his lip curled. "If you had any love for my brother, you would take me into the dungeon."

Al sighed. "What's going on?"

"I'll tell you on the way."

Outside the tower, Alistair worked to keep his rage in check. He was ready to rip the Council chambers to the ground. A crowd had gathered in front of the tower entrance. Two guards struggled to keep the mob back.

Al and Dominick pushed their way to the gate.

"Captain Alcott?"

"Cain, why are you away from your post?" Alistair asked as he pushed to the front.

"We've been reassigned. They put us with another company two days ago."

"What the fuck are they doing?" he asked, now at the tower entrance.

"I don't know, sir," Cain said. "You need access below?"

Al nodded. The gate rose, and he and Dominick slipped inside. A reeking musk of bodies and dirt wafted from below. It had never smelled this bad before.

"They also started executions." Dominick heaved, pulling his robe above his nose.

"That's not new."

"Daily!"

Fuck. "How many?"

"Dozens," Dominick said as they trekked downward. "The Council's paranoid. Claiming each prisoner is a spy."

Dom had explained they needed to find his friend. Alistair wasn't sure what level they would have placed him in, so they'd planned to work their way down. Now they reached the first set of cells. Each contained coven members. The stench of death was so pungent that Al wondered how many of them were alive. "Who's carrying them out?"

Dominick stopped for a second and rubbed his forehead. "The Council is condemning, but the aliato are completing the executions."

Alistair looked at his best friend's baby brother. Dust coated his hair. His eyes were bloodshot, and his movements were jerky. Al hesitated. He wanted to force Dom to return to the surface and rest, but he knew the oracle would put up a fight Al really didn't have the energy for.

The next level down, the coven prisoners were more lively. They reached through the cell bars with dirty hands, begging for food, crying for release. Each had a set of onyx manacles wrapped too tightly around their wrists. They must be terrified. The onyx ripped away their magic.

Another level down were the interrogation rooms. Warded walls prevented any noise from escaping. Alistair and Dominick peeked into every small window to see who was inside. The first three were empty; the fourth held Ophelia.

She was alone. Eyes closed, cross-legged on the floor. Her hands lay open in her lap, and her mouth was moving.

He sighed.

What would his father make of him now? Bringing witches to their deaths, abandoning everyone he loved. Allowing himself to be used as a pawn in the Council's plans. He should be ashamed of himself.

Ophelia snapped her eyes open, held up three fingers, and pointed to the wall leading farther into the tower. Alistair gave her an apologetic smile, and she returned it.

"Dom." He pointed down the hall. Dom ran ahead of him. He must have found who he was looking for, because the noise that came from the warlock was one of pure emotional agony.

When Al reached him, Dominick was clawing at the door. Inside the cell, a warlock lay motionless on the ground.

"Theo!" Dominick cried out, slamming his palm against the window.

Al grabbed him around the neck and covered his mouth.

"Be quiet," he hissed in his ear. "He can't hear you. It's warded."

Dominick stopped squirming, and Alistair let him go. He watched Dominick cry at the door, punching, throwing his magic at it, but it was useless.

"Come on, say your goodbyes." The stare Dom gave him was deadly. Al hadn't meant forever, but they had to leave, and soon. He took a few steps back to give them a semblance of privacy.

"Look at me, please," Dominick begged at the door. "Al, look, he's alive." His face was joyous, but he quickly crumbled to see his friend's state. The warlock's eyes were black and swollen, his nose shattered, leaning too far toward his right cheek.

Dominick put his palm to the door. "I'll get you out."

Alistair looked away, embarrassed to be interrupting such an intimate moment between the two of them. He remembered when Colton told him of Dominick's preferences. He'd been a little put off, blaming his discomfort on his parents' conservative views, but as they'd grown older, he'd understood that love was love. Colton was always supportive of Dom, so why should Al be any different?

Dominick kissed the pads of his fingertips and laid them on the glass. Theo mirrored him and smiled, splitting his lip further. The battered warlock's cheeks were stained with heavy tears, and his desperation was clear.

This wasn't a promise.

This was a goodbye.

"I don't want to leave him," Dominick croaked.

"We need the incantation to get him out. If you're caught down here, they'll lock you up too. We need to develop a plan. I have to get Sera, and we can figure this out all together."

"No, Sera can't come here. Galene said she isn't safe."

"I don't think any of us are very safe right now if there is a demon army at our doorstep." Al blew out a breath, trying to calm himself. "Lavinia wants her back, and I've got to trust Sera's mother will make sure she's protected."

Dominick scoffed. "Doubtful." He glared at the warlock. "Fine, let's get her."

Al gave them another moment alone, then they started toward the surface.

They were almost at ground level when three large warlocks, Chair Blackwell, and an aliato entered the dungeons. Alistair bowed deeply to the chair, and thankfully Dominick followed his lead. The aliato warrior was menacing: his chest puffed out, his bright white wings lifted well above the damp floor. The light-bringer let out something like a snarl as they passed.

Nausea rolled through Al. He knew which interrogation room they were headed to and what would happen to the witch inside.

Ophelia had known what she was getting into when she'd agreed to comply with the Council's wishes. He'd done his duty, and now she would suffer the consequences. It wasn't his fault.

Then why did he feel so sick?

CHAPTER SIXTY

DOMINICK

His hands wouldn't stop shaking.

Theo, his Theo, was… Dom couldn't think it. His condition was barbaric. His beautiful face marred and bloody. They had beaten him, tortured him.

Alistair instructed the guards to lift the steel gate from the tower's entrance. As soon as Dom was able to pass, he ran and vomited in the bushes. "I've got to get to Sera's room. There's a book…"

"Do I want to know what's in this book?" Al asked.

Dominick wiped his mouth. If they destroyed the evidence, Theo might have a chance. A mastria had probably already broken into Theo's mind, but at least there wouldn't be physical proof. The last thing he wanted to do was get Al mixed up in this. "Do I want to know what went on in the Council chambers?"

Al shook his head.

"Then no, you really, really don't want to know what's in it." The streets were bare of anything living. Most of the coven seemed to have escaped into the Citadel proper. Crackling flames and sulfur surrounded them, and still, projectiles crashed. Most of the Citadel was stone or marble; the worst damage wouldn't be from fire but to the buildings themselves.

"I'm going to get Sera, but I'm doing it somewhere that's not going to collapse any minute."

"Doesn't seem to be anywhere safe to me," Dom said.

"We'll go outside the Ogdelo." Al had his hands on his hips.

"And how do you know the main complex won't fall?"

Alistair just shook his head. "Remember what you just said about what I heard in the Council chambers?"

Dominick rolled his eyes.

"They won't let the main complex fall. That's all you need to know."

"Fine."

They trudged past the barracks, then the Council chambers. Dom and Al walked another stretch of block, and then there was silence.

He slowed while Alistair looked skyward, worry etched deep in his brow. The clear dome of the coven guardians' barrier had been re-warded high above them. Cheers erupted far ahead in the Menage.

They shouldn't have let the barrier fall in the first place. Dom knew of the strange hours the coven guardians kept. His father had been one for his entire life. A guardian was always on duty.

Al had an air of violence about him. Clenched jaw, tight fists: he looked like he had when he was younger and brawled with Colton. Dom was grateful Alistair had come home. It almost felt normal—almost.

"I want to see what's going on," Al said and jogged toward the cheering.

The amphitheater was packed. Everyone seemed to have sheltered within the structure during the attack. Slews of witches and warlocks, some bleeding, others attempting to soothe children, sat in seats across each level.

Chair Renata stood atop the platform in the middle of the arena. Her voice boomed. "Coven members! We've had a trying day. The barrier fell, that is apparent, but with the help of our allies, the aliato, we are safe once again."

The crowd was near deafening. Alistair raised his brows in question at the mention of allies. Dominick listened on.

"We owe our lives to these beings, and in return, we accept their aid and influence on the Council. May I present to you the newest Council member, Chair Raphael."

Dominick sucked in a breath as the winged being crossed the stage. Only then did he realize that Council Elder Corbin was not among them. "Chair Corbin hasn't publicly stepped down," Dom whispered to Alistair.

Al shook his head and put a finger to his lips. "Not here."

The new chair, Raphael, addressed the crowd. "May the glory of God bless those who worship the light. May the earth yield its life for the sake of the Holy. May your sacrifice not be in vain..."

How was the coven not seeing this? The crowd hung on his every word, as if the being wasn't spewing blasphemy against their entire race. There was only one God the coven worshipped, and that was Shadow. She was the Holy.

It had taken over an hour to get out of the Menage and around the Ogdelo. The garden was as beautiful as it had ever been, flowers blooming, topiaries tall and regal. It was as if that piece of the Citadel hadn't been touched.

Smoke curled high into the sky, and Dominick flinched every time a new projectile crashed into the wards.

"We're here. Now go get her," he said to Alistair. He needed to get Theo out of there, and if somehow Sera could convince her mother to let Theo go, then he'd take it. It would be the least she could do for the information he'd given her.

If Theo hadn't looked for Nora's thread in the pool, then none of this would have happened. He wouldn't have noticed that there were discrepancies...

"You're not going to do anything stupid while I'm gone, are you?"

"My parents' house is rubble, my lover is imprisoned... I've got nothing left *to* do."

Alistair pointed at him, his arms bulging, his eyes icy. "You do not move from here until I get back. Do not try and get into the tower without my help."

"I'm not an idiot. Now are you going to—" The warlock was gone before he could get the rest of his sentence out.

For the first time in twenty-four hours, Dominick pulled in a deep breath. His muscles twitched. He couldn't remember the last time he'd eaten, not that he'd be able to keep anything down until he knew Theo was safe. Theo... his poor Theo.

It was supposed to be joyous. He'd prepared an entire speech about how happy he was, despite all the shit around them.

Dom lifted a kernel of his magic. "Shadow, I don't know if you can hear me or even give a shit, but if you are out there somewhere, help me get him out." In answer, his magic was sucked from the very air into the ether and on to the goddess.

Dominick dozed in the shade of a phallic-looking topiary, desperate to escape the hot sun overhead. He let himself hope a little, think about what they would do as soon as he got Theo out of there. The healer first, although he'd need to be discreet if they didn't get full approval from the Council.

He'd break in. Between the three of them, they'd figure it out. They'd get through this. They all would. Theo, Sera, Nora, and Al. Hope: It was all he had left.

A fluttering of wings had him cracking an eyelid. A raven with a rolled-up piece of paper in its beak. The bird hopped over to him, threw the paper in his lap, and squawked.

"What in the world?" he whispered.

Dom unrolled it, and Sera's looping script covered the page.

Dominick,

Alistair shared news of the war and what happened to Colton. You must be devastated. I can't imagine what your parents are going through... what you're going through. I am so sorry I can't be there, but you and I know the Council won't help me get Nora back now that we are in active conflict. I've become allies with someone who can help. I can't promise when I'll be back, if ever, but I'll try. I love you. Keep your head up, and mind the bird.

—Sera

Dominick stared at the paper, reading it over and over again.

Mind the fucking bird?!

Screaming in frustration, he kicked at the raven, which hopped just out of reach. "I am going to fucking kill you, Sera!"

"Hey!" A Legion guard approached him. "What's your business here?"

Dominick cursed inwardly and pushed his hair back. "Didn't realize I needed to have business here to take a small break in a public area."

The guard shrugged. He looked just as defeated as Dom felt. "Suppose you don't." Dominick smirked. "You'll either need to move or head inside, though. There'll be another traitor getting their due tomorrow evening."

A knot formed in his throat. "Any word on who?" His pulse pounded in his ears.

"No, the Council likes to keep it close to their chest."

Dominick nodded and stood. "I'll leave you to it, then." The guard strolled back into the arena, and Dom kept to the dwindling shade.

As soon as the guard was out of sight, Alistair materialized, panting, with his hands on his knees. "She's gone."

"I know." Dominick crossed his arms.

"The fuck you mean you know?"

Dominick sidestepped, revealing the raven, which seemed to be growing in size as it croaked at the two of them.

"Oh."

"Oh?" Dominick asked. "Oh? Sera has a bird, and your response is *Oh*?"

Alistair stood to his full height, stretching his neck. "A lot has happened. That bird is her familiar. Don't ask me how she got one because I don't know, and now she's most likely halfway to the underworld with a demon lord."

"A demon *lord*?" Dominick hissed.

"Believe me, I'm not happy about it. The bastard ruined everything." Alistair's jaw ticked. His features were growing more stern.

"You fell for her, didn't you?" Dom asked.

"As if I had been pushed off the fucking ramparts." Al wiped his forearm across his forehead. "I need a wash and a drink."

"Let's see if my place is still standing. Then we can figure out how to get Theo out."

Chapter Sixty-One

Seraphina

*C*ursed. *You are cursed to be barred from my lands, from my home.*

Sera was dreaming; she had to have been, because she didn't understand what she was seeing. A silhouette of a woman stood before a giant ball of red flame.

You may curse me, but you will never rid yourself of me. I am eternal. I am the dark.

Sera jolted awake. Night and dew coated the grass inside the tent. They'd ridden late into the night, barely a word shared between them. Vasso had been deep in his own mind, brooding and miserable.

But he'd set up an impressive camp, and instead of a fire and hard ground, Vasso had erected an entire tent out of nothing, even constructing soft cots to sleep in—not that it helped her sleep.

"I will not let you do to her what you've done to me," Vasso called into the dark.

"Vasso?"

Sera rose from her cot and crossed the tent, reknotting the scarf he'd gifted her around her hair. The moonslight streaked through the tent's flap, giving her just enough light to see him. His eyes were squeezed tight, and his hands balled into fists. Every muscle was taut, as if he were fighting something.

"I don't care that I've defied you. Deal with it," he gritted through a clenched jaw.

Slowly, she approached him. Sera hated being startled awake, especially if she was in the throes of a nightmare. Leaning beside his cot, she caressed his temple with her finger.

He started talking in his sleep again. "She will not be—"

"Shhh, Vasso, it's okay."

His eyes flew open. Bloodred irises pierced her, and then his hand clamped around her throat.

"It's me!" she choked. "Vasso, it's me."

He didn't see her. No recognition, only rage. His lip curled, snarling, and he stood, pulling her up with him. Her toes no longer touched the grass. Where his fingers gripped, her neck burned like hot iron.

"Vasso," she choked. The edges of her vision pulsed. She couldn't breathe, she couldn't breathe!

He snarled. Steam radiated from his body, those bloodred eyes bore into hers, and his hand gripped tighter.

You know what to do, her magic said.

Sera let go of his arm and cast out her vatra, weaving eels of darkness from her hand, twisting and writhing around his body. The bands burned into the flesh of his shoulders and across his naked torso, wrapping him, squeezing the air from him.

In an instant, she was on the wet grass within the tent. "Vasso," she said between coughs, but he didn't hear her. A rabid animal was all she could think of as he strained against her bonds.

Snik cried out and ran to her side.

"It's okay," she said, touching her throat. The goblin pulled on the hem of her clothes, attempting to drag her out of the tent.

"*Puti la restca jadna*." Vasso bared his teeth at her. His dark mother language sounded like a curse. He was enthralled, under a spell—something. He wouldn't do this, not to her.

Sera pulled on that tether deep in her chest, pulled it so tight she wondered if it would snap. As she clenched her hand into a fist, her bonds around Vasso became tighter. Vasso hissed.

"Come back to me." She didn't sound herself.

The demon lord snarled. "*Te sie moj.*"

He had said that before. Outside of Crowpass, right before he said...

Sera took a deep breath, the cool air burning her throat. It had to work. "Subdina," she whispered.

Vasso's head snapped back. He inhaled a deep, gasping breath, then went limp.

"Vasso?" she called to him. He'd stopped fighting at least.

"Forgive me," he whispered. The demon lord dropped to his knees, his moons-gray eyes searing into her. "Please, Seraphina, forgive me." He lifted his hands to touch her, but then pulled them back.

She didn't touch him. She wanted to desperately. To run her fingers through his hair, tell him everything was going to be okay. "First, you need to tell me what happened. Who were you talking to?"

His chin quivered. "It's hard to explain."

"You'd better figure it out real fast, Vasso. Was someone dreamwalking?"

He crumpled into himself. "I am summoned in my dreams."

"By who?"

"The one I am bound to."

On her first day as a keeper, Seraphina had looked into the archives for the oldest tome someone of her rank could pull. It was riddled with the old language and vague interpretations. Descriptions of torture, examples of demons' preferred killing methods all lined the page, but she remembered one about being bound. Only the most powerful could bind another to themselves.

The texts stated that the practice was barbaric and had been outlawed by the demon king tens of thousands of years ago. But here in front of her, this beautiful broken man... Sera lifted his chin, hoping she'd read a lie in the lines of his face.

There was only anguish.

"Who?" She'd kill them. With her own two hands, she would break their bones and set them alight. He should be bound to no one.

He is fated to you.

"I cannot say." A single tear slid down his cheek. "Please, Seraphina, forgive me." He kissed the back of her hand.

"Are you a danger to me?" she asked. She knew the answer: They'd be each other's greatest love or their downfall. It was carved into her heart, into the tether that bound them together. He was as much a danger to her as she was to him. Sera swiped her thumb along the scar she had given him.

He didn't answer.

"I forgive you," she said.

He stood, took her hand in his, and pulled her outside into the moonslight. Ever so gently, he lifted her chin to see the damage he'd done. Vasso cursed. "Can I heal you?"

"That'd be wonderful," she said. Her throat was swelling, and each word felt like a blade.

Vasso lowered his lips and kissed every fingerprint he'd left. Sera's skin broke out in goose bumps. Soothing warmth spread through her, easing the bruised muscle. His lips trailed to her jaw, to her temple, then to her forehead.

"You didn't use your mouth when you healed Al," she said.

He smiled against her brow. "The Mesar is nowhere near as beautiful as you."

"Such a charmer."

He snorted. "You should go back to bed."

Snik whined in agreement from the flap of the tent.

"What about you?"

"I'm going to walk. Check on Ponic and Navine, I'll see you in the morning."

She understood the need to get away, to work off whatever internal fight he was having with either himself or his bonded. Moons, this was so much worse than she'd thought. She'd made not one bargain but two with him, and what did that mean if she broke it? Were there proxy bonds?

What she wouldn't give for Galene and the library right about now.

"Okay," she said.

Snuggled back in her cot, she watched Vasso through the gap between the panels of the tent. He must have thought she couldn't see him, for he fisted his hands and flexed every muscle in his back, neck, and arms. Steam rose from his skin, but before she could see any more, he walked away.

They rode hard that morning. Vasso stayed silent about what happened last night. He was being summoned and bound, but by whom? The cease-fire had ended. It was surprising that a seemingly *very* powerful demon lord was gallivanting on the surface instead of being below with generals.

Sera had a sneaking suspicion it had to do with her.

Off the bank of a wide river with harsh terrain on the opposite side, Vasso stopped Ponic. "We'll camp here for the evening."

Sera's thighs ached. Navine was a good horse, attentive and calm. It didn't matter, though. Sera wasn't used to hours on horseback.

"Go on, Snik," she said, letting the goblin drop to the ground and scamper into the woods.

"You're next," Vasso said, holding out his hands.

She let him take her, grateful she didn't need to rely on her own legs to dismount. His hands gripping her waist sent a rush through her, which radiated from where his thumb met a sliver of skin. Vasso's nostrils flared.

"What's wrong?" she asked.

"It seems that despite my healing last night, you still bruised."

She touched her neck. "Well, it feels fine." Vasso began to walk away, and Sera reached out, wrapping her hand around the brand she had given him. "Don't blame yourself for this. I know what it's like being stuck in a nightmare. I shouldn't have tried to wake you."

"You shouldn't be having nightmares."

Sera shrugged. "It's been a stressful few months." A warm breeze came from the south. The smell of brine was in the air, and it made her heart clench. Home, it was the scent of home. Gone was the dense forest that surrounded the Lanac Mountains. Across the wide river, east of the mountains, was a barren landscape of sand and black rock.

"Does it talk to you?" he asked.

"My magic? Sometimes."

Vasso rubbed his hand over his mouth.

"I just figured that was part of it. Is that the Deadlands?" she asked.

"The edge of them, yes." In a few flicks of his wrist, the tent was erected. "We need to talk."

"About?"

"I don't want to bring you to Gehenna."

Thump.

Her heart pounded.

Thump.

A rush of blood ran through her, and she lifted the lid off her well of power. "What do you mean you don't want to bring me to Gehenna?" She pointed to her brand peeking out from underneath his rolled sleeve. "We made a bargain."

"And I'll happily be indebted to you." There was a softness to him in the sinking sun, more than she'd ever seen while in the manor. It enraged her.

She didn't need to be coddled. She had power, and if last night was any indication, she was getting damn good at controlling it. So much had already gotten in the way, and she was so close. The Deadlands were right across the river. "You don't get to decide when this bargain is called in... I do. You're taking me."

"Subdina." He stepped toward her.

"Stop calling me that!" Sera shot her magic out, lassoing his foot and yanking him high above her head. He hung upside down in her volatile darkness, face level with hers. "I have a job to do. I have to get Nora out of the underworld." Her darkness snapped inside her, and this unrelenting hate bubbled, all aimed at him. "She could be hurt! Rotting in some cage!"

"She's not," he said.

"How do you know?"

"Put me down and I'll tell you."

She dropped him. She didn't care that the wind had been knocked out of him or that he needed to lie there for a second to catch his breath. "Speak," she said.

Vasso coughed. "I made... inquires."

"You had information about Nora this entire time and didn't tell me?" Flames surged to her palms. Her mist rolled off her in a fury. She was so dangerously close to setting him on fire.

Try.

"Who would you have believed? Me, or Ophelia pulling threads?"

Sera screamed and pounced on him. Vasso grunted, tumbling backward. She aimed for his cheek with her fist, but before she could make contact, he blocked, curled forward, and twisted.

Her breath came in desperate pants. How dare he? After everything they shared, he must have known how worried she'd been about Nora.

Vasso pinned her wrists to the ground, sinking his hips into hers.

She *burned*.

"Will you calm down?" His voice was low, and he was fucking smiling.

Sera fought to pull her wrists from his grip.

"You need to calm down. Your eyes—"

"I don't care about how beautiful my eyes are. I want to fucking throttle you." She bucked her hips underneath him, and he smirked. Rotating her fingers, she flung out two claws, aiming for his sides to push him off her.

"No—" He cast his magic over both of them, blocking hers from hitting its mark. Sera's rage turned to something primal and hot as their magic touched. "Now, if you'd calm down, I would tell you that your eyes right now are wholly black."

She stopped moving, and he pressed his hips harder into hers. "What do you mean they're black?"

"They're black, even the veins surrounding them."

One more thing she had to figure out. Wonderful. "Get off me."

"Not until you calm down and your eyes go back to normal."

Every pant had her chest rubbing against his. His darkness shrouded them from the outside world. "I'm fine," she said, taking in a deep breath.

"Are you sure you won't attack me again?" Vasso's question hinted at humor. She could feel his heart pounding in his chest, but his lips... She couldn't look away. Nor quench the urge to pull the lower one into her mouth and bite.

Sera nodded. He inspected her eyes, and when he seemed satisfied, he lifted himself off her.

It wasn't wise, what she did next. And maybe she was a bit impulsive, but as soon as he was off her, she threw an onslaught of magic at him, launching him ten feet into the air.

Before she could get on both feet, he threw his darkness out and ripped her to him.

"Let me go," she gritted.

Vasso threw her over his shoulder as if she were a sack of grain.

Sera punched and kicked, but he didn't flinch once. The grass beneath his boots changed to dirt, then rock, then pebbles. "Where are you taking me?"

"To cool you off."

She was falling, then the river engulfed her.

CHAPTER SIXTY-TWO

SERAPHINA

Part of her wanted to let the current take her away. Wash her out to sea with the mer. Maybe a deadly sea monster like the kraken or the leviathan would eat her whole, and she could cease to exist. No more death magic, no more guilt for not getting to Nora, no more shame for not having enough witch magic. There was no time for that, though.

Sera burst from the water. "You asshole!" Pulling her hair from her face, she stood in the soft sand and rock of the riverbed. Cool water ran from her hair down her arms. Her leather pants collected it like a water skin, sloshing as she made her way back to the shore.

Vasso's boots were already off. Then his shirt, and Sera did her best not to sigh as his rippling muscles glistened. His shoulders were sun-kissed from riding shirtless the day before, but the rest of him was as sleek as a mountain cat. Where Alistair was bulky, Vasso was defined, athletic.

But he didn't stop there.

Next, the demon lord proceeded to unbutton his trousers.

"What are you doing?"

"Going for a dip." With one fluid movement, he was naked. Gloriously naked. Sera stared at the man as if she were dying of thirst and he was the last brew on the continent.

She didn't even bother to close her gaping mouth as he waded into the river and dove into the current.

"Are you just going to stand there?" he yelled from the middle of the river, his mouth curved in delight.

She was no stranger to the male form. Quite fond of it, actually, and Vasso was an exquisite representation of it. Sera shuddered, remembering his body pressed against hers. The way his kiss had awakened some deep desire, ripping it to the surface, something her soul craved. Now that he was staring at her, a pleading eagerness in his eyes...

How long had she wanted a warlock to look at her that way? To feel a connection deeper than something temporary? She hadn't had anyone since this darkness awakened, fearing that whoever she got close to would run.

But Vasso, he was made of the dark.

She pulled the black shirt he'd made for her over her head. Kicking off her boots, she unbuttoned her pants, peeling the wet leather away from her hips, agonizingly slow.

Vasso's devious smile faded to a straight line. By the time she stepped out of her pants, his eyes were blazing red.

She let her undergarments fall into the pile of soaked clothing and sauntered into the cool water.

He'd never been so still around her. So silent, so incredibly predatory, lying in wait to see if she would get close enough to catch. Water lapped at her knees. Droplets fell from her hair, down her back. The slight breeze against her wet skin had her breaking out in goose bumps, and Vasso's eyes dropped to her chest.

A tug on the tether almost made her miss a step while she waded toward him. More than just one quick pull, he was reeling her in, and she was pretty sure it was due to his pure want and not because he actually meant to.

"Tell me everything you know about Nora." She'd play this game only if she got the information she needed out of him first.

He lifted his hand to his mouth before slicking back his wet hair. Without a response, he dropped under the surface.

Sera paddled against the light current.

Back above the surface, Vasso's eyes still blazed red, but he seemed a bit calmer than moments before.

"She's not in the lower dungeons. She has her own room, which is still guarded, but she's fed well and has a designated guard."

"So she's eating? She's all right?"

"No one has harmed her that I'm aware of," he said.

How strange. What was the point in kidnapping her in the first place if they were going to treat her like a guest? "Do you know why he took her?"

Vasso swam closer. "There is a rumor about a prophecy, a witch bride. I think Supay assumed that because she opened a portal to the underworld, your sister was to be that witch."

"Shit," she said.

"What?"

"It wasn't her who opened it, or well, it was, but…" She didn't know how much she should tell him. "My magic, it escaped me that day. It clung to her portal like a magnet. I had no control over it; it just reacted."

"Tell me about you and Honora," he said as he swam in a lazy circle.

"Why?"

"I want to know more about you."

"A question for a question?" She raised a brow at him. She wanted to see if he'd reveal what she needed to know.

Vasso assessed her.

She'd heard stories about the mer that made her wonder whether they, too, derived from demons. From the way Vasso glided in the water, she'd believe it.

"All right, you answer first," he said.

"I call her Nora. She's three years younger than me. A pain in my side for most of my life, though we've started to grow closer. She's so powerful and kind, thoughtful, smart—well, in the book sense—and didn't deserve what happened to her."

"I'm sorry," Vasso whispered, avoiding her gaze. Sera stood, her feet sinking into the smooth silt. She leaned against the current.

"Why don't you want to bring me to Gehenna?"

Vasso groaned. She couldn't help but smile at the trap he'd walked into.

He swam to her and stood. She looked up at him, at the hesitation in his gaze. "The one I am bound to—" He winced. "She wants—"

Vasso groaned and shook his head.

"She wants—" he gasped.

"Stop." Sera gripped his shoulders. A bead of black blood dripped from his nose. "Not if it hurts you this much." He let out a breath of relief.

"Do you have siblings?" she asked, trying to change the subject and stop whatever entity was ripping into his brain. He *was* bound. There had to be another way to find out the information without him getting hurt. Vasso wiped the blood from his nose.

"Not really, no."

Sera snorted. "What do you mean, not really?"

"It's difficult to explain. I wasn't exactly born in the sense that you were."

"You had a father and a mother, correct?"

"Yes," he said. One side of his mouth tilted upward. "And now I get to ask you three questions."

She splashed him. "That's not fair."

"A question for a question, Subdina."

She dared to get closer. "What does *Subdina* mean?" She was almost breathless. He seemed to be fighting himself, not whatever was lying in wait in his mind.

"Destiny." The word came out throaty and raw. She was weightless. He had called her his destiny from the first time he'd seen her. He'd known for that long that they were fated. Stroking her breastbone, she remembered the shocking pang that had rocked through her.

But he'd given her time to learn. To try and understand what this was between them. He had let her choose her course: Mortal enemy or lover. Executioner or inamorata. At times, she had wanted to be both. It was written... fated.

Vasso reached out his hand, just below the surface, beckoning, just like he'd done in the woods at Crowpass. That same feeling of being pulled toward something greater than herself ran through her. This time, she took his hand.

He pulled her to him, and that unsaid question lay in his eyes again. He'd looked at her the same way when they mounted the horses, and when he told her he didn't want to bring her to the underworld.

His lips hovered above hers. "It's your choice, Seraphina. I won't try to convince you one way or the other, but know this... The moment I saw you, that was it for me. Looking at you felt like dying and regenerating at the same time. You in the dirt, your feet bleeding, watching the forest creatures—just like I do. And I felt that tug in my chest." He raised his hand to his chest and tapped two fingers in time with his heart. *Thump, thump. Thump, thump.* "I knew."

She needed to be closer, wanted his heart to align with hers. "Why didn't you tell me sooner? After the images with Ophelia?"

"Because I wasn't sure you wanted the same. I knew you had feelings for the warlock."

"It was nothing like this." The words came out on an exhale. She didn't want to talk anymore, and wrapped her arms around his neck. Vasso lowered them into the water.

She wanted to feel. To feel something she knew only he could give her. Leaning forward, she brushed her lips against his, tightening her thighs, grinding herself into his length.

His composure broke with a moan, and he gripped the back of her head.

"Touch me," she whispered into a kiss. He ran a finger from her chin down her neck.

Sera leaned far enough back so he could grip her breast. The calluses on his palm, which grazed over her nipple, had her gasping. Pushing herself up with her thighs, Sera arched, and Vasso happily obliged.

She was burning. A drumming ache pulsed at the apex of her thighs. She ground herself against him to try and relieve it.

Aching want.

Desperate need.

She wanted it all, wanted it now. Vasso groaned again as if he could hear her. The sound vibrated through her as his tongue teased the hard bud of her nipple. When she wasn't sure he could worship her anymore, he bit down.

She gasped.

Her throbbing grew heavier, needier. More, she needed so much more. Every inch of her skin felt like it was on fire, and she would burn herself alive for him if she could.

His lips were back on hers. She vowed herself, to anyone who might be listening, that she'd learn every texture of his mouth, of his body. Reaching between them, she palmed his length.

"Fucking gods," Vasso cursed.

His grip on her ass was so tight that she was sure it would leave a bruise. Fuck, she'd beg him to bruise her. As she ran her hand from his base to tip, the river water created a delicious friction against his skin.

Vasso broke their kiss, and Sera whimpered at the lack of contact.

He looked up and cursed after a loud boom of thunder clapped in the distance. Heavy drops of rain bounced against the river's surface.

He lifted her to him and started carrying her toward the bank.

"Where are we going?" The clouds were angry, blotting out most of the sky to the west.

"I'm not done with you, Subdina. Not in the least. But I'm also not taking the chance that you get electrocuted before I get to taste you."

Sera shifted in his hands, and he let her down at the river's edge. Rain poured in buckets, and she ran to the tent, giggling.

CHAPTER SIXTY-THREE

ALISTAIR

With enough drinks in him to take a bit of the edge off, Alistair sank into Dominick's tiny bathtub. Working the soap into a lather, he washed off his arms and face the dust from a day of moving rubble and restoring homes. Everything had gone to shit.

When he traveled to Vasso's manor the day before, he'd been frantic, checking every room twice. With every hour that passed, his stomach sank.

He knew where she was going. The only thing giving him ease was the brand on his ribs. That demon would *have* to protect her with his life if required.

None of that negated the fact that Lavinia wanted her daughter back, and Lavinia was the key to getting Theo out of prison. He could tell Dominick hadn't slept much the past two days. The oracle was unstable, emotional—rightly so—but also a liability.

Unfortunately, Sera was already gone.

It had been harder than he anticipated to explain to Dominick that Sera was riding off into the unknown with the enemy. He saw the hurt in his eyes, then a hardened look of resentment.

She was with a demon, and a demon had killed Colton.

Al dumped a bucket of cool water over his head. Once dried and dressed in his dust-covered uniform, he exited.

"Let's go," Dominick said. He'd been set on getting Theo out all day. Too many times Al had explained that there were protocols and guard changes, and later would be better.

Al took two steps, grabbed Dominick's arm, and traveled them to a hidden alcove near the tower.

"Asshole," Dom got out before hurling into a bush.

Al patted his back twice and looked around for witnesses. "You'll get used to it."

The oracle righted himself and wiped his mouth on his sleeve. They were thirty paces from the tower entrance when Alistair stopped short. "I don't know these guards."

"That shouldn't matter, since you're a captain and the Council's private pet."

He curled his lip. "I'm not their pet."

"Okay, okay."

Alistair rolled his shoulders, cracked his neck, and approached the guards. "I need admittance."

The two guards looked at each other, then at the bars sewn on the shoulder of his Legion uniform. "I'm sorry, Captain, we've been instructed not to let anyone pass. It came directly from the Council."

Al thinned his lips to a straight line. "I'm here on behalf of the Council. I need to interrogate a prisoner."

The guards continued to look puzzled. "Forgive us, sir, but we didn't have orders..."

"I am ordering you now." He put every ounce of authority into his next words. "Open the door."

"But, sir, there aren't any prisoners left. They emptied the cells. Anyone captive was led to the Menage an hour ago."

Dominick sprinted toward the amphitheater before the guard could say another word. Alistair thanked both the guards, walked far enough that he was hidden, and traveled to the entrance where Dom was headed.

The oracle's eyes went wide right before he slammed into Alistair's chest. "You need to be calm."

Dom broke free of his grip. "You be fucking calm. The man I love is in there." The oracle paused as if he hadn't meant to say it.

"Exactly, and if you don't want to end up on that podium next to him, we need to blend in and come up with a plan."

"Travel in and get him," Dom insisted.

"I don't even know where he is."

Dominick huffed, pushing past him into the arena.

The sun had retreated for the day, and all three moons were full, positioned low in the sky. Al had somehow forgotten that tonight was solstice. The entire coven would be up through the night, trickling into the Menage for the celebration. He and Dom made their way to the Daedeth level but kept close to the exit.

There were no visible prisoners on or around the presentation platform, but a large tent had been erected toward the back of the arena's dirt floor. They had to be in there. But under what type of guard, he had no idea. He'd only gotten a glimpse of Theo, and finding him among a slew of broken bodies wouldn't be easy, nor quick.

It didn't help that he hadn't reported to Lavinia or the Council all day, and the fact that no one had come after him yet left him on edge.

The crowd changed and cheered as the five elders crossed the stage. Thorne led them, then came Blackwell. Renata was in the middle, as always; she was followed by the aliato, and finally Lavinia. All of them were dressed in coven-blue robes for the celebration. Each of the elders sat upon their thrones, except Renata, who readied herself to address the crowd.

He couldn't stop watching Lavinia, wondering if she'd orchestrated every move Renata was making. There was no way Lavinia would be able to keep a continuous hold on all four members. Although from what Dom had mentioned about Raphael being in the mastria's residence, he supposed she only needed to worry about three. Regardless, controlling three of them was a feat.

"Solarni coven!" Renata's voice boomed. "Happy summer solstice!"

Al mustered a small clap, keeping his eye on Dom. The warlock sat there, hollow, and Al nudged his friend's brother into applause. He didn't want to chance someone watching them, mastria or otherwise.

"We have a treat for you tonight." Renata smiled, and the four other Council members mirrored it. Lavinia was definitely in charge. "For years, a treasonous witch has been working against us. Some previous Council members thought it wise to let her live." The crowd booed, and Renata's smile widened. "We have found her. We bring her before you today to pay for her crimes."

Two guards pulled a figure between them up the steps. A chain was wrapped around her ankles with so little slack it prevented her from stepping high enough to reach the platform. The guards gripped her beneath her arms and dragged her up the remaining steps.

Al flinched at each thud of her shins against marble.

They threw Ophelia to her knees in front of the chairs.

The crowd seemed hungry for a retribution they didn't understand, nor care to. Every one of the Council members looked placated... except Thorne. The typical rosy color of her cheeks was gone. The corner of her mouth ticked downward instead of up.

"Stand, witch!" Chair Renata ordered.

Slowly, Ophelia raised herself to her feet, and Alistair's stomach lurched when he saw her face. They'd shaved her head, and raw wounds showed in open patches across her scalp. Her eyes were swollen and purple, her nose bent and bloody. Her lip split down the middle as if it had been done with a knife. The bottom half of her jaw was painted a yellowish green, and below it, she wore a simple frock covered in dirt and blood. Alistair scanned the length of her and swallowed when he got to her hands. Missing fingers, for sure, but he couldn't tell how many with how tightly she kept her fists clenched.

All that, and she still held her head high while Renata spoke.

"Ophelia Fray, you have been sentenced to death for your actions against the Council and coven. These include coercion, selling secrets to the enemy, conspiring against your kind, and the manipulation of our most vulnerable. You have violated the sacred laws of Solarni."

The aliato, Raphael, rose from his gilded throne and pulled his sword from its scabbard. Magic emanated from the blade as he took his stance directly behind Ophelia.

Renata's voice rang out. "Kneel."

Ophelia closed her eyes and began moving her lips. But she did not kneel.

The crowd chanted. "Kneel, kneel, kneel."

Al shifted closer to Dom, who had been stunned into silence. Alistair could only imagine the thoughts rushing through his head as he pictured Theo there instead of Ophelia.

Al placed his hand on the warlock's shoulder.

"Kneel!" Renata bellowed.

Ophelia's eyes snapped open. They were wild, a glowing aqua. The oracle raised her hands high above her head, and in one fell swoop, she broke apart the onyx manacles that bound her wrists.

Alistair stood. It should have been impossible. The onyx should have eaten away at her magic. There should be none left.

"Puti la, Nubenia, iz vas lanca."

Release me, Nubenia, from your chains.

A pillar of blue magic swirled around the oracle, surrounding her.

Renata reared back.

It was impossible—impossible, but he was seeing it with his own eyes. Raphael swung his sword at the magical force surrounding Ophelia. Before he could strike her down, the witch disintegrated.

A surge of power erupted from the spot where she stood.

Alistair stepped in front of Dominick, shielding him from the blast wave of raw magic that rushed over the entire Menage. The heat of it seared his skin even behind his shield, and those seated closest to the platform were blown back. The entire first row of spectators in the lower level was dead, their bodies burned to char on the floor.

"Get up," he yelled over the screams of coven members desperate to get out of the exit. It was pandemonium. He ripped Dominick to his feet. "Try not to puke."

In an instant, they were at the base of the marble staircase. If there had been a way, he would have thanked the witch. Ophelia's distraction was exactly what he needed to find Theo.

"Captain Alcott! Over here!" Chair Thorne motioned for him to come to her. Dominick gagged but kept up. The chair's eyebrows had been seared off, and she was holding the sleeve of her robe close to keep her arm elevated. "Follow me," she said.

"Where is the aliato?" Al asked.

"I have no idea," Chair Thorne said, looking over her shoulder as if the winged beast would appear.

Thorne led them to the tent on the far end of the arena and pulled back the flap. Alistair coughed at the stench. It reeked of piss and unwashed bodies. The rotting scent of festering wounds surrounded almost every coven member inside.

"Can you move them?" Chair Thorne asked, her face filled with panic. She must have barely gotten off the platform before Ophelia exploded. That arm was definitely broken.

"All of them?" he asked.

"Get as many of them out as possible, Captain. That's an order!"

"Where do you want me to bring them?"

"Anywhere, as long as it's far away from the Citadel and Lavinia Wildrick." Thorne's jaw clenched.

Alistair nodded, delicately took her wrist in his hand, and pushed a flow of healing magic into her. She sighed against the pain. "Don't puke."

CHAPTER SIXTY-FOUR

ALISTAIR

After a fold through space, he landed in the main chamber of Vasso's manor. He let go of Thorne once he knew she was steady and left.

One by one, he grabbed hands, shoulders, and arms and traveled his people to the underground sanctuary. By the tenth journey back to the manor, the floor was slick with vomit. Thorne was doing her best to get the prisoners into chairs and furnishings in the main chamber.

The next blink, he changed courses, bringing the prisoners to the mirroring pool, and once that was full, to the dining room.

Everything was burning. His chest, arms, face, every organ within his body, but he didn't stop. He wouldn't stop.

The next time he appeared in the tent inside the Menage, Dominick was standing in front of a crowd that had amassed.

"We need to find Theo."

"I'm trying to get as many out as I can." He grabbed the upper arm of a young witch and blinked from the tent to the manor.

"I can't find him," Dom said as he appeared again.

"You're going to have to. I've got to get more out." This time, he held the hand of an elderly warlock who must have been close to dust.

Tent.

Manor.

Tent.

Manor.

"Alistair!" Dominick's choked voice reached him. Al pushed his way between the coven members, begging for safety. There was screaming outside the tent, and he knew that his time for getting these people out was diminishing. Dom was on the ground, cradling a warlock's head.

"You've got to take him," Dominick begged. "Please, Al."

Crouching next to the warlock, Al slid his arms beneath Theo's legs and back. He was too light. From what Dominick had said, they'd only had him for a few days. It was like every ounce of liquid or magic had been pulled from him. His robes were soiled, and the pure anguish in Dominick's face had Al swallowing a lump in his throat. Theo was too far gone. Dom knew it.

In the blink from the tent to the manor, Alistair gingerly placed the warlock on a bed, turning his head to the side so he wouldn't aspirate vomit.

Al didn't have much magic left. Only a few more blinks before he'd burn out. But still, he conjured a bead of healing magic and placed it on the warlock's chest. He prayed it'd be enough.

Back in the tent, Dominick wasn't where he had left him.

Screams grew louder. The pounding of feet against the arena's dirt floor, accompanied by the sounds of swords zinging through the air, beat into his already aching head.

Al wasn't sure who was fighting whom at this point.

"You." He pointed to a warlock. Before his hand hit his shoulder, something burst through the opposite side of the tent with a rip of blade through canvas. Raphael entered in a bloody rage, striking down anyone who lay in his path.

Al grabbed a witch and a warlock and traveled them at the same time. He threw them in the hallway between his and Sera's room and traveled back.

When his feet hit the dirt floor, he was stopped by piercing pain. The tip of Raphael's blade rested just above the hollow of his throat. The aliato curled his lip, his otherworldly face defiled by a sneer. And those blue eyes blazed through him.

"Your parents were traitors. It shouldn't surprise me that you are as well."

Al didn't have time to process what he'd said. His father had been a great soldier, never once abandoning his post. The aliato's snarl had Alistair raising his hands. Raphael's wings were charred in spots, leaving dark craters between the white fluff of feathers. He wouldn't be able to fly like that, at least.

The carnage the aliato had left behind him started to stream toward Al's feet.

Shadow, he thought. *Please don't let any of that blood be Dominick's.*

"The Creator will make an example out of you. You and your kind. You will all be dust soon."

Alistair didn't speak, didn't dare move, but between the light-bringer's wings, he saw Dominick step closer. Raphael pressed his blade deeper into Al's throat. A dribble of hot blood flowed down his chest.

"Anything to say, *Mesar*?" Raphael asked.

Dom inched closer.

All Al needed was a touch, and they'd be out of there. "I hope to be the one to cut those wings from your back," he sneered.

Dominick yelped, slipping in the blood at their feet.

A mighty caw perforated his ears, and Raven slammed his claws into the aliato's face. The light-bringer roared, swinging his sword. Al ducked, healed the cut on his neck, and slipped toward Dominick.

In one quick movement, he, Dominick, and Raven all crashed onto the floor of Sera's room in the manor.

Dominick retched, crawling his way to Theo. Barely on the bed, the warlock cradled his love in his arms.

"Suppose I should be thanking you," Al said to the black bird, and opened the door to his room. "Though I don't know how you grabbed me in time."

Raven flapped its wings.

"What's this?" Al held out his hand, and the bird dropped something from its beak. "Oh, that's fucking nasty," Al said, inspecting the bright blue eye in his hand. "Well done."

He rolled the eye up into a piece of cloth to deal with later. He was exhausted. Truly, he didn't know how he was still standing. His legs shook as he rummaged through the small writing desk. He took out a sheet of paper and a quill, then scratched a note.

"I need you to take this to Sera and Vasso."

He handed it to the bird and let it out the door. At least now Vasso would know they were there. He limped toward the bed and dropped.

Before his head hit the pillow, he was asleep.

CHAPTER SIXTY-FIVE

SERAPHINA

Sera couldn't get into the tent quick enough. She was soaked from head to toe, shivering from the freezing rain or anticipation—she couldn't decide which, and settled on both. It was definitely both.

The need between her legs was becoming unbearable, and the temptation to strip off her undergarments and relieve the ache herself was more than she'd ever admit out loud. Plus, she couldn't stop the image of Vasso ripping those garments down with his teeth from circulating through her mind.

He barged into the tent, sopping wet, holding their soaked clothes in front of his groin in modesty, as if she hadn't just been cupping him.

It looked like every line on his body had been placed by the goddess herself, from his chiseled abs to the V-shaped cuts around his hips. Sera licked her top lip.

"*Udari la dolve, Nula.*" His voice was a deep rasp. "You're fucking breathtaking."

"You and all these archaic words."

He grinned. Shadow, he was gorgeous.

"Now," she said. "Get over here and finish what you promised."

Vasso's eyes grew a shade of red she'd never seen before, so red they were almost black. Her toes curled as she waited for him to move.

Thunder shook the tent as Vasso took a step toward her. "Is that a demand, Nula?" He dropped their wet clothes in a heap.

Sera swallowed at the sight of him. "And what if it is?"

Another clap of thunder, and Snik barreled in. The goblin screeched and hissed, taking shelter underneath one of the cots.

"Snik!" Sera screamed, snatching a blanket and wrapping herself in it. Vasso's posture changed. Turning away, the demon raised his head and sniffed. "Vasso?"

His head snapped to her, and she reared back at the look on his face. Every muscle was taut. Veins bulged from his neck.

"Is everything all right?" she asked.

Sera blinked, and where there had been nothing but smooth pale skin over toned muscle, there was now reinforced leather. A snap of his finger, and she was dressed the same. There was no mistaking it: The padding and extra layers on her arms felt like armor.

"Vasso, tell me what's going on."

"There's something foul on the wind."

A howling gust ripped through the tent, and Snik cried. "Come here, boy." Sera pulled the goblin to her chest.

"Stay here" was all Vasso said. Then he left.

She huffed. "What's a witch got to do to get laid around here?"

The goblin grumbled, and she couldn't help but laugh.

Outside the tent, the sky grew dark. Thick, angry storm clouds blotted out the dusk sky. Bolts of lightning traced their underbellies in violent succession.

Beyond the bank, the river raged. Logs floated downstream, and the onslaught of rain churned up the dirt from the riverbed, making the water muddy.

At least one of them had had the sense to get out of there in time. If she'd had her way, they'd still be wrapped in each other's arms, floating halfway to the ocean by now.

A burst of light, then a crack, had her jumping.

"Oh, shit," she said. Holding Snik to her, she raced to the cots on the other side of the tent, right before a tree toppled over, collapsing one of its corners.

"What is he doing out there?" she asked.

Snik cried.

"Stay here," she yelled over the wind. "If it gets worse, you run and find a burrow or something to shelter in."

The goblin nodded, and Sera stepped into the storm.

Rain pelted her cheeks. In the flashes of light, she searched for his white hair. This was not the way she wanted to end the day, searching for him in the dark, in the rain, during a freak storm.

As Sera crested the hill, she saw him standing defiantly in front of a giant.

She'd seen this creature before, in her tomes: the totrus. As mythical as the leviathan. The giant had three heads. The one in the center was speaking to Vasso; the other two watched, spitting flames and shards of ice. Behind it, the storm raged. Lightning pierced the ground, leaving smoke behind.

Sera ducked into the tall grass, keeping her head low. Blades of grass stung her cheeks and hands as she made her way toward him.

Whatever they were spitting at each other, Vasso was getting heated. He held out his hands, clenching his fists. Air rushed around him, tousling the tall grass. He whipped the wind into a cyclone.

"Shadow…" she said to herself. *That* was power, raw, unfiltered power. No witch or warlock could manipulate the weather, no matter what spell they chanted.

Sera blocked her eyes from the wind. Rain plastered everything around her, drenching the soil. Neither Vasso nor the totrus moved.

"Supay demands it," the beast snarled at Vasso. "All demon lords are to present themselves to the steward." The beast's voice boomed, almost as loud as the thunder around them.

"I will go when I am damn well ready." Cruelty underlined Vasso's statement. It was a tone she'd never heard from him—one she never wanted to hear again—but it befit his title of a demon lord. "You tell Supay if he has an issue with it, come himself."

The three heads snarled in unison.

Up close, she realized that the giant was at least three times taller than Vasso. Its heavy arms hung like clubs at its side. Vasso moved his own arm, and his cyclone moved with it, growing in twisting black wind.

The totrus slammed his hands to the ground, and all three mouths roared again. The head that breathed fire spat bright red flames, igniting the meadow.

Vasso snarled and moved his arm, pushing the cyclone toward the giant. "I do not wish to hurt you!" Vasso screamed over the wind. "Give Supay my message and leave me."

The crackle of embers and heat wafted toward her on the wind.

Sera kept her hand over her mouth to keep from screaming as a bolt of lightning crashed down a few feet away.

"Go back, totrus."

"I cannot, Lord Vasso, unless you are with me." He pounded his fist on the ground. Sera lost her balance, falling to her knees. She crawled in the grass, heading for Vasso.

"So be it," Vasso said.

The beast swung his massive arms but missed. The lord was holding back. She'd seen what he had done to that demon horde in the woods after they'd attacked her. He could easily burn this beast to ash. So why didn't he?

Vasso's black flames raged in a wave to extinguish the fire the beast had set. He'd turned his head only for a second, and the totrus swung a full-grown tree like a sword.

"Vasso!" Sera screamed so hard her throat burned. He turned just in time, his eyes like red saucers, then dissolved into a puddle of mist.

Sera cursed as the giant directed his attention at her. Would she be able to face this thing on her own? She let out a breath when Vasso appeared out of a pool of darkness in front of her.

"Get back to the tent!" he screamed over the crash of thunder. "Seraphina, go!"

It was too late. The totrus ran toward them, the log high above his head. He took a mighty swing.

"Oh, Shadow," she whispered before Vasso scooped her in his arms and twisted. Both of them flew backward. Sera screamed in agony. That bond between them ripped. His beautiful face—limp, and the totrus was reaching for him.

"No!" she screamed.

Sera ripped her arm free and threw a ball of black flame at the beast's hand. The thing reeled back, shrieking a sound that rattled her teeth. Shimmying from underneath Vasso, she got to her feet.

A line of fire raged beyond the giant, and beyond it, the cyclone stayed in one spot, spinning—waiting for a command.

The beast watched her. All six eyes were wide, its mouths snarling as her mist poured from her arms. "You are not meant for this power," it raged.

"Maybe not, but it's mine now." Sera pulled a flame in each hand. "*Barijara*," she said, and her barrier snapped around her body. She wished she had her enhancer; the shield would probably last longer. But right now her only task was to prevent this thing from taking Vasso—her Vasso.

"He belongs below!"

"You will not touch him."

The giant's shoulders tensed, his massive knuckles turned white around the log. "I will not let a witch stand in my way."

"Your mistake." A whirling hiss of flame and anger ripped through her body. Drawing on that deep well of power within her, she summoned her vatra and hurled her darkness at the beast. A hiss of flames on skin steeped the air in a noxious, acrid odor.

The totrus tried to dodge but failed.

Mythical beast or not, no one was going to touch Vasso. Not unless she was dead. Spinning, she wrapped her magic around her hand, creating that scourge that had given Vasso his scar. This time, she lined it with her flame.

Sera took her place, standing guard over Vasso's broken body. She rubbed her hand over the leather protecting her sternum, willing that pain to go away. Willing the feel of Vasso to come back, their tether to pull tight.

A trembling beneath her feet had her swaying. The totrus tumbled to the ground, momentarily knocked down by the quake. Sera dropped beside the demon lord. She wiped the rain and dirt from his forehead. "Wake up," she said, cradling his head. "You need to wake up."

Suddenly, Sera gasped. Her hands were on either side of his face. It had been this. This was the image she'd seen. He wouldn't die by her hand at all... he'd die here... now.

"Don't you dare fucking die on me." She shook him.

A blinding blue light far to the west speared the darkness. Like a pillar, a beacon direct to the moons. Almost as soon as the pillar was there... it was gone.

The ground shook harder.

A wave of power rushed over them; her barrier disintegrated. Vibrating and volatile. The totrus screeched, and Sera covered her ears with her hands.

What a sight this made.

The flames grew and grew, devouring the meadow almost from under them. Vasso's cyclone raged and built. The totrus bumbled to his feet.

Sera held tight to her scourge.

Destiny. You are his destiny... follow it, her magic said. Sera looked down at the limp demon lord. *Use it, control it.*

She placed her hand in the center of his chest. Reaching for wind, for him, she pulled, and the cyclone moved.

"Impossible," the beast raged. "Supay will kill you."

"Let him try." Sera yanked hard on that magic. And just like she'd commanded the scourge in her hand—it obeyed. The twister barreled through the field, ripping the giant from the earth.

Around and around he went. Red flame and ice swirled.

"*Vatera*," she said, and threw her flames into the swirling mass of wind. The beast's howl had her wincing. In a few seconds, it was done. She'd killed it.

Seraphina fell to her knees.

"Get up," she cried over him. The heat from the totrus's flames grew closer.

You can do it, her magic said.

This power in her felt new, raw, and potent. That bond between them: She reached for it, followed it with her mind, and placed her palm back on his chest. Something between them clicked, and an old, powerful magic poured into her. She could taste the earth and the air. The crackle of lightning, even the rain in the clouds, called to her. She was one with them, with Eraphon itself.

Hello, Osveknik. Who her magic was talking to, she had no idea.

Sera lifted her hand to the cyclone. "Quiet." Ever so slowly, the phenomenon came to a halt, the black flame within it gone.

Coaxing her vatra against the fire, she urged her black flames to put it out. The rain had slowed, but with each push of her magic, every ember dampened. She'd never been in control like this before, never been able to stop the destruction.

When the last bit of flame was extinguished, she picked up Vasso with four tendrils of her mist and rushed to the tent.

CHAPTER SIXTY-SIX

SERAPHINA

Vasso floated behind her on a platform of mist. The downpour had reduced to a drizzle. The booming thunder was now a rumble; gone were the crashes of lightning.

"Snik?" Sera called out. The goblin rushed from the dilapidated tent. Her hands shook something fierce, but as those little green arms wrapped tight around her legs, she felt a smidgen of relief. "Stick close to him."

Sera lowered her magic to the ground, and Snik whined over Vasso.

"*Vatera*," she called to her magic, throwing ropes of shadow toward the fallen tree that had knocked down the corner of the tent. She tossed the trunk and branches into the river. Thankfully, some of Vasso's magic was still working, and their shelter popped up in place.

Slowly, she maneuvered Vasso above a cot before setting him down gently.

You are advancing.

She didn't want to acknowledge that voice in her head, but she had to agree. Something had just clicked. Easy as breathing, her magic came to her now.

Snik whined, grasping Vasso's hand.

So still. He was so still. Barely a rise and fall of his chest. Her stomach sank. "Vasso, I need you to wake up," she said. Her chin was trembling as hard as her hands. He couldn't die.

How would she do this without him? Not only getting to Nora, but... life. Over the weeks she'd spent training and getting to know the demon lord, she'd relied on him like an anchor. Even now, she felt like she was falling. Blaming these feelings on fate was cheap. For so long she'd searched for someone who understood her, and here was her opposite, her equal, a twin flame.

Giving in to whatever they were would probably ruin her forever. But first, she needed him not to die.

Sera traced his brow with her fingers, down the side of his cheek, over his lips.

She had to keep telling herself that he was breathing, he was still alive. But Shadow damn him, why had he done it? He hadn't needed to save her, just get out of the way.

Settling herself in the damp grass, Sera rested her head against his cot. Rubbing her chest, she remembered the pain when the totrus hit him. It still ached, like that fateful line between them was being sawed away. But deep and buried, entwined through the ventricles of her heart, it was there.

Vasso coughed. "Subdina?"

"Thank Shadow, you're all right," she whispered, inspecting him closer.

"Did you save me?" He gave her a weak smile.

"I thought you were dead. I thought that giant was going to take you."

He coughed again. "To be fair, your distraction is what got me injured in the first place. Something I have not been in centuries."

She snorted.

Vasso ran his knuckles across her cheek. She couldn't help but push those stray strands of hair back. Wave after wave of emotion rocked her. Fear, anger, sadness, relief, all of it manifesting in the tears now rolling down her cheeks.

"Nula, do not cry."

"I thought I lost you."

Vasso winced before scooting over to make room in his cot.

"You're going to hurt yourself," she said.

"Nothing but bruises. My spine has already knit itself back together. Lie with me."

"I'm soaked."

"If I had it my way, you'd always be soaked around me."

"Vasso!"

He chuckled and snapped his fingers. Gone were her heavy wet leathers. Now, his oversize gray satin nightshirt hung to her knees. "I know you can make these fit me."

"They're perfect how they are." He motioned for her to come closer.

Sera carefully lay beside him, nuzzling the crook of his neck. Smelling his skin, absorbing his warmth. "Don't you ever do that again," she said.

"What? Make jokes about how wet I dream of making you?" Vasso wrapped his arms around her.

She huffed a laugh. "Die on me, you idiot."

"All right, I'll let it be your choice then."

CHAPTER SIXTY-SEVEN

DOMINICK

Every time Dominick closed his eyes, he saw flashes of the scattered bodies and blood that had lined the tent floor. Sword slashing, maimed prisoners, his coven.

To then be traveled to such an opulent room was unnerving. A four-poster bed, red velvet duvet, and carpet. Tapestries on the wall, candles burning in sconces—it was beautiful. And Theo was here, so this was where Dom stayed.

"Don't leave me," he whispered, cradling Theo's head. His sandy blond hair felt like straw against his palm. "There is so much more we need to do, to see."

Sleep pulled at him, but he refused to give in.

Instead, Dominick sat there soothing him for hours. He told him every childhood memory he could think of. He told him about his first crush, when he lost his virginity. His first day as an oracle.

"Do you remember the first time we met?" Dom's back ached something fierce, but he refused to move. "You directed me to the correct pool because I had my head too far up my own ass to find the training pool." He chuckled to himself. "I thought you were cute. Convinced myself you were too quiet, bashful." He rubbed a salve the singular healer had left him across Theo's dry lips. "Let's be honest, I was loud enough for both of us."

He desperately wished that he hadn't noticed the way Theo's breaths were further and further apart.

Dom's voice cracked. "You haven't even met Sera."

Leaning down, he kissed Theo's forehead, each one of his bruised eyelids. The Council had broken him. Battered him and tortured him, leaving him for dead.

Breath after breath came in gasps. Dominick pulled Theo to his chest, cradling him in his arms.

Shadow, it hurt. It hurt so fucking much.

"I love you, Theodore Sano." It had been the biggest surprise when the words slipped out of his mouth. But they'd been true.

If only his love could heal him. If only there was something he could do to save him. He'd bargain. He'd trade his life if only someone would take it.

Theo exhaled for the final time, going slack in his arms.

"I love you, and you never got to hear me say it—not even once."

CHAPTER SIXTY-EIGHT

SERAPHINA

She was screaming, and he was dying.

Over and over. Falling off the cliff where they'd watched the sun rise over Plaranina, stabbed through the heart, roasted alive in a vat of molten lava, and every time, she'd tried to save him and failed.

Over and over, it played in her dreams—a new kind of nightmare.

Sera startled awake, only to be met with the scrunched brows of the man she'd just watched be crushed to death hovering above her.

"You shouldn't have nightmares, Subdina."

"Well, tell that to Shadow. Isn't she the one who controls the dream realm?" Sera rubbed her eyes.

He chuckled. "Shadow hasn't been answering prayers for a couple of thousand years."

"What are you talking about? Where does our magic go, then?"

He shrugged, then bent his head down to nuzzle her neck. Unable to help herself, Sera purred under him. They'd slept all night together; still, it wasn't enough. Apparently Vasso thought so too. The brush of his teeth down her throat was enough to send her writhing.

"We should stay here." His lips dragged against the skin above her collarbone. "I'll build us a castle, just us..."

Now that was a dream. One in which she could see herself so clearly. The two of them together, laughing over a glass of wine, reading books, her screaming his name while he took her under the rising moons. Shadow, she wanted it. Maybe that made her a bad sister, but to be free of responsibilities without guilt? A dream.

"You know fate has other plans," she said.

Vasso sighed and rested his chin on her chest. Those moons-gray eyes smoldered into her. "Have I ever told you how much I hate prophecies?"

Sera tucked her chin and kissed his forehead. "Vasso, as much as I'm enjoying the sight of you between my tits, I really have to pee."

Reluctantly, he lifted himself off her.

It was bright outside—brighter than it should have been for the morning sun. She left the tent to relieve herself, then returned to a new pair of black leather pants folded on her cot. Underneath was an intricate reinforced corset with shoulder protection. Vasso was nowhere in sight.

"He thinks of everything, doesn't he?" she said with a smile.

Snik stretched and yawned, leaving her to change in private. She slipped the corset over her head. The leather was pliable, the fit snug, but it was thick enough to prevent someone slashing through, at least on the first swipe. It covered her stomach and chest, making her feel like a warrior, and she admired the detail on the shoulder pads.

The flap of the tent lifted, and Snik walked in holding a black raven feather.

Shit, Raven.

She'd forgotten entirely about her familiar. But the more pressing question was why Dominick hadn't yet sent word back. The Citadel must be a flurry of activity. The Legion preparing for war, the streets bustling with nervous coven members. She'd never been exposed to the city in war mode and could only imagine the chaos.

Sheathing the two daggers Alistair had left her at her hips, she clasped the enhancer to her palm. Today they'd enter the Deadlands, and she didn't want to be unprepared ever again.

In the sunlight, Vasso was tying on forearm braces that matched her leather corset. "Last night you looked like a river goddess, but today you look like a general." His eyes roamed over her body. Heat rushed to her cheeks.

"I didn't think the rivers had goddesses."

"There have been many deities on Eraphon. Most have lost their following and have abandoned us. But I promise you this... you would outshine all of them." He approached and lifted her chin. "Have I ever told you that I love it when you blush?"

The heat across her face doubled. "You know, *Lord* Vasso, I think you envision me as some innocent maiden. I assure you, I'm more experienced than you think."

His eyes flashed red. Then he kissed her, and the shiver of pleasure that went through her had her pressing into him. His lips were like velvet, and the way he breathed her in had her wishing she'd taken him up on his offer to stay.

"Delicious," he murmured into her mouth.

Sera giggled and pushed him away. "How are we going to get to Port Sidnah? Ponic and Navine ran off in the storm."

Vasso smiled. She caught her breath at the beauty of him. He whistled, and heavy hoofbeats pounded in the distance.

The elken king crested the knoll. "He says you may call him Hondor."

"Nice to see you again, Hondor."

"He says he's happy to see you as well."

"It amazes me you can speak with them." Hondor's fur was silken between her fingers as she petted his shoulder. He was a magnificent animal.

"You learn a lot when you've had over three centuries to roam above ground," Vasso said, then took her hand. "Up you go." He lifted her onto Hondor's shoulders, then placed Snik in front of her.

"What about you?"

Vasso smirked, then hopped up behind her. She didn't know whether she should be turned on or comforted. He wrapped his arm around her, his palm splayed on her stomach, his lips on her ear. "Are you ready, Nula?"

Ready wasn't the word for it. Sera adjusted herself to lean back into his chest. "Another pet name?"

He chuckled low in her ear. "I'll take that as a yes then."

With a click of his tongue, they were off.

When fighting the agbris, she hadn't had time to appreciate the animal's grace and majestic form. Elken almost glided above the ground, weaving around each tree and branch in a perfectly timed dance. And with every leap, her body rubbed against Vasso's, sending a jolt through her.

She knew he was having a hard time containing himself as well. His hand had dropped from her stomach to the waistband of her leather pants. His thumb lazily dipped below, in a question or promise, she wasn't sure. All Sera knew was that she was drenched. Still, their conversation yesterday, before everything went to shit, rang in her mind.

He didn't want to bring her to Gehenna. He was bound, but by whom she didn't know. Part of her had hoped that he'd changed his mind. That maybe he would petition the steward for her. Use his power as a lord to ask for mercy. Was that too much to wish for?

***

After hours of torture, the elken leaped across a narrow point in the river, and they were officially in the Deadlands.

Hondor pranced as if the sand burned his hooves. Vasso shushed him.

"So this is the Deadlands?" Sera asked. Tall dunes obscured the view to the south, but everywhere else was nothing but sand and black rock.

Farther to the north, she could make out an outcrop of buildings, though they were too far to see how many and what condition they were in.

"We'll walk from here." Vasso slid off the elken. He reached for Snik, who happily jumped into his arms, then Vasso held his hands out to her.

Sera smirked as she leaned forward. She didn't miss the way he slowly set her down, making sure that she had contact with his body the whole way to the ground. His sweat, that woody smell of ash, surrounded her. She'd bottle it up if she could.

"Real smooth."

"I've got a few tricks up my sleeve."

Shadow help her; she wanted to know them all. Every trick, every moan, every lick, every touch.

Vasso patted Hondor on his shoulder, and the elken took off.

They trudged through the sand, Snik scampering, chasing insects into holes, and slowly made their way up the dunes.

The sun was an inferno. She wished she had kept her Citadel trousers instead of the thick black leather ensemble Vasso had made for her. Sweat beaded and slid down the creases of her legs and back. Anywhere the outfit wasn't touching skin was a puddle of perspiration. She wiped her brow with her forearm.

Vasso shook his head. "You'll have to adapt before you go underground."

"I thought it would be cooler underground?"

"Some parts, but not Gehenna. It's basically built around Eraphon's heart."

"You'll just have to make me some new clothes, then."

He smiled at her so genuinely that she felt that tug between them pull taut. "It's an honor." With a snap of his fingers, her black leather pants, boots, and shirt turned into a long white linen skirt and sandals. A thin camisole covered her torso, and she didn't even mind its immodest sheerness. She groaned, twirling in the breeze. The sea air hit her sweaty legs, giving instant relief.

"You should have done that an hour ago."

"And missed the delight of watching you twirl?" Vasso smirked, then snapped again, changing into a white shirt and a pair of linen trousers to match hers.

"You ever going to teach me that trick?"

"We don't have the *exact* same magic, Subdina."

He didn't remember what had happened the night before.

She flicked her wrist and thought of the wind she had manipulated, recalling what it had felt like.

Sera rotated her wrists in a winding motion. The purple amethyst from her enhancer glittered in her palm, and just as she'd envisioned, a tiny whirlwind formed between them.

His face went pale. "How?"

"Last night, when you were hurt, something happened... between us." She gulped. "There was a quake, and then a blue beam of power shot up to the sky in the west. When it went out, I could manipulate your magic. It doesn't feel like mine. It's as if I'm borrowing from you."

"So it's done, then. They've killed Ophelia."

Her heart seized in her chest. So soon? They'd left only days ago. "But the magic, I felt it."

"She told me she made a deal, and it seems like Eraphon made good on her promise." He rubbed the sweat from his brow.

"What kind of deal?"

"You know as much as I do how stubborn she was. Come on."

He extended his hand, and she took it. This was war. That's what Al had said, as if that was a good enough excuse to kill an innocent woman.

Vasso helped her to the top of a dune. Sera's breath caught at the sight of the azure water. It was more vibrant than the ocean at home. The same color as that beam of light that had extended into the night sky.

"Is—um—is the water safe?" For so long she'd wanted to touch the ocean, and now it felt like a small conciliation against the weight of Ophelia's death.

"Go ahead," he whispered.

Waves lapped against her shins, then up to her hips in a rhythm only the moons chanted to the stars. The rocking eased some of the burden on her chest, and the water… it was everything Sera expected it to be.

Strong arms wrapped around her. His heartbeat ticked in an opposite beat to the rising tide.

"We met forty years ago. Ophelia was holed up in this dilapidated cottage like a feral cat. She'd been shunned by your coven for twenty years at that point." Sera stayed silent. "I didn't know what to make of her, but she had already been made aware of me. She was always writing in that dusty book of hers, leaning over bowls of water. I think that's why she loved the pools so much. She hadn't had access to them for so long."

The weight of his chin on her shoulder was soothing against the unease in her heart. The smoothness of his cheek and the warmth of his breath on her ear brought tears to her eyes. It was ending. The safety of his arms.

"She talked about you the most, though."

"Me?" Sera asked.

"She was excited to meet you." He chuckled, the vibration humming through her. "We traveled together sometimes. When she met me at my manor after a long absence, explaining that it was time to start preparing, we worked and planned."

"For what?"

"A better world." She could feel his smile against her cheek. "Let's get out of the water. I feel like mer bait."

This life was short. She'd experienced loss, heartbreak, destruction, and death. It wasn't that she wanted to save her sister because it was the right thing to do; perhaps, deep down, it was an escape of her own. To be away from the coven, away from harming the ones she loved over and over again.

Vasso settled in the sand. She sat in the space between his legs, cocooning into him, and watched the sunset. Wrapped in the arms of her destiny while her sister suffered, while Dominick suffered.

So long she had waited to belong, and now that she was here, she couldn't help but feel guilt creep in. Why should she get what she wanted while so many others didn't?

"This is what I wanted to show you." Vasso pointed out over the water. As the sun dipped below the horizon, the sky burst into an array of colors, mirroring the pools' threads Ophelia had so desperately loved. Orange, blue, yellow, rose, indigo, purple: It was all there, swaying in a magical form of light. "Sunrises over Plaranina are beautiful, but nothing compares to a sunset over Sidnah."

"It's as if she's here."

"She's somewhere. I doubt we are rid of that witch yet." He pulled her tight to him.

Sera waited for the sky to turn dark, soaking in every second of the sensations of his arms around her. "Will you take me?"

He sighed. "I think we could come up with a better plan than charging into the depths of Gehenna and trading you for your sister."

"Do you have something up your sleeve you'd care to share?"

"I need time to think, to plan."

"Vasso, you said yourself that you and Ophelia had been planning. If there is nothing, then I need to go, with or without you."

He stiffened behind her. "I'm not letting you set foot underground without me."

Oh, he was being stubborn.

Raven landed in the sand beside her, threw a note into her lap, and croaked so loud she winced. "Where have you been?" Sera unrolled the paper, but the scribble wasn't Dominick's.

They killed Ophelia. The Council has gone mad and has been torturing innocents. I traveled out as many as I could. Tell Vasso we're holed up in his manor. It's a mess, but I didn't have anywhere else to take them.
—Alistair
P.S. You need to know that Dominick is not well.

CHAPTER SIXTY-NINE

SERAPHINA

S era handed Vasso the note.

"Shit," he said. He stood and pulled Sera up with him. A moment later, their tent was set up at the base of the dune.

"I have a bad feeling about this," she said.

Vasso nodded, then whistled into the wind. A shadow sprite appeared, its body almost translucent. Its delicate wings fluttered so fast she could barely see them, its arms and legs too long and gangly for the rest of its body.

"I knew it."

He smirked. "Tell the domovoi to welcome the witches and warlocks. Provide them with anything they may need." The sprite flitted away on a puff of darkness.

"How do you have immediate access to shadow sprites?"

"The perks of being a lord." He whistled, and another appeared. "Get to my contact in the Citadel for a status report." This sprite kissed Vasso's cheek before it left.

Sera paced, wringing her fingers one by one. "Should I be jealous?" she asked.

"Never."

"This isn't good, Vasso. Whatever time you thought we had to make a new plan is gone now." They had to leave as soon as possible before things got worse. Before Supay decided that Nora wasn't worth keeping around, prophecy or not. And what did Al mean by the Council having gone mad? Torture? It had never been out of the realm of possibility with the elders. They'd thrown innocents in the tower before.

A stone dropped from the pit of her stomach down to her ankles. Alistair was concerned... Alistair. The Mesar... the one who reported directly to Renata... Oh, Shadow.

"I'm not rushing anything. Let me hear back from my contact in the Citadel, then we can discuss."

"Do I want to know who that is?" she asked.

He sighed, materializing her pack from a pocket of space. "I think it would be best for all parties concerned that you do not."

She kept pacing. If Al had needed to get them out, it wasn't good. She was sure he had almost burned himself out doing so. And what did he mean, Dominick wasn't doing well? Was he hurt? Sick?

"Everything will be fine, Nula. I'll make sure they're taken care of."

"Where's Snik?" Her brain was going too fast to keep up with the amount of information coming in.

"He ran out maybe twenty minutes ago. Probably chasing some rodent." Vasso ripped a bush up by its roots, lit it on fire, and set it into the sand. She supposed that was one way to start a campfire. "What can I do to make you feel better?"

Moons, she didn't think anything would. Except for... "I think you should tell me what you know about Gehenna. All I've done is read about it in books." Information seemed to settle her, no matter the circumstance.

He sighed and rubbed his brow. "Us demons, all different Dark Ones roam freely below. It's not just goblins like Snik. There are fouler things in the dark. Trolls, lords, the agbris, golems—every creature you've ever heard of is down there somewhere."

She swallowed hard. If he wasn't coming with her, she'd be so fucked.

"I've only befriended one of the furies; the other two are vile. Then there are the souls at the Shadow gates. Sometimes the beasties give me trouble, but not usually."

She sat in the sand and stared into the flames. The crackle of leaves and small branches twisted in on each other as they burned. "You mean like the totrus."

Vasso sat beside her, their shoulders touching. "You asked once about our life cycle. Demons can live for centuries, sometimes up to a millennium, but that doesn't mean we don't die. To reach our full power, our souls regenerate."

"Like the agbris." The way they had stitched themselves back together after she and Al killed them still made her shiver.

"The more powerful the demon, the more regenerations."

"Did you..." She didn't know how to ask. "With the totrus?"

"No, that didn't kill me. The bastard just knocked me out."

But *she* had killed *it*. The giant had been reduced to ash as soon as she lit it aflame.

"How many times have you died?" she asked.

"Oh, I'd say once every decade or so."

"Over thirty times!"

He laughed. "I didn't lie when I said I was the most dangerous thing in those woods. And before you ask, no... we don't know how many lives we get." His voice got quiet. "But I fear I'm at the end."

A shadow sprite materialized at his ear, its wings fluttered furiously. Vasso's jaw turned as sharp as a blade.

"What is it?"

"Thank you," he said to the sprite, then turned those moons-gray eyes on her. "The Citadel—it seems there was an attack. Many of the inner buildings had been leveled, especially in the lower quarter."

Her world stilled. All those coven members she'd taken care of over the years. Bringing them packages of elixirs and basic food. It couldn't all be gone. "What are the casualties?"

"It seems that was only the first wave. When Ophelia had her moment, she took out two Council members. Renata and Blackwell. Thorne, or at least her body, seems to be missing."

"Shadow…" Her people. How could Ophelia have done this to her people? Wrapping her arms around herself, Sera rocked. No wonder Dominick wasn't doing well. Colton, then the Citadel… She couldn't imagine it, couldn't picture what the destruction looked like.

How many of her people were dead, and for what reason were they torturing innocents?

"You must be hungry. I'll find us something to eat." He stalked past the dunes into the night.

She unpacked and repacked her bag, but the later it got, the more nervous she became. Two daggers, two summoning stones, one Legion uniform, two pairs of socks, a bedroll, and her cloak. Everything was there. She needed to ask Vasso for some different clothes, another set of reinforced leathers, maybe.

As she rolled one of the round summoning stones in her palm, her heart ached. She hadn't thought of Alistair at all the past few days. And the loyal brute had saved Dominick. He saved as many coven members as he could.

But he couldn't save her, not this time.

She dropped the enchanted stone into her pack.

Sera wanted to cry and scream and tear the world apart.

You could, her magic chimed. *You have the power now.*

"I don't want to destroy. I just want to live my life peacefully with the people I love," she said.

That was not written. All you have is this time, use it Seraphina.

A slight tug on the tether wrapping her heart had her looking up. Vasso was shirtless—her favorite version of him—and carried an animal of some kind. Snik tottered behind him, holding a desert hare by the ears.

A bead of sweat rolled down Vasso's lean muscles as he prepared the meat.

Statues in the artifacts vault had nothing on him. He was chiseled with perfect definition. He took a drink from a waterskin, and the sheen on his chest, over his abs, had her licking her lips.

Vasso's eyes turned reddish when he glanced at her, as if he already knew, as if he could sense what she wanted. Sera bit her lip. It was her last night above ground, alive... who knew. And she wasn't about to let it go to waste.

Hips swaying, she walked toward him. Sera placed a finger on his chest and ran her nail down the groove between his rock-hard abs. Vasso sucked in a breath as she made eye contact, then lifted her finger to her mouth and sucked his salty sweat from it.

"Seraphina." Her name on his lips had her heart beating faster. "Don't continue unless you mean it." His voice was low and dark—desire burned in his eyes, igniting her core.

The thread wrapped around her heart, tying her to him, pulled taut.

She slipped her finger in his waistband and pulled him toward her. The warmth of his mouth on hers had the universe standing still. For three heartbeats, he restrained himself. Three heartbeats of quivering muscle beneath her palms, then he broke. He kissed her hard and deep, teeth clashing, and that tongue, that mighty tongue of his, was consuming her. Sera arched into him, spiraling with the need to be touched. Devoured.

Loved.

He broke the kiss just long enough to nibble on her jaw. Sera moaned at the sensation. Vasso gripped the back of her head and whispered in her ear.

"From the moment I saw you, I wanted you bare to me. I wanted to fuck you with your hair falling around you like the goddess you are." He sucked on her earlobe, dragged his teeth over the sensitive skin on her neck. Then back to her mouth.

His hands glided down her back and gripped her ass to him, giving her a taste of friction that she needed so desperately. She moaned for it, craved it. He hoisted her up, and Sera wrapped her legs around his waist and squeezed. Vasso let out a guttural purr from the back of his throat as if he'd been starving for years.

Vasso carried her inside the tent. The cots were gone, replaced with a single large bed. She clung to him as if her life depended on it, refusing to break their kiss. With one quick motion, he ripped the camisole off her and set the white linen skirt aflame.

"I'll make you more," he assured her.

She didn't care if she never wore clothes again, as long as he kept touching her. Vasso ground his hips into hers, only the thin fabric of his trousers between them. She couldn't control her moan as he kissed the hollow at the base of her throat, tracing the curve of her breast with his fingertips. Vasso pressed the length of his body against her again, then rubbed his callused palm over her nipple as it pebbled.

She arched for his grasp, but he pulled away.

"I am going to take my time with you," he said. He traced the grooves of her glistening stomach and every rib with the tips of his fingers. She shuddered.

"Vasso." Her voice was thick as she ran her fingers through his snow-white hair.

"My name from your lips is better than any music, any prayer, Nula." Vasso sucked her nipple into his mouth, trailing his fingertips down her stomach. The drag of his lips and tongue against her hardened bud made her molten.

Every ounce of doubt evaporated when the back of his knuckle glided across her bundle of nerves. She sucked in a breath as he pushed lower and sank two glorious fingers into her. She gasped—she was so wet, so tight, they practically filled her on their own. Her hips bucked beneath his hand, and she whimpered.

A roll of his tongue, and he bit down. Sera moaned and pushed his head lower. She needed him lower.

Ropes of shadow bound her hands, lifting them above her head.

"You're cruel," she said on a soft sigh and tipped her head back, arching for him. The sensation that coiled within her from his fingers had her panting. It had been so long since she was this needy. Shadow, she didn't think she'd ever writhed beneath someone like this.

"You have no idea."

Sera huffed in frustration as he slid his fingers out of her.

"So impatient," he said and lowered his tongue to her clit. One swipe had her bucking again, and he groaned. "You taste just as I expected you to. Utterly divine."

Over and over again, he lapped at her. The pressure building had her gasping for air, for release, for something she couldn't name. She was so close. Sera pulled against his bonds, and he released her.

She gripped a handful of Vasso's hair and made him look at her as she ground herself into his mouth. His groan vibrated through her, his eyes grew so dark they were almost black, and he plunged two fingers into her once more.

"It was this," he rasped against her sex. "This was the image of you that Ophelia had shown me. The image I'd pleasure myself to every night. And when I saw you in person, I knew it would never be enough, not until I tasted you."

Another slow agonizing rake of his tongue, and she exploded.

"Fuck me," she said.

"What was that, Nula?" he asked with a wicked smile. He brought his dripping fingers to his mouth and sucked them clean.

"I said, fuck me," she panted.

"As you wish." He grabbed his pants and slid them down his hips, letting his length break free. He rubbed the tip on her entrance, barely giving her a moment, then impaled her.

She cried out, more in pleasure than pain, at the sensation of him stretching her. Sera let her head fall back as he thrust into her over and over again.

"You're so fucking perfect." He pulled out and slammed back into her. Pressing another bruising kiss to her lips, he whispered, "And you're mine."

Sera moaned as he drove deeper. Her need coiled tight in her belly.

"Don't you ever forget it, Seraphina. You were made for me," he growled.

She was going to die from her own pleasure, and she didn't care. His hands glided over her in worship. Every inch of his skin against hers was ecstasy. Every roll of his tongue, every word he whispered in her ear, had her spiraling. She clung to him, raking her nails down his back, staring into that beautiful face.

"That's it." He pounded harder, circling her clit with his thumb, and she screamed. She clenched around him, her nails tearing into his back, and rode every wave rolling through her. Shadow, she never wanted this to end. He worked her body as if he were made for this task alone.

"Fuck, Seraphina," he cried, then came undone, pumping into her until they were both spent.

He held himself on his forearms and kissed her. Their breaths mingling, both coming down from their trance. Sera clung to him, trailing her fingertips over the raised lines her nails had just made.

When he pulled away to look at her, there was such tenderness in his features, such admiration, so many words unspoken. And deep in her chest, wrapped around that fateful thread, was something she was scared to name. She searched his gaze, and in those strong features was tenderness so deep it made her eyes well up with tears.

Vasso kissed them away. She traced the length of his spine, refusing to let go... and never before had she wished that she could stop time.

CHAPTER SEVENTY

SERAPHINA

She slipped on Vasso's nightshirt, letting the sleeves fall past her fingers. The demon lord lay on his side, watching her.

The tether between them—she'd always envisioned it as a rope. But each time she met his gaze, it changed from fibers to steel links.

Sera lay back down beside him and caressed the curve of his cheek. Her fingertip followed his strong jawline to his chin, then down his corded throat. His eyes never left her. Not while she learned every dip and curve, committing them to memory so that even in the darkness of death, she'd be able to find him by touch alone.

"Can you feel it?" he asked, lips pursed with worry.

"Yes," she said.

Something had changed—some cosmic shift between them. The thread was now a chain. Placing her hand on his chest, she looked into his beautiful moons-gray eyes and told him, "I feel you."

Vasso pushed a stray curl from her face, tucking it behind her ear. The contact sent bliss deep into her skin.

"Tell me we'll make it. That I'll be able to rescue Nora, and then you'll build me that castle. Tell me we can hide away until we turn to dust."

His dark brows scrunched tight. "I won't lie to you. That isn't something I can promise, Nula. Eventually, Supay will come for me. Send every monster created to get me belowground."

"And what makes you so important? Don't your wards need to be ruled?"

Vasso gave her a sad smile. "Alas, they do."

She twined her fingers with his, rubbing her thumb across the calluses he loved to pick at. "When it's done, when Nora is out, regardless of what that looks like, what would you want?"

"Besides this, every waking second?" He rolled on his back, searching for the answer in the canvas ceiling. "I've built my life around my duty and prophecies. I've been expected to follow both. And honestly, I've never really thought what I could be, what I could do if I had the chance."

Her heart ached for him.

"But if you'd be willing to"—he swallowed, then stared deep into her eyes—"I'd like to figure it out together."

"I'd like that too." Sera kissed him. Their lips together felt right. She should be ashamed of how hard and fast she was falling, but who was she to question fate?

Pulling him on top of her, she nurtured that bond connecting them. Skin brushing against skin, nothing between them but the sounds of their own ragged breaths falling over each other like fresh-fallen snow. And when he had her screaming his name for the whole world to hear... Seraphina Wildrick decided there would be nothing better than to be loved by him.

❦

Sera woke up to an empty bed and voices in the distance.

Slipping on the satin sleeping clothes he'd left her, she smiled at the new leather armor he'd constructed. Carved into the thick black leather of the shoulder pads and corset were floral designs. He knew how to make her feel beautiful, even before a battle, it seemed.

The air was cool off the ocean. For a second, she stood in the dark, breathing in the salt and breaking waves. The voices grew, and Sera followed them.

On the other side of the dune, he was shirtless, hair tousled from lovemaking, and the way the moonbeams gleamed off his chest made her needy for him all over again. His companion was lurking in the shadows. Sera couldn't make out anything about them, only that the voice was decidedly female.

"Are you going to tell her?"

"Eventually, that's my intention, yes," Vasso responded.

"And how do you think she's going to take it when she finds out you're the reason her sister is captive?"

Her heart froze. Her lungs fumbled their air.

No.

Sera swayed, hands sinking deep into the sand for stability before a rush of blood to her head made her wince.

No.

Do not break, her magic said.

On shaky legs, she made her way back to the tent. The crashing of waves covered the sound of her heaving. How? How had she been so fucking stupid?

Her flames surged within her as her disbelief morphed into rage. She had given herself to him. Body, yes... but her heart, her soul.

Sera ripped off his sleeping clothes and pulled on her Legion uniform. As much as she wanted to leave them, she threw the leathers into her pack.

"You fucking knew," she said to her magic.

Yes.

"This entire time?" Tears leaked from the corners of her eyes. She threw her pack on her shoulder and ran out into the night.

It was written.

She was an utter fool. Every word her mother had called her came rushing back. *Spineless. Sniveling. Deficient. I do not care if you die; bring her back to me.*

Sera slipped up a dune. As she continued west into the Deadlands, she felt with misty tendrils over rock and sand for a doorway, a gate, anything. She'd do it without him. How dare he? How dare he!

She choked down her bile.

Some things must come to pass.

A collection of tumbleweed moved. Snik emerged, bleary eyed.

"You need to get me into Gehenna, now."

Snik looked back in the direction of the camp and whined.

Her voice caught in her throat. "There is no time. We can't trust him."

He was the reason Nora was imprisoned. She didn't know how yet or why, but the statement had been clear as day—*when she finds out you're the reason her sister is captive.* Her chest ached.

Snik grabbed her hand with his green claw and rubbed his face within it. With a yip, he galloped across the barren lands with only the moons as their guide.

Gripping her raven pendant, she heard its familiar caw in response.

She'd get down there, then she'd make a plan.

She followed the goblin over rocks as he approached a small pile of boulders. Pointing and yipping, he gripped the rock and pulled. Sera helped him, and deep in the sand was a hole.

"In there?" she asked. The goblin nodded.

Sera hesitated. It looked barely big enough for her to fit through.

That chain was pulling, and pulling. She placed her hand over her chest when a roar rippled over the desert. Screeching animals ran in a flurry past them.

Panic clawed at her throat.

This wasn't her.

She knew now what he meant when he said he could feel her terror. Her chest was being chiseled apart. Her knees sank in the soft sand. She gasped, willing the pain to subside.

He is angry.

"No shit," she said.

Snik whined and looked down the hole. Again, that chain pulled.

Vasso was hunting her. He was using the fated thread between them to find her. Sera glanced at the small shaft. He couldn't fit.

Tightening the straps of her pack, she dangled her feet over the lip. Another roar shook the ground. Sera didn't wait and slid into the abyss.

CHAPTER SEVENTY-ONE

SERAPHINA

Falling and falling and falling.

She screamed out as the stone walls widened. There was light at her feet, and she gripped the straps of her pack so tight her knuckles burned. Snik howled from above.

Oh, how she wished it'd been a normal doorway with stairs.

The shaft opened to a cavern. The floor was still a long way down.

"*Barijara*," she said, and prayed it would protect her from breaking anything. Sera hit the ground hard on her side, striking a mound of sand that had evidently collected from above.

"Fuck," she choked. Each inhale brought with it a stabbing pain along her right side. A second later, Snik landed directly on top of her.

Gulping for breath, she tossed Snik off her and rolled onto her hands and knees. Through bleary eyes, she took in her surroundings.

Torches affixed to the carved stone walls lit the space. A well-worn footpath wound between stalagmites as thick as trees. The fact she hadn't been impaled was nothing short of a miracle.

"Why..." she called out. "Why did it have to be him?" If Sera could have chosen a single person in this world to be honest with her, it would have been him.

Maybe it was the distance between them, maybe it was the overwhelming desire to kill him, but the panic was lessening. Sera leaned against one of the damp stalagmites and fought to catch her breath, to bury the pain in her side.

He'd lied. The wall he'd slowly torn down, the one that had encased her heart, was now reinforced with stone. Sera wiped her nose on her sleeve.

Shadows danced in the torchlight along the walls.

"Do you know the way?" she asked Snik.

He nodded.

With a croak, Raven landed on her shoulder. "Glad you could join us."

Sera slipped out of her uniform, not raising her arm any more than she needed to. She slipped on the leather armor Vasso had made her, though she wished she could bring herself to burn it, and pulled the strings tight to support her maybe broken, definitely bruised ribs. Next she slipped on the leather pants and sheathed the daggers Al had given her at her hips. And lastly, cursing much too loudly, she raised her hands above her head and braided her hair.

Snik led her down the worn path into a tunnel. His massive ears were constantly flicking, picking up movement she couldn't hear. Raven stayed perched on her shoulder.

"All right, you two, let's go get Nora."

She walked and walked. Drips of water sang against stone, and if she wasn't so scared, she would have found the sound divine.

Do not be scared.

"Easy for you to say."

We are home now. Where we belong.

With every breath, her side throbbed, and for the first time since he left, she wished Alistair were with her. If only for his healing power. She couldn't imagine the warlock underground. The very air would probably give him welts.

Sera kept her hands ready at her sides as she followed the narrow path. Her eyes darted to the shadows. They moved unnaturally—toward the light instead of away—like something solid would. But every time she turned her head, they disappeared.

Sera stopped short and leaned against the stone.

Her heart thrashed, and a cold sweat beaded on her palms. Terror flooded through her. Vasso was still frantic.

"Eeeech?"

"Keep going, I'm fine."

They'd been going for hours without encountering a single demon, creature, or anything else. It was odd, considering what Vasso had described to her.

Her steps bounced off the stone walls. The slightest touch to her ribs, even through her armor, had her doubling in pain.

Snik growled.

"What is it?" She listened as a faint rumble went through the ground.

Raven glided through the cavern directly toward the sound of stomping ahead of them.

"Come back, you stupid bird."

The bird ignored her, making an eerie knocking noise. There was a fork up ahead. A light was moving toward them from the right tunnel, but Raven had gone left.

"I hope you don't get us killed," she whispered. Each breath was a blade in her side as she ran toward her familiar.

The rumbles were footsteps that shook the caves.

"*Pronaki jadna,*" a voice as deep as the sea grumbled. Two trolls rounded the corner. Snik clung to her legs.

Their bodies swayed on warty feet. Sera glanced at the one holding the torch high above its head. Its eyes were milky white. These were cave trolls, adapted to live only underground. They didn't need torchlight to see. They could hunt her in the dark if they wanted to.

Sweat rolled down the sides of her face.

They were almost out of sight when one stopped. Her heart was pounding, her vatra thrashing, and the troll lifted its bulbous nose to the air and sniffed. Her chin trembled. It felt like an invisible hand was gripping her throat as she held her breath.

Please don't turn. Please don't turn.

The troll with the torch turned. Light danced along the wall mere feet from her.

Closer.

Closer.

The beast roared.

"Run!" she screamed to Snik.

Sera reached for her barrier magic. The power wound its way up her arm out of the enhancer. "*Barijara.*" A blue bubble of protection surrounded her and Snik.

They dashed into the darkness. Her side was splitting, and her legs burned as she ran, but she kept going. The blue bubble around them flickered as the club crashed into it.

She pushed faster, Snik galloping ahead. The cave walls expanded. She expected they were in another chamber.

Sera skidded to a stop before slamming into a wall of black stone.

A fierce burn ripped through her, and her barrier magic was sucked from her veins, through bone, and muscle, and skin. Then it was gone.

Sera shook out her shoulders and opened her well of vatra. Her darkness roiled under the surface, lying in wait. Snik whimpered.

"Hide," she yelled to Snik.

The trolls were almost on them. Their milky eyes and snarling fangs looked harsh in the shadows of the torch. The darkness stirred and snapped through her veins, enveloping her.

Show them.

Sera summoned her scourge. Black mist poured from her feet, blanketing the cave floor in a thick fog. The troll holding the torch took two steps before igniting into a black flame and disintegrating into a pile of ash.

Her hands shook, the flames in them trembling. She hadn't done that.

The other troll looked at her and roared.

"*Te klek pred vas, Dama,*" a deep voice drawled.

The massive troll shivered and sank to the ground, lowering its head to the cavern floor. Its fallen torch played with the shadows as the man walked forward. With each step, a building rage rose within Sera.

"You should have waited for me." Vasso's face was granite. He floated a mage light above his head, illuminating the chamber, and snapped out an order in the old tongue. His voice was stern, but this close, she could feel his true emotions. Panic, anger, relief, and... no, she wouldn't name that one. Not after what he'd done.

The troll whimpered and exited the tunnel.

"Nula—"

She didn't want to talk. She didn't want him near her. Sera swung her whip through the air, and Vasso blasted his power out to keep it from striking. She wanted to hate him. She wanted to kill him for lying to her.

Snik charged at the demon lord, growling and ripping at Vasso's leg. He snapped his fingers, and the goblin froze in midair, as if he were stone.

"You asshole!" Unsheathing her daggers, she charged. She was rage, undiluted rage, every ounce of her body hummed with it, and the carved floral inlays of the daggers sat true in her hands.

Vasso leaned out of the way, spinning to face her. "Looks like I should have been teaching you more than magic."

Sera screamed and went after him. He didn't understand what his betrayal had done to her.

Vasso ducked away from her swings, deflected her jabs, and stopped her at every move. Her side was screaming at her to stop; the stretch of her ribs with every inhale was searing.

"You've hurt yourself."

"Why would you care?" Her inky mist fell from her, its tendrils reaching, ready to snatch at him with her command. What she couldn't figure out was why he wasn't deflecting her.

"If you're done trying to play assassin, I'd like to talk."

Twisting in a circle, she rotated her dagger before he could move out of the way and made contact with his forearm as he blocked.

He hissed. "That hurt."

"Good," she snarled. She wanted him to bleed. She wanted him to feel every ounce of agony he had caused her after hearing what he'd said on the dunes. Her rage fueled her, hot and deep. Sera swung again, but Vasso gripped her forearm. A sharp pain bit through her wrist as he bent it back.

"Ahhh," she cried. Then he spun her. His arms were unyielding, no matter how hard she tried to break free of him. His chest rose and fell in rapid breaths as he ripped the other dagger from her hand. Her ribs screamed in pain.

"Enough." His tone was dangerous, low, and guttural.

"No." She slammed her head back, hoping to make a connection with his nose, but he tilted out of the way. He was too damned fast, and she was no fighter. Especially since she could barely breathe.

"What did I do?" The anguish in his voice gave her pause. He had to have known she'd heard him, heard his lie for what it was. He had to have felt her pain when she heard what that demon said. *How do you think she's going to take it when she finds out you're the reason her sister is captive?*

"I heard you," she spat. "You could have gotten her out of here! Brought her to me!"

He let her go, and she twisted to face him. His eyes were bloodred as they bore into her. "I ordered her to be released! As soon as I heard. I swear it."

"Well, maybe you should have come in person," she spat and picked up her daggers. It was no use. She'd never win against him. They both knew it. "What were you supposed to tell me?"

His eyes snapped to hers. "What?"

"I heard you. By the dunes, whoever you were with asked if you would tell me something. What is it? That you were too much of a coward to help me? That you would rather watch me suffer than help?"

It shouldn't matter to her. Not really, but she wanted to know. She was desperate for hope that maybe, just maybe, something was preventing him from doing the right thing. That there was redemption.

"Us. I was going to tell you about us." His body was rigid.

"There is no us," she gritted.

There was the slightest twitch to his brow.

"You betrayed me. There could never be an us." The moment she said it, she wished she hadn't. She wished she'd gobbled the words back without him hearing. That she could turn back time.

"Oh, that's rich. You know it's not going to be that easy, not anymore. Not when I've tasted you. Not when I've listened to those beautiful breathy pleas, or the way you scream my name."

Her body acted in treason as heat pooled between her thighs. "I can still kill you," she sneered.

"Not with those moves you can't."

"Maybe I'm choosing demise, then." She understood why her hatred could burn so hot for him. She could end him if she wanted to, was fated to do so, according to his words and Ophelia's. "Put Snik back."

Vasso snapped his fingers, and the goblin rushed to her side, whimpering. She lowered herself to hug him, no matter how much her side protested. "I won't let him hurt you again."

Vasso rolled his eyes. "I didn't hurt him."

Her body tensed as she marched past him. Conjuring her magic, she raised the giant torch next to the ashes that had once been a troll.

"Where are you going?" Vasso asked. The muscle in his cheek twitched. A menacing look crossed his face despite the cool mask he was wearing to cover it. Good. He was pissed too.

"I'm going to save my sister since you won't." As much as she hated him in that moment, a bit of her was relieved by his looming, broody presence behind her. Sera stomped toward her pack, the contents of which had been scattered across the cave when she dropped it.

There was nothing left to save, so she continued without it.

CHAPTER SEVENTY-TWO

ALISTAIR

He hadn't gotten a spare moment with Chair Thorne since he'd thrown her in the main chamber. Alistair didn't even know what to call her now. She obviously wasn't aligned with the Council. Shit. Half the Council was dead now.

Blackwell and Renata had been incinerated.

Shadow only knew what was happening within the walls at that moment. If he didn't think he'd be caught immediately, he'd travel back for Mr. and Mrs. Benero.

Al passed the makeshift healer's wing. The prisoners had only minor cuts and bruises now, thanks to him and the one healer he'd saved. Most breaks had been repaired, more or less. Wrists were still deformed, as were many knuckles and fingers. All the prisoners were poorly nourished.

The domovoi had no qualms about his new guests. Al's note must have reached the demon lord, and he was thankful for the warm welcome. They'd have been sitting ducks in the woods.

He went to check on Dominick and Theo. He had tried to give them some privacy, but Dom was in bad shape, and so was Theo. In fact, by the look of it, Theo had been the worst off of all the prisoners.

"Dominick?" he called out and knocked on the door. After a few moments of silence, he peeked in.

Dominick sat on the bed, holding Theo in his arms, rocking forward and back. Theo's skin was tinged gray, and the lack of movement in his chest told Al what he needed to know.

"Dominick," Al said softly. He put a hand on his shoulder, trying to stop him from rocking.

"No." Dom's voice was strangled.

"He's gone," he said. Dom didn't acknowledge him.

Al assessed his friend. Bloodshot eyes, with a whisper of beard coating his cheeks. He smelled like he hadn't washed in days.

"He's not gone," Dominick whispered.

"He is, brother." He took Theo's body from Dom's grasp and laid him back on the bed, then pulled Dominick up to his feet. There was such sorrow in his friend's eyes that he pulled him to his chest.

Dom shook in his arms, heavy sobs that racked through his body. Al squeezed tighter and did the same thing for Dominick that Sera did for him. Al wouldn't let him bear this alone. Colton was gone, his parents, and now Sera. He wouldn't let Dom fall too.

"I'll ask the healer to come and tend to him," Al said.

"I will wash him," Dom said. "I'll prepare him."

Alistair grabbed the chair near the desk and sat Dominick down. Entering the bathing chamber, he gathered a basin of hot water and a sponge. Sera had left some fragrant soap behind, and he added it to the water.

He left Dominick to do his task alone. Al had heard it could be soothing to prepare the dead, even though they were burned anyway. He'd heard it was a way to say goodbye. Hopefully it would bring his friend some peace.

Chair Thorne had been holed up in Vasso's study. The room was on the smaller side, and the house demons had probably cleared out anything that the owner deemed sensitive and stored elsewhere. But it was private and a start.

"Chair Thorne." Alistair bowed his head.

"We have no use for that title here." She rubbed her eyes. This was the most disheveled he'd ever seen the witch. Usually her red hair was pin-straight, flush with her chin. The white streak he remembered just being in the front seemed to have crawled over the rest of her scalp. Thorne had aged a decade in a day.

"Some of the house demons have agreed to take watch," Al said. "Not all of them can be trusted. We encountered a nasty set outside the manor, but those inside never gave us any trouble."

"I see," Thorne said, massaging her temples.

Alistair sat in the chair opposite her. "What happened?"

"It started slow. The Council votes on every decision. At first, I didn't notice the changes in opinion, not even in myself. That is, until Briar stepped down and Lavinia was appointed."

"Was Briar forced out of the role?" Council members had the right to govern until death. For there to be a transfer of power was unusual.

Thorne shook her head. "I don't think so. She was old and felt her life ending. Corbin, on the other hand, was..." She closed her eyes and sighed. "I still don't know what they did to him."

Al rubbed his hand across his chin. This was worse than he thought. Demons were after them, and now the Citadel. "We need a plan."

"We need to get more witches and warlocks out. Without the populace, we are nothing. There is no doubt in my mind that they have warded against you. Otherwise, I would have already asked you to start traveling," Thorne said.

"Lord Vasso's reach runs far. I don't think the Council was entirely wrong about traitors within the Citadel walls. If we can get the word out, if they can escape the fortress, I can get to them. I won't risk traveling directly in. Not yet."

Thorne nodded. "Let's try to get another message out to this lord." Alistair rose from his seat and bowed. "We are equals now, Alcott. Please stop with the formalities."

As he went to take his place on patrol, a lesser demon handed him a rolled-up piece of paper. He still didn't know how they came and went undetected.

Make yourselves at home. That was all the note said.

He didn't like being there in Vasso's space. It smelled wrong, felt wrong. He had told Sera that his magic changed while he was here, though he couldn't figure out what about it had. He still had full use of his abilities. Nothing hindered him. He didn't feel sick... just off.

Maybe she was right about it being a side effect of the parasite, or the fact that he was surrounded constantly by demonic things.

He thought about that moment. He was so sure they would die, cornered against the rock. He would have traveled above and burned out entirely for her. He wanted one kiss, but he still thought himself a bastard for taking it. His only regret was that he hadn't gotten a chance to tell her how he felt before it went to shit—not really.

The moment she'd set her eyes on Vasso, something had changed in her. She seemed brighter and more alive around him. Al had been jealous. She'd been right about that. He wanted to be that spark for her, the one to set her alight and make her happy.

A bolt of energy ran through him like white lightning. Al's eyes rolled into the back of his head, and he saw a dark cave. She was deep underground, but the summoning crystal had worked. She needed him. The raised dagger of his bargain itched on his ribs, as if he needed a reminder of what he's promised Vasso.

But he wasn't doing it for him, only her. A beacon in his mind had him honed in exactly on where she'd crushed the crystal, deep in the heart of Gehenna. And here he'd thought standing within this manor was uncomfortable.

"Shit," he said, rubbing his brow. There was only one way to find out. Alistair dressed in his Mesar uniform and armed himself until he clinked with each step.

"Dom?" He cracked the door. Theo's body was gone, and Dominick lay on his side, facing away from him. "Dominick, are you all right?" Of course he wasn't all right. But his friend didn't retort with a sarcastic quip or jab.

"You need to get up. Sera summoned me. I won't leave you like this." He didn't move. Alistair clenched his teeth. "Dom."

"I don't care," Dominick said, barely a whisper.

"Don't you want to see Sera?"

"No."

He needed time. Alistair sighed and shut the door behind him. Outside, he asked the healer to check in on Dominick every hour.

"Yes, Mesar." The healer curtsied, her head dipping low. Moons, he hated the attention this uniform got him.

Double-checking every pocket and sheath, he prepared himself. Sera had made it to Gehenna. That stubborn witch had done it. He was almost proud of her, but a layer of terror underlay that pride. She had asked for his help, leading him into a den of demons.

Nothing was easy with her.

Alistair sent an offering to Shadow, then vanished.

CHAPTER SEVENTY-THREE

SERAPHINA

The cavern tunnels were vast, and Vasso continued to trudge silently behind Sera. She assumed she was headed in the right direction, since he hadn't corrected her path. Knowing how much he'd kept from her, she should've been more worried that he'd lead her astray, but here they were.

"Are you going to let me heal you?" he asked.

She winced. She was in so much pain, but the thought of having him touch her right now made her blood boil. "No."

She was surprised he stayed. Her heart and her head went back and forth on whether or not she wanted him there.

Snik stayed close to her side, looking back at Vasso every few paces, scowling and hissing. She didn't blame the goblin in the least. Vasso had fucking frozen him.

She walked on, suppressing a pained groan, and rubbed at her chest. That damn braided thread wanted their souls to mend. If she could rip her heart out and live, she would have lit it on fire in front of him to get rid of the constant ache. Just to show him how serious she was.

The deeper they trekked through the stone tunnels, the more humid it became. She reached for her barrier magic over and over, but it never materialized. Unfortunately, Sera had only one person she could ask.

"What's wrong with my magic?"

"Now you'll talk to me? When you need something?" His voice was steel. Well, she had known better, hadn't she? Still, that tether tugged.

Wiping away the sweat that beaded on her hairline, she continued walking, vowing not to allow his attitude to affect her.

"When the rebellion began, the stronghold was relocated to this part of Gehenna. Onyx nullifies witch and warlock magic. Well, at least the majority of their magic. Veins run through much of the stone here."

"Convenient. I'm assuming that's why Raven has also disappeared?" she asked, glancing back at him, but Vasso was looking past her. Snik's ears perked, and he growled at whatever lay ahead.

Vasso hushed him.

"Keep silent," he commanded. "Whatever you do, do not use your vatra magic." He stepped in front of her. Sera unsheathed her daggers as quietly as possible and dropped to Snik's level.

"You need to get out of here."

The goblin whined.

"I won't let you get hurt. Please go to the manor and help Alistair. He needs you. That's an order." She held her arms out, and her loyal green friend hugged her. "Thank you for everything." He cooed and stroked her braid. Big, soggy tears lined his large brown eyes.

"I love you, too, buddy." She would not cry. Not now. Let her make her bargain with Supay; then she could wallow until the end of her sorry life.

Vasso whispered, "Stay in the shadows and try to keep from being seen." He dropped his shoulders, held his chin high, and glided forward with that effortless swagger.

Backing herself against the wall, she sidestepped toward the cave's opening, keeping to the shadows. Ahead, the chamber was well lit. Torches lined the upper walls, showcasing the giant spears of rock descending from the ceiling. In the center of the room stood a lone figure.

She recognized the demon lord's face. It appeared in her nightmares constantly, along with Nora's screams.

"Your Majesty, it has been an age. Welcome home." The sneer Supay gave Vasso contradicted his welcoming words.

"Majesty?" Sera whispered.

Ahh, and now you know.

"I figured it was time to take back what is mine." Vasso's words dripped arrogance toward the demon before him. Her body hummed.

"Here to take back your throne?" Supay paced lazily in front of Vasso.

"Here to ensure you obey an order when I declare it, Supay."

Supay's eyes blazed red. "It took only three hundred years. I thought the temptation of a bride would bring you back, but apparently not."

Tension clogged the cavity in her torso, but the words weren't lost. Ophelia had said Supay was the interim ruler for the true heir.

It was Vasso.

That's what that woman had meant when she said *you're the reason her sister is captive.* Sera's stomach rolled. A bride. They were going to marry Nora off against her will?

Sera stared at his back, and she could have sworn his shoulder twitched with an apology before their connection fluttered with sorrow.

"Better late than never," Vasso said and crossed his arms.

"Indeed." Supay waved his hand, and hundreds of shades emerged from the walls like ink being poured into the sea. The agbris pranced on all fours, filing in from the sides, pacing in wait behind Supay. *Click. Click. Click.* Their jaws chomped behind their skull masks, their parasite-infested claws screeching across stone.

Supay glowered, and then all of them launched at Vasso.

His magic shot out of him like rays of the sun, burning through the onslaught of creatures, reducing them to ash.

Those who could resurrect did so like a phoenix.

"Who allowed you to command the shades?" Vasso roared. The beings threw themselves at him over and over.

"Shadow is lost. They belong to Her now," Supay taunted.

Sera's magic laughed at that. *Foolish.*

Vasso fought with such surety that he looked more like he was dancing than killing. He dodged every intended strike and countered with blasts of black flame. He was magnificent. Each movement was controlled as wave after wave came down upon him—the shades, agbris, other foul and harrowing beasts with talons and tusks that circled the cavern walls. They were endless, and the more bodies that lay scorched on the ground, the pile of ash growing around him, the more vicious they became.

Sera's vatra danced in her veins, aching to get out and help, and it was impossible to stay still. Vasso roared, and she could see where he'd been sliced on the forearm—the same place she had slashed him with her dagger just hours ago. His eyes blazed red. Steam rose from his collar.

Silence. She could hear nothing but the frantic thumping pulse in her ears as the demons watched Vasso's face and neck stretch.

His clothing fell in scraps from his growing body until only a horned monster was left. The monster in front of her roared. Sera slammed her hands over her ears.

He was twice his human size. His skin a deep bloodred, with black spikes like natural armor covering every inch of him. Two enormous wings with talons protruded from his back. She was terrified and awed all at once.

He was the king of destruction and chaos—the king of Gehenna.

"Kill him!" Supay screamed.

Terror lodged itself in her throat, and with every pound of her heart, her ribs throbbed. Vasso's beast form flung the lesser demons across the cavern.

"Oh no," she wheezed, gripping her side. Something was very, very wrong.

Vasso glanced in her direction.

Sera took in his blazing eyes and fangs, the pure power that was him. He didn't even need his magic in that form. She knew it was him—she could see it in the lines of his brows. But it didn't stop the fear that racked her body.

A grimace crossed his monstrous face. But down the tether between them—it was shame. Shame and sorrow.

Sera slid into the dark cavern, away from him and the carnage, unable to take her eyes from the ash and flame and blood that painted the walls of the great chamber. Vasso could take care of himself. She needed to find Nora.

Sera turned down a narrow passageway, tracing her hand down the wall in the dark.

"I'm coming, Nora," she said.

She couldn't see a thing.

You should learn to create a light, her magic said.

"I'll get right on that." Sera winced and held her side.

Rough hands grabbed her arm. Sera ripped Alistair's dagger from its sheath so fast she surprised herself, then sliced the demon across the throat.

Ash rained to the ground. Three shades appeared, filtering the little light through a haze of shadow. She attacked, but cried out as her wrist hit the stone wall on the other side of the passageway.

You cannot harm the shades that way.

"*Vatera.*" Sera pushed her black flame at them. The shades' screams were nothing more than a whistled exhale.

"Oh fuck," Sera said and hunched forward.

More shades surrounded her. They whispered to each other in excited rustles and purrs.

Ja sadi doma, her darkness whispered back.

Sera was about to throw out more flames when pain erupted across the base of her skull.

Her brain sloshed. Her body crumpled to the wet ground. They were ripping her arms behind her back, and she whimpered from the pressure on her side.

"Let go."

Her ribs screamed, but her head pounded with the pulse of an icepick stabbing over and over and over. Hands gripped her under her armpits, and the shades pulled her back toward the fight.

Somewhere deep in her subconscious, she could hear the murmurs of her magic. The words moved, frantic, drowning, against the beat of her heart.

Sera cried out. With every jump of her pulse, a warm stream of blood gushed from the back of her head. Rolling, rolling, rolling down the nape of her neck. She winced from the blinding light of the main chamber, where black blood had congealed with ash in a circular offering to Eraphon herself.

Vasso panted. That massive red barrel chest rose and fell while the monsters around him kept lunging, snarling, licking his blood from their claws.

Sera squinted between the double vision. She could swear there were more than a few cuts on him.

THEY HAVE HURT HIM.

Something primal within her awakened, and she snarled. He was hers. Hers to maim or kill. No one else should have touched him.

"*Vatera!*" Sera screamed, and she launched her magic through the chamber like the threads from Ophelia's pool. Serpentlike spears twisted and turned, aiming, stabbing, slicing, finding their marks. Any shade, demon, or creature that surrounded him burned.

A chorus of shrieks went up in cantillation.

Sera's eyes locked with his, and down that fateful line between them... was pride. So much pride washed through her that she couldn't stop the smile, the tears. How long? How long had she wanted someone to cherish what she was? To belong?

Her mother, her sister... Dominick, Al, Galene... it wasn't any of them. It was Vasso. Her destiny.

"What do we have here?" Supay emerged from a dark corner of the cavern.

Vasso roared. But it was too late—she was falling. The only thing that saved her from splitting her forehead wide on the unforgiving stone was Supay's hand around her throat.

She felt her heart clench, and then a hollow cry of defeat rushed through her.

He couldn't give up. He had to get out of there.

"Let her go." Vasso's transformed voice was as harsh as his exterior.

"Now, why would I let a prize like this slip away? This makes more sense." Supay sniffed the blood dripping down her neck. "You're much more powerful than your sister." His grip tightened, constricting her airway further.

"Release her!" The walls shook. Small rocks and stalactites speared the mounds of ash around them. Vasso's vatra seeped from him, so uncontrolled that it scaled the walls. The tendrils reached out, snatching shades by the throats. Sera's mind swam in circles, the cavern tilting, and the only thing she could focus on was Vasso.

"What will you give me for her?" Supay asked, running a finger down her cheek.

"Me. You can have me."

"No," she rasped.

"Young love. How romantic. Change back, and I'll release her." More guards marched forward, weapons and claws at the ready.

Vasso dropped his massive black wings into the blood and bodies. Sera reached for the thread that bound them, went into her heart, and tried to tell him to let her die.

Save Honora, she screamed down whatever fated bond they had. Tears ran down her cheeks as she begged for him to understand, to release Nora and get her home.

Vasso's massive shoulders sank, and he shook his head in answer. His clawed hand held a flame, and he placed it to his stomach.

Skin and horns, claws and muscle melted. What lay beneath was a stripped Vasso—her Vasso—bruised and scarred. He rose to his knees, gasping for air. The beatings he'd taken and the amount of magic he'd used had carried a heavy toll.

"Secure him." The remaining demons hesitated before stepping forward. "Cowards." Supay threw his hand out and knocked Vasso unconscious.

As he released Sera, she gasped for breath and reached for her magic. "I'll fucking kill you," she choked out.

Supay sneered. "Just another entitled witch."

The steward of Gehenna snapped his fingers, and then there was nothing.

CHAPTER SEVENTY-FOUR

SERAPHINA

er head pounded. Sera blinked a few times, attempting to focus. Wherever she was, the ground was warm. Like sunbaked stone. All there was above her was a black abyss. Churning darkness simmering where the ceiling should be.

Everything hurt. Every breath, every twitch and blink. Fuck... Everything.

Sera rolled to her side and worked to sit upright. There was a strange smell here—ancient, sweet, something she recognized from the demonic relics in the keeper wing, but there it had been only hints.

Across the room was a dais, and on each side of the throne—a throne perched atop a pile of skulls—a body levitated. Both looked asleep. Vasso floated on one side, Honora on the other.

A cry lodged in Sera's throat as she sat up.

The pressure change in her skull made it unbearable. Each breath in was like a shard of glass in her lungs. Every inch of her was in agony.

"Careful," Supay drawled. "You wouldn't want to hurt yourself further."

She pulled flames to her palms. Black mist rolled from her feet. Fuck what Vasso said. She'd roast this fucker alive.

"Fascinating." Supay approached her, his hands clasped behind his back. The tailored jacket he wore didn't have a speck of ash or blood on it. She wondered how long she'd been out. "I thought at first that carnage had been Prince Vasilios's doing. I almost didn't believe them when the shades whispered to me that *you* had the chosen ones' power." Supay circled her.

She flared her magic and slowly, painfully, rose to her feet.

"I wouldn't try to use that on me. If I die, they die." He pointed to her sister and Vasso.

"What do you want from me?" she said through clenched teeth. The throne room swayed.

"I'd like to make a bargain," he said.

"You sure that's wise?" she asked as he circled her.

Supay grinned. "You're smarter than you look, but I trust myself to make a sound one."

Honora was floating midair. Her hair overpowered her too-thin frame. She was covered in bruises, and dark circles hung below her eyes. Sera took a step toward her, but Supay tsked.

Get her out. I don't care what you have to do. Just bring her home. Her mother's voice echoed around her. Moons, Nora looked awful. What had they been doing to her? Sera swallowed her guilt as best she could. She'd taken too long.

Vasso looked worse, if that was possible. They'd clothed him, at least, but the gash on his arm was open, and deep purple bruises coated every part of his body.

Taking a deep breath, she was caught off guard when a hacking cough barreled through her. The spasm of her diaphragm sent a blinding pain through her side. And across the stone at her feet, sprayed before her, were bright red droplets. Sera wiped her mouth with the back of her hand. It came back smeared crimson.

She was going to die. There was no getting around it now, with the amount of blood that she could feel down her back, clotted and caked from her head wound, to the rib that had apparently punctured her lungs. She was going to die. But there was one more thing she could do.

"What's the bargain?"

"Kill Vasso, and I'll release Honora. Refuse, and I'll kill them both." He shrugged.

It didn't make sense. Either way, Vasso would die. "Why do I have to kill him? You do it."

"Being the steward of the realm has been exhausting. The first two hundred years were fun—pulling strings, making demands, playing war with your precious Council. But I'm old and wish to leave the burden to the rightful heir. He can deal with Eraphon's demands. Plus, I'd rather not be on his shit list the moment he wakes up."

Vasso floated in the air next to the black throne. She could see him sitting atop it with his gorgeous smile, or with stern brows, passing judgment. He was the change in leadership. He was to be king and the rightful ruler of Gehenna. He'd be fair, considerate, even. Vasso cared about the beings in this world and what happened to them.

Maybe Vasso becoming king would be a good thing?

"Eraphon is sick of his games. She assured me he has a soul left to resurrect, and Eraphon is always right." Supay summoned a dagger, scrutinizing the pommel. Sera swayed and took a step to catch herself. He was speaking as if the planet were a person. He pointed the dagger's tip at Vasso. "He is her favorite, you know."

Vasso was bound. Of course. The king of Gehenna was Eraphon's champion. He was bound to... the world.

Sera's head swirled. Taking shallow breaths, she looked at him. He had one soul left. Vasso had been concerned he might be at his end—but if Eraphon had said so, she could free Nora. No harm, no foul.

"Will you let your sister die?" Supay was getting impatient.

"She goes free," Sera whispered.

Supay hissed and looked at his forearm. A raised raven brand took shape. "You can brand too?"

Supay clenched his fist, and Vasso floated to the ground at her feet. His breath barely fluttered. When she dropped to her knees beside him, he didn't wake.

Supay held out the dagger. Touching her lower back, she felt the raised scar from her bargain with Vasso.

Fate.

Love or demise.

He was still, and so ungodly breathtaking, even broken and bruised, it was killing her just to look at him. Sera leaned forward and kissed both of his cheeks.

"I need to get her home," she said, her voice trembling.

Sera pulled on the thread between them, letting her tears fall. "I don't know if you can hear me. And if you can, I hope you know how sorry I am. I hope you can forgive me for trading you." She brushed his hair away from his forehead. "You once said"—her lip trembled—"that it was a mercy, that *I* was mercy, and I pray that you see it that way. I'll come back, I promise."

Sera gripped the cold hilt in her hand. To lift her arm was agonizing. The tip of the blade trembled inches above his chest.

This was for Nora. To get her sister out. Then when he came back, she'd make it up to him. Sera didn't know how, but she would.

"Do it!" Supay screamed behind her.

"I'm sorry." She let her tears fall and stabbed him directly in the heart.

Vasso's eyes snapped open. He gasped. A wet, hollow sound. The moment his eyes locked on hers, a searing pain gripped her heart. Sera screamed in agony, collapsing over him. Excruciating pain cut through her. The throbbing in her head disappeared in comparison.

The threads that had entwined them from the moment she'd seen him were being ripped from her, severed by the blade sticking out of him.

Vasso cried out. She wasn't sure whose pain racked her body, but the pull that kept him linked to her frayed, and with every spasm of his impaled heart, it tore further.

Supay walked around them, watching their writhing. "Interesting."

Vasso's blood pooled, soaking into her hair and clothes. Sera reached for her barrier magic. It was there, warm and whole. She almost wept in relief. From her raised hand, she created a dome surrounding them. She wouldn't let Supay near him.

Vasso was still trying to draw air.

"I'm sorry," she cried. "I'm so sorry." He reached his hand out and cupped her face.

"Nula," he gasped. She could feel his heart slowing. "We are destined." Vasso's voice waned. "When it came to you... I wouldn't have changed it."

Sera sobbed as he coughed up black blood. He reached his fingertips to her cheek, attempting to wipe the splatter from her face. Sera took his hand in hers, kissing his knuckles. This was worse than dying. How could she? What could she say, do, to make this better?

"I'll always return to you..." He coughed again, his breath ragged. "Remind..."

"Shh, it's okay. It's all right." Her heart shattered.

"Our destiny." He took his final breath. The last strand of that fated link between them snapped.

He'd come back, he'd be okay, she'd see him again. They would be together again and leave the pettiness behind.

Love or demise, her magic said.

Somehow, she'd accomplished both.

Everything hurt. Her voice, her head—there wasn't a part of her that didn't radiate pain. Dots invaded her vision in waves. She'd be spent soon, but before she took her last agonizing breath, she'd see her sister free. "Let her go," she said. She wouldn't look at the monster behind her. Didn't want to see the satisfaction on his face at her pain.

"But of course," Supay said. "Though I suppose I should tell you about your sister's bargain. For your benefit, of course." Honora drifted to the floor. "She agreed to stay in exchange for your life."

No.

"You lied!" Sera screamed, which immediately triggered a coughing fit. Blood coated her tongue as she tried to take in a deep enough breath. She dropped the barrier between her and her sister. Her body was in agony, but Sera hauled herself to her feet.

"On the contrary, she will be free to roam as long as she doesn't leave the confines of this realm."

Nora stirred.

Sera grasped her side and limped toward her sister. Nora's eyes opened. There was recognition... recognition that gave way to terror.

Another step. Nora's name was on the tip of Sera's tongue. In a blink, Alistair appeared before her, and they were gone.

Chapter Seventy-Five

Alistair

Through time and space, he had sealed the crack in her skull. Her broken ribs were easier to heal, but she had lost a lot of blood. He was surprised she could still stand, but at least she wouldn't be in so much pain when they landed. Alistair traveled them back to his bedchamber within the manor.

As soon as they materialized, she pushed out of his arms. Two perfect, sizzling handprints somehow burned through his armor into his chest.

"How dare you!" she screamed at him. "You took me from her! From them!"

A knot formed in his stomach. Her eyes, once a vibrant mix of emerald and sage, had been replaced by an abyss of black. Dark as coal. A thick, swirling mist the color of night seeped from her feet, engulfing the floor in its eerie shroud. It seeped over his ankles, burning his legs.

Sera sank to her knees and sobbed into her hands. "You took me from her," she cried.

Alistair knelt in front of her. He bit his cheek and ignored the pain of her magic running over him. "He was going to kill you, Sera. I couldn't let him," he said as softly as he could, daring to push the stray curls away from her face. His fingers burned from her skin, but he didn't stop. She was barely breathing between sobs. He put his arms around her, and she fell into him.

It was never Snik.

When Alistair arrived in the tunnel, he'd fallen to his knees in agony, his magic sucked from him. He'd tried to travel before it was gone, but it was no use. Beside him Sera's pack had been strewed all over the cave. He'd found the summoning stone, noticing the hairline crack, but no Sera. Following the sound of a fight, he'd watched as a foul beast slashed through demons. Close to a hundred lay dead at his feet. He didn't know how, but he knew that beast was Vasso, something he'd thought was possible only in horror stories. In all his years as the Mesar, he'd never come across the beast form of a demon lord.

But then... but then... Seraphina had unleashed her true power. Such lethal accuracy. In that moment, she had looked like a goddess of death.

Al had almost fallen to his knees for her. But then that demon had her throat.

There had been no magic in his veins. There wasn't a chance he could have fought him with just a sword. But fuck, he had wanted to.

He'd followed the demons as they dragged Sera's and Vasso's bodies from the room, keeping a fair distance between them to give him time to assess. By the time he found the throne room, the trap was set.

The closer he got to her, the more magic he could feel seep into his veins. When she stumbled toward Nora, he watched Supay pull a sword from thin air. Then he ran.

By the grace of Shadow herself, the rest of his magic surged back, and he traveled to her.

He was sure his legs were covered in boils. There were welts on his cheek from her, but he stayed silent and stroked her hair. "Dominick needs you," he whispered. "He's not well, and Sera, I need you to pull back your magic for me."

She rasped, "Oh, Al, I'm so sorry." In a moment, the mist was gone, and she looked at him, frightened. "You're not going to tell, are you?"

"We have much bigger issues at the moment. We'll get to Nora, I promise, but I need you to help Dominick."

Sera sniffled and wiped her face and nose with her hands. "Okay," she said, her voice rawer than it had been inside the throne room.

He grabbed her hand and led her to the bathing chamber. "You're caked with blood, Minnow," he said softly. He ran a bath and left the room, giving her privacy.

She had demon blood. There was no denying it. Demon blood and fucking demon magic.

He was teaching her.

The thought echoed through him, accompanied by a cold sweat. She had only *just* revealed her power, but Vasso had trained her. Al almost laughed at the fact that he wasn't the only one who had kept secrets.

Sera cracked the door, wearing one of his Legion tunics. His stomach tightened at the sight of her. She looked like a dream, one he had envisioned for weeks, and now, knowing what she really was, one he understood would never come true.

Shaking his head, he led her to the door and knocked. Dom didn't respond. He'd kill the healer if she hadn't checked in on him like he'd asked. He wasn't fit to be alone.

"Let me try." Sera cracked the door. "Dom?" she said. The figure on the bed didn't move at the sound of her voice. Sera crossed the room, climbed into bed, and held Dominick to her chest. The warlock's shoulders shook.

At least he was alive.

Closing the door, Al left the two to heal each other.

He needed to inform Thorne of the imminent transfer of power and how that could affect magic. But walking through the halls, he couldn't get the image of her black, flaming hands and mist from his mind.

She shared fucking power with the future king of Gehenna.

Alistair found Thorne investigating the exit near the training area where he'd watched Sera sneak out on more than one occasion.

"This leads above ground?" Thorne asked in her pragmatic way.

"Sera can open it. I've seen her do it." He wouldn't tell Thorne yet how.

"You found her, then?"

He nodded.

"Good. Tomorrow, we can begin planning." Thorne turned, facing back toward the main chambers.

"Wait, Thorne." He turned to follow her. "While helping Sera, I obtained information indicating that a power transfer will soon occur in the demon realm."

Thorne pursed her lips but didn't look at him. "The master oracle told us that a few months ago. Do you know who it is?"

He swallowed. "The owner of this keep."

She stopped short and whirled on him. "You mean to tell me we are stationed in the king of Gehenna's personal manor?"

"He's an ally," Al said, rubbing the stubble on his chin. All he wanted to do was sleep, but Thorne had taken a double shift while he was gone. "Plus, we have something he wants."

"What is that?" Thorne asked.

"Seraphina."

"What would a demon king want with a low-level witch?"

"More than you know," Alistair answered.

CHAPTER SEVENTY-SIX

DOMINICK

Dominick thought he had imagined Sera's voice. Since washing Theo, he'd started hearing things that weren't there. Whispers and calls. He was going mad.

It wasn't until her arms were around him, when she whispered in his ear that she missed and loved him, that he believed she was real. At that moment, he fell apart, and she held him as he broke.

He didn't know how long they'd lain together crying. After a while, Seraphina started to talk. He listened to her talk about her time with the demon lord, about her sister, about the oracle who'd erupted into blue light.

When she was done, he wiped the tears from her cheeks.

Dominick choked on his words when he told her of Theo, how he had been beaten and brutalized for two days. As he and Alistair had rushed to get him out of the tower, and how Dom had cradled his corpse long after Theo took his last breath, praying to Shadow to bring him back.

Sera cried for him, cried because he didn't have tears left when he described his brother's burning, how his parents were now trapped in the Citadel. But when he was done, a small weight had been lifted from him. Minimal compared to the boulder that still held him down, but it was something.

"I've missed you so much," he croaked. A headache had formed behind his eyes from everything he had put his exhausted body through the past few days. "Will you stay with me? I don't want to be alone."

"Always," she whispered. "But you need to wash. You're ripe."

"All right," he said and made his way to the bathing chamber. His bones ached. He felt like he'd aged a century in a month. Removing his clothes, he glanced at himself in the mirror.

He was in bad shape. Lowering himself into the hot water, he soaked his aching bones and closed his eyes.

Upon opening them, he screamed at the witch standing before him. "Who the fuck are you?"

The witch smiled.

Sera burst through the door. "Everything okay?"

"No." He pointed to the corner and covered himself with his other hand. "Who is this witch?"

"Where?"

"Right there." He pointed again. The witch smiled at him and raised a brow.

"Dom, I don't see anyone."

"Tell her it's Ophelia," the witch said, her voice ethereal, something dark and other about it.

Dominick stared at the strange witch, then back at Sera. "She said her name is Ophelia?" Sera's eyes went wide as she looked to the corner.

"Dom, she's dead. That's the oracle I was telling you about."

He watched the shade in front of him roll her eyes. She wasn't even see-through. Shades were supposed to be see-through, right? Ophelia was wearing oracle robes, her hair long, her face no longer battered and bruised. He hadn't even recognized her as the witch he'd seen on that platform.

"Tell her that I am fully aware of what happened, and she needn't remind me." Ophelia straightened her robes.

He repeated her words to Sera. Seraphina just rolled her eyes in return.

Dom cleared his throat. "I need you both to leave."

Sera nodded and closed the door behind her. The witch in front of him raised her brow. "You sure I can't watch?" the shade said.

Dominick responded through gritted teeth. "Sorry, babe, you're not my type."

"Suit yourself." The oracle shrugged and left.

"Wait!" he pleaded. "Theo, can I see Theo?"

Ophelia's eyes grew sad. "Maybe one day," she said and disappeared.

Dom hated to admit it, but the bath did feel good. It hadn't brightened his spirits, but it did ease some of the ache in his bones. He wrapped a towel around his waist and inspected the clothes that Sera had laid out for him.

"These are too big," he said.

"They're Al's. I refuse to let you put on dirty clothes." She held his gray robes an arm's length away and dropped them outside the door, apparently for a demonic laundry service. "Where's Ophelia?"

"Not here."

Sera huffed. "I know where she'll be."

Dominick followed Sera through the halls. He held his breath as he gazed at the mirrored pool. The far wall was illuminated by moonstone, a rare rock said to be found at the bottom of the ocean. Its glow bounced off the walls, making the chamber feel almost holy. There, at the center of the pool, was Ophelia.

"She's here," he said. Sera looked to the center platform, giving the shade a small smile as if she could see her. "The pool is magnificent," he said. "How long has it been here?"

"I'm not sure. Before the war started, that's for sure, but I was never able to determine an exact date," Ophelia answered. "Maybe you will."

"I'll let the two of you get acquainted," Sera said, leaving him alone with the ghost.

He admired the colors twisting beneath the surface and stepped next to Ophelia.

"What have you learned from the master oracle?"

"Not much. Weather predictions, crop yields—I had just been moved to lifelines before we ended up here." He swallowed at the thought. The only reason he'd been promoted was because Theo had been imprisoned.

"Seems like I'll be stuck here longer than I thought." Ophelia threw her hands up in defeat.

"Why haven't you moved on?"

"Never mind," she said and motioned to the pool. "Pull a life."

Dominick raised his arms and closed his eyes. A red column formed, extending from the pool to the cave ceiling. He let out a breath. His mother was still safe and alive.

"Good, pull your father now."

"How did you—"

"Don't ask, warlock," she snapped before he could finish his thought. "Just do."

Dominick pulled a new column of blue. His father had frayed ends, gaps, and damage to the threads. His brow furrowed.

"Hmm, not so good," Ophelia said.

She instructed him to use his magic repeatedly, requesting the lives of people he knew and some he didn't.

"This was a good test," she said. "Get some rest. We'll start fresh tomorrow."

Dominick walked back to his room. Theo's face kept popping into his mind. The way he laughed, his lopsided grin. A wave of grief washed over him, heavy as an anvil, and he burst into tears.

He opened the bedroom door to find Sera curled on her side, already asleep. They'd been through so much together, and then apart. He was certain more was to come—more death, brutality, and war. His father wasn't well, if those threads were any indication. He needed Al to get his parents out as soon as possible.

He swallowed his tears and snuck into bed, trying hard not to disturb her. Just before he closed his eyes, he heard Theo whisper his name.

Frantic, he looked for the voice, willing him to materialize. "Theo?" he whispered. No one was there.

Lying in bed, he let his tears soak the pillow. Dominick focused on Sera's breathing. He wasn't alone, not with Seraphina here. And after a time, he drifted to sleep.

CHAPTER SEVENTY-SEVEN

SERAPHINA

The soles of her feet padded against the stone manor floor. It was quiet. Most of the coven members that Alistair had saved—almost fifty of them—were still asleep. It was late, but she'd awoken to the barest hint of a pull in her chest. She told herself it was a phantom pain. That it had been too long without him.

Still, Sera had not grieved him. She refused.

She bottled all that emotion up and pushed it down while she took care of Dominick. When she met with Alistair and Chair Thorne, she learned about the dysfunction and the role her mother had played with the Council. The deaths. The aliato placing themselves in a throne. It was all so backward.

Over the last three days, she had found no books or records on regeneration. And with each passing hour… her hope dwindled.

It had been days, and she'd found nothing.

But then there was another tug.

As soon as she snuck out of the room she shared with Dom, Sera threw out her mist in a wiry tendril and let it lead her.

She followed the smoke as it curved down a hall she'd never seen before. It was warmer in this part of the manor. The tunnels looked newly carved. As she turned down a new hall, a set of black doors appeared. Shadows and black flames encircled the frame. Carved depictions of demons and castle guardians adorned the doors. The handle was cool to the touch, but it wouldn't turn.

"I wonder..." Sera blew an ember at the stone doors. The flame joined the flickers beside it, and just like the exit to the training grounds, the door slid open.

Sera let out a cry when she realized where she was.

Sandalwood and ash breezed by her—a familiar haunting she'd thought she'd never smell again.

A rich desk was piled high with books and ledgers. Fur rugs were strategically placed around the room between chairs and other sitting areas. A chandelier lit and began to dance across the ceiling.

On the far side of the room was a four-poster bed. More demon forms were carved into the posts. The sheets were black satin, and Sera laughed to herself, wiping her nose on her sleeve. Of course he'd have satin sheets.

Rich tapestries lined the walls on either side of the bed, depicting scenes from the first battles—ones she had seen only in the oldest books in the keeper wing. A closet door cracked, and Sera went inside. She breathed in his scent. Rack after rack of black evening wear, training leathers, and shirts lined the walls. She found one of Vasso's gray satin sleeping shirts in a drawer and slipped it on.

Sera padded her way to the bed and curled up in his sheets. His scent, his closeness—it was the first time she'd been able to take a deep breath since leaving him behind.

Things had gotten so muddled. Not that anything in her life had been easy, but Vasso had changed her. He had made her better, stronger. A lasting mark that she'd have till the end of her days. But what she wouldn't give to have him here with her now.

Her hand glided over the satin pillowcase.

Thump.

She gasped.

Thump.

Sera ran her hand over her chest. The manor began to shake, and the chandelier above her swung violently. Small pebbles fell from the stone ceiling.

She cried at the rushing heat that sparkled through her chest, then laughed when she felt the threads she'd thought had disappeared start to knit themselves back together. They crisscrossed through the chambers of her heart. A flash of power ripped through the stone, the continent, the planet.

Power—his power—buzzed through her limbs. More than she'd ever held within her body before. A well with no bottom somehow dove deeper.

Sera choked back tears and spoke aloud, for no one but Shadow to hear. "He's alive."

EPILOGUE
VASSO

The way magic ripples through a planet when a new King comes to power is so destructive that one may ask why that planet would wish for it in the first place.

Why, when demons are already so close to being immortal, would Eraphon choose to crack herself wide for a new ruler of her people? One might never know unless they spoke directly with the world herself.

Wake.

He stirred. For so long, he'd buried that voice down. Deep into the cracks of his subconscious, she stayed buried, only speaking to him in his dreams. But this pain. He wasn't dreaming. He was reborn.

Water dripped from the ceiling above. It trickled down the walls, carrying sediment and minerals from the rivers and lakes far above.

I said, Wake, King Vasilios.

Sour coated his mouth and tongue. A reverberating ache and searing burn coursed through his arms and legs. Someone had killed him, and thus he had regenerated.

But how?

It does not matter how, only that you are whole.

"Ugh," Vasso groaned into an empty black cavern. It was a chore to turn onto his side. "I didn't agree to let you out of your hole, Eraphon."

You have no choice now, Vasilios. You are of full power; we are one.

"Let me find a knife, and I'll remedy that."

Eraphon went silent, and Vasso chuckled to himself, despite the throbbing in his head. Each new breath brought a deeper ache to his lungs. How much had he grown in this new generation?

His groans echoed off the walls back to him. The sound stirred a commotion of light and shuffling from the cave entrance. Vasso squinted against the oncoming torches. The shades, although curious, quickly scattered from the procession of demons.

His destiny.

There was no more putting it off.

"Your Majesty," his old adviser bowed low.

The tendons and ligaments in his arms pulled and snapped as he sat up on the cold, damp cave floor.

"You couldn't have put me in a bed, Supay?" Vasso growled and rubbed his eyes with the heels of his palms.

"Forgive us, your majesty. Your regeneration was taking a long time. Eraphon...she—"

Vasso held up his hand for silence. Of course, she requested that he wake up cold, dark, and sore. But for Shadow's sake, why did his chest hurt so much?

Do not speak of her.

Vasso ran his hands through his hair. It was short. Much shorter than he liked it.

Dinah came forward, bowed, and extended her hand to help him. Then, he saw it: a raised, angry demon brand, one in the shape of a raven.

"Who dared to brand me?" he seethed.

The demons, including his adviser, flinched. Only Dinah stood true and straight, ever the soldier, his fury. If there was one thing he could count on in all his years, it was her, and her steadiness.

It does not matter.

"Who?" he asked again, ignoring his commander's voice in his head. He was taller in this new form, almost a head and a half above his friend. She looked the same, blood red hair shorn to her collarbone.

Yes. Ever the soldier.

"Do you not remember?" Dinah asked him. Her brows were furrowed something fierce, a stitch of panic on her tongue. "What was the last thing you remember?"

Vasso thought back. Memories of a tent after a battle came forward. One, he thought he'd survive. That didn't seem to be the case. The words of the prophecy rang through his ears. He would be the downfall of the realm. He would be the last Demon King. Then there was nothing.

"The battle of Okaterth."

His creatures, his lords and ladies, gawked at him as if he were mad. Vasso growled in response.

"Your Majesty," Dinah lowered her voice. "That was one hundred years ago."

Pronunciation Guide

Citadel:

Jedan YEH-dan

Dobro doh-broh

Daedeth DAY-deth

Menage may-NAHZH

Ogdelo Og-del-oh

Darine DAH-reen

Characters:

Seraphina sar-ah-FEE-nah

Honora huh-NORA

Lavinia luh-VIN-ee-uh

Dominick DOM-uh-nick

Alistair AL-ist-air

Ophelia oh-FEEL-ee-ah

Vasso VAH-so

Supay soo-pay

Snik sn-ick

Galene guh-LEE-nee

Theodore THEE-uh-dor

Raphael RAF-ay-uhl

Creatures:

Elken EL-ken

Agbris AHG-bris

THE VATRA WITCH

Totrus   tot-ruhs
Vuk   vuhk
Aliato   ah·lee·AH·toh

If you loved **The Vatra Witch**, please give a review your favorite book apps.
Preorder Honora's story **The Kidnapped Novice** now!

ACKNOWLEDGEMENTS

This book was the greatest labor of love. There are so many people who helped make it the piece of art it is today, and I would not have been able to do it without anyone on this list.

First and foremost, I'd like to thank my husband. There has never been a person in my life who has cared as much about my dreams as you do. Thank you for giving me the space, time, and permission to follow them.

To my editor, Elyse. Not only have you gone above and beyond with your guidance, expertise, and care, but you're a lovely person whom I could learn from endlessly. Thank you for the boosts of confidence, your hard questions, and your pushes to take this book to the next level.

To my critique partners. Thank you, thank you, thank you. Thank you for reading my slop. For holding my hand through the first iterations of this book and any other story I threw at you. Thank you for your encouragement, your tough love, and your friendship. This would not be where it is without S.J. Snyder, Margot Grey, T. Minx, Chloe Cooley, Elysia Rourke, Indigo Rue, and "Kim Club" Kim Holland.

And my beta readers: All-star never said no to a request to read: Rebecca Baramidze! Plus, Gaylene Salazar, Gibson Monk, Chris V, Jim Rose, H.G. Kim, Hilary Hext, Megan Lawyer, Chaos Kellogg, Monika Trzcinski, and Rachel Savage. Your enthusiasm and notes helped mold the clay, and I hope you love this version of The Vatra Witch.

The most specialist of thanks to the wonderful Karmel M. Fausett. Not only were your notes helpful, but your TikTok videos and support, even at the beta stage, made my heart soar and gave me the confidence to keep going. You're a treasure.

The beautiful cover was completed by Alex McLaughlin at Nox Cover Designs. Alex's attention to detail and working with me on this book and the future covers in the series has been such a wonderful experience.

About the Author

Born and raised in Upstate New York, G.V. Hext can usually be found either writing, reading, or snuggling with one of her pets. Her love for fantasy and romance catapulted her into worlds of mystery and heartbreak, both of which she embraces in her books. She hopes you agree.
Keep up to date with all the news:
www.gvhext.com